KING
JOHN

EDMOND MANNING

Warning
This book contains two sexually explicit scenes and adult language that may be considered offensive to some readers. Main characters have mind-blowing sex. Please store your books wisely, where they cannot be accessed by underage readers.

Author: Edmond Manning
Copy Editor: Jonathan Penn, Romantic Penn Publication Services
Cover Artist: L.C. Chase

www.pickwickink.com
pickwickeditor@gmail.com general inquiries

ISBN: 978-0-9890979-9-4

Also available in ebook
ISBN: 978-0-9890979-8-7

KING
JOHN

EDMOND MANNING

To King Tony the Defender
We will meet again, brother, on the ancestral fields

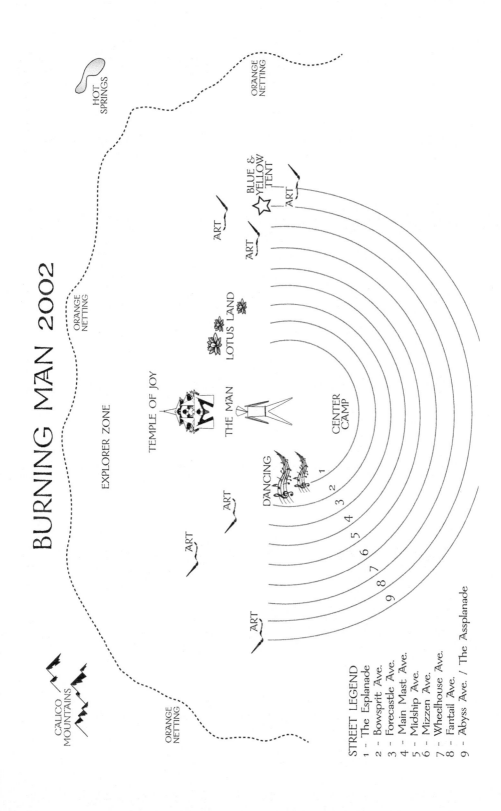

BURNING MAN 2002

CALICO MOUNTAINS

HOT SPRINGS

ORANGE NETTING

ORANGE NETTING

ORANGE NETTING

EXPLORER ZONE

TEMPLE OF JOY

THE MAN

LOTUS LAND

DANCING

CENTER CAMP

ART

ART

ART

ART

ART

ART

BLUE & YELLOW TENT

STREET LEGEND
1 - The Esplanade
2 - Bowsprit Ave.
3 - Forecastle Ave.
4 - Main Mast Ave.
5 - Midship Ave.
6 - Mizzen Ave.
7 - Wheelhouse Ave.
8 - Fantail Ave.
9 - Abyss Ave. / The Assplanade

The motto on the Black Rock Gazette's masthead:

Welcome to Nowhere.
Its name is whatever you name it.
Its wealth is whatever you bring.
Next week it will be gone, but next week might as well be never.
You are here now.

The events of this novel take place in 2002.

ONE

I am Bedouin.

I walk the hard-packed desert in my canyon-brown jubba, the thin cotton gown flitting over the tops of my exposed feet, tickling them. The scorching heat rises through the barren earth, through my sandals, slowly cooking me on this oven-blasted day. A sturdy rope belt, woven from camel wool, wraps around my waist twice; the excess swings at my side almost like a lasso. My canvas water bag sloshes against my thigh. A shorter length of camel wool secures my headdress, its fabric brushing my cheeks, flowing down my shoulders and back, protecting me from the brutal desert rays.

I could die out here. We could all die out here.

Sunstroke. Dehydration. A deep flesh wound could kill, so far from civilization and hospitals. The desert cares nothing about our survival. This is my world.

I am Bedouin.

"Excuse me," says a man wearing furry brown pants meant to represent goat's hind quarters. His feet are cloven hooves. "What do you call that thing on your head? My friend doesn't believe me."

"It's a keffiyeh. Traditional Middle Eastern headdress."

"See?" says the half-goat to his friend, a fuzzy rabbit from the waist up and below, well, just a white jockstrap and bunny slippers.

"Okay, okay, you were right."

They thank me and walk away.

I am Bedouin.

I travel with my thick staff, observing these people—my people—pondering their multifaceted fates. The sun celebrants, the fire worshippers, the partiers, the burn-outs, the techno-geeks, aging hippies, acrobats, sculptors, welders, performance artists, colossal dreamers, and the in-over-their-heads vacationers. The Mad Maxers. They all come to escape. They come to experience something they cannot find anywhere else but this desert.

Also, they come to get laid.

We are Burning Man.

Despite living here for five days, I still haven't picked my Bedouin name. I haven't had the need. Haven't talked to many people. But I do like to pretend to be someone else. Should I be…Vinicio Vanabalay? What? No, that sounds almost Italian. A terrible Bedouin name. I need a more Arabic-sounding name. What about…Vanaco. No. How about….Vintalmach. Ick. No, that's a mess of letters flung together without any regard for their personal safety. This is hard. The Arabic alphabet contains no letter *v*. In their language, my name couldn't possibly exist.

V. The touchpoint of two *l*'s clashing, meeting by rooftop in the dead of night, two ninja swords—*No.*

Enough on the word stuff.

I step aside to let twins pass me, not twins exactly, but dressed as twin bumblebees, both women holding martini glasses and singing. I will head down Mizzen Avenue and see what I might barter for lunch. Who needs the services of the traveling Bedouin, Vinicio Vanabalay? *No, dummy.* Too Italian.

I chat with cheerful folks who offer a trampoline to passersby, the chance to jump into the blistering sky. I politely decline. I pass southern white trash who have recreated a run-down trailer camp. They call, "Hey, foreigner," in their friendliest redneck accents. They invite me to join them. I bow. I pass a squirrel theme camp, which is pleasantly odd. Ahead on the left I see Camp Cuddleville, where lingering hugs evolve into nonsexual intimacy in the shade of their RV's awning. May have to return there tomorrow. I pass the Fun Time Death Camp and Wine Bistro. Seems hopping already.

A block later, one guy snarls at me, "Go home, towel head." I bow to him. I expected comments like that so recently after 9/11. I intentionally chose an Arab costume this year to generate and share goodwill. We all lost lives, landmarks, and trust in our world. We must regrow our tolerance—nurture a sturdier crop this time. The world gets smaller each week. We must grow to meet this new, unfolding era with patience and love.

A medium-height, black woman in a flashing silver skirt—some space-age polymer wrapped around her in sensuous folds—argues loudly with a taller man: white, mid-twenties, shirtless, with sunburnt shoulders. I don't know why I think *former fraternity guy*, but I do. First impressions. Her naked breasts support dozens of silver necklaces, which fall over and shelter them, yet draw the eye to the heavy curves of their undersides, revealing thickness and perfection. She defines austere elegance in this harsh environment.

The man's blonde spikes suggest more haircare product than the haphazard, windblown appearance most burners share. I see his abandoned robot-something costume a few feet away—same silver material as hers—already layered in playa dust.

She yells. He sloshes his beverage, gesturing wildly, and snarks back. She screams louder. He shrinks from her—only for a second—redoubling his yell. Interesting. A few people stop, a small crowd forming. I see others dressed similarly, probably from the same camp, whispering, deciding whether to intervene.

Common enough scene, drunken rowdiness or random expression of fierce emotions, but perhaps I am needed. I stroll right between them. I must distract them from their rage.

I jerk my staff above my head and I out-shout them both. "'*Nobody fucks with the Butterfly King!*' he would cry in his resonant voice—and all rejoiced when he thundered those words, for this meant he would take action against an injustice to his people, and so many considered themselves *his* people."

It works, for they pause long enough to gape at me.

"The Butterfly King ruled with the gentlest touch, not ruling at all, merely a hand on a shoulder, the soft awareness of his presence behind you as you blew out your birthday candles, letting you know he shared in your wish, whatever it might be. He sometimes paid the rent for those who could not afford it. Those fired from their jobs often found fresh roses delivered the next morning, compliments of him. Next time you go to New York, look for a new kind of graffiti, not spray-painted. Look for the yarn butterflies. This king taught me the lightest feather touch will enable a certain magic to emerge, and this feather-touch ability he bequeathed me, a simple Bedouin. I stand in your service to see if I might offer you butterflies of your own."

"What?" The frat man is annoyed. "No. Go the fuck away, dude. Private conversation."

"Of course, of course," I say and bow before them. "Sahib, I am yours to command, yet might I suggest with four minutes of your time, I could change your life direction, making your fights softer and more loving. Four minutes is all I ask. This, and you must answer my every question with truth."

"Go the fuck away," he repeats, his emphasis harder.

"No, stay," she says. "Help us. Four minutes?"

She wants me to stay, if only to defy him. She's spoiling for the fight. Still, it's an invitation to stay.

"Yes, beautiful lady, four minutes, if you both agree. And you *both* must answer whatever I ask, however I ask it."

She glowers at her lover. "Stay. We agree."

He scowls and takes a slug of his drink. Foam sloshes over the side, suggesting beer. I don't work with drunk people, but I don't think he's wasted. He's merely enjoying a cold one—or possibly warm one—as they explore the city streets. Yeah, he's okay. More importantly, I measured her reaction when I said "beautiful lady." I believe I know her story.

"My name is Vinicio Vanabalay."

Why didn't I invent a better name?

"I am an Italian expatriate, wandering the desert, searching for treasures buried in this barren land. Throughout my journey, I help those in need. Please, good people, what are your names?"

"Helena."

He grimaces at me. "Alan. This is bullshit."

"Are you two dating?"

They answer in the affirmative.

"For this next question, you must both answer quickly. Ready? Ready, Alan? Okay. Are you in love?"

"Yes," Alan says.

"Yes," Helena says.

They look at each other and this simple declaration changes the energy between them. Neither one hesitated to answer the question.

"And, Helena, why do you argue today?"

She says, "We partied all night. We drank until dawn. I think we should lay low today, take a day off. Sleep."

"I see."

I don't care about the fight. It doesn't matter. I want to surprise Alan and I need him to drop his guard.

She says, "He wants to go meet friends at the Temple of Joy, people we already saw—"

Alan cuts her off sharply. "I didn't come here to be no burner vampire. You have to—"

I flip around, instantly furious, yelling my loudest. "Enough of your fucking bullshit, Alan!"

His chest inflates, and he rises to his full height, ready to scream back in my face. Too late. I saw him flinch when I yelled. I saw the split-second hurt in his eyes.

Alan sputters, "You *goddamn, motherfu—*"

I raise my hands, as if in surrender to his fury, and say, "Stop. That was a test. I got what I needed. Alan, who yelled at you? The way I did?"

He stops short, bewildered by my sudden change. "Listen, asshole—"

"Father? Mother? Yes—right there, friend. You twitched when I said the word 'mother.' Your mom yelled at you. You ever yell back?"

Gritting his teeth, he speaks. "Fucking pop psycho bullshit. Hel, we're not taking relationship advice from some burner turd Arab."

I bow before him. "Shalom, shalom, my good sir. You promised me you would answer my questions. I ask again, did you ever yell back?"

I drop to one knee, recreating a child-parent dynamic with him. He won't yell at me while I gaze up with a pleading expression. He won't let himself become *her*, the woman who raged at him. I say, "Please, *please*. My question to you. Did you ever yell back?"

He huffs and says, "Helena, if you're not going to leave with me—"

I must interrupt.

"It was awful. You loved her deeply, but even as a child, you possessed enough awareness to never yell back. You knew defending yourself would make it worse.

She said things, terrible things about you, what a mistake you were, how you ruined her dreams."

His head jerks away from us both, staring at something far away.

I know how this works. I can guess at what a mother who didn't understand boundaries might yell at her kid. I employ the fourth pillar of kinging. Make your leap, and read the results. I step closer.

"Alan, she unloaded her fury on you. And yet, you took care of her. You never yelled back. Isn't that right?"

"Alan," Helena says. Her voice trembles. She reaches out and places a hand on his neck. "Did you ever yell back?"

Captured at last, his face turns to her and his eyes grow confused, angry and soft at the same time.

"This is bullshit." After a long pause, he looks away. "No."

A small, hurt sound escapes her.

That is all we will hear from him.

I rise from my kneeling position.

"Helena, when you yell at him, he feels like he's dying. He feels powerless again. But this time, he's not going down without a fight. For as long as you two date, you will never, *ever* successfully win an argument by yelling. You will lose. He will lose. You both lose, every time. If you want to date him, you'll have to find a way to feel furious with him that doesn't involve yelling. Scream into a pillow. Yell into the desert and let the wind carry your rage far away. When you're ready, be angry, but stay even-toned with him. Yell, and you've already lost."

Alan juts out his chin defiantly. "Don't talk about me."

His girlfriend pulls him into a hug, squeezes him, and says, "I won't yell, babe. I won't yell."

His arms find their way around her, casually at first, as if he hugs her to comfort her. But something changes and he buries his face in her neck and squeezes harder.

From this soft place, I can do her work.

"Alan, meet Helena. You may have noticed she is hot. She is smoking hot. She knows it. Men have dated her because she is smoking hot and then dumped her when she became a real person. They didn't want to put up with her attitudes and anger, her days when she felt unhappy. They thought she should behave as a trophy girlfriend ought to behave. Although she's smart enough to know that's their issue, not hers, she still believes she failed. She doesn't trust you're going to be around a week from now. She doesn't trust your love. She fights with you to prove her suspicions—that you will get tired of her being a real person and leave. Earlier, you said you loved her. Was that true? Do you love her?"

While holding her, he says, "I do."

"Every day for a year, you must tell her you love her. Every single day. Not the same time of day, and not in the same way. You don't have to give a speech. You don't have to give reasons. But every single day, you must say the words 'I love you' to her. . Do this daily without fail for one year and she will trust you. The words don't matter as much as your commitment to the year. Do you want to date her for the next year?"

"Yes."

She pulls back from him. Helena has been crying.

"Helena, you must find a way to fight without yelling. Alan, every day for a year, you must say you love her. If you two can do this, the butterflies will come."

Helena wipes her face, nods, and pulls her hair out of her eyes. "I won't yell."

"And now, according to Bedouin culture, we drink."

Alan says, "I thought you were Italian?"

"I'm working out my backstory." I hold my canvas water pouch out to her. "It's water."

She takes it from me—still crying, and laughing at herself now—removes the plug and takes a healthy swig. She passes it to Alan, who remains serious through these motions. He moves to put it to his lips but pauses, looking into her eyes as he says, "I love you."

He drinks.

Then he hands the canvas back to me and I take a swig too. You can never drink enough water out here on the playa.

I speak my final words as I wrap the pouch strap around my shoulder and neck. "Amongst my people, we honor each other after a fight, after bruised feelings transform into something lighter with wings. You create butterflies in this desert wasteland with every kiss. I will show you. You may decide if it fits your circumstance. Helena?" I reach toward her. "Your hand?"

She offers her right one willingly, and under the bright sun, I take it and turn it over to reveal a chalky-white palm, covered in playa dust like everything else. I kiss the underside of her thumb, the thenar...*something*. I knew the name at one point, the muscle right under the thumb. The king's kiss.

"If it feels right to you, Helena, kiss Alan right here, under the thumb."

Helena turns to her lover and reaches for his hand. He smiles.

My cue to sneak away, while those two remain engaged with each other, and the meager crowd surrounding us disbands. Best to leave before questions arise.

Surprising how easy it is to disappear here in the desert, with no trees, no geography to speak of, no place to hide. Well, except among the ocean of people. I am engulfed within seconds, passing three or four in long white gowns similar to mine, followed by a topless woman in a nun's veil. For a split-second, I see a man licking a Popsicle stick, fingers red. I love the crowd at Burning Man, old and young, naked and clothed, the costumed, and the burnouts who dress like Chicago bike messengers on the longest assignment ever. Not far away, a man sits back in an old La-Z-Boy recliner, motorized to drive him around. Don't see that every day.

I am Bedouin. I have many places to visit, many people to see. True, I do not know who they are at this time. But I must meet them. And damn it, I've got to invent a better name than Vinicio Vanabalay.

A young Asian woman jumps in front of me, sporting a spiked, yellow fauxhawk and glittery green eye shadow extending beyond her eyelids, curling downward into flowery spikes on her cheek. She holds melting red ice in front of me, chilly droplets dripping from her fingers.

"Cherry Popsicle, Arab man?"

I nod solemnly. "Yes, please."

She hands me the ice pop, red stickiness running down my fingers as they touch hers.

"Pretty lady, may I do anything for you in return?"

She says, "Kiss me."

She turns her face and indicates the bronzed cheek not covered in sparkly green makeup. I lean in to touch my lips to her soft skin, silently blessing this sparkle pony who decided to make my day better.

She bounces away, eager to distribute her prizes before they melt. Over her shoulder, she says, "Be wonderful."

I will try, Sparkle Pony. I will try.

A school of mermaids passes me, a dozen of them, green streaks in their hair, flowers behind their ears, carrying scaly tails of shimmery blue, like wedding gown trains.

I suck the red juices and glance around Black Rock City, taking in the outrageous, volatile clan gathered in this Nevada desert, the seventeenth year of Burning Man. The Floating World—this year's theme—dictates the art, the street names, even the costumes. Well, to some degree. The barren, crusty playa is our ocean, a boundless dead sea. A million dust granules, finer than sand, our ocean spray.

Out in the real world, everyone's life is shaped by the need to bob the waves and survive reality, gasping for air in the impossible deluge of everyday sensations, modern life experiences. Endless daily chores, information overload, and conflicting moral impulses over minutiae constantly waterlog us, splashing reality into our throats. Drowning us.

Here in the desert, we gather to resist drowning, clear our heads, attempt to ride uncharted waves, instead of simply reacting to life. Or…maybe not. Maybe we celebrate the opposite. To drown. To surrender to the inevitable, sinking beneath thick waters to King Poseidon's ancient ocean floor—this barren bedrock—dancing and swaying like seaweed tethered to the bottom.

Both can be true at Burning Man. Anything is true if you want it to be.

That Popsicle tasted yummy. I add the stick to my carrying bag. It is now my responsibility to carry this moop out of the desert. Matter Out Of Place. *Moop.*

I suck my cherry fingers clean. Don't get started on the word *moop*. Don't do it. Think of the ocean.

The ocean, the ocean, the sea, the sea. *Sea.*

C.

C is the Capital constantly changing, from Capital to capriciously curvy and always upended. A cup you can sit in until it rights itself on its side, spilling over, then back again, becoming a *u*, a *u* you float in until you can *c* it, an ocean of floating in your tea cup. It's obvious *c* and *u* are unique cousins, sharing sibilant sibling parents, an *S* in common who broke into children. You see? *u c?*

Quit it.

Quit doing that, Vin. Don't let yourself. Think about something else. Look around.

I am surrounded.

It's impossible to catalog the thousands of people, some naked, some close to that state, others body-painted with handprints on their thighs. This very second, I am passed by a constant parade of burners on bikes, beat-up bikes, tall bikes, and now, at this second, a man bicycles by, wearing a top hat and a wedding veil and camo shorts. A cloud of churned dust chases in his wake. No point chiding him. The hard crust in this ancient lake bed is dust-free until you step on it. With each footstep, every crunch, alkaline dust is manufactured. More than *see* the white dust, I *feel* it sting my cheeks.

"I beg pardon, Bedouin man."

A man at my side touches my elbow. I turn, half expecting to see Alan or Helena. It's not.

This man is fair, his hair mostly red-brown—more brown perhaps than I first perceived—and his face dusted lightly with freckles. Shirtless and wearing a purple sarong. Thirty, maybe? Thirty-three? He fits my definition of postathletic, someone who used to work out, maybe used to be chiseled but decided that's simply not his style anymore. I hope he slathered his pale skin in sunscreen. Hopefully, he sunscreened the tops of his ears, which stick out a bit. Did he stop me for a reason? Did I drop my Popsicle stick?

He smiles, nervously, as if he must deliver bad news. "I waited until you finished your Popsicle."

Waited?

"May I help you?"

He smiles, broadly now. "It's you. The king maker."

What?

I shake my head and smile. "No, friend, you're thinking of someone else."

How does he know me?

"No," he says. "It's definitely you. Your eyes flinched, a little. Almost imperceptibly, but I was watching for a tell. It's *you*, mate. You're the king maker."

He's English. English accent. Do I know any English guys from Burning Man? I chuckle. "Sorry, friend. You mistake me. I am a simple Bedouin."

He says, "Also, you didn't ask me who or what a king maker was. You instantly denied it. Which means you already know what I mean when I say 'king maker.'"

My heart beats faster. What does he want?

"Shalom," I say, bowing.

I turn away, careful not to appear too eager to leave. If I stride too hard, it will look like I wish to escape. If I give any sign of confirmation, he will chase me. Instead, I pleasantly meander, just another burner appreciating theme camps, lost in a crowd. Chill, Vin. But hurry. Get away from him. I hear a xylophone nearby, maybe three or four of them, a xylophone band. The music sounds like the letter *x* to me. I'd stop and listen, but I have to get away from this guy. He was cute, though. I like a guy with big ears.

I travel only one more block before I see the same shirtless man, in his purple sarong, standing in the makeshift street before me. How the fuck did he manage to get in front of me? I approach him slowly, and he watches my every step, anticipating my racing away. When I get close, he speaks.

"You'll find the English are not easily dissuaded. I worked arse over elbows for two full burns searching for you. Finally gave it up this year."

"'Arse over elbows' isn't British slang."

"English slang," he says. "It is if an English person says it."

He grins at me, happy and lopsided.

Is he crazy? Is he...unhinged? Something feels off-kilter about this situation. Something isn't right.

He laughs. "I invented it. You like, yeah?"

Ah. *That's* it. He's not English. Everything swirling around him says "not from England." Years spent analyzing split-second reactions means I know things almost immediately, and I often don't know how I know it. I can't articulate why I'm so sure, but he's not English. So, why pretend?

I say, "Although no forests grow nearby, metaphorically, you're barking up the wrong tree."

"The king's kiss, mate," he says. "I witnessed what you did. As I passed those two fighting, I heard you cry out 'nobody fucks with the Butterfly King.' After two burns searching for you, I had become attuned, listening for any overheard conversations of *kings*. I know other Found Kings come here. The rumor is, they use Burning Man to gather and make plans in secret."

"Rumors, huh?"

"Burners talk."

My heart pounds. How the hell do I get out of this?

"You mistake me." My resolve grows weaker.

He folds his arms before him. "Which begs a few questions, yeah? Why is it important to these Found Ones to gather in secret? What are they planning?"

I try to appear bored. "You lost me."

It's true. Some Found Kings come to Burning Man every year. Liam told me Perry's coming this year, which terrifies me. I don't know if I'm ready to see him, though three have years passed. Am I over him?

People navigate around us, and as it's clear he's not letting me go, we move out of the main pathway. We are passed by pirates, nymphs, and four men in tutus. A man wearing a Batman cloak and bat headgear strides past us without pants or underwear. Ah, shirt cocking. Kinda weird, but it's all good. Radical acceptance.

He says, "Three years ago right here, I met Liam, the Dolphin King, late one night around a fire drum. He revealed to me, and a few others, his extraordinary tale—his forty hours spent with a garage mechanic who promised to reveal his true kingship."

I say nothing.

"You kinged Liam. Right here at Burning Man. All of us standing around the fire drum could somehow sense the truth of it, though none of us knew what a *kinging* was. The longer into the night he spoke, the more Liam transformed, like some half god revealing himself. He finished his tale as the sun rose, so we all held hands to greet the dawn. I can't tell you how this night impacted me."

I say, "You were doing drugs, weren't you?"

"Yes." He doesn't hesitate in his reply. "But I wasn't hallucinating. I know what I saw."

I'm not sure what to say.

"Please, mate," he says. "I spent the next two years searching for you, yeah? No leads. As a bit of a last resort, I found Liam's restaurant in San Francisco. He refused to put me in touch. He told me, 'that's not how it works.' Said hunting for you disrespected the *organics*. I said, bollocks, and once again, I searched at the next burn. No results. This year, I decided to enjoy myself. Forget about finding the king maker. Then, I *happen* to stroll by as you're yelling a king story and teaching two people the king's kiss. How is that possible?" He takes a step closer. His eyes are earnest. "Please don't tell me I'm wrong, or it's not you. For two burns, I searched. Please be honest with me."

Something feels off in what he told me. On the other hand, he's not wrong. Lying to him is not the right move. I must respect his journey.

Though I fear I know what he will want from me, I must let it happen. "Okay. You found me. What do you want?"

Standing close, I see his eyes fill with tears. "Would you—would you king me?"

Damn it. I knew he would ask.

I evaluate him more closely than I have before.

Not particularly tall, not particularly short. He's handsome—well, handsome to me—but I dig guys who are rather nontraditionally handsome. I like his big ears and straight, long nose. For a moment, I flash upon Perry Mangin, one of the most movie-star handsome men I've ever met, and I can't resist comparing the two. By contrast, this man is plain, but plain is my favorite flavor. The shape of his arched brows, raised in hope, appeals to me. His flushed expression, the raw hunger. Pale and rugby solid, reddish-brown hair glowing in the desert sun.

He searched for me at Burning Man for two years? He's got the fire.

What does my heart say?

Nothing.

Well, that's clear.

I shake my head. "No. I'm sorry, friend."

I turn and head back in my former direction.

"Please," he says, from behind me. "I'll do anything."

Over my shoulder, I say, "I'm sorry you spent time looking for me. I answered your question."

I am sorry. I wish him well. But this can't happen.

Coming at me, there's a man clad in leather pants carrying a—*holy shit, a live snake*—no, wait, it's a snake-painted inner tube hanging around his neck. The snake appears to be eating its own tail. Probably an inner tube from a bike tire. Accompanying him, two more bald guys with inner tube serpents. Yikes, those snakes look completely realistic.

Feather boy, feather girl, feather camp I guess, ahead to the right. A remote control car with a tumbleweed attached to the top races across the street. Cute. I smell pizza. Oh, that's right. Somewhere ahead is the Pizza Sluts camp. I ate there my second night. A Goth accordion player pulls his instrument apart and wheezes the two sides together, making it complain bitterly, possibly about the heat. Burning Man attracts people who like to bond over hardships. When you talk about the weather out here, you're talking about life and death.

The crowd surrounds me, and I feel deliciously lost, floating along, observing theme camps on Mizzen Avenue, wandering across the street labeled as 240 degrees. Maybe I should wander through Center Camp and assist lost noobs. Sit. Chat. Drop off a few coins. I see a camp ahead, Spices and Vices. They're serving lunch, and I feel hungry. Perhaps I will visit those friendly tuna guys from Oregon. Damn good tuna. And a fresh tuna melt at Burning Man? Impossibly delicious.

Two blocks later, after crossing the 220-degree street, I see a guy on stilts. I like stilts. *Stilts* is a word standing tall with *l*'s and *t*'s in it, *i* to keep it—

Damn it, there he is again. Purple Sarong Man.

He's standing right there, in front of me. *Again!* How does he keep getting in front of me? I approach him, and he nods at me, juts his chin in recognition. The gesture feels very English. Except, he's not English. I'm sure of it.

He says, "I want to be clear, yeah? I know what this means. I know it means sacrifice and doing whatever you say for the whole time we spend together. I know. I accept those terms."

I stare at him, vexed. How do I end this?

"Please reconsider."

Despite our immersion in a sea of people, he speaks with an intensity and ease suggesting we're completely isolated. Our own private island.

"I'll do anything."

"I'm sorry. I don't decide to king a man on a whim."

"Bollocks. You kinged Liam at Burning Man many years ago, and you didn't know your intentions until after you spent time with him and received whatever message you get to *king him*. Spend time with me."

"Did Liam tell you we were almost killed?"

"He did, yeah. He was beyond terrified. Every worst fear came true. He said he never felt more alive, more aware of the connectivity in all things. He saw things in the desert he could not explain. He heard unearthly music. He told us *he remembered* but would not articulate what exactly he remembered."

"He probably heard a zither. They make unearthly—"

With his eyes, he scolds me for lying. "No. You know that wasn't it."

I've got to convince him he does not want this. "You're missing the point about almost *dying*. Liam and I almost got killed. I can't do stuff like the old days. I've made commitments to nonviolence, to keeping my men safe."

"We will be safe. You can find a way."

"I don't know anything about you. I don't know what kind of person you are. I don't know if you and I have enough of a spark, any chemistry, a—"

"Okay, okay," he says, raising his hands as if approaching a wild dog. "We will figure it out. Ask me anything. I will tell you anything about me. Give me a chance."

Should I?

I don't think I will king him. I'm not getting any vibes to suggest *yes*. In fact, I'm sure I will *not* king him. But perhaps I have another gift to offer. He's so persistent. He's trying to be patient with me, though he wants this so badly. It's a pretty sweet form of love. It's been years since I tried a Burning Man kinging. The kings will help. Most likely, they have plans of their own—secret stuff—and I'd be crashing their party. *No. That's not true, and you know it.* They'd eagerly help with a kinging. Aric told me they still haven't figured out how to cross a man over. They'd want to participate, to observe and learn.

I could see Perry. My Alcatraz king. My heart thuds with love for him.

I've got to snap out of this feeling, this maudlin gray while standing in sunlight, come back to the here and now. Come back, Vin. I let myself study this strange man in his purple sarong, pretending to be English. Who is he? What are we meant to be for each other?

He clears his throat. "Please? I'm a famous Burning Man artist, and I made three of this year's installations, including that one with the shark fins swimming in concentric circles around the life raft. The feeding frenzy."

"You made that? You're lying."

"Of course I'm lying." He appears almost cross with me. "I said that so you'd think I was cool and you'd want to hang out together. Let's hang out together."

I smile. I love his moxie.

I say, "First, what do you think of the letter x?"

"X?"

"Yeah, as a letter. Any opinions as to its personality?"

"What am I supposed to think?" he asks quickly with a surprised frown. "Always in a tuxedo at expensive parties in Essex, X-rated parties, in his black tux driving a BMW X5. What do I think? X is a badass."

I say, "Walk with me."

TWO

I say, "Here's the plan. Let's skip not knowing each other. Pretend we've been friends for three years. Point out the observations you would make to your intimate friends as we explore Mizzen Avenue. Can you do that? I suspect yes. You seem to be a go-with-it kind of guy."

"No problem. Cheers for the invite."

We head in my original direction.

"What do you think of this year's theme, The Floating World?"

"S'alright," he says. "Don't care much about the theme any year, I suppose, but I won't whinge. I 'specially don't care for the way they named the cross streets after compass degrees, I'll tell you that. So irritating! Why should I have to say, 'two hundred and eighty degrees,' to describe a cross street? It's a cock-up."

"Where were you for Tuesday's whiteout?"

Another fun, shared topic for burners—desert disasters. The infrequent, unpredictable rains that come flooding from the sky, disappearing as quickly and mysteriously as they manifest, crushing tents and creating instant mud lakes. The wind is no idle threat, either. Two years ago, strong winds knocked over an RV. People were inside. Ambulances were needed for the casualties. During Tuesday's ten minute whiteout, so much thick dust scoured us, I had to scoop out the interior of my tent by the handful.

As we discuss how we survived the whiteout and the chaos we witnessed firsthand, I realize I don't know this man's name. Does it matter? A name is nothing more than a word we slap on ourselves and swear to the world, "this is me." They're so one-dimensional, a ridiculous summary of nothing but whatever we file under that heading. So, who cares if I don't know his name? Real names mean little to Burning Man friends.

He asks, "Were you planning on going to the Black Sabbath Pancake Breakfast the morning after the burn?"

"I might. Hadn't planned that far ahead. I hear Porn and Eggs over on Bowsprit is doing something special that morning, too."

He points out a man who has ocean waves tattooed on the lower half of his legs—every square inch.

"What do you think it means?" he asks. "Should we go ask? Or pass by?"

I like how he entertains options besides intruding on the man's solitude.

"Let's wonder," I say. "Let others ask. In the meantime, let's speculate. Do you think he was raised near an ocean?"

"Maybe," he says. "Could be metaphorical. No matter where he's at, he's always relaxing on a beach, standing in water."

"Yes, that fits. What about this theory? What if, three years ago he went kayaking and..."

We eventually decide the man's tats celebrate some triumph, though we disagree on the exact victory. I say he fought off a school of sharks and won. My new friend imagines more of a time-traveling-on-a-giant-squid scenario, which I like. We chat for another two blocks, and I find myself enjoying Purple Sarong Man. I haven't witnessed his compassion for others, but I could see us hanging out. I can't quite fathom the motivation for this English impersonation, yet I enjoy his accent. It's fake, but he's damn good at it.

We stumble into a camp devoted to selling used lawnmowers, and a shirtless salesman wearing a wide, polka-dotted tie invites us to sit in lawn chairs and rest. So we do. While we sit, he brings us each a cold glass of water, two cubes of ice. Ice is a rare luxury here. For me, this is the best part of Burning Man, the lovely bits of kindness floating everywhere around us.

My new English friend says, "Did you hang out at the Dice Bar at all last year?"

"No. I walked by a few times and always saw a line to get in, so I never made it."

"Totally crazy," he says. "The owner organized an ongoing drama every evening with this Hawaiian-themed camp. They became the Hawaiian mafia. Each night, the mafia thugs stopped by with a new threat, culminating the night after The Man burned. The mafia burst in and threw pineapple chunks at everyone, making machine gun sounds. We all pretended to be gunned down. It was fucking hilarious. Everyone was lying there, dying, moaning, and some bugger yelled out, 'I'm dying. Get me some vodka.'"

I laugh. He's good at voices.

He laughs, too, and says, "Someone else cries out, 'sawed in half with bullets. Cosmo, please.' Pretty soon everyone's yelling out drink orders and where they were shot. Soon, we all get up, this dead horde, you know, stiffly, sorely. Instead of being zombies, we all got drinks at the bar and talked about our deaths. How it felt, our last thoughts. Between karaoke numbers, people took the mic and gave self-eulogies, some quite moving. All fucking night, people got pissed and talked about death. Quite lovely."

"That sounds fun."

He says, "It was. One of those times where you feel you belong here, like the universe is magic, and you were meant to chill out with these exact people. Strangers consoled each other on the loss of life, yeah? Meant it, too. It was...it was intense. But brilliant fun, too, you know? It's a Burning Man thing."

I ask, "Do you believe in a magical universe?"

"No," he says right away and then pauses. "I want to. I mean, sometimes I believe. You experience extraordinary moments and you think, 'life is brilliant,' but it always seems to fade, doesn't it? The rent on your flat is due. You have to work some shite project. Your lover reveals himself to be a nutter, and instead of feeling lucky and blessed to have loved at all, you bloody hate life, feeling nothing is fair in the world."

I get his perspective. Many believe life will one day be sparkly and joyful all the time—*after* we "arrive," in some hard-to-describe way. Pain will not hurt and sadness will find someone else. Magic should save us. It's hard to stop searching for one happy elixir of life. Does he think his King Weekend will fix everything?

I say, "Sounds like you went through a bad breakup."

He snickers. "Aren't they all?"

"Getting kinged doesn't eliminate bad breakups. Or the necessity of paying rent."

He smiles a crooked smile at me. "I accept that. Cheese and toast."

"I'm not familiar with that expression."

"I'm being cheeky. Made that one up, too. I like seeing which invented phrases I can pass off as an authentic expression. It amuses me."

He's got balls, I'll give him that.

"I like playing with words," he says.

"I noticed."

Wait—he likes playing with words?

Did he say that to win me over? Does he know more about me than he lets on? Or does...or does he simply like words, as he said? Okay, Vin. Dial down the paranoia. And yet, it's not all paranoia. He didn't run into me organically. He lied about that. What else is a lie?

We drink our water in silence, and he passes another test of mine: to see if he can simply be. When our cups are empty—our ice sucked into nonexistence—our eyes meet to confirm it's time to go. We stand. The shirtless man with the fat necktie comes to us to ask if we have considered buying one of their spectacular showcase models.

"Check out the GTZ4000XL Magnum 4500 DZ5," he coos, pointing at the decades-old frame of the severely dented lawnmower that proudly stands front and center in their show area.

He gets on one knee and pretends to rub away dust with a hankie.

"It's nice," I say, rubbing my chin. "But we wanted something with an engine. And a handle."

"Wheels would be nice," says my new friend.

"No, no," our dazzling salesman protests, caressing the frame. "You're seeing this all wrong. Many years left in this beauty. Top of the line."

"It looks like a rusted turtle shell," I say. "And the turtle left."

"Oh, darling," says my faux-English friend, putting his arm through mine. "What do you care, yeah? I'm the one who does all the mowing at our house." He cocks his head and turns to our salesman. "Like I can get *this one* into the garden. Him and his stamp collection."

We both smirk, and I play the role of injured stamp collector. Our salesman plays along, giving up eventually, promising, "You won't find these bargains elsewhere."

We thank him for the water and the chance to rest, and he bows—a thespian concluding his role.

After rummaging under my jubba for the fanny pack I carry around my waist, I find the object of my search and present him with a gold coin.

"No money," he says with surprise and perhaps a smidge of irritation.

I'm violating a sacred Burning Man tenet. No currency is exchanged here except for buying ice and coffee at the Center Camp tent. To attempt to buy food or water is an offense to the giver, reducing his generosity to crass consumerism. Out here in the desert, we live in abundance. Generosity is our currency.

I continue to hold the coin in front of me. "I apologize and intend no offense, my hospitable lawn-mowing friend. Check it over, sahib, and note it carries no currency markings."

"It's heavy," he says, taking it.

"Heavy, good sahib, as it bears the burden of granting wishes. You now hold a wishing coin, you see, imbued with the height of Roman power. On this side, the goddess of abundance, Copia, and on the other, Nero. Wish for whatever bounty you desire in your life, but beware selfish wishes born of an emperor's ego. Selfish wishes have a knack for coming true in unexpected ways."

He frowns. "This isn't a real Roman coin, is it?"

I smile. "I enjoy making up stories."

Our salesman wraps the coin in his fist and holds it to the sky. "With the goddess Copia as my witness, my wish shall be non-beer-related."

My purple-sarong friend and I say good-bye and amble down the street, hot dust curling around our feet. A line of men, naked except for their rainbow-painted skin, cross in front of us, causing us to step aside as they hustle by, laughing and shouting.

After we pass a gaggle of nuns, I say, "Is it me or are there a lot of nuns at Burning Man every year? Do you think they're rebelling, or recruiting?"

"Recruiting," he says. "Go where the sin is. Actually, I talked to a bird last year who said nun's habits keep your hair cooler, out of the sun. Cheap, too."

Makes sense.

Men and women in Santa hats pass us singing. This is a good opportunity for my proposition.

"Okay, new purple-sarong friend, here's my idea. I will ask you three questions. Your heartfelt honesty does not guarantee I will say 'yes' to a King Weekend.

However, answering with even the *slightest* dishonesty will assuredly disqualify you, and at this point, I barely need reasons to disqualify you. Understand?"

His eyes get slightly bigger. "Yes, King Maker."

"Please do not call me that. I do not make kings. I cannot *make* kings."

"I don't know your name."

"You don't need to know it. Nor I yours. We may never meet after this conversation. Today, we both had a conversation with a nameless man we came upon in the desert."

"This...this is..." he sputters, and it's obvious he doesn't appreciate my answer. "I don't mind if you know my name."

"Don't tell me. Let circumstance dictate when our names are revealed. This is a dance. You've already proven—several times—you're attuned to reading people. So, I shouldn't have to repeat this next statement. From now on, you follow my dance moves. Let me lead. Exchanging names isn't forbidden but telling me yours in this moment is like stepping on my toes. You want me to come to this decision *organically* and give you full consideration, right? Answer with unflinching honesty and let things unfold."

He nods. "Okay. I will. May I ask you a few questions, too? I don't know much about King Weekends, or you. Only what I learned through Liam's story." Hastily, he adds, "I'm not making a demand. I'm asking if I *may* ask you a few questions."

"I may not answer, but yes, you may ask. Let's keep wandering and observing. I'm enjoying this time together."

He sighs with relief.

We continue down Mizzen Avenue, and the road curves again to reveal more campsites and one or two upcoming theme camps. With over thirty thousand people expected to attend this year's Burning Man, we can entertain ourselves for days just by walking the streets.

"It's weird not knowing your name," he says. "What if I want to get your attention? Should I say, 'Hey you'?"

"You know, I struggled to come up with a good Burning Man name for myself. The result of my brainstorm was Vinicio Vanabalay."

"That sounds Italian, not Arabic."

"I *know*. I'm not great at inventing names."

He chuckles at this, and before either of us responds, a lady calls out from her lawn chair, raising her plastic cup. "Go home, Arab. Never forget 9/11!"

I bow to her and continue along the way.

"Why didn't you say something?" he asks.

"She seemed drunk. Not worth it. Okay, my first question. Why does this matter so much to you, getting kinged? You spent two burns seeking me and found Liam in his restaurant in San Francisco. Obviously, this is important."

Another sparkle pony approaches, platinum-blond hair and dressed as a cheerleader, her gaze glued to my shirtless companion. As she saunters past, she says, "Yummy." Four Asian men dressed as Ghostbusters jog past us, armed with poltergeist equipment, which appears to be Super Soakers.

Burning Man is a never-ending parade, one spectacle after another. No wonder I picked Burning Man as the site for my first real kinging. This place is insane. When the San Francisco Cacophony Society first wore costumes to this event back in 1990, they had no idea the legacy to follow. Costumes matter.

"Yes," he says. "It's important. I've spent a great deal of time questioning this myself. I'm not sure what I expect you to do for me. I am a lawyer who doesn't like the law, heavily in debt to my alma mater. I never should have gone to school in the States. I'm a wanker. Stupidest decision I ever made. Could have become a barrister for free back home. So, I work. I come home. I try to do yoga or read. I get high. I go to parties. Is this it? Work for some toff until I retire? There must be more. There has to be."

He's earnest. This answer is truth. But it's not his truest truth. There's more going on here. We stroll in silence while people yell and laugh around us. Dust interrupts us again. We keep our mouths closed, and a tuba player in full band uniform attempts to shield his instrument from the onslaught, the very definition of futility. After a moment, we're free to speak again.

I say, "Go deeper."

I trust he knows what this means.

His voice trembles. "I didn't seek you because I need help with a career change. I'm not asking because I'm bored. Not exactly. Not looking for something to believe in. I'm saying I *already* believe. When Liam told the story of *The Lost and Founds*, I felt a punch to my sternum in a way I cannot explain. Every man is the one true king...I *know* that's true, yet I can't quite taste it. I hate asking you to king me, I would much rather demand it. Or use my lawyer skills to persuade you. Something tells me you aren't persuadable, and I hate that, too."

He's too...solicitous. Not every Englishman possesses a stiff upper lip, but there's a quality here that's hard to define, a boundary he keeps crossing. Will I ask him why he masquerades as English? Will he give me an honest answer?

No. There's a more pressing question.

I pull him to the side, off our gritty road, allowing more burners on bikes to pass our slow wanderings.

"I need to see your face for the second question. Ready?"

He studies me with cautious surprise and nods.

"I know you lied about finding me *organically*. You didn't happen to stumble upon me when I met Helena and Alan. Tell the truth."

His face instantly assumes a certain defensiveness, someone wrongfully accused, but I must cut him off before he speaks a word.

"Remember, if you lie, there's no chance I will consider a King Weekend."

He reads my serious, probing expression, and I read the microshifts in his face. In a split-second, he decides to tell the truth. I see it. It's all right there.

"Okay," he says cautiously. "I did not find you organically. I lied. Wandering around Burning Man for two years didn't work, so I decided to try a different approach. At one point in his story, Liam accidentally let your last name slip. I don't think he realized he'd said it aloud. He was careful to reveal nothing about your appearance, and he referred to you only as 'the mechanic.' I knew I couldn't find you in the real world, but here? Maybe. This year, I found a volunteer to bribe, someone who could get me access to the entire campsite registration. She found me all campsites registered under the name 'Vanbly.' There were exactly two. One is a married couple. The other was you. I followed you for a full day wondering how to introduce myself. Suddenly, you yelled about the Butterfly King. I took the opportunity."

I study his expression. I say, "Good."

He squints. "How did you know?"

"I'm not sure. I could just tell. I guess you weren't excited enough when you *accidentally* ran into me. If you truly had been searching for two burns— and it mattered this much—I think you'd have stuttered more, displayed more nervousness. Something. You seemed too calm."

He grins weakly. "Side effect of being English, I suppose."

I cross my arms. "Yeah, about that. You do realize, *if* I king you, all your bullshit lies will tumble out. *All* of them."

He meets my gaze with firmness. "I apologize for the flutter on how I ran into you."

"Flutter?"

"Means gamble. I gambled. I struggled with how approach you because I know I was wrong, bribing and whatnot. Bloody invasive and rude. Now, that's all pear-shaped, too. Beyond that lie—which I am sorry for—I won't tell you another."

You're not English!

How can he stand here and tell me he's not lying? His eyes deny me, refuse to capitulate. He's a lawyer, so I have no doubt he's got an airtight case. Undoubtedly, he's memorized all the details of his English "hometown," wherever that is, and relevant facts about the motherland. Slang, language, London, customs. Attending college and law school in the United States would explain his bastardization of his native tongue when he accidentally slips. I won't catch him easily.

Returning his stare, I say, "I need you to know. All the lies."

He remains unflustered, staring into me, but his eyes are locked tight, a fortresses I will not penetrate.

Oh.

We've been standing close and I've studied his eyes, but I didn't notice them. I mean, I didn't *see*. They're stunning, hazel, greenish-brown with flecks of gold. Magnificent, really. Observing them this close, I see the patterns, like a blurry constellation, faraway radiant gold, an entire milky way orbiting a black, demanding sun. His eyes contain universes, and I did not notice. I was so busy trying to catch him.

"Star light, star bright, first star I see tonight." I hear myself murmur the words between us, and as if in response, the desert wind rises, swirling a friendly tornado around us, around everyone. His hands rise to protect his vision, reminding me to do the same. Pointless, of course, as the dust gets everywhere, in everything, becomes everything. Five days on the playa and we are nothing but dust. Still, I try to protect the eyes, the one tool indispensable for desert survival. If you can't see, you die.

When we wipe our faces and resume our gaze, he no longer possesses that confrontational glower. He appears chaste and slightly nervous again.

"I have a question or two for you," he says. "Is sex an essential part of your King Weekend? Is it a requirement?"

Hell, yes, it's required. It's one of the ways I spin all my love into a man. But wait a minute, Vin. Is it *necessary*? Stop and consider this. *Necessary* versus highly desirable. Couldn't I love a man without fucking him?

"Let's talk about this. I love sex. I love making love to the man I'm kinging. With you, I feel a strong spark of attraction I would enjoy converting into physical expression. I love your cute ears and your hazel eyes. Until a moment ago, I didn't realize how dazzling your eyes are, and I am beginning to think you might be like your eyes—a lot more than you first appear. You hear me?"

"Yeah," he says glumly.

"Hang on. I didn't say deal breaker."

"Okay," he says, a tad more hopeful.

It's a small shift.

"Were you ever sexually abused as a kid, or young person?"

"No," he says with some surprise.

The red glint to his hair gleams in raw sunlight.

"I'm serious. It will fuck things between us if you lie about sexual abuse."

"I'm not lying," he says, and his earnestness returns, which I already find endearing. The sincerity on his face reminds me of peanut butter, somehow. A creamy expression from his hazel eyes? A nutty—I dunno. I don't know what to feel about this guy. Beyond his eyes, he reminds me of peanut butter.

"Make me a peanut butter promise you don't have sexual abuse in your past."

I hold out my pinky to seal the deal.

"Peanut butter promise," he says, equally serious, raising his pinky.

We interlock them and pinky swear.

"So why don't you want to have sex? Be honest. Not attracted?"

"No," he says with haste. "*Attracted*. Definitely attracted. Remember when I said I experienced a bad breakup, yeah? Complete nutter. Left me in shambles. It's put me off sex for the past eight months. If I thought we might have sex this weekend, I'd worry nonstop and wonder if I were ready. It's stressing me out to think about it. But. I will follow your lead. I know I must absolutely comply in all ways, so, I'm trying to steady myself for it."

I chuckle. "Bracing yourself for sex. That's hot."

He looks at me with sadness. "I'm not ready."

"You've given me another variable to consider. Touch and affection are powerful ways to love you. Not exclusively for the sexual healing aspect—and don't pretend to me you don't know sex is healing."

He recoils. A useful reveal. Sex damaged him.

I say, "What about touching without sex? May I touch you?"

"Yes," he says, conciliatory in his tone, yet I know it's not authentic. Not entirely. He's nervous.

"We need to test these boundaries. I'm going to get close to you. Touch you. If we're going to hang out, I need to determine the line I cannot cross. If I cross said line, you *must* speak out, telling me it feels too sexual."

This makes him breathe easier. Without a shirt on, I see his whole body take a breath, sucking in hot sunlight. The agreement about sex mattered a great deal. What happened to him?

"Keep in mind, friend, I need to get physically close all weekend. You've gotta let me sidle next to you, to whisper in your ear. If it feels like sex, and you get nervous, say so. But if my standing close makes you nervous because I make you feel jumpy, you might have to accept it. Physical proximity is not sex."

"Brilliant," he says with deeper relief. "Cheers."

"Let's step to the side."

We walk until we reach a section of road a little less fabulous, where burners hang out in their campsites, appreciating what's all around them yet enjoying a quieter experience. Less people traffic and more space to loiter. Behind us and to the right, a very hairy Alice in Wonderland straps on his blond wig. Wearing a blue twirly dress, Army boots, and sporting a five-day stubble, he certainly puts a unique spin on this childhood favorite.

I take the Purple Sarong Man's two hands in mine and clear my throat. "How's this?"

He squints at me and says, "I can barely see. Sun's in my eyes."

"Mine, too. Roughly noon. We're both blind."

"Right," he says. "This is good. Standing here holding hands. This—I appreciate this. I appreciate you're not pushing me on sex."

"I'm not promising anything, stud. I'm not convinced I can king you without sex, but I'll definitely think about it. Might be an interesting challenge, actually. Now, I'm going to step closer. How's this? May I stand this close?"

"Yes," he says.

I pull his hands to my shoulders. "How about this?"

"Easy peasy."

Still the English accent. I underestimated his commitment. This English persona is a bigger deal than I supposed. The secret to his King Weekend might lie right there—getting him to reveal he's not English.

I place his hand on my chest. "How about now?"

"Yes, fine," and he says this with breezy confidence, so I know we're not near the edge.

I touch and stroke his neck, caress his cheek with my fingertips, and slow dance, all successfully bypassing his boundaries. Can I king a guy without having sex? How do I feel about that? No sex? I *like* this guy. A lot, already. He made me his stamp-collecting husband. He thinks I am the kind of man who collects stamps? Of course I wanna have sex with him.

I move my lips close to his. The desert heat is a stick of gum we're clutching between us. The air smells acrid, burning my nostril hairs, or else the heat is from him. One of us ate an embarrassing amount of fire for lunch.

"Still okay?"

"It's close," he says, nervous, and his tongue darts to lick his lips. "I'd consider kissing part of sex, yeah?"

My hand finds its way to his angular jawline. A person might describe his jaw as "hard planed," softened by the smooth skin and the sweat dripping from him. He is so beautiful.

"Part your lips, yes, like that. Are you all right? If I talk into your mouth but do not kiss you?"

"This makes me anxious," he says.

I take a step back. "Okay. We found the line."

He nods with relief.

"We're not done. I have a few more intimacy tests."

We hug. I'm surprised when he lets me hold him from behind, wrapping my arms around his front, hands on his stomach. We stay like this a moment, swaying together, watching a parade of Maxers trudge by.

"I invented a word for all the burners who look like extras from a Mad Max movie. Have you seen those movies?"

"Yeah."

"So, you know the type. Old clothes, creatively wrapped scarves protecting body parts from the sun, water pouches, crusty handkerchiefs wrapped around their hands. Appearing both futuristic and dirt-poor."

He chuckles. "I know it."

"I call them Maxers."

"Cheers," he says. "Good word."

Is that how an English person uses the word cheers? I dunno. He likes me holding him. I feel him nestling into me. I don't think his sex resistance is physical. This is emotional. He got hurt during sex.

"I can't control my erection," I say. "If we're hanging out this close and I bone up—I get hard—you won't be expected to relieve me, but I refuse to deny myself a good hard-on."

"Right. Might feel a bit dodgy for me. Uncomfortable."

"Perhaps it will. But no sex will follow."

"Okay," he says, unconvinced.

"If I show up tomorrow evening, I will respect your boundaries. I haven't promised anything yet. I might decide I can't king a man without sex. Or maybe the issue isn't sex. I may not hear the 'king him' voice inside me. So, all this conversation may be for nothing. We don't know."

"Yeah, yeah. I bloody hear you."

"Okay. I won't say it again. I need you to know—"

"Message received." He extricates from my arms and turns to face me. "Okay, my turn. While we're spending time together, may I take notes?"

"No."

"Why not?"

"Writing about the experience gets in the way of *having* the experience."

"But I will want to write down observations. Conversations. A journal. I won't write all the time."

"Nope. Nothing. No voice recorder or notebook."

"What if I forget something?"

"Then you forget."

"What if I want to king a man myself and I need to remember what you said?"

I laugh. "I seriously doubt reading from your journal will help. Half the time, I don't know what I'm saying, or where this all comes from. Next question."

"Can I smoke pot?"

"No."

"I meant, can *we* smoke pot. I would share."

"Nope."

"Just thought it might help create a nice mellow vibe."

"No pot. No alcohol. What else?"

"May I ask questions while we're spending time together or must I follow every order without understanding why?"

"I'd strongly prefer no questions. Strongly. I'm not saying, 'don't communicate.' If you want a water break or need to sit out of the sun, speak out. Obviously, we'll chat all weekend like normal people do."

"You don't want me asking questions about what you're doing or saying?"

"Same as pot. Same as note-taking. You can't have an experience if you're doing everything possible to get out of the experience, moment to moment. Pot and note-taking are a definite no. Can you ask questions? If not asking means you're going to obsess for six hours, sure, ask the damn question. I might choose not to answer it. Or I might ask you why you think you need an answer. You'll be the one under scrutiny. Bottom line. If possible, don't ask."

"I don't understand why my asking questions about the experience—"

I say, "My third and final question, and then I'll let you go."

He looks anxious. "Mate, we've hardly spent any time together."

"Enough time for me to know I like you."

He says, "I have so many more questions."

"Nah, you really don't. Besides, I won't stay answering questions for another two hours when I have some serious pondering to do."

"What should I wear?"

"Whatever's comfortable. We'll have to return to our tents for water, maybe heavier clothes at night, so you'll have the opportunity to change clothes. Bring whatever water you would carry if you decided to amble around Black Rock City for a few hours."

The dust blows between us, reminding us both of the wisdom in my words.

I say, "My third question. What's your favorite color?"

His eyes fill with tears. "I don't know. I stopped caring about favorite colors a long time ago. Don't you think it a bit off, to not have a favorite color? To not *remember* one's favorite color, yeah?"

I'm surprised by the raw truth in these words, the way tears came instantly. It's harder to cry in the desert. The body conserves water. Yet, they came to him so readily, I suspect being around me is putting him under much greater stress than he's letting on. He wants this. He wants this bad.

I reach for his right ear and caress the outside ridge between my thumb and forefinger. "Much better answer to the question of why you want this King Weekend. To get your colors back."

A tear falls.

"Also, please tell me you're wearing enough sunscreen."

He wipes his face and says, "I am."

"Head? Back of neck? On your ears, too?"

"Yes."

"Good."

I turn to leave.

A man approaches us. Well, technically, the Ace of Clubs approaches us. The giant playing card covers both his front and back. Glancing around, it's apparent he's part of the Alice in Wonderland crew assembling nearby. I see a couple other aces and some face cards. They carry long lances.

Looooooooong laaaaaaaaaaaaaaaaaaances.

"Hey guys," he says. "Help me out? I need someone to secure the straps of the card on my back."

"Absolutely." I indicate Purple Sarong Man. "He'll help you."

"Wait! I have more questions." Purple Sarong Man smiles, but I see he is irked—with a *k* up his ass—because he wanted more time with me, and now he's got an assignment.

I back away from the two of them. "If I'm going to king you, I'll meet you tomorrow at six p.m."

The Ace of Clubs says, "Thanks, man. They're hard to fasten in the back."

Purple Sarong Man says, "*Wait.* Where should I meet you?"

His voice is almost shrill. He's not happy about me leaving.

I grin. "Where do you think? Where does anybody meet?"

I turn and walk away.

I know nothing about his compassion. That seems significant. I dunno. Maybe I overestimate its importance as the spark. Maybe it's always present, and I should assume everyone has it, instead of insisting I witness a firsthand demonstration. Maybe I don't need to see it. The more skilled I become at kinging men, the more of my own rules I find myself breaking. Of course, we didn't have cause for him to show compassion. He seemed cool about respecting people as we wandered down Mizzen. That's something, right?

"Once there was a tribe of men, a tribe populated entirely of kings!"

I hear the words yelled and turn around.

He stands behind the Ace of Clubs man. The playing card's arms are extended while he gets buckled up.

I hear my new friend say, "Hang on, mate."

Louder, he yells to me, "Every man was the one true king and every woman, the one true queen. Odd you may think and wonder how any work got done in such a society with everyone making rules. But these were not those kind of kings."

He shoots me a crooked grin. I nod and smile. How does he know the exact words?

He watches me backing away and yells, "My name is Alistair!"

I nod. I turn away.

Alistair is good.

If I were faking English, I'd have gone with Nigel, but I suppose that's a bit over the top.

THREE

Hands on my hips, I survey the city.

Black Rock City.

I observe a thousand dusty campsites and two thousand more behind them, all impacted by the same swirling singular wind, sweeping in from the barren playa far behind me. I watch it crash against the nearest tents, unstoppable as it curls into open nylon flaps and RV doors. Dust settles on food and drinks, shoulders and shoes. From this vantage point, I inspect our temporary metropolis rising from the dead earth each year—a city erected with engineering precision for a festival idealizing chaos.

That's Burning Man for you, the unlikely attraction of polar opposites. Abundance amidst the scarcest, deadliest landscape known to man. Chaos brings life. Burning equals renewal. And naked, joyful hope arises every year from people who have almost given up on the outside world.

Burning Man has changed over the years.

The first few years I attended felt strange. Many people knew each other from the San Francisco Cacophony Society or were part of Larry's crew, those who had erected The Man for years on a San Francisco beach. Even with that smaller attendance, I could blend in unnoticed for a weekend. Well, usually. The first year out here, I got caught limping back into camp the morning after The Man had burned, as people packed up to go home. The questions began. Who are you? Who here knows you? What were you doing in the desert all night?

What was I doing?

Freezing, mostly.

Given the cold, I don't remember why I woke up naked the next morning. Hell, I don't remember why I decided to go into the desert the previous night. Maybe to stare at the Milky Way? I remember the freezing temperatures, how small and insignificant I felt, how liberating it was to fully realize I am so unimportant and... and then I awoke naked, my clothes folded neatly in a pile near my feet, which of course I must have done. Sleepwalked, maybe.

I didn't enjoy the probing questions, and I didn't want to confess the truth—I was lost and cold and couldn't find my way home. Those early organizers kept grilling me, and I'm sure it seemed suspicious, my inability to answer them. They eventually forced me to reveal I knew nobody prior to the event. I subscribed to the Cacophony Society's newsletter and decided to join the fun. But that guy, Ranger Ron, he did not like me. He didn't call himself that back then. There were no rangers. But he's the lead ranger now. Or if not the lead, one of the top two guys.

"What were you doing out there?" he asked me over and over.

I shook my head, over and over. "I don't know," I kept saying. "I don't remember."

I skipped in 1991, feeling I had drawn a little too much attention to myself. By the time I returned to Burning Man, the crowd had tripled in size. I could haunt the playa easily. First year back I impersonated a media technician from HBO. That was fun. Steered clear of the organizers like Ranger Ron as much as possible. Still, he eventually found me. I guess it was the third year of my return, he stopped me in the street, spun me around, and said, "It's you, isn't it?"

My heart pounded as I walked away. He recognized me?

I denied it.

He followed me for the next half hour. I found a friendly camp where I interacted casually, pretending to be part of their crew. They were baffled but played along. Ranger Ron did not approach me directly and eventually left. To this day, I avoid him. Though I doubt he remembers me, Ranger Ron still makes me uneasy.

The next year, I kinged Lucian during Burning Man. The next year, Liam. After that, well, I no longer required this makeshift community as unwitting collaborators—the bleary lovers and drunken misfits, the artists, the welders, the watchers, gun hoarders and sun-baking goddesses. I learned how to bring the love beyond this desert. I could king men in real cities.

And now? Well, now I am a wandering Bedouin in a city that spans seven miles across.

These are my people, those who live on the fringe. Those who don't always have a home, a job, a place in the world. Of course these days, the Burning Man tribe includes wealthy trust fund partiers, middle-class adventurers, and bored tech guys trying to get laid. Everything changed mid-90s, when the Silicon Valley dot-commer adopted Burning Man as a networking opportunity. But, *shalom*, they must be made to feel welcome. Radical acceptance. This makeshift city—its rich kids, freaks, and paupers—is still the closest thing I know to a home.

Another hot breath of desert air hisses against me, stinging my nose hair, urging me into the city. I cover my eyes until it's safe to gaze around again.

Burning Man evolves but this playa remains unchanged.

Every single year, the wind discolors the brightest art cars and the flashiest theme camps, repainting them a dull sandstone, until the air clears again, and everyone coughs out the desert's latest offering. From here, the capital, the very throne of Burning Man, I see how far, how deep, the perfect order penetrates the city. Perfect alignment, the city built in a vast curve—about three-quarters of a circle. It makes me wonder how easy it could be to navigate real cities if someone were permitted to do what is done here each year: dictate the city layout using a compass and geometry. If that were possible, I wouldn't get so lost in London.

Last chance to reconsider: will I ask Alistair about London? Will I spend time trying to trip him up? Nah. I've been over this many times. Trying to force his confession won't stir his vulnerability, only make him more defensive. I could work to expose him, but where's the victory if I win and he loses? No kingship there. He must choose to tell me.

Though still plenty bright right now—only six o'clock—I see lamplighters gathering, wearing their ceremonial robes, bearing yokes of kerosene. With the sun running in slow motion to the horizon, manufactured light will not be needed for hours. They obviously enjoy their gift of service, and I'm guessing they gather early to discuss their plans, or perhaps to lounge with others like them. They are one of the many volunteer groups who keep Black Rock City running.

Far off, I see La Contessa fucking around, lurching forward, sailing a few hundred feet at dangerous speeds, then screeching to a halt. Deathtrap on wheels. Who'd have thought you could build a half-sized replica of a Spanish galleon pirate ship on a school bus and drive it around the desert? I had fun with those guys the other day, but I doubt they took my advice about keeping the engine clean. They are marching band guys, not car guys. Far away, I see another mutant car, this one a great white whale. A giant shark car. Junker cars spray painted with messages or the anarchy symbol. Another three dozen mutant vehicles circle outside the city, too distant for me to recognize their exact creativity. I watch them drive in looping arcs through the permitted area, like koi fish in a pond, darting artfully, aware they are watched and admired. Hmm. They are coy koi.

I decide right now, standing here, I am captain of the known world. The Floating World. I stand before the lighthouse, this wooden structure serving as a pedestal. On it stands, well, *him*. Oh, right. Who am I kidding? I'm not the captain of The Floating World. He is.

The Man.

The enormous wooden man, the mayor of Black Rock City, rising forty feet into the air, the faceless humanoid construction we choose to worship as our trusty commander until Saturday night, when we set him on fire and shout into the black night, "Burn! Burn! Burn!"

Everyone screams. We will scream for his destruction. Those guys over there and those women wearing lobster claws. They will scream. Those reclining on beach towels, studying Burning Man with big fruity drinks.

We're tough on the mayor.

Another Bedouin, dressed similarly to me, approaches the lighthouse. He's more of a wealthy oil sheik, mirrored sunglasses and a long gold cord wrapped around his keffiyeh. Apparently, my costume was not so unique.

A man and a woman approach the lighthouse holding hands. Both have cameras.

I ask, "Would you two like to be photographed together?"

"Sure," she says and pulls back her orange hair. "Thank you."

We position them in a few traditional tourist photos, but after a minute, I encourage him to kiss her, *really* kiss her. I snap a few of those for them, too. We part.

When the new sheik speaks, his voice is surprisingly heavy, thick with a fake Middle Eastern accent. "Shalom. I seek the Italian expatriate, the one they call Vinicio."

Ha. It's Alistair.

I put my hands on my hips and stare into the distance, chin proudly jutting forward. "It is I, Vinicio Vanabalay. Blamed for a crime I did not commit—"

"Lame," he says.

"Seeking justice for my slain family—"

"Nope." He raises his hands. "Not unless you're Russell Crowe. How about this? Spice trader. Seeking the elusive, um, xenoxx plant, yeah? With three *x*'s."

"Spell it."

"*X-e-n-o-x-x.*"

"Nice. Go on."

"Well, you're searching for the xenoxx plant, while trying to uncover the truth about your father, a spice trader like yourself, who disappeared mysteriously."

"How is that better than my slain family?"

"Mysterious is better. Everyone knows. You're primarily searching for the xenoxx plant. The plots are intertwined."

"Okay. What's the xenoxx plant do?"

"Um, healing properties? Don't you think, yeah? Exotic plants often heal some rare disease."

Healing properties. Interesting.

"Taken under advisement. Nice threads by the way. You didn't have to dress like that."

He holds his jubba between his fingers, pulling it away and whipping the fabric around his legs as I admire it. "I traded two boxes of chocolate biscuits and two gallons of water for this. Bloody energy bars for the gold cord. If we had talked more yesterday, I could have asked more questions about what to wear."

"I told you to wear something comfortable."

"I had more questions than that."

"I believe I warned you I would not answer some questions."

"Yeah, but—"

"Did I know you had a million more questions? Yes. Did I let you sit with them for a full day, like the stink of rotting road kill? Yes. Lord Alistair, had it occurred to you this stewing—which you now pretend to be so cheerful about, while obviously it bothers you very *much*, thank you—was a necessary part of your kinging?"

"Why?"

I pull off my keffiyeh, exposing my full face. "Quit asking questions."

"Why?"

He pulls off his keffiyeh and his sunglasses, revealing his earnest, inquiring face. The kind of open, boyish-man's face you'd trust in a courtroom to tell you the truth.

He says, "Answer me this *one* and I'll stop. I just—I want to know why leaving me ill-prepared for this experience was essential. Hear me out, yeah? Meeting you here wasn't as easy as I thought. The last twenty-four hours have been a rollercoaster. When I saw you standing here, my heart panicked, and I almost backed out, despite having searched so long. You don't know how scary this is. I've heard stories, and not only from Liam. You unravel people. You break them. It's scary to say *yes* to a mystery weekend with all your questions unanswered. Do you understand?"

"I do."

"I mentioned, I'm a lawyer, yeah? Lawyers don't go to court unprepared. This is all wonky."

He's articulate, self-aware, and honest. Good. This is good. I can be frank.

I say, "Thank you for your honesty."

"Where's the harm, mate, in answering one question?"

I run my hand over the blond stubble on my skull, flinging sweat from the back of my head. The sun remains powerful, even as it strolls toward its own setting.

I say, "Where's the harm, *mate*? Well, there's a price. A price you must pay to hear the true answer to your question."

"What's the price?"

"That's a different question. Either pay the price and get your full answer, or no answer, no consequences."

"I want the answer," he says, squinting. "I'm not trying to be a tosser. But it's bothering me."

"Absolutely," I say. "You should know once this question is no longer stressing you, another will take its place. Then another. Then more. I don't think you'll feel the satisfaction you expect. Still, if you want, I'll answer you and reveal the damage. Sound good?"

He nods.

"Let's sit in the shade for a moment. Other side of the lighthouse."

We head to the east side, which provides meager shade in the shadow of The Man. I sit on a wooden bench, tracing the exterior, and he joins me. We hear people tromping around the platform above us, laughing, occasionally calling to friends. From here, we regard a few of the larger interactive art pieces erected in the desert. Beyond the art, far away, the Calico Mountains. Still, no human-made art outclasses the sun, the best and biggest artistry in this competition.

"I'm sorry you're nervous about hanging out with me. I understand what you went through to come today was difficult. I get it, because I intentionally made it hard. Tell me this. If I'd sat with you yesterday and answered all your questions for the next two hours, would you have felt better?"

"Yes."

"And what would you have done with information I provided."

"I would have analyzed it for better understanding of a King Weekend and if such a weekend felt right for me. I would feel more confident about my personal and emotional safety. As far as today, I could relax and enjoy my time with you instead of feeling anxious."

"Okay, so more information would have helped you relax. Helped you make the decision to show up."

"Yes."

"No. Not true. The amount of information didn't impact your decision. We know this to be true because here you are."

"Specious reasoning."

"Ah, lawyer talk. With additional information, the lawyer in you could think, think, think until you dug escape tunnels for every question I might ask. That's what you would have done with my answers."

"I wouldn't say that, no. Valuable analysis, yes. But not—"

"Liar."

He bristles.

"Alistair, you're not someone who lies to yourself often, so let my accusation sting a little. You lie to the outside world, but you don't lie to yourself. You pride yourself on that. My point is, with your questions unanswered, you grew your trust. You stretched a muscle inside you which you forget to exercise."

He puts his elbows on his knees and says, "Trust."

"That's what you grew in the past twenty-four hours, living with unanswered questions. You grew your faith. One way to grow your crop of faith is to grow it incrementally, force your heart open an inch at a time. I once kinged an Illinois farmer. I pried open his trust inch by fucking inch. All weekend, inch by inch. Inside his crusty exterior hid this amazing man waiting for someone to find him. Your King Weekend won't work that way because you're completely different."

"How?"

"Well, you strike me as the kind of man who grows in explosive bursts. Nudge a man like you in the right direction and you go barreling toward the kingdom gates. Drawback is, the more a man like you knows about how his kingship works, the more he intellectualizes the experience. It decreases his odds of crossing over. Now that you know I intentionally attempted to grow your trust, every time a similar opportunity presents itself this weekend—a time when you could spontaneously act from compassion or faith—you'll think twice. How should I act? What would someone with trust do? What would a king do? You won't know your true reaction. You've just lost the opportunity for unconscious authenticity. Receiving the answer to your big question—that I was trying to grow your trust in a huge leap—has suddenly made it a lot harder for you to reach your kingship."

"Wait. I wasn't trying to wreck the weekend, I only wanted to know why—"

"Now you do. *And* you've paid the price. Compared to five minutes ago, you're now less likely to become a Found King."

"Bullocks!" he cries. "I didn't...You didn't..."

He stands and paces a few feet away. He returns and stands in front of me.

I watch his shocked expression with grim satisfaction. This works. He's a question-asking machine. I didn't realize we'd start the weekend with a lighthouse duel. I can use this to learn how far to push him. *En garde!*

"You're lying, Vin. That is some dodgy behavior right there, telling me a lie straight off."

"Not lying. You lost a huge advantage. You lost it because you insisted on an immediate answer."

He paces in front of me. "But, you have to king me. Or you fail."

I shrug but then realize he can't see gestures under my robe, so I say, "Okay. So I fail."

He sputters.

I say, "Years ago, I used to worry about failing. I used to worry it was entirely my responsibility to cross a guy over. It's not. It's yours. *Especially* you, Alistair. You tracked me down. Begged me to consider you. Make no mistake, I'm only here because I want to be. I love your smarts and word play, and I see how earnestly your king wants to dance in sunlight. I *want* to stand with you for the next thirty-nine and a half hours. But this is your King Weekend. I am a guide. Nothing more."

"So, I might not get kinged."

"Correct."

"Because I already know too much about what you're trying to do."

"Yup. On the positive side, you demanded an answer from me and you got one."

"Well, what kind of bloody tosser—"

"Hey, you insisted. I explained a price would be paid. You didn't care. Yesterday I *strongly advised* against asking questions. Remember?"

He takes a step or two away, out of shade, into raw sunlight.

This King Weekend will be easier than I thought.

Turns out Alistair is a windup toy, and if I tweak him the right way, he does all the work himself, lumbering across the playa with his jumble of half analysis, unanswered questions, and wrong conclusions.

He turns around. "How big a deal was this?"

"I don't understand."

"By what percentage did I influence the outcome? Like, by fifty percent or by, like, seven percent?"

I'm imagining him with one of those giant metallic keys sticking out of his back right now.

Crank, crank, crank.

I stand. "Oh, look. As predicted, another demanding question marches in to replace the one recently answered. If you want, we could calculate percentages, but it would mean I'd tell you more about the weekend. Which, of course, would change the percentage *while* we were estimating it, so in the end, the exact number wouldn't be accurate. Is that what you want?"

"I can't believe how hard you are fucking with me."

"Hi, Alistair. My name is Vin Vanbly. Welcome to your King Weekend."

He huffs out an angry chuckle. "Well, at least I now know your name."

I don't mind calling him Alistair, though it's not his real name. Everyone gets to wear costumes at Burning Man. The name *Alistair* is a clever disguise, and I enjoy disguises.

"So, what now? How can I repair the damage?"

"You can't. Think of this weekend as a trip across one of those ancient rope bridges in a South American jungle. Rarely used. As you cross those wooden slats, a taut vine snaps, or a plank cracks beneath your weight. We've barely started our journey together, and already you've insisted on slashing a few ropey vines. They were important. All you can do moving forward is to step carefully. You know how you snap more vines? Break more boards beneath your feet? *Ask more questions.*"

He shakes his head. "I don't like the rope bridge. I don't like heights, especially."

Good to know. I'll use this image all weekend.

His face retains a default stunned surprise, like he's found himself holding a gasoline-soaked, flaming torch, while behind him, his own home is consumed by a raging inferno. He wishes to ask "how could this happen?" But he knows. Most men understand how they set their very lives on fire. Even so, they remain incredulous that everything is burning.

I must go easier on him.

"Alistair, feel ready for a little love?"

The worry on his face is its own answer. "Very much so."

"Okay, first, let's go around to the other side."

I take his hand and lead him. He offers no resistance, which is something. When we face the sun, on the west side of The Man, I move behind him, and he lets me put my arms around his waist, my hands meeting in front of his stomach. I pull him to me, minimizing the space between us. I bend down enough to rest my chin on his shoulder. I must bring him some measure of peace. Not too much. I want him to worry; I want him to stew. Just not too much.

My eyes go fuzzy trying to distinguish the land mass far to the west, so much naked desert intervenes. Almost behind us, off to my right, I see rainbow-painted men, biking to the art installations. I want to advise them to check out the Golden Tower, all the different urine shades, but they don't need my advice. You take care of yourself out here.

I take a deep breath. "Take a deep breath with me."

We inhale, exhale together.

I'd prefer to feel his skin against mine. These Bedouin costumes are not the sexiest clothing.

After several deep inhales and exhales, he says, "I know I'm a bit prickly. Cheers for showing. Means a lot to me."

"You're welcome."

"I really want to ask why you decided to come. What made you say 'yes,' and if you got the message to king me, as you have with others."

Although he didn't use a question mark, he thought he could just slip that in? No way.

"Alistair, look at the pretty flower garden over there."

He says, "They're lotuses."

"Yeah, okay. Take a deep breath and appreciate it for a minute. It's nature."

"Not nature. They're carved out of wood."

"Alistair, take a deep breath. Why must you fight everything?"

"I'm a lawyer."

"Not on the playa. You're free of your profession. Why are you still lawyering?"

He flinches and says, "I don't know."

"Okay, good. Let go of knowing why and take a deep breath."

We breathe together.

"Look around."

This hunk of earth, a hundred and forty-three miles from Reno, is unlike other deserts. No vegetation. No animal life, save for the rare lizard fleeing desperately, as if it knows it does not belong. Not even snakes and scorpions. You'd think they'd appreciate a deadly environment. No cactuses with cute pineapple-yellow flowers peeking out. Nothing. The playa is a giant floodplain for the infrequent deluge, an overbaked sheet cake or a crumbly brownie crust, miles and miles long.

We watch the garden of giant lotus sculptures, the art installations a hundred yards beyond, and the obscenely fat sun, attempting to lower itself without crushing the earth. Between us and the sunset, nothing but scorched, parched earth.

"Alistair, in your insistence on having your question answered, you forgot something important."

He waits for me to continue. I squeeze him tighter.

"You're here. You're *here*."

He says nothing.

"You chose faith. Without answers, without the security you crave, you chose trust. You're so frightened by that choice, you couldn't help but—first thing—attempt to undermine it with questions. You don't like trusting with your heart, yet you're desperate to experience it. A million sharp-edged questions can't chip away this undeniable truth: you are here. You chose trust."

"You're not being a wanker just to make me feel better, yeah?"

"I am not. We established I don't mind gutting you with the truth. I will also eagerly share the truth if it heals."

He says, "Dog's bit that stew, for sure."

I ponder what he might mean but decide not to indulge him.

He chuckles. "One of the phrases I made up."

I thought it might be. It's a brilliant part of his cover, really, his wacky habit of coining new phrases. If he repeats some English phrase wrong, mispronounces or doesn't use the right Cockney rhyme scheme, well, most Americans—including me—wouldn't know. Yet, with true Anglophiles, he could pass off a mistake as one of his kooky inventions. I don't know if he does this *Alistair* character outside of Burning Man, but I assume so. He's too skilled at it. He didn't break character when he was genuinely upset with me. What happens if he runs into a true Englishman? Can they tell right away? I have so many questions of my own.

"Let's visit Lotus Land."

I tug his hand, and he follows. We cross the playa and only the occasional crunch beneath our feet distracts us from our journey. This stretch of earth has borne a thousand footprints in the last five days, a thousand times a thousand, stomping the alkaline crust into submissive dust, which means not every step creates sound.

The lotuses are extraordinary. I visited them a few days ago. From curved wooden poles, arcing gracefully fifteen feet above us, heavy lily pads and wooden flowers touch the sky. Metal stems might support the lotus more effectively, but efficiency is not the chief consideration. Saturday night, the mayor of Black Rock City burns. Sunday, the temples and its art gardens will follow The Man into orange destruction. Monday, we pack up and go home.

Alistair wanders under a lily pad, letting his face find shade. Shade is everything out here. You go to it instinctively, recognizing it as lifesaving. Which makes this sculpture true genius. It's a shade station for anyone fucking around out in the desert all day. It can't cover your whole body, but gives your face a break from the grueling sun.

I join him, hiding under a nearby petal.

With a slightly acidic tone, Alistair says, "So?"

I play dumb. I look around. "So?"

"What do we do out here? How do we *begin*?"

"Begin what?"

"The King Week—"

He sees my face and stops talking.

"You're fucking with me."

"I am."

His face is tight. He's not great at hiding his frustration.

We face each other in silence.

After a moment or two, he asks, "Well?"

"Well what?"

"Well, we're standing here under these giant lotus leaves doing nothing. Is there a plan?"

"Oh, there's a plan."

"Good."

I say, "Did you know the lotus symbolizes purity and spontaneous generation? Hence, they are frequently used as symbols to represent divine birth."

"Didn't know that," he says through gritted teeth. "How interesting."

I point to the flowers on nearby stems. "Purple lotuses are rarely depicted. White is more common. Purple represents spirituality and mysticism. Combined with the divine birth symbolism, purple often represents an unforeseen arrival of divine energy. When a purple lotus appears, watch out. You will still be surprised, but at least you'll know a divine surprise is coming."

He hasn't budged. Arms still crossed.

We wait in silence. I glance at the sun. Still crawling downward. Still not touching the horizon. Sunset takes forever in the desert.

"So, what's the plan?"

"The plan, Alistair, is to wait until you to stop asking questions. That's the plan. Seems we need more time."

He glances down again. "Bloody hell."

I step to him. I put my hands on his shoulders and he squints at me, his face no longer protected by the lily pad's shade.

"Take off your left shoe."

"Why?"

"*Alistair.*"

"Okay, okay."

He leans against me for support and reaches under the long folds of his robe to find a sneakered foot. He pries off his left gym shoe, holding it up and staring at me expectantly. Without words, I crouch down, lift my own jubba, and unlace my left boot. I tug it free and face him, holding it by the long laces.

"Now what?"

"Alistair." My voice is a warning.

He huffs. "Yes, fine. No bloody questions."

We remain silent, each of us holding footwear, me waiting until I see it, something, some shift, some signal of his submission. Even after all these years, I'm not sure I could name what I seek until I find it, until it happens. A softening in the eyes, a gulp and the shift in the Adam's apple. The hiss of breath through parted lips. Shoulders unclench. With every man it's different. Yet, with every man it's the same. We do not like to submit. We refuse to give in. It feels like a betrayal of our masculine power to lower one's gaze and say, "I will," when the will is not your own. This is true of the butchest gays, as well as those who sashay into the kingdom. Even those men who love submission have difficulty surrendering when it isn't what they planned on doing anyway.

I stare at his gorgeous green-and-brown eyes, flecked with a thousand stars. His eyes beam their intelligence my way, and I want to explain intelligence has little to do with submission. But this is not the time for words. Spontaneously, he stutters a halted laugh. *That's it.* His submission, masked by a slight guffaw. He shifts from one foot to the other, another clear sign he's willing to wait for as long as I might command. Good for him.

"And now," I say with great formality, "let us turn and throw our shoes in the direction of the east, the direction of new beginnings, with a prayer for love and divine birth."

Without further conversation, he takes a step away from me and hurls his sneaker, shot put style, over his shoulder. I twirl my boot laces several times over my head and release, chasing the trajectory of his, until it too crashes to the earth with a soft crunch.

We watch the inert shoes, and I wait for him to ask his question, but he remains silent. *Good job, Alistair.* More burners arrive in Lotus Land, a small group of women and two of the naked rainbow men. I have no idea if these are the men we saw earlier, or if they're new colors. After two or three minutes pass, with us staring at our shoes twenty and thirty feet away, I feel it's time to speak.

"Good job. You didn't ask, 'Why the hell did we do that?'"

"I wanted to. But I will try not to ask questions."

If I'm not mistaken, there's a touch of humility in his words.

"The reward for your not asking questions is an explanation. Why'd we do that? No reason."

"No reason," he says.

"No reason. None. Alistair, our whole time together, I'm going to demand that you do stupid stuff. Unreasonable requests. Smart as you are, I must insist you be an idiot with me. Will you be an idiot with me?"

He cracks a smile, the first authentic smile I've seen since we met. "Yes."

I like his soft, proud "yes." I will turn this into a cheerleading moment.

I grab him by the shoulders and shake him. "Alistair, will you become *the biggest idiot* you've ever been?"

"Yes!" he cries.

"Yes!" I roar in response and hook my thumbs under my armpits, pumping my arms. "To supreme idiocy!"

"*To idiocy,*" he shouts and pumps his arms, mimicking mine.

We grin at each other and flap our wings enthusiastically, as if they could lift us from the ground.

He keeps pumping, watching me for a cue as to our next move.

I jerk around in small, tight circles, jerking my head back and forth. Alistair follows suit. We dance our spontaneous chicken dance in silence under the purple lotus.

One of the naked rainbow men walks to us. He's painted navy blue. "What are you guys doing?"

"Celebrating idiocy," I say. "We're chickens."

"Why?"

Alistair pumps his arms furiously and says, "Because we're idiots."

Navy Blue says, "Can anyone dance?"

I say, "If you can celebrate your own idiocy, join in."

He considers this. "I painted my penis and balls blue and there's no showering out here. I qualify."

Navy Blue pumps his arms, joining us in our imaginary pen. He adds squawking.

"Your body is a lovely shade," Alistair says. "Evenly done. Looks brilliant."

Another few burners wander by, some stopping to admire the purple lotus petals. Some ignore us. One guy says, "Very nice."

The dance dies naturally, our idiocy spent, and we thank our cobalt friend for joining us.

We hobble to our shoes, pick them up, and as we relace, a sandal clad man approaches us, curly black hair. I do not know him. He wears cutoff jeans and shells around his neck. When he reaches me, without words, he hands me a folded note. I read it, stare into the distance. Alistair watches with interest, still wiping dust from inside his shoe, a futile gesture.

"Pen?"

The young man produces one, and I indicate I would like to use his back as my writing table. He bends over. I scribble my response. The whole exchange is over in less than a minute. I am pleased that, during this entire exchange, Alistair does not ask a single question. Damn. I'm worried if I keep using that name, I will come to think of him as *Alistair*, when he is clearly someone more.

Without a word, the seashell man heads back toward Black Rock City.

"We can go now," I say, pointing at our next destination.

"The Temple of Joy, yeah? That wasn't a question, just confirmation."

"No problem. And, yes. The Temple of Joy. We couldn't go there until everything was made ready for us. Now, we officially begin your King Weekend."

"What?" His surprise is not small. "We hadn't officially started? What the hell was the lotus stuff, the big lecture on questions and...what were we doing?"

I say, "Nothing. Just being idiots."

I walk toward the Temple of Joy.

FOUR

I can't think of a better location for a Temple of Joy than in a barren desert. Here, where joy is needed most. Amidst the flat lack of, well, everything, rises an Asian-inspired wooden delicacy, its highest spire stretching one hundred glorious feet above us, defying the ecosystem's dictate to stay flat, dead, and lifeless. Everything out here must be extreme to appear significant against the vast emptiness in every direction. The Temple succeeds.

The informational plaque explains every piece came from leftover plywood taken from children's dinosaur assembly kits, the ones you find at nature stores. Every wooden bit was cut to intersect other pieces, minimum nails necessary. Each lacy, carved panel permits air and light to flow through, so the entire structure resembles a house of dainty curlicues. As we draw closer, only a couple hundred feet away, I once again ponder the many arcs, curves, and patterns. Could the architects have embedded a secret story in the exterior? Maybe. The structure inspires the contemplation of mystery.

Extending immediately behind The Man, a wide colonnade, a quarter-mile long, invites burners to approach slowly—no, reverently—allowing the Temple of Joy to gradually reveal its exquisite majesty. Towering, formidable columns adorn the colonnade, flaming lamps atop each column. After midnight, when darkness digests the playa, walking this promenade feels like approaching your afterlife. Step closer, and discover your final destination.

We will approach from the wrong angle to stroll the promenade. I see dozens wandering back and forth to the temple. A popular destination.

Alistair catches up to me. "Okay, so I think you owe me one answer, yeah? One answer. That's it. The part about me being further away from my kingship—me making it harder on myself—if we hadn't officially started my King Weekend, was that true? Were you bullshitting me because of, well, *idiocy*?"

"I guess you'll find out."

"How? When?"

"Your first opportunity to demonstrate trust, you'll question yourself and your motives. If you act authentically, and you're honest with yourself, you'll know. If you don't, you'll know that, too. You are the one person to whom you cannot afford to lie, so you'll know if what I said was true. Now, a question for you. Why ask me that question when you knew eventually you would have answered it yourself?"

"Well, I hadn't—"

"You would have figured it out. If you had patience."

"Bloody patience. Why do people assume the English are patient little fobs who would rather wait than act? It's a stereotype."

I laugh.

Considering his whole Alistair personality is a farce, getting annoyed over this seems a bit absurd. Although, he assumed this English identity for a reason. He's trying to love them by proclaiming, "See? I could be one of you." Yeah, I guess I understand how he'd get offended by slights in their direction.

"Why did you laugh?"

I'm not the one who will confront him about being English. He will out himself. "I laughed because something amused me. You could probably figure that out too, if you were honest with yourself."

Although I will not call him out on his English deception, I will not play his game. I will not pretend I don't know. We will not discuss it, though he will certainly try to bait me into discussion.

With every step closer, the temple's delicate wooden folds twist the sunlight and shadows, creating the illusion of movement, like black ghosts flitting through the rafters, listening to the prayers offered below.

I say, "Those beginning a powerful journey often visit temples first, naming their hopes for a successful outcome. I remember two best friends, King Charles the Diamond and Ivan, the King of Cats. Their legendary exploits traveling from kingdom to kingdom, well, it started at a temple much like this."

"Why was he named the King of Cats?"

Given our recent conversation, I chuckle. "Seriously?"

"Bullocks," he says grumbling. "Forget I asked."

"Don't be cross, Alistair. We're almost at the Temple of Joy at Burning Man, on the cusp of great adventures. You asked me to king you, and here I am. This is exactly what you wanted, irritations and frustrations excepted. How are you not filled with joy?"

"Yes, but—" He pauses. "I don't mean to sound ungrateful. I'm grateful. But..."

"...but it's hard."

"No," he says quickly and then says, "Yeah, all right then. It's hard. When Liam described his weekend, he said you forced him to talk to people, to interact, yeah? You made him sing a duet one night in front of a crowd."

"Yes. For Liam, interacting with people exhausted him. Singing before a small crowd was one of the worst horrors he could imagine. You have no problem with people, no problem playing, so our sojourn takes a completely different path. What do you think of the word *sojourn*?"

"You barely know me. What makes you so sure?"

I stop walking. "*Really?* Another question?"

He gets quiet.

Can't you see it, Alistair, the answer right in front of you? Your questions do not bother me. However, the lack of answers drives you nuts, which is how, together, you and I will unearth your secrets. Together we will dig for treasure in the hard-crusted playa. The sharp tip of each unanswered question bites the earth a bit deeper, digging, digging, digging. Keep questioning, my friend. But don't expect answers from me.

I wonder if I should use this moment to nudge him onto the right path, without giving too much away.

"Alistair, instead of asking me questions aloud, try asking yourself, 'Why must I have this answer? What will knowing the answer give me?'"

As we renew our stroll, I say, "King Charles the Diamond and Ivan, the King of Cats, had been best friends for many years, ever since the day Charles taught Ivan to play duck, duck, gray duck."

Alistair chuckles gruffly. "Gray duck? What the fook is that?"

"In Minnesota, they call it duck, duck, gray duck."

"Why?"

"I don't know. It's fucked up."

"But why *gray* duck? Isn't it duck, duck, goose?"

"Normally, yes."

He says, "Why would you run from a gray duck, yeah? It's the American geese you've got to watch out for, they're mean as hell."

"Minnesota is weird. But King Charles taught Ivan to play other games as well. Ivan's childhood, spent working the family's farm in Russia, did not allow much time for children's games. He worked hard, cutting hay and feeding chickens with his brothers. He was primarily responsible for the family vegetable garden, and his success determined how well the family ate all winter. He loved his family and loved the farm, yet he always harbored a distant longing for another childhood, one where he played and colored and spent full afternoons wandering along a creek. As an adult, Charles taught him to play."

"Is that why he was called King of Cats? Because he liked to play?"

I'll ignore it.

"The two men decided to test their friendship by journeying together, a *dangerous* journey, across mountains and deserts, risking all for unknown outcomes."

"This story would be better if they secretly loved each other but were afraid to speak it."

"Perhaps it would. Who is to say they weren't?"

"And Charles the Diamond was hung."

"Oh, definitely he was. He had a sixteen-inch cock, incredibly thick and veiny. And it could talk."

"Now you're being an arsehole."

"Well then, quit making suggestions and let me tell the story."

We arrive.

We stand before the temple. I ask him his impressions.

He says, "The color reminds me of biscuits. Slightly undercooked, yeah? Lightly golden, perfectly soft in the center, and waiting for an enormous pint of milk for dunking. Do you get those famous Danish butter biscuits here in the States? The ones with the intricate patterns?"

Here in the States? Oh, brother.

"I like your cookie interpretation. Perhaps this cookie temple was baked by a foodie witch who wanted to draw more sophisticated-tasting children into the woods, more than a gingerbread house might attract."

"Barmy," he says, shaking his head. "That is arse over elbows."

"No, no," I say in protest. "No, you're missing the point. The children are really tasty. Grown-up flavors, like cumin and cinnamon-spiced pot roast. The kind of tasty children who know multiple languages."

"Bugger, that's demented."

Standing outside the wide back entrance, we pause for a moment to listen to grungy guitarists leaning against one wall.

I nod at them. "Maxers."

He snorts.

Their accompanists in this moment are shirtless drummers, nodding and bobbing, slapping their canvases softly with bare hands. It's hard to say who leads whom in this tune. A half-dozen burners appreciate their attempted synchronicity, and like us, move on after a moment or two, eager to explore the interior.

We join four dozen other delicious children already lured inside, admiring the delicate wooden folds, moving slowly through dappled sunlight, tracing curved joints with our fingers. This art is very much hands-on. Inside, the wooden surfaces are lavishly vandalized, graffiti written in marker, and instead of pleas from desperate children seeking escape, we find notes of love, joy, and sorrow.

Help me fight multiple sclerosis.

With gratitude for falling in love.

I want to serve people as a doctor. Prayers for medical school acceptance.

More beer!!

Please don't let Kevin die. I love my brother.

Help me get laid this week.

Not every note tugs at the heartstrings.

But to read the earnest scribbles is to witness the exact moment when hope takes flight, a sparrow flying straight up, its intended destination either some higher power, or perhaps gaining altitude to better dive-bomb the one below who needs hope the most. It feels strangely intimate, too intimate, to read prayers for deceased parents, entreaties for true love, for release from constant pain, or even the deeply felt gratitude for some life-changing blessing. How dare we?

Are we the seekers in this temple, or are we the gods, deciding which requests to approve? I feel confused.

I miss you every day, mom.

For all burners to party safely.

The dream of equality.

Please help my daughter find her way out of heroin and into sobriety.

As we shuffle along, Alistair nudges me to review one or two, and we read them together. I do the same. He nods grimly at the daughter lost to heroin. The joy in this temple is derived from its ethereal construction, its improbable location in desolation, not from these writings, remembrance and suffering. Photos embellish some notes—thumbtacked on—hoping to strengthen the initial prayer.

I turn to him and say, "Once there was a tribe of men, a tribe populated entirely of kings. Odd, you may think, and wonder how any work got done in such a society with everyone making rules. But these were not those kinds of kings."

Alastair blasts me a wide smile. "Right on."

"In this tribe, all brothers were rightful owners of the kingdom. You might come across King Ryan the Protector or King Galen the Courier on your way to visit King Jamie the Dancer. They loved freely and with open hearts. Some lying with other kings and some seeking women as their queens. I met one such king, a queen seeker, named King Malcom the Restorer, an African giant whose powerful voice commanded love and goodness from those who had abandoned their true selves."

A youngish woman—maybe late twenties—with straight, brown hair stops near us and puts her hands on both our shoulders. She says nothing, but nods at me, encouragement to continue. Why not? It's Burning Man. Anything goes.

"The orchards were full of ripe, luscious peaches; the beer brewed amber and frothy. King Nareeb, the Baker of Gifts, delivered blueberry pies and fresh, buttery croissants. You could often find King Jimbo the Bruiser stomping across the countryside tracking Kalista, his beloved falcon. His best pal, the King of Curiosity, played at his side, sword fighting with corn husks and coleading A Curious Army into elaborate, ridiculous conflicts."

"The queens of this land were fearsome to behold," says our new friend, looking at Alastair. "Muscular women who didn't need men, yet sometimes used them for pleasure. They established an ecstasy dome, where Queen Sheeba the Fierce and Queen Marilyn the Extremely Baked would oversee fist-to-fist combat, followed by hours of lovemaking. Many of these queens had broken noses from their hard battles."

She turns to me. "How'd I do?"

"It's more violent than I'd like, but I appreciate the assist."

She smiles. "I'm high."

She turns away, bumping into a young couple and apologizing before gliding into the crowd.

"Was *she* the big thing you needed to prep at the temple?" Alistair asks. "The Queen of Extremely Baked?"

I laugh. "She was an eager participant. You'd be surprised how many people want to play with the story."

Alistair looks around. "Okay, not her, obviously, but I imagine there's a clue here, some clue I'm supposed to uncover. Is it in a note? In a prayer?"

In addition to the graffiti, hundreds of notes, scrawled on squares of colored construction paper, are tucked in corners of wooden joints. At either end of the temple, tables holding markers and paper invite additional prayers.

"No," Alistair says, glancing around. "It would take us hours to find it. It must be...it's something more obvious. Right?"

"Pardon me, is that a question?"

Alistair frowns. "I'm getting quite irked by every word coming from my mouth being criticized."

"I'm not criticizing. I'm observing you. Reflecting back to you."

Alistair says, "Fine. No questions. Let's wander around and read more notes."

I nod. "Sounds good."

I need a job.

I want a girlfriend, one who really loves me.

Help me to be strong.

I miss you, D.M. Three years gone.

I'm not popular, and it makes me sad.

I'm not sure how many more I can ingest. The suffering in this world can be hard to absorb. I recognize its value in making me softer. But just how much pummeling can a person take? Change the topic.

"I gotta be honest with you, Alistair. Capital *M* is not my favorite letter. Check out this one. *Make Me More Loving.* Make Me More. See? Capital *M* should have its arms crossed instead of pointed straight down, because it demands everything. *M* is a thug. Make. Me. More. Those are a bunch of bullies."

"I think you're missing the bigger issue," he says. "I love that it's a fuck-you prayer to God or Buddha or whoever. *Make me.* It's your job to make this happen. Not mine. Yours."

"Yes, exactly. This is capital *M*'s influence."

Alistair laughs. "I thought your word obsession was just the letter *x*. You have opinions on all the letters?"

"Pick a letter."

"The letter *r*."

"Big or little *r*?"

"Both."

"Capital *R* thinks it's so damn hot. Gaze upon me for I am Regal and Royalty, yet forget not that I'm Ravenous too, and I will devour you, because I control Reality. I can't say much good about his son, *r*. It's not lowercase *r*'s fault he was raised in a household with Rigidity and Raging Reprobates. Capital *R* is a shitty father. Maybe it's not reasonable, but I try to steer clear of the son, too."

"Slipped in *reasonable*, yeah?"

"Thank you for noticing."

"You used a lowercase *r*-word to represent—"

"Ha. You just used an *r*-word yourself. Just now. It's not so easy to avoid the son. He's very repeatable."

"You're mentally ill."

"How revealing in that regard."

He laughs. "There is no finite to your madness." Alistair takes another step or two and stops. Turns to me. "Do you believe in God? In some higher power?"

I think about this from time to time. I've seen the evidence. People's kindness, the love inside almost everyone, always bigger than the actual person, so, yeah, I've seen evidence. Still, I feel like I'm standing outside a great castle, lurking in the shadows of the courtyard, watching the inside revelers celebrating joyful news. I see the joy through the open windows. But I'm not at the party, so I can't quiet say yes.

"I don't know about God. I believe in colors."

"Colors."

"Colors. Pink and purple go together beautifully. How can we explain that? I love every shade of green. Behind color theory looms science. Our optic nerve and the spectral range, light waves, and stuff. I know it. I've read it. But science can't explain losing your breath in front of a painting. I believe pink loves purple for a lovely irrational, nonscientific reason. Are colors poetry or science? I don't know. I don't care. I like emerald green in tree tops. Shakes of cobalt blue make me gasp. I believe."

"Noted. God is colors."

"You? What do you believe?"

"I think if there's a higher power out there, he—or she, or Ganesha—sucks ass for leaving us in the dark. I'm like the prayer we just read. *Make Me* believe. If you're real, God, fine, do something. Otherwise, fuck off. I'm an atheist."

"Actually, your willingness to believe makes you agnostic."

"Maybe agnostic years ago, but my willingness to believe expired. Agnostic. Atheist. I'm sure you have an opinion about the letter *A*."

"Ah, yes, now there's a lowercase letter who didn't turn out like his or her upstanding parent. Had such a good home life, too."

We bump into others, all of us reading, reflecting, wondering about the multitude of lives we're trying to understand through short notes. Come Sunday night, all this will be ash. Everything burns.

Alistair says, "I will try to ask fewer questions, yeah? I want you to know I'm listening to you."

"You asked me if I believed in God, less than three minutes ago."

He reaches out to put his hand on my arm, stopping me. "I know. I'm going to stop. I will. But before I do, I have another question for you."

"Color me shocked."

We face each other. His pensive eyes watch me carefully.

He says, "I'm going to ask but you don't have to answer. Did you already pick my king name? Have you already decided? Because if not, I have a request."

"Let's hear your request."

"Well, the request doesn't matter if you already picked out my king name. So, have you?"

"Tell me your request without demanding I answer your question."

He opens his mouth to speak and stops. Then, he says, "I want a really unique one. Different from all the others. Like, *so* different people have to say it twice to make sure they heard it correctly the first time."

"A name different from every other king."

"Yes. I hope I'm not being too egotistical. I just...it would be nice to have something special, yeah?"

I ponder this. I hadn't officially decided on his king name. A few possibilities presented themselves, but I didn't experience that *ping* of recognition I get when I come upon the exact right name. I felt I needed to know him better. Maybe this is why? Maybe I am to take his request into consideration. My King Weekends are more flexible than ever. Should I be flexible on this point?

We stand still, and slow-moving lines of devotees pass us, nuns, white-hatted women, a guy in a slutty prom dress, others in colorful spandex, and uncountable numbers missing some important piece of clothing: shirts, shorts, or in one older gentleman's case, everything but swimming goggles. He's stark nude. Huh.

Alistair says, "I understand this is your specialty, so horses for courses. I'm *requesting*, not demanding, to make it feel utterly unique."

"I'll consider it."

Alistair's face brightens considerably. "Brilliant. Thank you."

"Horses for courses?"

"Technically, it means to each his own. I meant to suggest, 'if it suits you, factor in my request.' I didn't invent horses for courses." After a pause, he says, "And by unique, I don't mean it's a French word or street slang or something silly, like the King of Willywumpus. I mean, *unique.*"

"Awfully demanding, don't you think?"

He laughs. "If you're going to ask, ask big. That's my motto."

No, Alistair. You just revealed your motto: *I am not unique.* I do not believe I am special as my own person, so I made myself English and gave myself a fake name to sound more interesting. Even faking English does not satisfy this deep-seated hunger, so I seek to become a king to be *truly* unique. But that's not good enough either. Among the kings, I wish to be more unique than any of them. He craves a level of distinction I cannot deliver. His King Weekend will be a huge disappointment, unless he stops seeking approval outside himself.

We have traversed the full length of the temple, which is admittedly only two dozen feet long, but it takes a while when you stop and read as we have done, and as everyone around us does. This end of the temple opens onto the promenade, and we survey the long road that leads straight back to The Man, watching over the city.

I say, "Let's go back down the opposite side."

We turn and get in line with everyone zombie shuffling forward, standing behind two men dressed as water gods, carrying tridents. They can't both be Poseidon. Though, at Burning Man, everything is possible. They sip from oversized plastic cups, and from their level of rowdiness, I assume it's not water.

"Still not sure why we're here," Alistair says. "Statement, not question. I will be English patient."

After a pause, he says, "See what I did there? *English patient?*"

"I saw. For your own dignity, I chose not to comment."

"C'mon. It was beautifully punned," he says and grins.

We come upon a few pieces of blank construction paper and some markers.

"Let's create an intention. Just as Charles the Diamond and Ivan, the King of Cats, did when they began their journey. We will each write something on paper, something we want from our time together."

"Alright," he says.

I hand him a sheet and he scribbles a note. I hold my paper, waiting for the right words to come. Something true. Something to bait him. When I finish, I ask to see his, and he hands it to me, grinning. *A unique king name.*

"All right, mate, let's see yours."

His grin dissipates when I hand him mine, and he studies me with those dreamy hazel eyes, big and unsure.

Help me find his love.

He reads it over and over. Something hit the mark. Regret? Confusion? Do I detect a swipe of sadness? I give him too much grief, I think. His unflappable English exterior is like many things in the desert, a mirage. An illusion. He's hurting in there. He's lonely. I have to love him.

I take his hand—the one holding my strip of paper—and turn it over, palm up. He does not resist as I bring my lips and his hand together. The king's kiss.

His voice trembles when he says, "What are you doing?"

"You know what I'm doing. I'm loving you."

We stare into each other.

He says, "I'm afraid of what you'll do to me."

A fat tear escapes—jumps from his lower lid, and races down his cheek.

He is truly a curious mixture of unflappable crust and exposed vulnerability.

I put his hand on my chest and say, "It's okay to be afraid, especially beginning a journey."

"Excuse me, Arabs," says a woman in seaweed wig. "Can you hand me a piece of paper? I need to dash a note to my gran."

We remove ourselves so she can access the supply of paper and markers, continuing our slow-walk through the temple. I keep his hand in my own. He squeezes back, my prayer paper sandwiched in our grasp.

We read the exposed pleas written in marker on the wood but do not unfold any more notes. Those, we leave tucked into crevices like temple birds, awaiting the right moment to take flight.

For Dad.

I want P to be happy.

Forgive me, Janet.

Anyone here gifting weed? I'm outside. Red shirt.

Brave souls, we will never forget you.

That must be in reference to those who died during the September 11th attacks last year. This temple is dedicated to them.

"Alistair, what happens if I come upon your king name—the one fitting you best—and it's ordinary? Should I ignore the truth of what I've discovered to accommodate your request?"

"How ordinary?"

"What if it's *King Alistair the Ordinary.*"

"Ow," he says. "Is that what you think of me?"

"A man's king name is not my impression of him. Well, I suppose it must be on some level, since the words come from my mouth. However, in my experience, a king name is more than a celebration. It's an expression of his greatest gift, and sometimes his greatest sorrow."

"Okay," he says stiffly.

"You don't believe me."

"No," he says, glancing at me nervously. "If I am honest, I call bollocks."

We pause behind a couple, naked except for their matching thigh-high boots.

"In the early nineties, I found the Butterfly King. He is a large man, a powerhouse, his personality a force of nature. I remember walking down wide New York City sidewalks next to him and people darting out of his way. He once told me his king name challenged him. He felt silly, almost ridiculous, associating himself with the very thing you might find doodled repeatedly on a thirteen-year-old girl's notebook. But he realized, over time, his king name offered him the opportunity to play, to take himself less seriously. To celebrate the ridiculous, beautiful whimsy all around him. Alistair, you would have no problem with his king name. Yet for him, it was a challenge. Despite the fluttering discomfort—pun intended—it sometimes causes him, he loves being the Butterfly King. So do you want your king name to resonate your deepest truth? Or do you want to feel unique?"

"Can't I have both?"

"You're answering my question with a question."

"I want the truth. I want the king name expressing my truth."

"Okay. I will accommodate your request the best I can, and I will not compromise. You have to accept that what I find may not fit your criteria."

He opens his mouth, and I sense another argument, but instead of speaking, he looks over my left shoulder and knocks the back of his hand on my chest.

He hisses, "*Look. That guy.*"

We stand near the backside of the temple where we first arrived. A man passes in front of us, maybe twenty-five, with short brown bangs suggesting a certain level of nerdishness. He folds his piece of paper and wedges it into a nook, same as the people around us. After depositing his prayer, he ambles away. Gym shorts, striped shirt. He looks uncomfortable, as if he's not sure he belongs here. If something happened between him and Alistair, I did not see it.

"It's *him*," he says, whispering.

"Who?"

He regards me with exasperation. "Gosh, I couldn't *possibly* know, Vin. Except I'm sure he's the reason we're in this Temple of Joy. He glanced at me several times before he took paper and wrote his message on it. He's the setup. You don't have to pretend."

I have no idea what gave him that idea. But I can play along.

Alistair says, "Right? Tell me I'm right."

In a tired voice, I say, "Yet another question, which you just promised you were finished asking."

"Bollocks," he says, growling, and reaching for the recently tucked note.

He unfolds it in front of us and we read it together. *I want to play.*

"A bit sad, yeah?"

I murmur a quiet assent.

Alistair says, "We have to help him."

"Yeah? Why so?"

"'Why so.' What an American thing to say. Because as kings we would help him. Right? This is what I'm supposed to do during our time together, learn how to help people, yeah? C'mon."

We carefully maneuver our way to the exit, the man's prayer in Alistair's hand. We touch strangers with a gentle, *please let me navigate around you when it's convenient*, and in this slow-moving chase, we follow him. He reaches the desert, and I see him raise his hand, protesting the dying sun. In a few feet, we will join him outside as well.

"Alistair, do you know what you'll say once we reach him?"

Alistair laughs. "No bloody clue. We will think of something together. I know it."

He leads me by the hand.

There is much to love about Alistair, or whoever he is. His fearlessness. The sheer audacity of his sparkling personality. He masks his true self with reckless confidence. Who dares faking an English identity during a weekend of submission and self-revelation? He wants to be discovered. He wants someone to find him, to reach beyond the iron fortifications he constructed, and see him. Love him. I know. We are cut from the same cloth.

We emerge, and I also raise my hand to the blinding sun, which punches me with its hard glare anyway. Our favorite star kisses the horizon, yet still blasts noontime rays with unconscious brutality.

"Mate, hold up." Alistair speaks as a lazy command, the right inflection to bring a stranger to a halt. He's got that English swagger down cold.

Holy shit. Wait, wait, *wait.* What if I'm wrong? *What if he's really English?*

"Mate," Alistair says. "Hold up. You just left the Temple of Joy, yeah?"

The man with brown bangs turns around and acts sheepish, as if he were a shoplifter confronted by department store security. "Yes, hello."

"Mate, thank you for stopping. We need to talk to you," Alistair says, clearly stalling.

"Yes, hello, sahib," I say, stepping up. "We are adventurers searching for the mighty xenoxx plant, three *x*'s, you see. We witnessed you in the Temple of Joy and realized at once you play an important role, critical to our success."

"Yes, yes," Alistair says, nodding at me. "Go on, then. Tell him."

I shoot him a wry smile, implying he's abandoned me to accomplish his dirty work.

"Sahib, sahiiiiiib," I say, because I like saying this particular word. "In our quest for the mighty xenoxx plant, we receive clues through our service to others. Have you heard of the mighty xenoxx?"

"No," our new friend says, the reluctance on his face revealing he now realizes this is some sort of game. He's not sure if he wants to play. He thinks we might be making fun of him.

Alistair says, "Xenoxx, healer to broken hearts, balm to many ruined dreams. Healant for lost causes."

"Plus it's good for your hands," I say. "Softens them but with a manly scent."

Alistair regards me coolly. "Really? Healer of broken hearts wasn't enough, yeah? It's also a cologne? Did you like *healant*, by the way? Made that up, yeah?"

I ignore him. "Sahib, we must assist your dream today. Alistair—"

"I believe you meant to call me *Humphries*," he says. "From now on."

"Yes, *Humphries*, the paper."

We present his prayer to him.

He now bears a sullen expression. "Not cool, guys. That was private."

"Sahib, *sahib*," I say.

"*Sahib, sahib*," Alistair adds in a pleading tone.

"Mistake not our intention. We wish to help you play. The word *sahiiiiiiib* is meant in respect, a word into which you cram a lot of *i*'s if you say it right, elongating the vowels, so it feels like young brothers, standing tall in a row. They're grinning."

Alistair says, "Okay, ignore him. He's nuts." He steps in front of me. "Mate, we came to help. In the gift economy at Burning Man, this is our gift. We help people who need assistance. Your prayer says you want to play. How do we make this happen?"

I remove my headdress so the man sees my full face, and Alistair does the same. What the hell was I doing, going off on the word *sahib* when this guy doesn't know me?

I say, "You're right. We should not have stolen your prayer. We intend no disrespect. My friend saw you and recognized you were important. How can we serve you, my king?"

He pulls himself together. "I'm doing fine."

He's not.

He puts his hands on his hips. "Thanks, but I don't need your help."

He does.

Of course, he has every right to refuse us. At his insistence, we will leave. I hope Alistair knows to back off. Still, we must give him every cause to say "yes," and only then will his "no" feel sincere.

I say, "You're doing okay?"

"Yeah."

"Did you come here to be *okay*? Or did you come to Burning Man for something magnificent? Didn't you show up to make glorious, life-savoring memories?"

Our new friend appraises me with surprised hurt, as if I'd insulted his manhood. Glad to see Alistair leaves this part to me.

I say, "I think you came here for more than *okay*. You came here for more, and it's not happening. Is this your first burn? No shame if it is, brother."

"No," he says coldly.

Virgin burners never bring enough water, or can't anticipate needing shade for a week in the desert. That's not their biggest surprise. No, they are shocked to discover the love fest—which Burning Man can be—does not happen without their active participation, their vulnerability and risk-taking. They often arrive ready to participate by watching from the sidelines. "Next year," they tell each other. "Next year, I'll be different." For that reason, "burgins" are considered the lowest on the playa food chain.

"It's my second year," he says with reluctance.

Alistair starts to say something. I silence him with a gesture.

We three stay silent. Silence will force his confession. While I stare, his eyes shift from mine to Alistair's and finally to the sun, as if he's afraid of cosmic eavesdroppers.

"Last year was more fun," he says. "My group and I planned a big theme camp. Shows for audiences, twice a day. I brought my keyboard and performed a lounge show. I mean, I was the piano player for the lounge acts."

"But not this year."

"Julie and Larry and a few other people couldn't come. I know you don't know those names. They organized us last year. A bunch of us came together again, so that's fun. At times. Everyone's off doing other stuff this year, hanging out with new groups. It's not like last year, spending all our time together."

We let our new friend's words thud to the cracked desert floor, the ugliness, the loneliness. Yes, there are worse tragedies in the world than a pianoless piano player who wants to play. But his heart is breaking because he expected love and got none, and *that* burden, whatever the circumstances, breaks us all.

Alistair says, "That is hard, mate. Rough going." To me, he says, "We need to find a piano for this man."

"No," says our piano player with extra energy. "Don't. I don't want to look like some pathetic loser with no friends. I have friends here. We partied two nights ago. I'm just not as good at making new friends as they are. You guys will embarrass me."

"We would never do that," Alistair insists.

"We are totally going to humiliate you," I say.

"Yes, humiliate you," Alistair says, nodding. With a hint of irritation he adds, "Because apparently this is something we kings do."

I nod at him. "What's your name?"

"John."

Alistair fires a hard look in my direction.

What did that mean?

I say, "John, we might humiliate you. We don't know how we're going to work this. In humiliating you, we're going to connect you with a camp in need of a piano player. We'll broker the introduction."

"No," he says firmly.

I make my own voice firm. "Stand here and watch the sun set. Or let us serve you and change your destiny. Your choice. Tell us to walk away and we will return your prayer to where it belongs. Unless, perhaps, your prayer happens to be right where it belongs at this second in Alistair—"

"Humphries," he says.

"Humphries' hand. Humphries saw you first and knew you were special. Now that we're talking to you, I see he was right."

He shifts from one foot to the other.

Alistair says, "How good are you? On the piano?"

John looks at Alistair. "Pretty good."

Howls fill the air around us.

Burners howl at the sunset. It's something we do. The sun dips low enough that it doesn't appear undecided anymore, truly ready to end this long day.

Alistair howls, so I howl. Gotta support my partner on the journey.

John attempts to howl but it's more of a low moan he hopes nobody will notice.

To worship the sun is to worship the very king- and queenship in all of us, the never-ending fire. Lost Ones worship the sun's rage and indiscriminate destruction. Found Ones worship the life-giving source that blesses all living creatures.

John looks from me to Alistair. "I don't know you guys."

I drop to one knee. "My Burning Man name is Vinicio Vanabalay, an Italian expatriate explorer in search of the elusive xenoxx plant. My real name is Vin. If you don't like what we're doing and you want me to stop, you use the name *Vin*. Everything stops. Otherwise, I am Vinicio."

"I don't know."

Alistair drops to his knee. "We're not drunk. We're not high. This is what we do. Let us serve you, John. Let us make your night memorable."

"I don't want to be humiliated." John speaks with a certain pout.

I nod. "Nobody does. Yet you must pay a price for getting what you want. The question is, John, what would you risk to create the kind of night you want?"

More burners howl. Air horns, car horns, bells, gongs...anything that can make noise will make noise, at least for the next hour. The entire city howls.

"Okay," he says reluctantly. "But I don't...I'm not great at acting or being weird. I can't do this thing with fake names and stories."

"Quiet, slave," Alistair says, and the vehemence surprises both John and me.

Alistair unknots the golden cord around his keffiyeh and says, "Vinicio, let us bind this slave's hands. Take him to Black Rock City where we perhaps trade him to a camp with a piano."

Alistair demands John's hands, which he offers, and Alistair binds them with the gold cord, not tight, but with enough loops and twists John's hands won't slip out. John might protest but it's already over. It's shady, the slavery angle, but I guess it could work. My unease is placated by the realization that Alistair now leads us. This could be interesting.

I say, "John, you okay with this? Will you trust us a bit?"

John chuckles and says, "Who are you guys? Why are you doing this?"

Alistair jerks the rope. "Come, slave. We must travel into the worst part of Black Rock City. The seedy underbelly."

"Actually," I say, "isn't all of Black Rock City the seedy underbelly?"

Alistair says in a stiff English affectation, "Quite."

I glance at the setting sun. "Wait. We should all howl one last time."

The howling continues all around us. It never stopped. So when we join in again, our voices, neither missed nor remembered, are nevertheless essential to the sunset Burning Man chorus.

Mutant cars honk.

Burners scream and cheer.

I hear cymbals crash together.

We all beat the desert. We live another day.

Alistair bellows out a mighty howl. I follow his lead and amp mine up, bigger, louder, infusing the desperation I sometimes feel escape me.

John joins us.

This time, I hear his true voice.

FIVE

Once around The Man, we approach the Esplanade, Black Rock City's main street. Spots on the Esplanade get awarded to popular, established communities who have earned a reputation as Essential Burning Man. These camps are the Sax Fifth Avenues and Calvin Kleins of this temporary city, though they would vehemently denounce any corporate comparisons. Camp Times Square—constructed entirely by New York burners—offers a slice of urban living to those who miss it. Every night is New Year's Eve for them. Good to see them back again, as well as the Intergalactic Virgins camp. They were fun last year, too. Up-and-comers make it on the Esplanade too, those who might draw large crowds. Impressive light shows or experiences, marvels of science, popular giveaways. Three days ago, I saw a Little Mermaid parody camp, complete with underwater drag queens offering desert makeovers in exchange for a song. Definitely catering to the Floating World theme.

But the Esplanade loves the night.

Near us, rave organizers start preparations for tonight's rowdy crowds, assembling giant silk screens, adjusting their strobe lights, and unloading their enormous speakers from vans, where they've been protected all day from the white, alkaline powder. I see tech-savvy women in kilts digging through massive toolboxes, and a handful of people in jump suits making calibrations to equipment for tonight's luminescent displays. I smell gasoline as machines are refueled. The whole street straps on its neon, preparing for the biggest party night of their lives. Just like last night. Two years ago I saw a few phosphorous tubes integrated with art installations, and now they're everywhere, turning the Esplanade into a bright-lights-carnival, each camp eager to impress each other with technology-inspired imagination.

"Let's go deeper into the city."

Alistair says, "Maybe Wheelhouse or Fantail. Start there?"

I nod.

He gets it.

Dance parties aside, any music venues along the Esplanade won't need last minute piano players. Working the Esplanade means high profile. They will have had their talent lined up for months, with backups to their backups. The odds of finding a camp requiring a piano player increase as we move farther back.

Our introduction to Wheelhouse Avenue is a Roman theme camp with many in full togas or sexy variations. A Roman with fire-red hair offers us a chalice of wine to celebrate the sun god's victorious charge into sunset.

"Apollo?" Alistair asks.

"Apollo was identified by the Greeks interchangeably with Helios, but in Roman mythology, it's Sol Invictus."

Alistair eagerly accepts and reaches for the wine. I interrupt and suggest perhaps we'd best sell our cargo while sober. We thank the Roman, who tilts his head back, and in a thunderous roar informs us—and everyone within shouting distance—of a fashion show featuring Roman gods and deities, showings at nine and eleven.

"Sip of wine wouldn't have hurt." Alistair throws me a friendly grumble. "Nobody's getting pissed."

Does he need a drink, or was he testing me? First and second pillars. Stay present. Then, follow the man; follow and lead. Alistair will show me where to go next. After all, he's literally leading.

Thinking of the four pillars makes me think of Julian, *beloved* Julian, my first Burning Man king. Julian was my third king. Took me quite a while to recover from the first kinging, before I felt ready to fulfill the mission they gave me. *Find them. Bring them home.*

Don't.

Don't dwell on it. Don't think of them.

Focus on finding a camp with a keyboard.

I love this time of day.

Burning Man is a twenty-four hour event. Over the next two hours, nightlife will erupt all over the playa, lasting until the night sky grows exhausted. But as the night revelers collapse under the weight of their own excesses, dawn worshippers emerge from their tents in the quiet darkness. Yoga devotees gather. Meditators claim their outdoor spots, like garden gnomes silently guarding us all. Soon after, morning people emerge—the desert bunnies, who love the camaraderie, the art, the freedom to live as themselves. They play, create art, befriend strangers, and drink water incessantly until, well, now.

The sun is only less than half below the horizon. Once it's gone, our community must demonstrate readiness for the enduring night. The next hour and a half before darkness falls is the quietest of the day. In every camp, members far-flung by day return to share food and booze and stories, and to rub aloe on each other's skin. They share today's best adventures about feeling alive on a molecular level, basking in the sunset gleams. It's an oddly wholesome hour of day, this make-your-family hour.

More people pass—Maxers, half nakeds, and but-for-the-hat nakeds, and then a woman dressed as Medusa. Two guys bike by us discussing ecstasy. Okay, maybe it's not *that* wholesome.

Over the street noise, I say, "John, what kind of music do you play? What sort of camp might interest you?"

"I don't know. I don't know this is a good idea, after all. I feel silly bound like this."

"You feel silly?" Alistair asks. "A minute ago, we passed a man whose clothing consisted of a gas mask and pink rubber boots. On the right, that unicorn camp's flag is the *sod off* finger turning into a horn. *You* feel silly? You're still sweeping the side of angels, friend."

"Sweeping the side of angels?" John asks.

"It's an English phrase," Alistair says, winking at me.

My stomach tightens.

Oh, shit. I am complicit in Alistair's deception. I don't mind if he pretends he's English. It doesn't bother me. However, I'm now his partner in deceiving others, because I know something they do not. I did not anticipate the awkwardness of this. I deceive people constantly. I lie about my name, my job, my everything. So why—when I do it—does it feel acceptable, but perpetuating his lie seems a step too far? I'll have to figure this out. I could try to persuade myself I have not seen concrete proof of his nationality. *Bullshit!* That's a coward's argument. I know what I know. I don't need proof. Like a dog, I sniff many different truths on him, none of them authentic Englishman.

We pass a few camps with happy partiers, who shout their fuck-you greetings with cheer, receiving us with the desert friendliness that is our due. We wave to them. I'm sure we appear to be from someone else's theme camp, the desert wanderers with a slave in tow. Ahead, a camp named PsychFakes proudly boasts futures told. They have rainbow flags everywhere on their tents, so I'm going with *gay* fake psychics. Or gay-friendly. Everyone is welcome, straights who boast rainbow flags and gays who bring their straight wives. I spy a keyboard, and we halt in front of their space, but it's obvious they are disassembling for the night.

Seeing our small party linger, one of the fake psychics says, "We'll be open tomorrow."

A wave of white dust rolls in, possibly from an art car driving fast a few blocks away. Can't see a car. But I heard the engine a few seconds ago, and this cloud is proof of its existence. All three of us turn our heads and cough, then continue our journey.

Without words, Alistair hands me the golden cord functioning as John's leash.

I ask John more detailed questions about his music, what he plays, because he never answered me. He reluctantly shares a few of his favorite styles.

Alistair interrupts. "We'd have more luck if we split up. I'll take Fantail Avenue for the next block and see what's up. Meet you in a block or two."

I say, "Wait. We should stick together."

"This will go faster," he says, and before I can argue, he's zipping down the 255-degree cross street, slipping away as if he were the escaped slave.

Alistair, what are you doing? Why must you fight me so hard?

"We don't have to do this," John says.

It's exactly this mentality I'd feared our splitting up would cause. John sees himself as a chore, a problem we aim to solve quickly. I must fix this so he knows he is truly wanted. Show him all my love.

"*Quiet*, slave. Do not question your wise masters. Humphries' and my plan involves you and me spending time alone so we can plan your audition. You said you're good, so let's talk about your range. How talented are you with improv?"

We chat.

We pass playa Maxers in grubby shirts and shorts as often as those in costume, but with so much surprising apparel it's hard to categorize all the people, to see every cascading wave of humanity pouring down the city street.

"I always think Burning Man looks like a casting call for the Mad Max movies," I say.

John grunts his agreement.

We discuss songs within his repertoire, and I explain the direction of my narration. He suggests a few good bits. If we can find an opportunity, we will present quite a show.

We pass a woman wearing enormous brown and white wings—genuine bird feathers, what must be thousands of them—carefully navigating the crowd as if she were unfamiliar with land-walking. A person like her was clearly meant to soar. These lunatics in costume work harder to celebrate their king- and queenship more than anyone I know.

We pass a phone booth, decommissioned from the real world, but authentic in every detail, complete with a door to fold yourself inside. There's a man inside, speaking into the disconnected receiver. The inscription across the exterior says, "Talk to God." There's a line to get in. Five people wait patiently.

When we reach the end of the next block, Alistair rejoins us.

"Brilliant news," he says before either of us speaks. "I found a 1980s-themed piano bar, one street over, in need of a keyboard player. I started jogging, looking for keyboards, and I found this place. It's next to the Desert Dead on Fantail Avenue. Come on."

"Sounds great," I say with cheer, feeling quite the opposite.

He's trying to solve a problem. This isn't the right energy. John isn't a problem. He's a friend. A king. I'll delay this while I figure out our next move.

I say, "You've been running, Humphries. Drink some water."

His face scrunches with confusion. "Oh, right. *Humphries*. I forgot my name."

"John, you, too. You drink next."

While Alistair raises my water pouch to his mouth, I catch John's gaze lingering to the right of us. I glance in the direction he's looking and spot a camp named Unlucky Pete's. The setup is a fat tiki hut—a lovely piece of shade during the day—a bar with four or five stools, and a small stage, which boasts a guitar case and two chairs.

Alistair explains his journey, how he ran—and I interrupt. "John? See something?"

John says, "No. I mean, I thought, yes, they have a stage and there's a guitar case out, but no keyboard."

"Let's find out."

I tug the rope and John grimaces his compliance.

Alistair says, "I already told the other place about John."

I say, "Good. Because this probably won't work out. Follow my lead."

Stepping over to the hut, I exclaim, "Sahib, sahib!" bowing deeply to the two gentlemen behind the bar.

"Sahib, sahib!" cries Alistair, and despite my irritation with him, I find myself relieved to have him back at my side. I like it when he's at my side.

I say, "We are poor traders of the desert variety."

Of the two men behind the bar, I now know which is in charge; the subtle shifts in body language give it away. I address the dark-haired man with his shirt hanging open. "Good sahib, if you would consider honoring my humble self with a question. Do you have a keyboard for your shows?"

"Were you here last night?"

"No, good sir."

Alistair said, "It was camels-drink-free night over at a sweet club on Bowsprit last night."

They chuckle.

The owner says, "Devon is our keyboard guy. He's not here, though. You know him?"

"No, sir, we do not. We are simple Bedouin travelers, travelers who have—"

"You guys want a beer?"

I say, "Kind sahib, we could not possibly impose."

Alistair says, "We could impose a *little*. One beer."

The bartender signals to his friend who dips below our line of sight.

"We will pass," I say, glancing at Alistair to communicate my wishes. "Thank you. Look at this slave, sahiiiib. He is useless! He cannot clean. He does not cook. He is terrible with camels."

"He cannot reinstall Windows when necessary," Alistair pretends to spit on the ground.

"He is truly the worst," I say. "His only redeeming quality is he plays keyboards quite well."

"Is that right?"

"Magnificently." Alistair spits on the ground again.

I spit on the ground to mimic Alistair. "Like an angel."

Alistair says, "For those of us who do not believe in angels, he plays like John Ogden, yeah?"

John says, "Ogden? Was he in Crosby, Stills, and Nash?"

Alistair mutters under his breath. "Fucking Americans."

"Sahib, sahiiiiiiiiiiiiiib," I cry.

"Sahhiiiiiiiiib, sahib," Alistair pleads.

I want to kiss Alistair in this moment for his ability to play, to match me and dive head first into this insanity.

"You play keyboards," the bartender says, nodding at John. "You any good?"

Alistair interjects with a snappish tone. "Do not speak to the merchandise directly. The only way to know is to hear him play."

Oh, that's good. Perfect way to make this happen.

When we make eye contact, I try my best to communicate, *Good job, Alistair. Good job.*

The bartender frowns. "Can't. It's Devon's keyboard. We don't fuck with it when he's not around. Sorry."

"Sahib, sahiiiiiiiiib," I say.

"Sahiiiiiiiiiiiiib, sahib," Alistair says, trailing behind.

"Thank you for your time," I say.

We drag John away with us.

The bartender once again offers us beer, but we decline. Well, I decline. Alistair looks at me hopefully. We discussed this. I'm not sure why he's pushing this boundary again.

As we near the 80's theme camp Alistair found, a few of the Desert Dead approach us, arms extended in zombie trance. The majority of their crew sits huddled together, apparently eating dinner. Looks like ramen noodles. Well, ramen noodles do look like brains, so who knows. One of the lumbering undead bears a tray of gray liquid in cups.

She moans and says, "Melted brains Jell-O shot?"

I thank her and decline.

She turns to Alistair and says, "You want another, sweetie?"

He stammers a polite refusal.

Yeah, I caught it, Alistair.

He had to have known we'd stroll right by her, so obviously, he wanted be caught. He may not have planned this, but he didn't *not* plan it either. An accidental intention. One of those "gosh, I didn't think you'd find out," while completely aligning the elements of discovery. Okay, so he's backing me into a role. I've seen this before. He wants me to be his watchdog. He wants me to take responsibility for policing him. He's a rule worshipper. If there are rules to his King Weekend, he can win, as long as he first learns how much he may bend them. Damn, less than two hours have passed since we started hanging out, and he's already testing every rule. I bet he's an amazing lawyer.

Tonight's stories will be perfect for him.

As promised, the 1980s come to greet us in the form of a slender, punky-type woman with a fat scrunchie in her tangled hair, reminding me of Cyndi Lauper's sage wisdom that girls just wanna have fun.

"Sahib, sahiiiiiiiiiiiiib," Alistair says, hands extended. He turns to me. "What's the female equivalent?"

"I don't know. *She*-hiiiiiib?"

Alistair says, "Sheeehib, sheeeeeeeehhhiiiiiiib!"

I follow immediately. "Shehib, sheeeehiiiiiiiiiiiiib!"

I like all those *i*'s together. They are brothers with their arms around each other's shoulders.

She crosses her arm. "I get it. You're Arab slave traders."

"I'm Italian, an expatriate named Vinicio Vanabalay."

"I'm a disgraced English baron, Humphries Smogswollow, so, we're not actually Arabs. That's a racist stereotype."

She smiles. "Oh, so now *I'm* the racist, huh?"

Alistair bows before her and says, "Shehib, sheeeeeeeehhhiiiiiiib!"

She chuckles. "Nice groveling. Who are you, third guy?"

He says, "My name is John Hemmer."

Alistair spits on the ground to his left and cries out, "Worthless!"

I spit on the ground to my right and match his enthusiasm. "Troublesome burden!"

She says, "I see. Well, he plays piano, right?"

"His only redeeming quality," I say. "We will arrange a demonstration. Humphries, untie the slave. We must show this kind shehib how useless he is."

As Alistair does this, a man steps out of the street traffic and hands me a piece of paper. Although I do not know him, I'm not surprised by his sudden appearance. He is a relay, helping me communicate with the Found Kings this weekend. A trickster like Alistair requires tricks.

I unfold the paper, shake my head with disgust, and take the pen offered by my new acquaintance. I write my reply, vehemently protesting the smell and texture. Then again, I've never been much of a fan of gorgonzola cheese. Alistair watches me with amusement but says nothing. He and our freed slave head to the hot pink stage, where a poster-sized photograph of singer Rick Astley adorns the center, with fake roses stapled to the bottom half, attempting to appear as if casually tossed at Rick's feet. A few feet on either side, George Michael and Michael Jackson posters flank Rick. It's a nice venue, gotta admit. They must attract a lot of people.

John tinkers with the keyboard. I join Alistair on stage.

"Was the note something related to my King Weekend?"

"Not everything is about *you*, Alistair."

"Sahiiib, sahiiiiiiiiiiiib," he says.

We chuckle, both knowing I will not explain despite his supplicating tone.

I say, "You're great at following my lead. I ask you to do so now. John and I worked out a few bits, so don't go far off script. Remember, this is about *him*."

"Of course," he says. "I know."

"I hope so."

"Hey, I *found* him this opportunity."

I hear hurt in his tone.

Good.

Prick the thumb for a drop of blood. Every good spell needs a sacrificial opening.

"Gather up," I cry, waving people from the street to come watch us. "Sahiiiiiiiiibs and sheeehiiiiiiiiiiiiibs!"

Alistair roars, "Sheeeehiiiiibs and sahiiiiiiiiiiiiiiiiiiiiiibs!"

John echoes our opening cries with deep, resonant cords from his keyboard, old-timey sounds suggesting every dramatic radio program ever. He plays the first chord tentatively, hesitancy in his fingers as he tests the sound. As we call to people, begging them to join us, confidence emerges in his choices.

People amass. They come from tents across the way. Burners finishing a pre-evening stroll find their way to us. I recognize a few costumes from earlier today, or related costumes, and wonder if we passed each other—any of these folks dressed as mermaids, or body-painted, or whatever they're wearing or not wearing.

"Come on then, *zombies*," Alistair cries, and dead-walks across the stage. "Drag your dead carcasses over here."

Well, Alistair ain't shy.

Grisly zombie music emerges from behind us, bones grinding against hard sockets—the stringiest tendons and misshapen muscles—moving up and down the keyboard. The dead in the camp next door become engaged in John's flesh-dragging music, and it turns out, yes, John can play.

Having successfully lured the walking dead, Alistair jumps to a new direction, like a true carnival barker, shouting, "Shehiiiiibs and sahiiiiiiiiiiiiiiibs!"

I shout, "Sahiiiibs and shehiiiiiiiiiiiiiiiiibs!"

Alistair doesn't lose his accent at all.

He announces the auspicious onset of a thrilling tale, the most adventurous, *wildest* tale, and pauses to say conversationally, "It's quite brilliant, really."

He glances at me for confirmation and, in doing so, passes me the reins.

My turn. Make it loud.

"Listen to a tale—a cautionary tale—for burners of all ages, a tale of madness in desert winds, of sorrowful prisons and acute dehydration, of gold coins and powerful curses laid upon a people. The adventures I tell today are of the legendary King Charles the Diamond and Ivan, the King of Cats, two mighty kings from the Lost and Founds."

Alistair throws up his arms. "The Lost and Founds!"

John mimics the cry, musically, and our ridiculous show comes together. I feel it. This is the best of Burning Man, like-minded folk creating art together.

I continue. "These are the tales of the Lost and Founds, for once there was a tribe where every man was the one true king."

I nudge Alistair, visibly, so everyone sees.

"Oh yes, and every woman the one true queen."

A smooth trumpeting comes from behind us, regal classical notes. John twindles or speedles between two notes with such laughing ease, I swear it justifies inventing those goofy two words. The notes speedle-eedle-eedle-eedle-eedle-eedle.

When his trill softens, I say, "Odd, you may think, and wonder how any work got done in such a society with everyone making rules. But these were not those kinds of kings."

Alastair says, "And queens, love. Don't forget the queens."

While John accompanies in something classical, I rattle off the names in the story, King Ryan the Protector and Malcolm the Restorer. So many more names, men whom I love.

"My, what pretty, *American*-sounding names," Alistair says with enough stiffness the joke works.

"King Liam," I suggest.

He snorts. "Irish. C'mon. Throw in a bloody *Basil* or *William* for god's sakes."

The audience chuckles.

In this fashion, we continue, me leading, him dancing around me, John's accompaniment sometimes following and sometimes leading us both. I relate how kings left the mighty kingdom and got lost. When I describe how Found Kings would depart on mighty quests searching for the lost ones, Alistair chimes in.

"As they left the southern gates, each one would be asked two questions. 'What would you risk to find a lost king? And what if he doesn't remember you?'"

How does he know these details so well? How does this story get passed around?

I take over. "King Charles the Diamond and Ivan the King of Cats decided to test their friendship by undertaking such a journey together, a dangerous journey, across mountains and deserts, risking all for unknown outcomes. Perhaps they would reclaim Lost Ones. Perhaps they would find the mysterious xenoxx plant, alleged to having healing properties. They came to the desert together, wondering what they would find."

Someone yells, "Ecstasy!"

Another voice yells, "Sex!"

"Mostly," I say, "they wandered."

John's plays, "Tiptoe Through the Tulips." Alistair and I share exaggerated shrugs, and then skip around the stage as the music commands. The music becomes a shade less optimistic as it evolves. Musically, John leads us to the true desert, scary and barren. Soon, we struggle across the stage as if it were the desert floor, and the piano reflects our exhaustion.

I clutch at my throat. "Water."

"Red Bull," Alistair says, gasping, and everyone laughs.

Alistair is the favorite, which is fantastic. He's the one-liner man, which permits him a bit of downtime during my lengthy explanations. This works. We're completely in sync.

"It was broiling under the desert sun."

John plays a single note, something sharp and low, allowing the echo to die before he strikes the same one again, repeating this hard note with the persistence of a single, scalding sun.

This earns him some applause and he grins. He knows how to command a stage.

"They hallucinated," I say loudly.

John plays "White Christmas."

A few people laugh as I glide on ice skates, and Alistair appears to ski downhill. Several people in our audience also ski or skate. A few others clap.

They're into it!

"The two kings came upon a splendid castle, a magnificent castle made of silver stone with a hint of pink marbling, which made it gleam like glass. It was called, in fact, Castle Gleam."

Alistair blocks his face from the castle as if it will burn his retinas.

"Not quite so gleamy," I say.

He allows himself to gaze at the imaginary castle but still keeps one hand raised.

"Nope, less gleamy. Like, forty-percent less gleam."

He drops the one hand and scowls. He adopts another posture.

"No, *more* gleamy. No, less than that."

In protest, he slumps and raises one hand in sullen protest, like an irritated traffic cop who doesn't give a fuck if you get run over.

"Perfect," I say.

The audience cheers and John plays game show victory music. Alistair throws both hands in the air, bowing to the audience who took his side in our argument.

"Inside Castle Gleam's expansive city, life drooped. The streets were full of markets and shopkeepers, open and busy, but the people seemed defeated. They went about their business, eyes cast down, ignoring the fragrant jasmine 'twined around market pillars, and ignoring the cheerful gurgle of the stream which bisected the city."

"Also, no Wi-Fi," Alistair adds. "Very dodgy signal."

Everybody laughs.

"Fuck Verizon," someone shouts.

"Fuck *Comcast*!" cries one of the zombies, and two others clap.

Better change the direction of this story. "They were brought before the king—"

John plays stately music.

"A mighty king—"

He plays something more forceful, dark undertones.

"The mightiest, most badass king who ever fucking lived, a *Burning Man king*."

As we planned, John switches to heavy metal.

Our audience screams for one of their own, a burner sitting on the throne. Others strolling on Fantail have stepped out of the street traffic to stay; we now perform before a good-sized crowd.

"Before this mighty king, the two champions stood and asked, 'Is there anything in this kingdom which ails you and your people? We noticed the sorrowful pall cast over your glorious, gleaming city.'"

Alistair steps forward and says, "Also, very pretty little stream running down the middle. Nice touch."

He steps back again, allowing me to take the lead.

"The mighty king spoke."

John plays a heavy metal riff.

"'Yes, brave wanderers. Our city lives in perpetual dismay. My beloved daughter is trapped in the prison beneath the city. She is the light of the kingdom. All who meet her love her. The entire kingdom reels with the sad knowledge she cannot be rescued.'"

John initiates a sadder piece, some light notes muted.

"'This is very sad,' said King Charles the Diamond."

John establishes a three-key sound to emulate diamonds, a hard glass sound, a tinkle, tinkle, tinkle.

As King Charles, I continue the story. "'Have you no keys for the prison below?' With grief in his voice, the mighty king spoke. 'Yes, we have the keys.'"

Alistair says, "Wait. You have the keys to the prison?"

I make my voice strong. "'Yes,' said the mighty king. 'But what good would that do?'"

John plays the heavy metal chord.

Alistair breaks character and says, "Wait, so you have the bloody key that opens her cell? The princess' cell?"

"Yes." I speak in the same strong voice and add a stately arm wave, a magnificent blessing across all the people.

Alistair says, "Why not use it?"

Acting as the burner king, I scratch my head. "I'm afraid I don't follow."

"The key? Why don't you go and open her cell? Let her out?"

"You lost me. You want the *key*? Why?"

Alistair bellows, "*Well, let her out of her cage!* If it's such a bloody aggro not having her around."

Interesting how he plays up the English angle.

No denying people love it, laughing and clapping for him.

"Yes," I say and wave my hand broadly. "All in the kingdom miss her terribly. We do not know what to do."

Alistair says, "Yes, but the key—"

I step in front of him and announce to all, "King Charles the Diamond—"

Tinkle, tinkle, tinkle.

"Said to the mighty king—"

Heavy metal chord.

"'Will you give us this key?'"

Tinkle, tinkle, tinkle.

"And the king said, 'Sure!'"

Heavy metal chord.

"Charles said, 'Cool.'"

Tinkle, tinkle, tinkle.

"The heavy metal king said, 'I'm not sure what good this will do you, but here you go.'"

Heavy metal chord.

"King Charles the Diamond said, 'Thanks!'"

Tinkle, tinkle, tinkle!

"The mighty king said, 'You're welcome.'"

People snicker at my unnecessary conversation, the way I make John dance to keep up. At the height of this insanity, I remind all of the King of Cats' presence, for which John has manufactured the sound of clumsy paws running down a keyboard.

Alistair asks, "Was it, by chance, about to storm?"

John—exhausted trying to keep up with me—finally cries out, "C'mon."

Everyone laughs and cheers.

"King Charles the Diamond and the Ivan, the King of Cats, crawled deep into the tunnels, wading through red and pink carnations many inches deep. They endured murals devoted to unicorns strolling through sunlit meadows. The princess was fourteen, and she liked her unicorns. The scent of popcorn wafted down the halls. The people could not rescue her, so they'd remade the prison into her own private palace."

John has been painting this girl's bedroom with pink musical notes, and she gets her own riff, a spunky little twist at the end of her chord, implying she is not the kind of prisoner to abandon the dream of freedom.

Alistair steps up. "Her name was quintessentially English, a respectable name—"

He pauses, waiting for me to insert the humor.

"Basil," I say loudly and cross my arms. "Princess Basil. Happy now?"

Alistair and I face off, and he crosses his arms. "You're committing to this?"

The crowd laughs.

"The two kings made their way to Princess Basil's cell. A dozen citizens stood ready to comfort her if this was, in fact, another false hope. Someone said, 'Are you sure about this? Using the *key*?' Charles and Ivan proclaimed their great confidence and inserted the key into the lock..."

Alistair mimes the story, pausing to grip the handle of the prison door, waiting for me to direct the next chapter in the story. John hangs out musically, trilling notes to define impatience.

"...and the door swung open! Princess Basil was saved!"

John trills all the way up the scale to celebratory music, a princess coming out of her pink and purple prison, being led up the curling stairs, up, up, up, as the townspeople join in the procession.

"The entire town accompanied the Princess Basil—"

John plays her spunky-twisted riff, now with a British inflection.

"—reunited with the mighty king."

Heavy metal.

"And the citizens rejoiced, celebrating the unconceivable ingenuity of King Charles the Diamond—"

Tinkle, tinkle, tinkle.

"As well as Ivan, the King of Cats."

Paws hopping down the keyboard.

"In gratitude, the mighty king gave them each a chest of gold to carry, and they left the kingdom, strolling back into the desert."

Clapping erupts. But we're not done.

"Sahiiibs and sheeehiiiiiiiiiiiiiiiiiiiiiibs," I cry, stopping the applause.

"Sheehiiibs and sahiiiiiiiiiiiiiiiiibs." Alistair imitates my tone and volume.

In a much more abbreviated tale, I demand the two adventurers head into the desert again, strolling with tulips, then suffering through sunstroke, and then hallucinating while Christmas music accompanies.

"They wandered and wandered, and they wandered..." I say and take a deep breath. "Then, they wandered and wandered—"

"No, they didn't," Alistair says impatiently. "Didn't they find another castle? Didn't *that* happen?"

A smattering of laughter and appreciative clapping follows.

"Sahiiib, sheeehiiiiiiiiiiiiiiiib," I say and bow, showing my deference to his turn in the story.

I describe how the two kings spot a mirage, a green and blue island, thick with trees, and almost jungle-like vegetation. In its center, King Charles and King Ivan discover a shiny obsidian palace, carved and polished, every interior room decorated in sunset orange to honor the freak volcano whose violent origins created this oasis.

Again, our story finds a city besieged by an unsolvable problem—this time, a lack of water. Dehydration would soon kill everyone in the kingdom.

John develops riffs an unquenchable musical thirst, which makes burners howl in acknowledgment of his skills.

"Their kind and willowy king explained all sky water fed the plants, their lush gardens. Rain was exclusively devoted to preserving their jungle. The people selflessly believed the tropical paradise must live on, even if they all perished. Their demise was so nigh they had all begun making plans for their interment."

Alistair rallies the zombie population by saying, "Show the rest of the crowd unquenchable thirst, as if brains were full of juicy water."

Our zombie audience attacks the rest of the watchers in slow-moving drags, eliciting happy squeals, and more trays of melted-brain Jell-O shots are distributed to all. We've turned an audience into a party.

"King Ivan, the King of Cats—"

Paws leap down the keyboard.

"Asked this willowy king—"

A trilling of a scale, like wind whipping a tree branch.

"'Do you have wells running deep into the earth?' 'Why, yes, of course,' said the willowy king. 'Full of drinkable water, if only we could reach it.' The King of Diamonds asked, 'Do you have buckets? Ropes?' The willowy king said, 'Yes, of course. But what good would that do?'"

Alistair explodes. "What the *bloody hell* is wrong with these wankers? Have they not heard of radical self-reliance?"

Our burners explode in cheers and laughter.

Alistair raises a hand to me and says, "I've got this, mate. They got the rope. They got the bloody bucket. The townspeople—very friendly, though a bit dim—gathered around the biggest well to protest and exclaim, 'We don't think this will work.'"

He swivels to me, eyebrows raised. "Yeah?"

I give him the thumbs-up and a head jerk to indicate John. *Include John. Include him!* What else can I do? Alistair owns the audience now. John plays cold, trickling plinks whenever the well is mentioned, but can't keep pace with Alistair's storytelling speed. Alistair is now accidentally excluding John, the man we are allegedly helping. Alistair lowers the bucket into the well, pulls up the pristine, clear water, sparkling in the sunlight, and announces that the kingdom celebrates with Nine Inch Nails. John freezes, unable to comply, and Alistair catches himself quickly to say, "I meant Barry fookin' Manilow."

John handles this request—bridging into "I Write The Songs."

"The kingdom rejoiced," Alistair cries, cutting loose on stage. "Show us how to celebrate!"

The audience responds to his energetic lead, and more than half dance while John plays Manilow. Alistair and I dance, presumably with the entire obsidian kingdom behind us, celebrating with giant mugs of cold water.

People begin singing the next few lyrics to the song.

After the dancing dies down a bit, I speak. "The willowy king presented the adventurers with more gold."

"Yes, yes, more bloody gold," Alistair says, facing the audience. "But the willowy king—"

John plays the willowy king riff.

Where is Alistair going?

He shoots me a smug grin. "The king said, 'Listen, you big adventurers, I have a question. Why do they call you the King of Cats? What's the backstory there?'"

Alistair puts me in a position where I have to deny the story, the essence of bad improv, or let him have his way. Okay, Alistair, you want this so badly. You got it.

I say, "Like his namesake, Ivan, the King of Cats, moved in such a way as to be described as 'sleek and silent.' Before anyone noticed he'd skulked into a room, he had already taken full measure of the circumstances. Some found him cuddly, others did not care for his hard stare. He could act before anyone realized action was needed. He upset the order of things, constantly knocking over breakable truths. He was no innocent. Nor was he malicious. Growing up poor on his Russian farm, his outlook was guarded. His best friend, King Charles, might be described as doglike in his innocence and courage. Ivan was known as the King of Cats for his fierce, feline protection of those he loved best."

Alistair smiles at me with soft reproach. "That wasn't so bad, yeah?"

I take the story back from him, finish the town's rejoicing, and promise great riches to whomever in our audience can find the moral of our stories. A zombie, with a white bone jutting out of his right arm, clamors to the makeshift stage, and—standing under Rick Astley—loudly proclaims, "Drink lots of water in the desert!"

The audience claps with hesitation, unsure if this morality feels like the right answer.

From under my thin, cotton jubba, I produce my fanny pack, jiggling it prominently before opening it to extract a gold coin.

"Sahiiiib, sahiiiiiiiiiiiiiiiiiib," I say, and Alistair follows with our trademark greeting.

Two or three members of our audience yell the same words back to us.

I say, "Thank you for coming on stage. We bequeath you a gold coin from King Charles and King Ivan's journey, a coin magically enhanced for its ability to solve problems and keep you safe during unexpected sandstorms."

The zombie accepts it with a polite bow, and as he returns to his brain-starved friends, another person reaches for Alistair's hand, wanting him to pull her onstage.

She's a sparkle pony, pretty and young, wearing a tight T-shirt proclaiming "Go Home," her hair pulled back into a bouncy ponytail. Once onstage, she yells out, "Sahiiib, *sahiiiiiiiiiiiiiiiiiiiiiiiiib!*"

Members of the audience cheer and laugh, yelling the words back at her.

She addresses both Alistair and the audience. "I think the moral of the story is we have to all love each other and solve each other's problems."

The audience prefers this fable's morality and they scream for her. She screams, too. Someone yells loudly, "Show us your tits." The audience's clapping dies after this.

She is awarded a gold coin, also imbued with magical properties, but before I elaborate, Alistair says loudly, "Also, it helps keep away pervs."

The audience laughs hard at this answer, and she does too, as she gives him a tight squeeze before thanking us both and dropping from the stage.

Alistair, Alistair, what have you done? You humiliated that man. While his wording was crude, and perhaps on some level he deserves your judgment, is he not also the one true king?

Alistair stands before the crowd, throwing his arms wide and yells, "Cheers, mates! Thank you for listening to our tale!"

Everyone claps, and John plays the appropriate flourishes, the old-timey radio sound to bookend our broadcast.

Alistair lifts his hands over his head. "*These are the lost and founds!*"

One final cheer rises through the crowd.

God help me. He drives me crazy, cornering me, defying me, and not focusing on John. I have to talk to him about all of this, but...but look at him. *Look!* The sunlight grows weaker but the power inside pours forth, his effervescent cheer as he waves good-bye to our audience, swirling around him like sand.

He turns to me and laughs. "That was brilliant! *You* were brilliant, Vin!"

I love him, and I don't even know his name.

Six

The three of us congratulate each other, quick words of praise as we leave the stage and make our way to our scrunchied hostess. We don't want to appear boastful. A few people congratulate us, tell us "great story," and the woman with the gold coin hugs Alistair again. He's got a fan.

Once our audience fully departs, our hostess says to John, "We have three sets tonight. We have about forty-five minutes between sets, and ideally, I'd like to fill that time with eighties music. If your repertoire is any good, we'd love to have you sit in. Dance pop, New Wave, whatever you want."

John says, "Oh. Well, I might not be the best person. I never learned much eighties music. I'm sorry."

"No worries," she says. "You guys were great fun. Can we offer you something, maybe some fruit? You guys drinking enough water?"

I say, "Water would be fantastic, thank you."

She smiles. "If I'm not mistaken, that's one of the morals of the story."

She asks us to wait. She leaves.

John says, "You guys, I can't spend the night playing Madonna and Duran Duran. I swear, I'll play anything else."

Alistair says, "No worries, mate. We will find you another session."

I can't read Alistair. Did he mean that sincerely? I think so. Perhaps I expected pouting, as he's the one who found this audition, yet right now he seems genuinely concerned with John's happiness. Points in his favor. With good cheer, Alistair discusses music John would find more palatable.

Wait. *Wait.* I have an idea about him. Could Alistair be like me? Is he—is he a *king finder*? Is he one, too?

A twenty-something shirtless guy in long shorts steps up. "Nice show. Where's your camp?"

"Don't have one," John says. "We were just messing around."

I'm surprised John spoke first, but scrutinizing his face and how he carries himself, I see he's different. He's out of his slump. He may not be as shy as I originally thought. After all, we met him when he was discouraged. His face isn't nearly as gloomy.

"You three are friends?" Long Shorts pulls his blond hair behind his ear.

"We are," I say, "though we met John an hour ago or so. We're taking him on auditions. We're his managers."

"Really," the guy says, and he sputters a laugh. "So you don't know these two Arabs?"

Alistair says, bowing, "Sahib, sahiiiiiiiiiiiib."

John smiles and says, "Not really. While we walked around together, we planned a few gags. The rest was us fucking around on stage."

I say, "John invented all the music, following our lead. The diamond sounds, the paws down the keyboard—all John. While we walked, I told him a few things, like that I wanted to communicate the broiling sun and he decided what to play."

"Amazing," our new friend says. "I'm in a nightclub two streets over on Mizzen Avenue. Come play with us tonight. We need keyboards. It's high audience participation, poetry, people talking, some karaoke. We need a guy who can do what you did, musical improv."

John glances our way. He might be seeking our permission with this glance, but I sense reluctance. He probably doesn't want to commit until he sees the situation and assesses a fit for himself. No problem.

"Sahiib, sahiiiiiiiiiiiib," I say and am echoed immediately by Alistair.

I drop into normal conversational tone again. "We'll check out your club. However, it's our decision as to whether he stays."

Alistair says, "He's our slave, yeah?"

Long Shorts raises his hands as if surrendering. "Totally. Your property."

John chuckles. "It's not all bad. I get off holidays and every other Saturday."

Alistair says, "Not Guy Fawkes Night, mate."

Our 80s hostess returns with four cups of water, and if she is surprised by the newcomer to our small group, she masks it well and hands him a water, likely the one she intended for herself. Her generosity is a reflex. We live in a gift economy.

We toast.

Our hostess introduces herself as Audrey, we chat about the success of this theme camp. The camp originally began as a mockery of terrible 80s songs, but genuine affection for that decade gradually evolved into something both commemorative and campy. We also discover Long Shorts has a name: Sistro. Many have Burning Man names, words they slap on their truest, wildest self. I remember a punk chick—avid firebug—who called herself The Storm. She managed a kidney dialysis center by day. In this light, Alistair's English persona cannot be considered too odd. Alistair is this man's burner identity. If he were ever found out, this is the one place where he could get away with saying, "I have always felt English on the inside. Let me be Alistair in your presence."

Burners would say, "Alistair. Cool."

Radical acceptance.

We thank Audrey for the water, the opportunity, and John walks with Sistro a few steps ahead so they can talk music and shows. We follow behind.

"Alistair, we need to talk. Three things. The alcohol, your ditching me, and forcing me to tell the King of Cats story."

"Oh, bloody hell," he grouses. "*Two* fucking shots."

"The alcohol was another two planks snapping. One under your footing right now, the other about ten paces ahead."

"You might be exaggerating your metaphor, mate," he says. "Only two drinks."

"It's not about the alcohol, though I don't want you buzzed. Right now, you're treading a narrow rope bridge swaying from side to side. Relaxing yourself with alcohol works against you. Big time. Also, lying to me breaks trust between us."

He grumbles.

"Alistair, you have to pursue this differently. I'm not the rule master trying to catch you at every turn. Don't back me into that corner. You make me into your boss, and there's no chance I can king you. Do you hear what I'm saying?"

We reach the cross street and turn toward Mizzen. John glances behind and I smile, jut out my chin to say "I'm here. We're still connected." He smiles and offers a slight head jerk at Sistro to indicate something positive.

Alistair stays quiet for a full minute.

I say, "Do you want this? Do you honestly want your kingship?"

"Yes," he says. "I bloody well do."

"Okay, then. Don't make me the rules guy. Do what I say. No smoking or drinking. Don't ask me questions. Follow my lead and step up your game because after watching your genius on stage a few moments ago, I know I'm working with a pro. You and I, we play with people easily. So don't think you're overly impressing me by manipulating me into revealing the King of Cats backstory. Your cleverness cost you another wooden plank. I had planned to keep that particular story on reserve for a time when you needed it most. Now it's gone. Right now, you're walking the path to remaining unkinged."

"Jesus and Mary," he says. "I get it. I'm sorry."

"I don't need you to be *sorry*, Alistair. I need you to understand the price you pay for getting your way. For choosing not to submit."

"I'm submitting."

"No, you're not. Only when you feel like it. You ran off this afternoon despite my saying I didn't want you to. During the second story, you hijacked the show and took the focus off John."

John and Sistro walk into a camp. We're here.

I say, "To be continued."

"No shite," he says.

Sistro's camp sits on the corner of Mizzen and the 195-degree cross street. I've been down Mizzen this week, but not this block. The camp is themeless. A cloth roof—which might be flannel sheets sewn together—pulled over a crude wooden stage made from shipping crates and metal poles. Nothing fancy. Several large tents behind their stage. A few mismatched tables, a short pillar candle on each one, already lit. This feels like a coffee house converting itself into a nightclub.

During our introductions to others in Sistro's camp, Alistair and I cry out, "*Sahib, sahiiiiiiiiiib,*" and we describe the pure worthlessness of John, followed by our spitting routine. Someone hands John a drink and guides him to the stage. A heavy, quilted pad, the kind used by moving companies, is removed from the keyboard, and John takes his place.

He tests out a few chords. The audio system is less intense than at the 80s theme camp gig, but the sound carries well. Passersby stop, half-interested in whether something's going to happen. At Burning Man, spontaneous art happens. Blink and you might miss it. The moment you ignore could be the one everyone remembers and discusses for the next year.

John is surrounded by his new camp mates. Well, if he decides to stay.

Alistair says, "Look, I didn't mean to ditch you this afternoon, I felt we could work smarter alone."

"Alistair, we're a *team.*"

"Hey, I got him the audition that eventually landed him *here.* If this works out, it's because of me."

"You treated John like he was a problem to solve. He felt it, too. Immediately after you left, he apologized for making work for us."

"That's not fair, Vin."

"You treated him like a problem. Not a king."

"*Bollocks.*"

"Alistair, I don't know how to emphasize this enough. You keep snapping planks out from under both our feet on this rope bridge."

"Enough of the rope bridge," he says, irritated. "Your little scare tactic isn't working anymore."

"Guys," John calls to us.

"To be continued," Alistair says.

How do I reach him? How do I explain I'm not trying to scare him, but warn him? Should I explain my suspicion he might be a king finder? No. It might create a false sense of entitlement or somehow make him think he's better than others. He's no more worthy than anyone else.

As we approach John, the two camp mates chatting with him take their leave and greet us in passing.

John says, "Can you guys stay and do a story? I want to make a good impression."

Alistair avoids looking at me and says, "Of course. You're our mate."

"Absolutely, John."

"These guys are cool," he says, nodding at his new friends. "Sistro and I talked music the whole way over here. This could work."

Alistair and I both express our excitement, and we rehash the first performance, what worked, what did not.

Sistro approaches and says, "John, how's your beer? You guys want one?"

Alistair says, "No."

I say, "John asked us to stay and do a story. What do you think?"

"Sure. Cool. Another king story?"

"Yes. The Lost and Founds."

Sistro nods and pulls hair behind his ear. "Cool. Sure on the beers?"

"Cheers," Alistair says. "But no."

"No thanks."

"Okay. Mics are on. Everything's set. Have fun."

I pull Alistair aside. "Are you and I okay? Can you still play with me and we'll work through the rest later?"

"I can play," he says. He appears contrite. "I am sorry to have disappointed you, Vin."

"I know you are. But you'll have to try harder. The bar is higher for you because you're, well, *you*. Your path is different from other men. You're unique."

He smiles at this intended compliment and turns to the burners milling near the intersection.

"Sheehiiiibs and sahiiiiiiiiiiiiiiiiiiiiiiiiiiibs!"

I echo his words. "Saahhiiiiiiiiiiiiiiiiiiiibs and shehiiiiiiiiiiiiiibs!"

Showtime.

I defer to Alistair, insisting he lead the way, as he provides the backstory to the Lost and Founds. John follows musically, throwing in some new riffs and reusing the successful ones from our first show. Alistair leads with grace, pulling in new listeners from among those strolling by, pointing at them and speaking lines like, "I can see you're wondering why some kings left the kingdom," and "I wonder what your queen name would be, Unicorn Girl in the blue top, if you remembered your *true* self."

John leads King Charles the Diamond and Ivan, the King of Cats, through the tulips, into the exhausting desert under the one-note sun, and beyond. A musical sandstorm hits next, sending Alistair and me careening around the stage. Desert hallucinations set in, and Alistair and I downhill ski together—side by side—as John plays Christmas music.

Alistair, gasping with sand choking his throat, says, "I believe I see a castle ahead."

John plays a hopeful tune, spirits rising.

This is my opportunity. Through art, I can express a topic impossible for me to discuss.

Facing the crowd of twenty-five or thirty people who have become engaged, I say, "As they approached the lands containing the faraway blue castle, Castle Forgiveness, they realized they must cross a rickety, ancient rope bridge to enter the kingdom."

Damn it. Why the fuck did I use Perry?

Alistair shoots me a *you're kidding* reaction, but John covers by making creaking wooden sounds emerge from his board while also teasing out a strained chord that suggests dizzying heights, earning a few impressed claps. John is good at this.

"The bridge bore broken planks, damaged recently, and more than a few of the vines meant to secure the way had been freshly snapped. The rope bridge hovered over a mighty chasm and the howling winds below—"

John makes the sound a wounded wolf might make.

Alistair jumps to the front. "'But I'm not afraid,' said King Charles the Diamond. 'I'll cross first.'"

Not what I intended, but this works.

Either Alistair leads John or John leads Alistair across the rope bridge, struggling, grasping. Through plunking keys, John mimics Alistair's leg breaking through a board. Crawling on stage, Alistair makes it to the other side and jumps up with energy. He takes a bow.

John celebrates this with a flourish.

Alistair turns to me with a self-satisfied smile. "That wasn't so hard. Even with a few planks missing. Your turn."

I say, "My king, I cannot."

Alistair frowns. In improv, you never say *no*.

Don't freak out. Talk normal. "The rope bridge is passable only for Found Kings. And I, Ivan, the King of Cats, must reveal a shocking secret."

John responds appropriately with a dun-dun-*duuuuuuuuuuuun*.

My eyes fill with tears. "I am a Lost King."

Alistair smirks and opens his mouth to respond but sees my face and stops.

"I've been trying to warn you. The more a man knows about his kingship, the less likely he himself will cross over. Those weren't idle threats. I can't cross over myself, because I know too much."

Alistair's face fills with surprise. "No. Vin..."

I hate the rope bridge metaphor! Why on earth did I keep using it? From this side, I feel panic when I talk about planks snapping, rope vines unknotting or stretching until their very tension makes a sound. I see the chasm of emptiness below me. I see my future, returning to the sewers to live out my days, and I think maybe I deserve that life. A life with the rats.

Alistair says, "Wait...wait. Use your Found King training to come with me, yeah?"

"I can't. It doesn't work like that."

True to my character, tears of frustration fall down my cheeks. I'm so goddamn tired of being lost. "With every kinging, I step further away from my own possibility of success. I have warned you a price must be paid for this knowledge. I am paying that price. My Lost King name is the Human Ghost. Ask Liam. Ask any of them. I will never be found."

Alistair says in an anguished voice, "No."

I'm so ashamed. Others tried to warn me about this. My big brother—who doesn't even believe—tried to warn me. I remember an argument we had seven years ago, a big one, and also the night I called him from New York City. That happened almost ten years ago, on Rance's weekend. I wouldn't listen. Why wouldn't I listen?

John kicks in with a sorrowful tune, a thick grief in low notes. He cannot see my face, but the audience reflects the strange seriousness, and I see one or two people whispering to their neighbors.

Alistair's face sags. "So, by saying 'yes' to this weekend with me—"

I interrupt him. "You must go on without me. See what can be done to alleviate suffering in this land."

"You're nutters. You're the bloody *guide*."

"Not a good one. I can't make you follow, no matter what I say or do."

Alistair falters. "Vin. I'm—I'm sorry."

John's not playing any music. Now, *I'm* the one guilty of making the show about me and not John. Does it matter that I did so intentionally, to work Alistair? Maybe not. Maybe I'm simply a different flavor of selfish.

I face the audience and spread my arms wide. "So, King Charles the Diamond continued the journey without his trusty companion, the King of Cats."

Tinkle, tinkle, tinkle.

Paws down the keyboard.

People may not have understood exactly what passed between us, yet their expressions reveal they felt the palpable tension. Time to exchange this for something lighter.

I wipe my face. "As he drew closer, Charles crossed field after field of the most extraordinary flowers, populated with the brightest oranges, the yellowest yellows. Unfortunately, no xenoxx plants. He found himself welcomed by a people kind to him, but suffering under a great sadness. Their mighty king, Perry the Forgiver, had been asleep for the longest time, an untold number of days and nights, and they feared, from the way he twitched in his sleep, he dreamt nightmares. Unfortunately, there was nothing they could do."

Why?

Why did I pick Perry? Because I'm nervous about seeing him? Sloppy, Vin. *Sloppy.*

I play the role of the grieving populace while Alistair—as King Charles—asks in a pointed manner, "Have any of you wankers tried waking him up?"

"No," I sadly report to the visiting king. "What good would that do?"

After exchanging a fleeting glance, Alistair takes the lead. "King Charles the Diamond went to the mighty Perry's bedroom. Saw his sleeping figure. Around the bed, many candles burned, offered in supplication. Quite the fire hazard, yeah? Very, very dangerous. But Charles the Diamond knew what needed doing."

Alistair leans over the imaginary bed and, in stage whisper, speaks to the audience. "Mighty king, sleeping king. Soon you will awaken. I must ask a favor, yeah? When you arise, I ask you to remember a friend of mine, a Lost King, stuck on the other end of a rope bridge he cannot cross. Take your king friends and go to him. Help him. Carry him over."

I find myself fighting tears.

A sudden wind blows down the street, through the camp, forcing us all to avert our faces from the stinging dust.

Alistair utilizes this wind as stage drama, waving his arms over the sleeping king, as if a magician about to saw his assistant in half. After the wind dies and the audience returns its attention to the stage once again, Alistair pretends to shake the sleeping man, saying, "Wake up, mate. Get the fook up."

The audience laughs.

My turn. "Much to the delight of the people, King Perry awoke! Nobody could believe Charles the Diamond's insane plan worked!"

Alistair points at the imaginary sleeping man with open arms, palms up. "I just fookin' woke him up is all. Don't shite yourself."

The audience laughs.

We finish the tale as we did the others, another chest of gold from another joyful kingdom. Alistair takes center stage as the story reaches its conclusion, and I toss him my bag of gold coins. He invites audience members to shout out their interpretations.

"Don't sleep at Burning Man!"

"Don't let someone lace your water with ecstasy!"

Before tossing the first coin, he explains its significance as a wishing coin, the same tale I told our lawnmower salesman yesterday. Alistair rewards the crowd's favorite answers and tosses a few coins.

We take our bows, John takes his, and half the crowd wanders, while some of them stay, eager to see what happens next.

We approach John, who smiles eagerly. "That was awesome."

"You were fantastic, John."

"Bloody amazing," Alistair says.

He grins under our praise, and we trade our favorite parts of the latest story. Sistro finishes a nearby conversation, and I see him heading our way. We've only got twenty seconds before he arrives.

I say, "Quick. John. What do you think of this place?"

John beams approvingly. "This is it. I want to stay." He adds hastily, "If that's okay."

"Sahiib, sahhiiiiiiiiiiiiiiiiiib!" Alistair throws his arms open wide. "Get your arse over here."

John comes around the piano to hug Alistair.

I cry out, "Sahhhiiiiiiiib, sahiiiiiiiiiiiiiiiiiiiiiiib!"

Sistro congratulates us on our story and reinvites John to stay. John agrees. Sistro laughs and turns to us, "Can your slave stay?"

Alistair spits to his left side. "He is worthless to us! Of course you may h ave him."

John considers us with an expression hard to gauge. "You guys are gonna leave."

"We are," I say.

A woman approaches and says, "Excuse me. Could you accompany me if I sing something?"

John says, "Yeah. Gimme a minute to say good-bye."

She apologizes and retreats a few steps. Sistro joins her and initiates a conversation. John stares at us without speaking.

I say, "You're going to have a magnificent night."

John blinks away a few tears.

Alistair puts his hand on John's shoulder. "Fuck your burn, mate."

John laughs at this standard salutation and wipes his eyes. "Yeah. You guys, too. Fuck your burn."

Seven

During the day, Black Rock City feels like a daddy longlegs spider, as each delicate step one takes is measured and careful to minimize contact with the scorched earth. At night, Black Rock City becomes a neon tarantula, cruising nimbly over the rugged terrain like a badass cross between a Jeep and a Ferrari.

Damn. I've imagined so many different kinds of cars having sex with each other and wondered about their resulting offspring, but I've never put a Jeep and a Ferrari together. Weird oversight. Yeah, a neon tarantula, that's their kid. Thick hairy legs, suggesting power and fierce fitness. The creature's spirit harbors no more malice than "leave me the fuck alone," yet this attitude is often mistaken for evil intention.

As intimidating as the desert is during the day, at night, Burning Man can seem downright sinister. The noise. The screaming. The howling in the distance. The raw language and the lack of clothing, lack of rules, lack of suburban civility. Oh, there's civility. Rules apply. But it's wilder. Maybe a tad more likely to create some trouble. Not to mention all the fire.

Right now, it's not quite night. The neon tarantula unfurls, testing its strength.

In the distance, the Fire Conclave practices. I know this by the unpredictable plumes of orange rocketing into the sky, racing straight up, gone almost immediately. Fire dancers emerge at this hour. They burn hoops, sticks, fans, torches. They spit the fire out of their mouths—anything to celebrate the glorious illumination, warmth, and power of life and destruction.

"Well, this is awkward," Alistair says.

I hadn't noticed our silence. I'd gotten caught up watching the transformation from day to night. I should pay more attention to Alistair, his every facial tic, as I have with men in the past. I should. But his is a different kind of King Weekend. The burden of crossing over is his, not mine.

"Awkward how?"

"Are you kidding? *Everything*. You agreed to king me. I had no idea it would... you know, have consequences."

"True."

"Why didn't you tell me?"

"It wasn't your burden to bear."

"Still...and you're truly a Lost King? You weren't baiting me?"

"No, I wasn't baiting you. Yes, for the first question."

We pass a juggler with glowing green balls, big ones, and two men with fake white beards, trailing to the ground. A woman sings loudly to herself as she passes. A dozen more people, more shapes than human forms, loom ahead of us until they saunter by. It's odd when you pass someone wearing a costume in the almost-dark. The unrecognizable contours are more suspect, more threatening. Then they get near, and you realize it's no threat, just three women with bones for hair.

Alistair says, "I feel terrible."

"Don't. This was my decision."

"Yes, but—"

"Alistair. This was *my* decision. I knew the consequences."

He sulks. "I feel bloody awful."

I stop walking. Pull him off Mizzen Avenue, out of the traffic. Everyone is headed somewhere except for us.

"Alistair, guess why I didn't tell you any of this? Guess what this knowledge does? It takes you off your path. It increases the pressure you put on yourself, it makes you more self-conscious of me, of us, of our relationship together, of any number of variables except the path to your own kingship."

Well, at least that's what I *hope* it's doing right now.

"But you did tell me. Just now."

"Yes. Because you're dangerously close to losing. You don't understand. You won't lose in the final hours of your King Weekend; it almost never comes down to the wire. You lose now, *tonight*, because I can't steer you into right direction this early, not with your lies and your covert agendas."

"What lies?"

You're not English!

"You had two shots. Tried to hide it. Remember?"

"Oh. Right. Sorry, mate."

"Alistair, you don't even *remember* you lied an hour ago. But it's not the drinks. Hell, I have a bottle of champagne for us to enjoy later. It's the disobedience. Not because everything I command is so important. *One* of my commands will be important, and you must obey without hesitation. It might be the only command all weekend that matters, but you won't do it if you spend all our time together debating which ones to follow."

The drivers of art cars flip their customized light switches, illuminating the colorful underbellies. Off to our left, a giant plume of fire races toward the sky and dies, disappears. While we were arguing, night arrived.

Through a break between camps, I see him. The Man.

At night, with wire-coated phosphorous wrapped in transmitter wires, surgically implanted throughout his entire frame, The Man glows, a battery-powered, violet-glowing skeleton, arms at his side. Last year, he was blue. Every night, he serves as our beacon, protection against the terrors of this alien landscape, this corner of desolate Mars we call the playa.

Lost at night?

Find The Man.

Follow him home.

And at the end of the week, watch him burn, burn, *burn*!

"I'm sorry, Vin."

"Stop being sorry. Stop feeling guilty. If you want to do something useful, honor the choice I made. I'm sacrificing for you this weekend. Honor my sacrifice by following my lead, my rules. Honor what you're here to do. Don't waste time with pity or guilt."

"Okay," he says. "I will. I will be better, yeah?"

"You don't have to be *better*. Let me carry my emotional burden, and I will let you carry yours. Honoring my choices means you let me into your heart. Choose to submit."

"I will. I promise. I'll do better."

Do better? He's still thinks it's about his performance. Maybe there's a way for me to use this. I have an idea.

"Alistair, you want to prove you're ready to change? Great. Here's a test. I'm going to tell you something. Don't argue with me. Don't disagree. Don't say anything. Let me say what I want to say without questions, without refuting me. Deal?"

"Yes. I can do that, mate."

"Great. Here goes. I know things about you, Alistair. I know things you don't want me to know. Or rather, things you *think* I don't know, I already know. By keeping these secrets, you think you're testing me. If I prove worthy, you might reveal them. Here's *my* secret: I don't care. Keep your secrets. I don't need to expose you or have you confess. I'm loving you anyway. I love the man who plays, with spontaneous abandon. The man who can work a crowd. The man who knew to say "fuck your burn" to John—the perfect good-bye. The man who improvised and asked King Perry to help me. You're kinder than you think you are. You're more ready for this than you know. You're so primed. Will you find your kingship? Maybe. I don't need to know your secrets, but as long as you don't let anyone in, you're trapped with them."

He says nothing.

I can barely see his face, but I don't think he flinched. All around us, soft phosphorous glows. Greens and purples, long tubing. Hairy legs. We stand in silence as the neon tarantula begins to scramble.

"Shall we walk?" I ask in my most pleasant tone.

We continue our path down Mizzen, and he says nothing.

Crank, crank, crank. His windup crank gets a few more turns.

After two minutes, he asks, "May I ask an unrelated question?"

"Sure. Of course, we discussed your question-asking habit multiple times, so I abdicate any further responsibility for advising you against it. You know the consequences. Ask away."

He is silent as we continue our stroll.

"Your question?"

"Never mind."

I feel I should force this moment. See if he circles back to his important question.

"Alistair, you hungry? I am. We should get a snack."

"Yeah, sure."

A robot passes us, two shirtless guys singing, a goddess woman. She's gone immediately, slipping into the night, but she was a goddess woman. At Burning Man, you simply accept that sometimes a goddess passes you, without your being able to articulate any details about her. Who was she?

At last, he asks, "Is this magic?"

"Is what?"

"Your King Weekends. You're a Lost King, but you wield some sort of magic, right?"

I snort. "No. No magic."

He says, "But *Liam*."

"Liam what?"

"The night he talked about his King Weekend. He changed. He transformed."

"You said you did drugs."

"Not hallucinogens. I know what I saw. We all saw it. He was more. He became more."

"More what?"

"I dunno. More of something. He...it's hard to articulate."

"You were on drugs."

Alistair stops. "Quit saying that. Don't dismiss my experience. You weren't there."

He's right. Maybe drugs had nothing to do with it. Or maybe being high is how to experience magic. What do I know?

I say, "I'm sorry. It's hard for me to ignore that you took drugs to alter your brain. I guess I have a prejudice around that. I wasn't there. I don't know what you saw."

"Thank you," he says. "I don't know what I saw either. *Something* happened. He described his king shirt, said it was crimson. But I already knew. Stars had been circling around him, and they glowed this deep maroon, but brighter. I can't explain it. How could I know his king shirt was crimson? So, I ask again. Are your King Weekends magic?"

"No. I mean, weird stuff happens sometimes, but I don't think I believe in *magic*."

"Why not?"

"I just don't."

"Have you seen the sparks? On the men you king?"

"Yes."

"You know something about those sparks, right?"

"I—"

I stop. I *what*?

I can tell when a man crosses over. Temporarily, I see the sparks, the light going in and out of him. I assume that's my eyes playing tricks on me, having to do with emotional intensity. On the other hand, I know an ancient tablet exists related to the Lost and Founds story. I've seen it in my brain. In New York, Rance exposed me to a Greek tablet, which made me, I dunno, black out or something. He said I spoke a sentence that—to this day—I don't remember. Then, there's Ryan and the kite. Suppose I've had enough experiences to convert me into a believer. But I don't believe. The world is too shitty. If magic exists, why do kids get abused and raped? Why doesn't magic intervene?

I say, "I don't believe in magic. As a kid, I believed for a while. Growing up in foster care, I had a rough couple of years. I used to wish for a magnificent king or handsome prince to rescue me. Nobody ever came. No magic wishes were granted."

"No king came for you, so you started making kings."

I frown. What is he implying? I invented all this stuff about kings to rescue me from my childhood?

I cross my arms. "I don't believe in magic."

Alistair says, "How do you explain what happened tonight with John?"

A light flicks on nearby in someone's camp. I see Alistair's earnest face. "Explain what?"

He says, "We meet him, I find him a camp to play in. It's not the right camp. There *happens* to be a guy wandering by at the right time who *happens* to need a piano player in his camp, and John *happens* to love it there. How do you explain this?"

I cross my arms. "Hundreds of people are walking the city right now. Hell, thousands. One is a guy who hears piano music. He's thinking of how he needs a piano player so he stops to listen. Sistro got lucky John was shopping for a stage, but honestly, it's equally as likely we stayed at the first camp John noticed, the one where they said their keyboard guy was away. Maybe that situation could have worked. So could a dozen other camps. Half a dozen, at least. Probability. Statistics. Not magic."

Alistair says, "What I saw with Liam was real, the crimson sparks, the way he was more stars than human at the end of the night. Maybe being a Lost King blinds you."

"I don't want to argue this. If there's any magic, it comes from ordinary people choosing to be their very best for each other. That's the only magic."

"Hey buddy," says a robot who joins us. "How's it going? I can't believe it's you."

He wears an ice bucket on his head, making him more like the Wizard of Oz tin man, than a glimpse into the future. His arms are encased in silver tubing, giving the impression of a cheap, knock-off Home Depot robot. I don't recognize him, despite his big grin. I can't quite see his eyes under that bucket.

"You're the Italian Arab working out your backstory, right?" He removes the ice bucket. "I'm Alan. You helped me and my girl yesterday. Helena."

"Alan!" I'm delighted to see him, and of course I recognize him now, sans bucket. His face is hard to see in the gathering darkness.

"Alan, this is my friend Alistair. Alistair, this is—"

"I know who he is," Alistair says with a surly tone. "I know *exactly* who he is. So, running into this guy, by accident, must be a complete coincidence, right? Nothing planned? No magic?"

"Not a coincidence," Alan says. "I've been looking for you, assuming you dressed the same. We never got to thank you, Hel and me. You disappeared."

Alistair smirks. "Like magic."

Although I don't think this is magic, still, it's surprising Alan found us in the dark. Organizers estimate over thirty thousand people here this year. Of course, we're on the same street where we saw him yesterday, so maybe his camp is nearby.

"What are you guys doing? Come over. Hang out with us."

I say, "Maybe later. We need to find some grub."

"Come back with me," Alan says. "I'll make you a sandwich and get you some fruit. C'mon. Helena would love to give you a hug."

"How lucky, yeah?" Alistair crosses his arms. "We *happened* to cross paths with Alan and he *happens* to provide dinner. Certainly not magic at all."

I cross my arms. "I could have planned this."

"Did you?"

"No."

Alistair remains smug.

Alan nods at Alistair. "What's up with English?"

"Beats me. Lead the way. We're really hungry."

Well, I'm hungry.

On the way to Alan's robot camp—which we learn is dedicated to sci-fi of the 1950s—we chat about yesterday's run-in. Alan eagerly asks how I guessed his relationship with his mom. I explain, best I can, my ability to read faces, read people, a lifelong skill cultivated through crippling loneliness. Well, I don't explain *how* the skill was cultivated. Most people don't care how my abilities developed. They care about the magic tricks.

We cross another two streets and head south on Mainmast Avenue, closer to the center of the city.

"Helena!" Alan yells when we get close to his camp. "Guess who I found? The Italian Arab king guy."

We learn their camp is affectionately known as Robot Zamp, and it's closed for the night, like so many others. A few midsize tents surround a main tarp and two smaller tarp shade structures—suburbs to the common space. Six or seven people sit under the big tarp, lounging and drinking. As we get closer, I see two of them busy organizing piles of clothes, rope, cans, and more, typical Burning Man supplies. I see clear tubs stacked in succession, loaded with supplies nobody wants saturated with dust. Robot costumes, maybe.

"Helena!"

She emerges from the largest tent wearing a tight red dress and army boots, big hoop earrings dangling. She sees us. Without words she wraps herself around me. When she finally releases me, she kisses me on the cheek.

"Thank you," she murmurs into my ear.

She takes a step back, and we hold each other's hands.

I say, "You look fabulous."

She laughs and says, "You look the same."

Alan circles behind her, wrapping his arms around her waist and says, "You do look fabulous."

I step aside. "This is Alistair. We met shortly after I met you. Tonight, he's my date."

Helena laughs. "Do you only date men dressed like yourself? That certainly narrows the dating pool."

For once, Alistair stammers and seems downright sheepish, which is funny to observe. His confidence knows no limits—his showmanship rocketed him to "carnival barker" status during our show with John. Now? He's like a shy ten-year-old.

"Good to meet you," Helena says. "King man, you left before we could thank you."

"You're welcome. It was my pleasure to meet you yesterday."

Alan says, "What's your name? Not your bullshit name."

"Vin Vanbly."

Close enough.

As others from Robot Zamp stroll over, Helena says, "This is him. This is the guy."

This mention increases their interest and friendliness; they shake both Alistair's and my hand vigorously, which clearly means they heard the tale. Alan explains we are guests for dinner, and despite the fact they've packed away dinner supplies already, he insists it's no trouble, *no trouble*, and steps away to prepare our meal. Several of their mutual friends joke about how they couldn't get Alan to help with dinner preparations any night thus far. We sit under their tarp asking questions about their sci-fi theme. Like some camps, they do not take their theme too seriously. It was mostly an excuse to wear reflective, cool costumes. Helena is a costume designer for a university theater department, as are two others in the group. Their coolers and hard plastic bins serve as benches, arranged in a semicircle. In the glow of a battery-powered lantern, Alan opens Tupperware and prepares peanut butter and jelly sandwiches, asking us if coconut water works for us, which it certainly does. Coconut water is great for rehydration.

Hydration is everything.

Helena sits next to Alistair and asks him how we met, what we're doing, our plans for the night. He answers her honestly without using the words "King Weekend." Like me, he's a master of dancing around the truth while telling the truth. Alistair glances at me and confesses he does not know our evening plans, but he trusts they will reveal themselves.

I say, "We don't have plans. What are you thinking, Alistair?"

"Me?"

"Yeah. How do you want to spend tonight?"

Alistair balks at this. "Isn't this your call? Your decision, yeah?"

"Well, it's *our* decision. I want your opinion."

"Come dancing with us," Helena says. "Come dance."

Alistair says, "I'm not sure we can. I believe we're supposed to help people all night. Vin?"

"Do you feel like dancing?"

Alan kneels nearby, peeling oranges for us. "Come with us. We'll have fun. Promise."

Alistair stands. "Vin, may I talk to you privately?"

"Sure. We'll be right back."

We step to the edge of their camp, almost in the road. Night patrols the city now, slipping between people out in their dancing clothes, hats covered in reflective ribbons, leotards, tutus, and occasionally birthday suits. Less nudity. It's cooling off. Bicycles illuminated in neon tubing navigate the streets carefully. Four muscle men wear glittering jockstraps. Kinda hot, actually. Everyone chatters excitedly, eager to explore the night's fire art, or chase down main attractions, such as Dr. Megavolt, La Contessa, or other mutant cars careening dangerously in the dark, spewing fire. I saw an octopus that spewed fire. That was cool.

He says, "I don't want to fuck up this choice. I want to do the right thing."

"Alistair, tonight is a free night. I have plans for us much later, but for the next few hours, we're free. Do you feel like dancing, or would you rather talk and wander?"

"Tell me what to do. I will obey."

"I appreciate your willingness, but there's some flexibility. Let's do what you feel like doing."

Alistair hesitates. "Am I supposed to choose dancing? Is that why we're here?"

"We're here for sandwiches."

"I'm not an idiot. There's some reason we're here. You planned for Alan to find us."

"I thought magic brought us here."

"I was trying to win an argument. Which I did, by the way. However, I assume you set this up. You and your guys exchanging notes. Are we supposed to fix something? Fix someone? Is it the tall guy with glasses who doesn't say much?"

"Alistair, what if we're here to eat their food and enjoy their company for a while? Kingship isn't about trying to fix everyone in the world."

"Well, what is it, then?" His tone is sharp. "I'm trying to figure out what you want from me and what to do. What's the lesson?"

"The lesson is whatever you want it to be."

Alan calls out, "Food's ready."

"C'mon. Let's eat."

Alistair hisses in the dark. "*Seriously*. Tell me what to do!"

"Alistair. Answer this question honestly. Do you want to go dancing?"

"I like to dance."

"Okay, so let's dance with these guys."

"I see. The lesson comes later, when we're hanging out, yeah?"

"Alistair, quit pressuring yourself. Kingship means something different for every man. Quit trying to box it up and get it *right*. C'mon. Chow time."

We return to the small group and Alan presents us with dinner: sandwiches, oranges, and coconut water.

Experienced burners know we eat less out here. They know how to pack foods to last a week with minimal odor. Minimal packaging, since there are no trash cans; you carry out your moop. Moop. Moopsie doopsie, do. *Stop it*.

Hydration is the biggest issue. If you spend the day riding bicycles or wandering the broad city, you gotta keep electrolytes hopping. Especially if you're going to drink and party at night. Energy-rich foods with little packaging is the smart choice. Coconut water is a great gift out here.

We thank him, and Alistair announces we'd relish the chance to go dancing. A few Robot Zamp members leave to finish changing clothes. Helena and Alan introduce two of their camp mates who show up in tight silver shorts and matching cut-off vests, making them the sluttiest looking astronauts on the playa. They call themselves Tuck and Nitro. I love Burning Man. Everybody gets superhero names.

Nitro expresses great shock that Alan made us dinner, and he bemoans the darkness preventing photographic evidence of this historic day.

Tuck asks, "Helena, did you nag him? Beg him? Scold him?"

Helena says, "Nope."

"Bribe him sexually?"

"Nope. He's getting that for free, later."

Alan growls a sexy Eartha Kitt response, and returns their ribbing with good-natured barbs, explaining if Tuck did something *worthy* of dinner, Alan would cook him a steak. After a few minutes of razzing, we do what burners do. We share our stories. Our first Burning Man, crazy adventures we've had over the years. Alistair tells his story about last year's Dice bar, the one he told me yesterday. Helena attended Dice bar one night last year and knew of the Hawaiian mafia plot, but was not present for the final night, the one which touched Alistair's heart. They enjoy his retelling. We discuss the whiteout from a few days ago and where we were when it hit.

Nitro says, "Have you seen the flaming bike rider? He'll be out tonight."

Apparently, one of this year's artists created a burnable stick man of human proportions, made of unknown material, and has him attached to a tandem bike, back seat. At night, the artist sets the second rider ablaze and rides around the playa. In the thick darkness, nobody sees the human rider in front, so it appears to everyone a literal burning man steers his bike across the playa.

"It's the bee's knees," Alistair says. "Absobloodylootely terrifying. I've seen it."

Everyone speculates on the material he uses to hold and conduct the fire.

Our sandwiches and oranges finished, Alan collects our plates, and even Helena seems impressed by his dedication to his role as waiter and maître d'. He ignores Nitro yelling "someone grab my camera," and after watching Alan a moment, Helena turns to us with wet eyes. She reaches for my hand.

"What you did," she says, and she stops speaking. A few seconds later, she says, "We talked all night."

We stare at each other, offering our best silent blessings in the halogen glow.

The moment is complete, and she laughs, wipes her face, and excuses herself. She wants to grab something from her tent before we head out into Black Rock City.

When Alan returns, Alistair asks me if he might gift Alan a wishing coin. Alan insists no need, dinner was his thank you for yesterday's gift from me. But when you live in a giving culture at Burning Man—a culture dedicated to appreciation—the thank-yous stack up. Luckily, the desert is big enough for all our gratitude. Alistair thanks Alan for the kindness shown to him as Vin's guest, and after collecting a coin from the sack, he presents it, telling the story of the wishing coin, embellishing with details including a genie trapped inside the image of Nero.

"It's heavy," Alan says.

Alistair nods solemnly. "The genie was a portly man before he got trapped in the coin."

As we prepare for our departure, back to the nightclubs along the Esplanade, Alan says, "You guys can't dance in those heavy robes and headpieces. It's too hot, and tonight's not going to get that cold. Leave them here. Grab them later."

We strip to our shorts and T-shirts, which feels fantastic. The sensation of warm breeze against my bare skin makes me almost shiver in appreciation. I feel unbound. I feel free. I will keep the bag of coins with me. We may want to give some away.

Alistair's T-shirt boasts the logo of some English football team, and I realize I haven't thought about his performance as a Brit for an hour or more. I guess I've come to accept him as English, this Burning Man identity. When we met John a few hours ago, I bristled and contemplated the morality of it, me as a collaborator in the lie. I guess I'm okay with it. Who am I to criticize? What about the lies I show the world?

Alistair and I may share another commonality. You adopt another persona, someone who could be you—is at least partially you—and after a while, you forget you're pretending. Maybe I can't become a Found King because I don't remember who lives underneath this façade. Maybe this isn't a façade and the real me is just really lost.

When the Robot Zamp group is ready to go, all eleven of us, Tuck informs us we must first toast with vodka.

Nitro raises the bottle and says, "Burning Man is like the child of Las Vegas and New Orleans' French Quarter."

Our small group murmurs an appreciation.

After his swig, he passes the bottle to Helena. She hesitates for only a moment. "Burning Man is like sweaty, noonday sex on a cliff's edge."

In a sexy, hopeful voice, Alan says, "Oh, baby."

We all laugh.

"Keep dreaming," she says, taking his hand. "It's a metaphor."

Alan passes on taking a swig. "Mmmmmm..." he says, imitating Homer Simpson. "Cliff sex."

He hands the bottle to Alistair, who in turn, looks at me.

"Go for it," I say.

He raises the bottle. "Burning Man at night is like the punk scene in Bristol during the late 1970s but with gifting and gratitude."

Tuck says, "You're way too young to have lived that."

"True," Alistair says. "Just playing along, mate."

He passes me the bottle. I take a sip. "I thought about this earlier. Burning Man at night is a neon tarantula."

Two women in our group do not care for my metaphor, so I switch and explain it's like a Jeep had sex with a Ferrari, which meets with more general approval.

After a few more toasts, we leave the camp and walk in a group.

Alistair takes my hand and squeezes it. "I liked the neon tarantula."

I squeeze back.

We hold hands.

I revel in how ordinary this feels, as if I could do this back home. Take a date out dancing. Hang out with friends. I can't. But here—here at Burning Man—freaks fit in. I'm one of the gang. I'm normal.

Burning Man is the closest I've ever come to family.

Burning Man is like home.

EIGHT

e dance.
We dance.
We dance.

First at one club, then another rave, farther down the Esplanade. Our group mostly stays together, taking head count when we think we're ready to move on. Tuck remains behind to keep dancing with a girl with pink hair. During a break, someone gifts us vodka shots, which Alistair declines.

I nudge him. "Go ahead if you want."

He politely declines again.

He's trying to be *good*. He wants his kingship revealed in rules, in right answers, in a sequence of steps performed the right way. I'm not surprised. A lawyer crafts a detailed outline to win an argument. There might be multiple ways to win in any court case, so he knows there's flexibility, yet he assumes a series of winning steps will cross him over. For some men, that's how it works. It's not the same for everyone.

Each club attempts to outdo its neighbors, bigger light displays, crazier themes, the wildest attractions. At Beasterville, we dance like animals, purring, licking, clawing, howling, supervised by hosts dressed as feral cats and sexy foxes. The Dalmatian costume man doesn't bounce with their sensual energy. He's just some guy in a dog costume who found his way home.

During a break we joke about Animal Control and how they'd love this party. Because no actual pets are permitted at Burning Man, Animal Control volunteers patrol the streets and occasionally abduct burners dressed in animal costumes, those they deem "strays." Strays are auctioned off just before sunset each day. Beasterville seems like a prime hunting grounds.

"I heard if nobody buys you at auction, they make you compete in a naked tetherball tournament," Nitro says, very pointedly staring at Alan.

Alan laughs. "It's not naked."

Helena says, "How did I not know this about you? They got you?"

"The first year I came, I was a penguin for a day. They said it was my own fault for being off-leash."

We move on to a heavy metal rave. Not our scene. We choose not to stay long. On our way to the next destination, a herd of bicyclers pedal toward us, each of them wearing a head lamp. In the pitch dark, it's like an army of cyclops approaching. They're singing a song I do not recognize. As they pass, one of them yells to our group, "Keep it strange!" Shouldn't be too hard to take that advice. On our right, a mortuary camp, calling themselves Last Chance, invites burners to rest comfortably in luxurious coffins to experience true sensory deprivation. The place is crowded with partiers on break and a number of black clad Maxers, pierced uncountable times. It's a Goth homeland.

Alan and Nitro disappear briefly and return with a new friend who gives us water from his supply. He agrees to stay and dance with us. Alan is so affable, so friendly. We are lucky he found us.

Huh. Maybe luck is magic.

At the 70s disco, we all do the hustle, and I work up a sweat. Alistair loves to dance, loves to match the music, the thumping base, with his body. Sometimes he grinds slowly, as if dancing underwater. Other time he meets Donna Summers' high-pitched notes with his own whirling dervishes. He throws his arms around me, pulling me into him, and suddenly his lips are inches from my own. I'm surprised he initiated this intimacy, but then again, no I'm not. He wants this. The reason for his no sex rule is not sexual abuse, nor is it because he doesn't enjoy his sensual body. He clearly does. I wrap my arms around his waist and, without kissing him, rub our noses together. When we're in sync, we're amazing.

A few minutes later, he yells at our friends to look up and spin, the night sky creating the most intense, brilliant disco ball planet earth could possibly imagine.

Oh, man, the stars.

They never fail to impress, their intensity, their willingness to be witnessed, bragging about their ongoing hydrogen collisions, pulsing with us as we spin, spin, spin.

On a break from disco mania, Alistair and I sway on the crowd's perimeter, allowing me to catch my breath. Alistair is in better shape for this. He grins at me constantly, telling me over and over, "This is fun. I'm having fun." Helena and Alan both remain in *Saturday Night Fever* mode, and their connection to each other is made sexier by both of them dirty dancing. Together, they get cheers. They must savor this—this level of exhibitionism. Good for them.

A man steps out of the shadows, which is nothing new. Tonight, everyone's in the shadows. However, this one hands me a folded piece of paper.

"Another mysterious piece of paper." Alistair wears an aloof expression. "I'm not going to ask."

I scan it quickly. "Our ride is here. We should go. Find the gang and bid them adieu."

His startled face is illuminated by glowing purple tubing, which gives him the appearance of a mad scientist. We dance our way through a crowd of seven or eight hundred, returning to the spot where we last saw them grind. It still takes a solid ten minutes before we spot Helena. Once I start making "taking off" gestures, she and Alan's faces grow alarmed. They shake their heads in disagreement.

"Stay," they both say over the pounding beats, though none of us hear the word spoken.

We get the gist.

I shake my head and point to my imaginary watch. "Time to go."

They leave the dance area with us, attempting additional coaxing, but I insist we have plans, late-night plans, and we mustn't keep them waiting. They reluctantly accept this.

I say, "Can we swing by tomorrow morning and grab our robes?"

This makes them happier. We will see each other in the morning.

We all hug.

Since we've been partying on the Esplanade, it's a short distance to The Man, radiating his purple approval. His violet bones vibrate with light, our powerful Mayor. We love you. We will destroy you.

Burn, burn, burn.

Alan was right—although chilly, it's not cold, not like the last two nights.

Alistair and I hold hands. We do not speak as we pass The Man and head deeper into the desert. I don't think I could feel happier. We experienced some rough moments earlier today, but this feels lovely, a night spent dancing with friends, and now we're off for some quality time alone. Behind us, the carnival screams, the colored lights and blaring chaos of a dozen raves attempting to attract attention from deep space. I wonder if it's working. Is anybody out there? If so, come here. Come to Burning Man. Come experience radical acceptance.

Alistair turns to me. "Hey, can I ask you a question?"

I try to keep my face neutral. "Sure."

He smiles. "Are you having fun?"

This makes me laugh. He's fucking with me. "I'm having fun. I'm having a great time."

"Me too," he says. "Me too."

We lean into each other as we stroll. I feel my dick stirring in my pants. He wants to dance, too. As I consider the many sexual things I'd love to do with Alistair, how I crave the taste of him, how I want to lie on top of him and wrap my arms around his pale chest, squeezing him—my thoughts are interrupted. *I know his king name!* Lotus Land lies directly before us, and the memory of our time there jars me into recognition. I know his king name. No question!

Ha. *No question.*

A few hundred yards beyond Lotus Land, our vehicle awaits, or rather, *vehicles*, plural. Two bicycles. They're nothing special, cheap mountain bikes, I guess, and I don't know who owns them. The kings promised to find whatever I need all weekend. I was told if someone didn't already possess it on-site, they'd run into town. Of course they'll have to run into town—nobody out here has four hundred Twinkies. They handle all the details, the supplies, the timing, the relays. Hell, I don't even know the men delivering the cheese notes. They're friends of the kings. The Found Ones know enough not to come themselves. Any contact with Alistair could influence him in one direction or another. They know how delicate this is. They remember.

Thinking of them makes my heart hurt.

The man standing next to our bicycles greets us and invites us to partake of a snack. He offers us bananas, a small baggie of M&Ms, a few organic granola bars, and two fruit cups. Alistair chooses the banana. I want the granola bar. Our polite host, a man probably in his thirties, wears vacation garb: a short-sleeved, button-down shirt of unremarkable pattern, blue cargo shorts, and hiking boots. He suggests we strip our food so he can collect our refuse.

Alistair says, "I can't believe we've been together all this time and you haven't gone off on the MOOP acronym."

"I'm over that word. I've done as much with it as I can. I wrote a moop poem a few years ago."

"Of course you did."

While we eat, the man hands me a folded note.

I read it.

"Do you have a pen?"

The man produces one without speaking. I wonder who he is, this man who agreed to meet us here late at night next to an art installation. What's his story? I write a terse reply ending with the words, *wrong, wrong, WRONG*! I underline the last one for emphasis. He accepts my answer without reading it and takes our garbage without eye contact. He turns toward Black Rock City. Alistair and I watch him retreat. His silence makes me think of him as a ghost, and the carnival city behind us, some sort of afterlife, though heaven or hell, I couldn't say. Probably heaven. He seemed like a nice guy.

Black Rock City is already far from the civilized world, and every second we pedal farther from its temporary civilization, the isolation grows. Man-made light recedes. Noise recedes. Our bike ride doesn't take long in terms of chronological time, six minutes, yet the physical distance seems like miles and miles. We reach the orange plastic netting, the stuff used for crowd control at sporting events. In this case, the fence is more symbolic than functional. Marking the desert boundary for Burning Man, it can barely hold itself erect. Burners are not allowed beyond this point. It's the law.

We dismount.

Alistair says, "You know they patrol this regularly. Multiple trucks, I think. Nobody is allowed beyond the orange fence."

"I know."

We wait.

I'm sure Alistair is bursting with questions, the biggest one being, "are we really going beyond it?"

Yes. We are.

To his credit, he does not ask.

We both turn to study faraway Black Rock City, surely a colorful mirage, a vague mass of blurry hues and occasional bursts of fire. For some reason, our remoteness makes me question humanity's existence. To see this many stars, this much wide-open black—along the horizon and in the sky—makes me believe nothingness is all. So much emptiness. We are but a tiny little carnival on a tiny little planet.

Someone approaches. I *feel* him in the darkness, his silent footsteps. I don't know how I know what I know these days. My abilities to read people, to understand what's happening instantly, it's growing. How can I know someone's coming when nobody is visible? I don't believe it's magic. I think this is connectivity. I think we're all connected, and the more attuned I become to the connection, the more I feel it. That's not magic. It's deep listening, nothing more.

I touch Alistair's arm. "Don't be afraid."

Seconds later, a shape emerges from the darkness, and a split second later, he is recognizable as human.

Under his breath, Alistair says, "Jesus bloody Christ."

It's the same guy who met us in Lotus Land this afternoon. He still wears cutoff jeans and shells around his neck. He's shirtless now, exposing a variety of tattoos. Wearing shoes this time, and carrying a step stool. Who had one of those?

From his back pocket, he pulls out a walkie-talkie. "They're here."

Alistair turns to me. "You have a lot of help."

"A number of men want to see you kinged."

He smiles broadly—so broadly that, even in this faint light, I see his face change. "Yeah?"

Alistair waits, expectantly.

He wants me to elaborate. He wants me to tell him he is special, the Found Kings at Burning Man recognize his greatness, and I believe in his greatness too. He believes if this message is repeated enough, perhaps one day he will also believe. The problem with a man like Alistair is no amount of praise, flattery, or loving from the outside will impact his core. Not love from me, not love from any of the kings.

There is only one love that can reach him.

The seashells man steps away and speaks quietly into the walkie-talkie. He gets his reply and turns to us. "Go. You have twelve minutes."

Alistair says, "What? No. No, Vin. *No*."

"We don't have time to argue. The people distracting the perimeter rangers estimate twelve minutes."

Alistair watches while Seashell Man and I spring into action. He unfolds the step stool. I climb it and quickly hop the sagging orange plastic. Seashell Man hands my bike over first, then Alistair's.

Alistair stands and watches numbly. He says, "No. I bloody can't."

"You must. It's our path."

"Vin, we could get banned from Burning Man, yeah? Not just this year, but always."

"What would you risk to find a lost king? And what if he doesn't remember you?"

Alistair glances back at the city. "Can't there be another way?"

"This is it. Time to decide how much you want your kingship."

"Wait," he says. "Let me think."

Alistair wants me to make a stronger case. I know. I've been here before. I remember trying to convince Perry to join me on Alcatraz. With King Nicholas the Rose, I spent almost an hour convincing him we needed to jump. Not Alistair. He could never be persuaded, not by external forces. Nobody gets through to him unless he chooses it. Every argument I make will get countered. Some men cannot be cajoled or seduced.

Alistair doesn't move.

I refuse to speak.

Seashell Man breaks the tension. In a quiet voice, he says, "I'd give anything to be invited. I don't want to remain a Lost King."

Alistair looks at him.

Shit. *They aren't supposed to interact with Alistair!* Hasn't this man been briefed?

"Only eight minutes left." Seashell Man disappears into the darkness, leaving behind the step stool.

Crap. I don't know if those words will help or hurt. He doesn't realize Alistair ricochets away from anything like pressure. This is why I make rules about who can speak and who can't, for these delicate moments. *Fuck.* Depending on how Alistair interprets that comment, this could be the end of our King Weekend!

"Vin," Alistair says, pleading.

"You must choose. Nobody's forcing you. Remember what I said about one key moment of obedience? Maybe it's this moment. Maybe if you hadn't spent all afternoon fighting me, you'd hop this netting with ease."

I fish out a gold coin from the sack tied to my belt and reach through, leaving it atop the stepladder. Though I'm pissed at Seashells Man for speaking, but his words touched my heart. I don't want stay among the Lost Kings either.

"We have six or seven minutes," I say.

I turn away and pedal into the darkness.

I feel him approaching, the same sensation of not feeling alone and not sure why. *Alistair's coming!* He reaches me, in fact, almost slams into me, because this space approaches total darkness. Other than a surprised *huff*, he says nothing.

We ride in silence.

At last, he says, "I can't see you. We might crash."

"Good point. Let's talk. Help us keep aware of each other. If your home were on fire, what would you grab first?"

"Why? Why does that matter?"

"I'm making small talk."

He does not answer this.

"If you were a flower—"

"Vin, we could get expelled from Burning Man for this. Permanently."

"Yes. For having this adventure."

"It's not an *adventure*. We're breaking Burning Man law."

"Which makes it an adventure."

"Which makes it illegal. I'm a fucking lawyer."

"Is it breaking a federal or state law to come out here? Or against a Burning Man regulation?"

He sputters. "How do you know where we're going?"

I say, "As long as we stay in a straight line, we'll arrive."

"Yes, but in the total darkness, how do you know we're still on a straight trajectory?"

So many questions.

I say, "It's magic."

He says nothing for a few more minutes. We listen to the mechanical grinding of the bike chains, the only sound for miles in any direction.

As we approach the banks of the hot springs, the terrain changes. We feel it through the wheels. Bumps. Small ruts. Then, rougher terrain. Soon, we feel patches of grass. Without light, our sensitivity to touch—even without direct contact with the earth—becomes something enhanced.

I hear running water, the hot springs gurgling, and we see the outlines of things. Water. Land. Sky. I continue to surprise myself by how much I take the visual for granted, to distinguish nuances in those features allowing us to walk with confidence.

God, I want this water. Too many days without a shower. Camp Shower Girls was great fun—loved being sponged down by those sweeties—but that was, what, three days ago? With clean water imminent, I permit myself to feel irritated by the grit coating me head to toe. *Clean!* I will be clean!

With no emotion, he says, "These are the forbidden hot springs."

"Ooo, it's dramatic when you call them 'forbidden.' There are two *d*'s in forbidden, which make it a doubly difficult word to break, especially with the *b* pointed the opposing direction. Only the friendly *i* prevents a conflict, but make no mistake—"

"We can't be here."

He sulks.

"Perhaps along the banks we will find a blooming xenoxx plant."

He grunts.

How many times have I had a conversation like this, a cheerful, law-breaking conversation with a resistant man? I suggest walking our bikes along the water's banks. He doesn't speak. I don't speak.

Farther down—a couple hundred yards I'd guess—I see a faint light, very faint, and I know it's ours. I asked them to leave a light, so we could find the tent. Alistair was right. We weren't traveling in a straight line. As we draw closer, Alistair lets out a big breath, as if he had been holding it.

I announce, "That light is our tent. Let's look inside."

He says nothing. The tent is standard fare—bigger than a pup tent and smaller than a four-person stand-up. As an avid camper, I should recognize the brand and make, but I'm tired and my brain doesn't want to function. It's orange. That's all I need to know right now. Hopefully, there's bedding inside.

We pull back the flaps, and Alistair says, "Oh."

I feel myself revive.

The tent's interior is everything I'd hoped it would be: the inside of a genie's bottle. Pillows everywhere. They aren't as exotic-colored and fringed as I might like. Mostly ordinary pillows, but instead of feeling critical, I remind myself that many people go without pillows tonight so Alistair can have this experience. Robin's-egg-blue sheets cover the air mattress, seductively crunched, inviting sensual play. Well, *that* won't happen on this no-sex weekend. Still, it's sexy in its suggestiveness. Dozens of beads, colored glass, and mirrored trinkets dangle from the interior tent rods, wrapping around each other, coloring the tent's roof with intrigue and texture. Compared to some of the luxurious hotels I've stayed in, this is low rent. But it's beautiful because strangers created this through careful attention and sacrifice. They sacrificed for us.

After appreciating this latest piece of art, I leave him staring at the interior.

I pull off my shirt. "Let's strip. Bathe."

Alistair says, "I hope the no-sex part of the weekend is still okay, yeah?"

His tone is more conciliatory. Good.

"Of course. Though we'll share the same tent and air mattress."

As I pull off my shorts, I spot a small black cylinder positioned at the tent's base. A flashlight. After stripping my lower half, I shine it around the area. In one corner, farther from the opening, I see a small ice chest and two plastic cups. I bring these to him. He's fully clothed, watching me.

"You get naked just like that," he says. "Don't even care."

"Care about what?"

"This! Being here! You don't know me, yeah? We've never seen each other naked."

"So?"

"We're on a date, mate. You just sort of...stripped it all off. No regard."

"Gotta be naked to skinny-dip."

He glances at the water. "This is how people die in American horror movies, yeah? Skinny-dipping."

"We're not in a horror movie. We're in a romance."

"But without sex."

"Romances sometimes skip sex. Now, let's see what treats they brought us."

Inside the cooler there's not much room, enough for a bottle of champagne, surrounded by the most precious commodity on the playa right now, glittering in my flashlight's beam: ice.

"Oh my god, ice! Do you want ice in your champagne? You *must*."

Anything cold is a blessing on the playa.

Alistair looks around helplessly.

While opening the bottle, I say, "Try saying the word *ice* slowly. You can't. *Ice*. It slips out of your hands before you can examine it. Ice! Ice! There it goes."

In the great silence all around us, the fizzing and hissing carbonation yells its presence.

"Before I turn off the flashlight, I'm setting your cup at your feet. It's full. I'm getting in the water."

He stays where he is.

I ease myself in, keeping the hand with my champagne above the water. I resist gasping at the mud squishing between my toes. I've swum here before. I know the bottom is thick, goopy. It's initially alarming when the fat, mysterious goo oozes through your toes, but I don't want to give him further cause to avoid this, so I keep my mouth shut and squeal internally. Ohhhh, so gross! *It's so gross!* The word *mud* fits the experience, the *m* dragging you down, the *uuuuuuuud* sound falling in fat, wet chunks out of your mouth with a grunt.

The water feels unusual, not one uniform temperature, which is an interesting sensation. I feel warmth on my upper chest and legs. The one submerged arm is perhaps the warmest of all. A cold current runs over my feet. The temp in this small pond varies depending on where you stand. You can swim to warmer or cooler areas. I sip my champagne. I wish he would join me.

I call out, "After all these days at Burning Man, you're going to skip the opportunity to bathe? Real water?"

Nothing.

I will enjoy a swim while he deliberates. I paddle back to shore to leave behind my now-empty cup. As I stand, the gloop oozing between my toes feels intriguing.

Cold. Sometimes the unfamiliar can be embraced. *Muuuuuu-u-u-u-u-uuuuud*, thick stuttering mud.

I return to the deep and sink beneath the surface. The uncanny distinctions in temperature remind me how I feel—still feel—about the men I have kinged, a thousand sensations against my skin, hot and cold at the same time, refreshing, invigorating, pulling and pushing me. If I swim into cold, it reminds me of Ryan, and how we loved each other beyond reason. I inch to my right, hot water, think of Rance, how I slept in his arms, warm and safe. How many years since I loved Jamie? I don't want to think about it. I haven't kinged a dancer in a long time.

"Oh bloody hell," I hear from the shore, muffled in sound. "It's squishy."

Well, he's in the water.

"Yeah, I deliberately did not mention the mud. Try saying the word this way, *mmuuuuuu-u-u-u-u-u-uuuuuuuud*."

"There could be crocodiles and such out here," he says.

"How much do you know about Nevada geography?"

"Nothing," he says. "Except this is probably crocodile infested."

"This is a crocodile-free pond. No alligators. No lizard people or serial killers. No snakes."

"How do you know?"

"I read books. I've read up on the area."

He wades in deeper.

Another man, I might feel tempted to tackle into the water, drag him deeper, writhing and tugging, laughing and splashing. Not Alistair. He must come on his own. As he lingers, I explain how hot springs work, how this pond is fed by both warm and cold currents. I explain how it's not all mud underfoot. In some parts, he will feel rock or a gravel footing.

Distracting him further, I relate this particular hot spring's Burning Man history, a gathering spot after The Man burned in early years. However, the numbers grew too many to sustain this spot without damaging the landscape. The Bureau of Land Management forbade its access during Burning Man.

"See?" he says testily. "Illegal."

I offer to bring him to a warm spot of the pond, one with a sandy footing.

"It's brilliant, really," he says. "Warm and cold at once."

Alistair comes around.

Within another minute, he's up to his neck, adjusting, still cooing about the raw mud squishing between his toes, but he's excited to be wet, to be clean, and to be *free*—temporarily at least—from playa dust.

We swim close to each other.

"Come with me," I say.

We swim to the other side, which I remember being warmer. It still is. Not hot tub temperatures, yet it's much more soothing than lukewarm, and the rock footing is stable. We stand and bask.

"Oh god," he says. "I forgot how bloody good *water* feels."

"Alistair, may I put my arms around you?"

He resists, says it would make him feel uncomfortable, and I let the matter drop.

Almost immediately, he says, "Changed my mind. Just for a moment."

I wade through the water until I'm next to him. "Turn around."

He does so, and I wrap my arms around his tummy, resting my chin on his shoulder.

He says, "No—"

"Sex." I end the sentence with him. "Got it. I want the intimacy of staring at the stars this way."

We gape in silence.

After what seems like ten minutes, he speaks. "Do you think there's life out there?"

We sway in the meager current—let ourselves be moved as the planet spins—and discuss extraterrestrials, which leads to talk of past, possible spaceship crashes on Earth, ancient Egypt, pyramids, radical healing, past lives, future lives, and crystals—all common fodder at Burning Man. You don't have to believe in any of them—he and I mostly do not—but the playa is where you discuss what you do not believe and admit you might be wrong. If a new friend discusses past lives around a fire drum, well, maybe it's your opportunity to practice radical acceptance. Burning Man is where magicians meet to share secrets under this impossible field of luminous stars, secrets about everything that might be true.

We take a champagne break on shore, refilling our cups, and when we're finished, Alistair splashes into the pond eagerly. He requests I hold him again in the warm spot. Despite no sex, we feel like lovers.

Alistair says, "Tell me something that nobody else knows about you, yeah? None of the other kings. A secret."

I ponder this. I know he wants this on his quest for originality, but do I play along? Why not. Why not give in to one of his demands. I expect so much from him. Doesn't take long to come up with an innocuous and cryptic answer.

"I've never kinged a man in March. In fact, I hate the month of March, so I probably never will."

"And you've kinged someone every other month of the year?"

"Yup."

"Is this because you don't like capital *M*? Seems a bit harsh."

"May also starts with *M*."

"True," he says. "So why not March?"

How to answer?

"Tell you what, Alistair. I'll answer if you insist. But I'd prefer not to explain, for it makes me sad. I love this sexy hot springs vibe with you and I want to be fully present. If you insist, I will tell, because it's not about holding back from you, it's about keeping my attention on you. Your call."

"Oh," he says.

After a moment of waiting for his answer, I feel him shift and lean his head back on me. "I love being here with you, too. Thank you."

We stay silent and in love.

A little later, he says, "I want to ask you something."

I wish he wouldn't.

"It's about me. Not about the kings or the weekend or magic."

I still wish he wouldn't. Let it unfold, Alistair. Let the universe unfold before you.

"Earlier you said you knew things about me. Things I didn't realize you knew."

"I did."

"What do you think you know?"

"Didn't I ask you specifically *not* to ask questions about that? Wasn't that the test?"

"Yeah, hours ago. I think I passed the test. You don't have to answer if it's still an ongoing test."

"May I offer you some feedback?"

"Uh oh." Alistair chuckles. "That's never good."

"You ask questions to test me. You're gauging how much to reveal. I suspect you do this with others. If you like someone—if they pass—you'll share yourself. It's a good way to protect your heart. We all guard ourselves when trying to determine a safe space. But right now, you know you're in a safe place. You *know*. You knew it when we goofed around on stage. You knew it when we danced close. You hopped the orange fence. You're letting me hold you, naked, because you trust it won't lead to sex. Quit asking questions. Tell me what you want to tell me. Take the risk."

His voice shakes. "I can't."

"You can. You don't have to. I won't force it out of you. But you *can*."

I hope he tells me he's not English. His big reveal may not be as shocking as he worries.

"I'm not a risk taker."

"Aren't you a lawyer?"

"Good lawyers minimize the risk-taking. They force the odds to their favor."

"Okay, well, choose to be a risk taker, *Alistair*. I know how it sounds, coming right on the heels of my refusing to talk about March. I sound like a hypocrite. In my situation, I'm willing to tell you but would prefer not to. Could you tell, if asked? Keep in mind, you don't have to tell me shit. I told you I'm not going to force revelations from you. I do have a request, though." I squeeze him tighter. "Stop testing me."

My hands wrapped around his stomach, my chin on his shoulder. I like squeezing him this way, feeling the weight of him in my arms. I make sure my cock does not ride up against his ass crack, inspiring me to get hard. Stay soft, Vin. Stay soft.

He makes a throat noise but says nothing. I squeeze his chest tighter. I kiss his shoulder.

Steam emerges from the water in long transparent arms, rising and signing secrets with wispy fingers before ascending and dissipating into a billion stars.

Is his fake English persona the reason why we aren't fooling around? Or is this about one of the other possibilities I've contemplated?

I speak right into his ear. "Here's your big chance. Why aren't we having sex?"

He takes a deep breath, coughing on his exhale, surprising him, forcing his next breath even bigger. After he finishes coughing, I mimic his breathing, tasting the raw air around us. When did it get so chilly?

His voice quivers when he speaks. "Eight months ago, I broke up with my cheating boyfriend. I believed we were monogamous, yeah?"

He takes another big breath, and I feel vibrations in the back of his lungs when he exhales.

"I discovered we weren't monogamous when I tested HIV positive."

He raises his hands over his face, as if hiding from this truth, and he cries. I turn him to face me, make tidal waves with my slow movements, and pull him into my arms. He howls almost right away, a darkness falling over him, the agony of revealing this secret that has shamed him.

I'm both surprised and not surprised. I wondered about HIV. Gave it some consideration yesterday afternoon. I'm so goddamn relieved it's not childhood sexual abuse. I mean, I believed him yesterday, but you never know what's buried beneath the surface. I reconsidered sexual abuse this afternoon, when he suggested we seek the healing xenoxx plant. Triple XXX. Obviously, he wanted healing in his sex life.

Thank god, it's only HIV.

I hold him.

While he cries, I feel my cock start to awaken. I try to ignore my thickening erection, which never works. Go away. *Quit happening!* His crying slows, ending abruptly. Unfortunately my cock grows hard against him, right under his balls, which is a weird nonverbal when the man you hold cries with grief. I warned him yesterday I couldn't be held responsible for spontaneous erections.

"Are you hard?"

"Yeah. Sorry."

Alistair pulls back, surprise on his midnight features. I know streams of tears run down his face, because I see stars reflected on his cheeks. "You're getting hard."

I start to pull away. "I'm sorry. Totally respecting the no sex rule. Spontaneous erection. Could not be helped."

We say nothing while he stares at me quizzically.

My dick has stopped getting harder, which is good. Not quite at full mast and also not quite so...insistent.

"Was my crying turning you on? Or do you have some sort of HIV fetish?"

"No. Your honesty turned me on. I'm guessing you haven't told many people about your status. You chose me for this honor. You chose *me*. That got me hard. Sorry."

"You have no problem with my status?"

"Alistair, it's 2002. It's not 1982. Not even 1992. You're not my first poz king."

"You have sex with them?"

I flex my body against his and try to make my voice sexy. "If they let me."

This makes him cry again, and he wraps his arms around my neck.

Oh Alistair. *Alistair.* Stop living alone.

Ha. Advice easier to give than take.

He releases me, bringing his hand from underwater to wipe his face. He steps back and wobbles, dipping deeper into the water. I reach out to steady him.

"You okay?"

"Yeah. Lost my footing."

Still English, even during this revelation. Unbelievable.

He says, "I know some neg guys won't care. Some will. This isn't about other people. I can't forgive myself. I trusted my boyfriend, and he made me...made me this."

"Made you *what*?"

"This." He considers before answering. "I felt proud of my negative status. I used condoms. I played safe, always. Maybe I judged HIV positive men—somehow they, well—made bad choices. A bit prejudiced, yeah? So when I discovered my new situation, I did not handle it well. This wasn't supposed to happen to me. We had both committed to monogamy."

Oh, man. This is suddenly very weird. The accent is gone. He's forgotten he's English. Does he realize what he's truly revealing? I can't acknowledge it. I don't want to catch him; I want him to volunteer it.

"I'm sorry, Alistair. Sorry for what you went through alone."

"Bloody hell," he says softly.

Aaaaaand it's back.

Obviously, this HIV status issue cuts him to the core, enough so for him to unconsciously forget to be English. I thought nothing could crack that exterior! But I get it. People who acquire one of life's extra burdens feel not only the weight of the burden itself but often how it was acquired. He trusted his heart. He trusted love. Now he has HIV. No wonder he doesn't want to open up.

"I haven't told anyone," he says. "One friend back home, only. Not my parents. Not any of Jerry's and my mutual friends. Not even friends who I know are poz. Men who would understand and comfort me."

"No dates, I take it."

He barks out a hard laugh. "Of course not. No shagging. Me and my fist. Even then, it's hard to watch porn without wondering, 'Is he poz? Does he know about his partner?' Always ruins it."

"Face away from me, and let me hold you."

He looks down. "I'm not ready for sex."

"No sex. Holding. Also, possibly, my semi-hard dick to remind you sex can be good. We won't discover that tonight, because, no sex."

He chuckles at this, and says, "All right."

We stay pressed together, my cock against him, which now softens, because I'm feeling his sadness for all the times I longed to be touched and felt I didn't deserve it. Tonight, we will not have physical sex, yet this counts as making love. Beneath the stars, amidst the silence of this magic hot springs, he and I make love.

He says, "I know I'm punishing myself. I just find it hard to believe I will never be HIV negative again. I can't get over the shock of it. I thought I would, as months passed. There's plenty of outreach for the newly poz but I did nothing—no therapy or community groups. I thought I'd go once I was more comfortable, that *eventually* I'd get more comfortable on my own. Somehow. Two months ago, I realized my celibacy could unintentionally stretch into years."

After another pause, he says, "The problem is me. My self-acceptance."

Isn't it always?

We stare at the night sky, the dark shapes around us, and mostly stay silent until we are ready to sleep. We trudge through the mud to shore, wiping our feet on the towels provided. Once inside the genie tent, he pulls my arm over him, wrapping himself. I cover us in blankets. It's officially cold. We listen to the slight tinkling of plastic and glass beads clinking against each other, and he dozes almost immediately.

When I close my eyes, I see stars.

Nothing but stars.

NINE

The tent shakes, making the glass and plastic baubles jingle. As irrational as it may be, my first blurry-eyed instinct is to think, *earthquake.*

"Guys, get up. You have to go. *Now.*"

The frantic voice jerks me awake. I can't sit up because my arms wrap around Alistair, who nestles into my stomach and snores softly.

"*Guys,*" the voice says again, louder and with more urgency.

I squeeze Alistair. "We're awake. We're moving. Alistair. *Wake up.* We have to go right now."

He moans and pushes back into me. Under any other circumstances, I would welcome this morning intimacy. He's rubbing his ass against my dick, and if I weren't worried about being kicked out of Burning Man, I'd be turned on. I shake him.

"Alistair, wake up. We have to leave right this second."

"Guys," the voice outside the tent says again. "We've got a limited window. Perimeter rangers are approaching the bus."

Alistair stumbles into consciousness as I crawl out the tent flap.

Behind me, I say, "Hurry. We only have a few minutes."

Outside the tent stands a sandy-haired man, reedy thin with a blond, scruffy beard. He's anxious and nodding at me. "Hey."

"Good morning. Thank you for your help."

He nods. "You have to hurry."

Alistair emerges, blurry and confused.

"C'mon, Alistair. We have to make this window. Catch up."

By the time he's dressed, I'm pedaling away.

Less than four minutes after waking, we furiously pump our mountain bikes back in the direction of Burning Man, though nothing from the camp is visible yet, just the bleak, faraway horizon already recharged with sweltering heat. The sun woke first, reminding all beings the long night was merely a short reprieve from today's scorching dominance. Must already be six-thirty or so. Maybe later.

"Vin, what's happening?"

"Pedal faster."

Soon, I see the orange line above the horizon. In two minutes, I will recognize its true shape. Which means anyone—*anyone* at Burning Man—could see two figures biking across the horizon. If we are reported by one of the many thousands of residents, and rangers catch us, we could be expelled.

"We'll never make it," Alistair says, slightly out of breath. "Someone will see us."

He's right. He inspires me to pedal faster. He picks up speed too and outpaces me, legs working furiously.

"We can make it. We have help," I say.

"Who?"

"Pirates." I point to our destination.

On the horizon, butted up against the orange fence, sits La Contessa. The mutant car—full-sized school bus actually—on which the wooden replica of an authentic pirate ship is built. The ship boasts a mast, ragged cloth sails, a crow's nest, and other authentic nautical stuff—details explained to me a few days ago, but I don't remember. Starburst sides and whatnot. Pirate, pirate. The word starts out sweetly, like pie, but midway through, it's ripped in half with a sabre, *raaaaaaaaate* down the middle. Pi-raaaaaaaates!

"What are—" he huffs, "—doing here?"

Take a deep breath and explain this. "La Contessa pretended to break down right at that section of the fence and called the perimeter patrol over to assist. Once we're on board, the ship gets mysteriously repaired and off we go."

"The rangers are already at the ship?"

"Yes, distracted on the other side so they won't see us board."

"Shit," Alistair says. "They're *right here*?"

"Yeah, talking to the captain. This is the best option to cross back so they don't catch us. The crew expects us, but we've got to get to the ship quickly."

Alistair grumbles, and I don't believe I'm meant to hear his exact reply.

As we pedal harder, shifting our weight from side to side, the ship appears to bob from left to right. I scan the horizon for anyone far away, pointing at us, running toward us, but nothing. We're going to make it. *We're going to make it!*

Oh shit. My heart feels like it's exploding.

Next to the ship, on *our* side of the fence, is a parked perimeter patrol vehicle. If anyone's in that SUV, we're dead. We're banned. I have a contingency plan for finishing his kinging outside Burning Man, but better to finish it here. We can't miss out on Burning Man. *Please let no one be in the SUV.* Oh god, what about Ranger Ron? I'd do anything to stay off his radar.

I see the ship's crew gathering where we're to climb aboard, two or three, and I want to scream not make it obvious. Calm down, Vin. You can't control everything. A thick rope with knots slithers over the side. I saw that rope a few days ago, when thrill-seeking pirates dangled from it behind the ship while the bus sped across the desert. Someone could die. This whole contraption really is a deathtrap on the high seas.

Our bikes skid to a stop right at the orange fence. Relief floods me. Nobody's in the ranger SUV. I'd worry about the dust we kicked up—it might attract attention—but I have no time for that particular concern. Without words, I grab the rope, pull it lower, and force it on Alistair. He gawks at me in disbelief but takes hold. He tries to climb the knots but doesn't make any progress, grasping for the next higher knot and failing. I stand behind him and push up on his ass. *This has to happen quickly!*

Even with my assistance, Alistair makes little progress. In a sudden jerk, he rises halfway up the ship's side. They're yanking him. They do this without words, or talk so quietly I hear little of it. I can definitely hear the murmur of voices on the other side of the ship.

"Wait," someone cries loudly from the far side.

Oh shit.

Alistair's legs are the last thing I see as he's hauled over, rescued from the ocean of playa dust around us. As soon as he disappears, hands reach down, snapping at me and pointing. Bikes. I grab mine and position the front wheel against the side, rolling it high enough to be grabbed by the man extended far over the rail. Someone must be holding his legs.

I hear the engine turn over—someone's starting La Contessa. They're clearly running out of excuses to distract the perimeter guards. *Hurry, fucking hurry!* The bike pedal scrapes the hull as it's roughly lifted over, and another pair of hands appears. The engine roars to life, and several loud cheers erupt from topside. I can't listen. I grab the second bike and roll it up the same way. Soon it disappears. Any second now, those rangers are going to walk around to my side of the boat.

"Thanks, *Rangers!*"

The voice which yelled this emphasized the last word, trying to warn us to move quickly.

The rope flops over the side again. I grab it, panicked. I can't get kicked out of Burning Man. *This is my home!* I jerk myself up, one knot and then another. Surprising how expulsion can be so motivating.

"Don't go so far out again. This is your third and final warning. We're gonna report this to the Department of Mutant Vehicles. You're going to wreck it for all mutant cars. Don't fuck around, guys."

"Hey," says a female voice sharply from elsewhere on board.

"And gals," says the ranger.

Hands reach over, desperate hands, grabbing my shirt collar, then belt—heaving me, like a giant marlin, onto the deck.

"Stay low," a man rasps in my ear. "Stay flat."

The rope lands on top of my legs with a soft thud.

Gasping for breath, listening to my heart pound, I notice the sand coating the deck. I'm already covered in it, the filmy grit sticking everywhere to my sweaty body and clothes. So much for feeling clean.

La Contessa lurches forward, and relief floods me. I turn my head to the side to see our bikes and Alistair, eyes wide like a surprised fish, only a few feet away, panting and staring at me.

Now that we're moving, I feel less panicked. I smile and mouth the words, "Good morning."

He grins back at me and rolls his eyes.

After a short time, our shipmates give us the all clear to stand. Nobody can speak easily over the engine's loud roar, so we nod pleasantly at our pirate comrades and they at us. The ship is long. There are at least twelve people on deck, everyone clinging to something for steadying support. We speed across the desert floor, bounced hard around a wooden ship atop a deregulated school bus, so it's not like we can wander the deck holding hands. I told these guys to better preserve the engine they should drive slower. Obviously, they love speed. One guy allows himself to roll along the deck, as if pummeled in a storm at sea. He laughs greedily. He's already got a bloody nose.

I crawl on hands and knees to Alistair. From a crouched position, grasping the side railing, we lift our heads to see the city. As soon as we do, great white clouds of dust assault us like ocean spray, but not nearly as refreshing. Simultaneously, we bring our heads down below the rail and cough. Oh god...I taste it in my lungs. How could I have forgotten that feeling, hot sand in your lungs? Today will be another hot, hot day.

We sneak peeks over the side, and through the spraying dust, the city of tents looms, our wooden mayor standing tall at the center, protecting everything. We don't drive too close to the city. There are rules about where the mutant cars are permitted. La Contessa already broke those rules once this morning to pick us up. Of course, the La Contessa crew enjoys breaking rules. They're pirates, after all.

At the far edge of town, beyond the assplanade, the ship slows down. I laugh to myself, feeling like a ten-year-old boy. *Assplanade.* That's what burners call the farthest outer street in Black Rock City. Alistair shakes his head in disbelief, his first real communication since our rescue at sea. Far down the boat, one of the pirates working the rigging yells, "*Land ho!*"

"I can't believe this," he says. "Do you know how many people chased this ship around Burning Man all week begging for rides? How did you manage this?"

"I fixed their engine a few days ago. In the real world, I'm a car mechanic."

"Oh, that's right. Liam called you 'the mechanic' when he told his story."

When the ship stops, the captain's head pops out of the hatch. He grins, introduces himself to Alistair as Captain Graybeard, and invites us to meet him below deck. He has no beard. No gray hair, only wavy brown. We clomp down the narrow stairs. They spared no expense down here, including two miniature crystal chandeliers, several eggplant-colored chaise lounges, and of course, an overstocked bar, everything firmly bolted or strapped down. A full length school bus carries the ship, so this cabin is bigger than one might expect. It's designed for parties.

Two oil paintings, a landscape and a bowl of fruit, suggest middle-class values, but the black jockstrap dangling from the fruit bowl painting's frame offers a less-than-wholesome Bohemian twist.

Including Captain Graybeard, six or seven shipboard guests already lounge in various corners of the room. There's a woman asleep on a chaise lounge, short maroon-striped hair. A man and woman chat with the captain, and I get the distinct impression our arrival ended some very heavy petting. The couple welcome us in friendly voices, but they seem distracted by each other. The five of us sit in a circle of comfy chairs, a few feet away from the sleeping guest.

"A toast," the captain cries out in his pirate voice, "to evading maritime law."

"Yarrrrrrrrg, Cap'n," cries one of his crew, raising his glass in salute.

The crewman is bald, shirtless, and seems quite drunk already. Or perhaps he's still drunk from last night. His lady friend seems less wobbly. She wears a flowery sundress, as if prepared for a garden party. Her right arm is covered in a sleeve of tattoos.

The captain insists on Gummy Bear shots to celebrate our success. While he pours amaretto into a shot glass filled with multicolored bears, they discuss the warning from the ranger and the lies Graybeard told to explain his presence so far out of the designated area. Alistair glances my way for confirmation regarding the shot, and I subtly nod. This is not my preferred morning wake-up, but we must respect the captain's prerogative on his own ship.

The three shipmates have questions about our journey last night to the hot springs: where we slept, how it felt to *feel* clean. We tease them with our descriptions, making them laugh about what out here is considered treasure—a water source. They ask Alistair and me how we know each other. Alistair fumbles, explaining we're Burning Man friends, and the woman tucks her legs under her body as she curls up next to her boyfriend.

"So, you're fuck buddies," she says.

Alistair blushes and stammers," No, not quite."

"You're blushing. You really are English, aren't you?"

Alistair says, "Tea. Queue. Bollocks. Bloody hell."

She smiles dreamily. "I thought you were faking it."

Alistair shoots me a friendly grin, and I'm not sure what he sees on my face, but the grin freezes. Did my surprise at her words somehow convey I know he's not English? I might have given something away.

I finish my shot so I can tilt my head back and avoid eye contact.

"To be honest, he's kinging me," Alistair says. "I'm on his King Weekend."

"A King Weekend," Captain Graybeard says with surprise, sitting forward, interested in the conversation again. "For real?"

Alistair looks to me.

"Yes," I say. "For real."

Nobody speaks. I'm sure they're expecting me to elaborate, but I have no desire for explanations. I'm growing uncomfortable with how many people know what I'm doing. How does word travel so far?

Graybeard says, "I've heard rumors. Burner talk. I assumed it was bullshit."

I nod.

Graybeard says, "That's it? You're not going to fucking say *anything*?"

"I'd rather not."

Graybeard sputters. "You fixed our bus a few days ago. You said you were a car mechanic. *You're* the king guy? You?"

"I guess so. We should get going. We are profoundly grateful for the lift this morning. You saved us."

Graybeard turns to Alistair. "What's happening? What is he doing to you?"

"It's surprisingly intense," Alistair says, reluctantly looking at me. "But he doesn't explain what's going on, so I can't describe it well. It's unsettling."

I stand. "We should go. Not impose on your hospitality any further."

With some reluctance, they show us to the exit. In what must be the world's most obvious attempt at distraction, I ask questions about the engine and how they've cared for it since my recent visit. He answers with what he knows, but obviously doesn't care much about the engine or preserving its performance. I know they came with two qualified mechanics. I happened to find a better way to keep sand out of the engine. They said they "owed me one."

As we stand outside, shaking hands, Captain Graybeard says, "So you're going to leave without telling me anything about the secret kings of Burning Man?"

I say, "That is not today's story. Perhaps one starlit night, Captain. We'll stroll your deck, and I will speak to you of a tribe where every man is a king, every woman the one true queen."

He pleads with Alistair, but Alistair shrugs and offers his own hand for the good-bye. "Brilliant ship, Captain."

Reluctantly, he says, "Thank you."

Already burners gather, admiring and waiting to speak with the captain.

A young man with long blond hair, wearing nothing but a pair of plaid shorts, says, "Can I get a ride? Please?"

A tall, lean man glides close on rollerblades and falls on his ass, kicking up dust. I don't understand the people who rollerblade out here. It doesn't seem to work well on this cracked, hard surface. Never stops them from trying.

Captain Graybeard looks as though he wants to argue with me, but apparently decides not to. "If you need anything, get word to me. Tell your messenger to say it's a request from the king man."

"Thank you. Very generous."

He and his crew disappear into the interior, hounded by admirers.

Alistair and I watch while La Contessa fires up her engine and peels away, faster than you'd think a school bus could move, covering us in clouds of pirate dust. We wave the dust away from our faces, as if that would do any good.

When the dust settles, I say, "I thought we could stop by my tent to stock up on water and food, and change clothes. We definitely have to slather ourselves with sunscreen, even if we wear our Arab robes all day. We don't have to wear those, I suppose. We could stash them. But you have to admit, they work—"

"You're not going to say anything about what just happened?"

I look at the retreating ship. "What just happened?"

"The *secret kings of Burning Man*? You don't think that deserves some explanation, some..."

"What?"

"I don't know. Something. *Something*."

"What's there to explain?"

"I don't know," Alistair says, shaking his head. "I don't know what the fuck is happening anymore. But I am catching on."

Okay. This is new, this almost smug quality on his face. What changed?

I say, "Let's get some water. I'm already parched. All that biking."

Alistair looks wistfully at the retreating pirate ship.

Quietly, he exhales the words like dust, "Well played."

Almost an hour later, we're out of my tent. My canvas water pouch is still at Alan and Helena's camp, so I grab my second one and refill it from the supply in my nearby truck. Of course, the water is warm but we could stop at Center Camp, buy ice, and make it cold. A cup of ice might be a refreshing delight to start our day. I should take him out for ice breakfast. Maybe he likes coffee. We could visit Java Whores. They have a morning ritual for coffee worshippers.

"How shall we spend our day together?"

"I dunno, Vin. Does it matter what I say or choose?"

"Do you need coffee this morning?"

"No."

A string of orange-robed monks pass us, and we step aside to let them pass with more ease. A ballerina follows them—a Frankenstein's bride ballerina—sheer black cloth wrapping her shoulders and a long train fluttering in the breeze behind her. She carries a black parasol. What a fascinating look. Who is she?

"Alistair, what do you think we should do?"

"I think it doesn't matter," he says. "I think you have every move planned."

"Oh yeah?"

Alistair says, "I figured you out, king man. You almost got me, back there on La Contessa. A dude who calls himself Captain Graybeard asks you if you're part of the *secret kings of Burning Man*. I heard those words and I thought, *magic*! But this—like all of your other little tricks—isn't magic. You planned it. You controlled it."

"I did, huh?"

"Of course. You arrange this flawless escape on a pirate ship—"

I bow. "Thank you. It was close, but thank you."

"And you told your pal, Captain Graybeard, to say these magic words. The *secret kings of Burning Man* and, like a sap, I gasped because, oh my, another clue to this amazing puzzle!"

"That was unplanned."

"Riiiiiight," Alistair says.

A gentle flurry of tambourine players pass, jiggling their instruments to produce a gentle tingling, perhaps a wake up for those hovering between sleep and reality.

"I totally underestimated you. I freely admit it. You got me."

I am not sure what to say to this. He's a magician like me. We're like two tops together—spinning around each other, making each other dizzy. Do I tell the simple truth? Or do I let him spin? His question requires careful consideration. So, is he spinning me, or am I spinning him?

Spin, spin, spin.

I'm going to stall for time.

"Do you like the word *spin*? The engineers behind this word's construction knew what they were doing. If you say it *fast*, the word twirls around on a lowercase *p*. Spin! Elongate it, like, *spiiiiiiiiiiiiiiiiiiiiiiin*, and the word is exhausting, and circular, and whirrs into an *n* that just won't nobble, nobble, wobble, nobbly stopple."

He crosses his arms. "I get it. The goofy word stuff. The guys who keep passing you notes. Keep me off-balance, keep me guessing. Make me think the weekend is about my decisions. We were always going dancing with Alan and Helena. Some random temple dude who happens to be nam—you're good."

What? What does *that* mean?

Wait, is this—he flicked his head at me when we met John yesterday. Something crossed his face, and I didn't understand. But I think he just confirmed it. *Alistair's real name is John.*

Oh, wow.

King John.

I'm talking to *King John*.

My heart thumps faster.

Although we're not moving particularly fast, we reach an intersection and stop. We should finish this conversation. Wrap this up. Don't get too excited. His name might not be John.

Ha-ha. *Yes*, it is. I know it is.

Alistair says, "I know now you and your people are behind everything."

How to handle this? He's not entirely wrong. I organized our escape, asking Graybeard for assistance this morning. But I didn't tell Graybeard what to say. Couldn't Alistair see the captain made me uncomfortable?

"Vin, you had three outfits my size in your tent. All clean and folded. *Tell me* you're not a control freak."

"Medium is a common size. I wanted you to be comfortable in fresh clothes today."

"Vin," he says, his voice a warning. "C'mon."

"Alistair, I'm not ready to talk about this. I'm trying to decide how much to tell you. You've drawn some erroneous conclusions, but you're not wrong about my being controlling. Let me figure out how much to reveal. I might have to tell you some truths about my real life in order for you to trust me, and I don't enjoy talking about myself. Can we stroll to Alan and Helena's camp to get our stuff? Pick up this conversation after?"

"Absolutely. Make no mistake, I still plan on going along with your King Weekend. I know you're manipulating me, but I also know you're being yourself, yeah?"

I take his hands. "I am. Alistair, please believe the reason I showed up is because I want to spend time loving you. After we parted two days ago, I first decided *no* to kinging you, because you present such complexities I didn't think I could cross you over. I like breaking into men's hearts. I also like breaking into buildings I shouldn't be inside. Yet, I have to recognize and acknowledge security systems too complex for me. You were too tricky for me to attempt. So, *no*.

"After making that decision, I couldn't stop thinking about you, your ingenuity in finding my campsite. I loved your boldness, your determination. After you found me, I tried to lose you twice, and your big heart refused to give up, though I suspect the lawyer in you suffered while you chose to risk that particular vulnerability."

Alistair smiles and looks down.

"You must be a damn good stalker, because I've got the twitchiness of a rat. I *know* when I'm being followed. Obviously, you impressed me in a few ways. After I initially decided *no*, I kept glimpsing a big fat *yes* peeking out, until I realized yes, yes, *yes*. I'm delighted to be with you. Yes, I manipulate you, well, *some*. Maybe not as much as you think, but some. Last night was real. That erection—"

"—was real," Alistair steps closer. "I know. You can't fake an honest body reaction. Your feelings were genuine. I know. I know how to show authenticity, too."

Wait, what?

Does *he* know *I* know Alistair is fake, and he's trying to communicate back to me that a whole lot of him is present in Alistair? Or, I'm reading waaaaaay too much into what he said. My head spins. This is the problem with kinging another magician. The air between us starts getting thick with implications, subtleties, and word magic—the most difficult magic. Okay. Maybe I believe in the magic of words. But that's it. That's the only magic.

We've been studying each other for a minute or two, searching each other's face for clues, insights. He knows how to read people, too.

Be graceful. Be open.

I say, "I propose a time-out."

A man three feet away bellows, "*Good morning, Burning Man!*"

Alistair turns and says in a loud hiss, "Hey, mate, *shut, your fookin' mouth.* People trying to sleep, you git."

The guy gives Alistair a thumbs-up.

Aaaaaand, Alistair is back. I thought we were approaching something honest.

He squeezes my hand and says, "Sorry. Bloody idiot. You proposed a time-out?"

"Yes. Let's get our clothes from last night, say hello to Alan and Helena. Then, restart this conversation. Or something like it. Once again, you're trying to get me to reveal things about your King Weekend, and this time I'm sorely tempted, because without your loving trust, none of this works. But there really is a price. I'm trying to protect you. The more faith you can preserve, the better."

"Well, don't reveal anything," he says. "I'm not asking for that. Let's...let's let this all sink in. I am trying to absorb how much you're behind these events."

"I swear, not as much as you think."

A man with face tattoos, sucking a lollipop, walks up to me. "I have a note for you, Mr. Vanbly."

I know I'm mumbling when I say, "Call me Vin."

Alistair crosses his arms. "Unbelievable. Tell me again you're not controlling everything."

Ugh. Bad timing.

The man nods, as if accepting a receipt for this communication, and shifts the lollipop to the right side. Army shorts. Metal-band shirt. I take the note and read it. I'm too flustered to deal with this.

"I don't have a response at this time. Maybe at the next intersection."

He nods and strolls away.

"Vin Vanbly. Is that even your real name?"

I hesitate.

His eyes widen. "*Oh my god*, it's not?"

"Yes, it's my name. It's the name I use in the world."

"Bloody unbelievable, Vin."

Okay, enough is enough.

I cock my head. "Really? Is it completely *unbelievable* someone would go by a name not exactly their own? Or might you have a decent ounce of understanding for why a person might do that."

I can spin the top, too.

Spin, spin, spin.

Alistair looks down the next block. "We're taking a time-out, yeah?"

Good. He's willing to back off. Since La Contessa, the dynamic between us has changed, moved by significant inches. If he now suspects I *know* Alistair is fake, this could go down one of four ways. Two ways, very bad. Let's think about this.

I say, "Yes. Time-out."

I take his hand and we begin walking.

"Dancing last night was fun," I say.

Alistair smiles. "I want to kiss you. I'm building up to it."

I grin back. "Ready when you are. You make the first move."

We don't have to worry about waking Alan, who paces his camp, shirtless and in running shorts, scanning the distance and pausing to stare in various directions. When he spots us, he appears both angry and relieved.

As soon as we get close, he speaks. "We have a problem."

Uh oh.

Alan says, "The gold coin."

Oh shit. Well, he found out. I had hoped no one would.

Alistair says, "What problem?"

Alan bores into me with his steely eyes. "It's real."

He stops speaking to let the news sink in. I'm ready with no reaction.

Alistair says, "It's real what?"

Alan says, "Is he in on it?"

I say, "No."

Alan turns to Alistair. "Real *gold*."

Why is Alan so serious, what's got him so rattled? It's real gold. So what?

Alan turns and yells toward their tent. "Hel, they're here. Get out here."

He faces us with a tangible, physical anticipation, as if he expects us to bolt and he's ready to chase. I want to tell him to relax. I'm not a runner. I don't understand why he's so upset.

Alistair says, "I don't understand. What's real gold?"

Alan frowns in my direction but speaks directly to Alistair. "After you guys left, we partied for a few more hours. Toward the end of the night, we took a break. Headed to this city block where people were chilling. Someone was passing out water. We got talking to these folks, introducing ourselves."

Helena emerges, T-shirt and shorts, no shoes. She's gorgeous, wow, really gorgeous. In the simplest attire, the most casual thing a person could wear, she is amazing. Such big, beautiful eyes.

"Vin," she says with a nod. "Alistair. We're upset. How could you do this?"

Alistair says, "I'm confused. What did we do?"

Alan says, "Vin involved us in whatever's going on here. His gold coin scam."

Alistair says, "What scam?"

Alan says, "I passed around your fake *wishing* coin and we all made wishes. One of the guys asked to see it twice. He was a coin guy. Had a buddy more expert than he was, so he went and got that dude. The gold coin you gave me is from ancient Rome. It's worth over three thousand dollars."

Alistair laughs at this, glancing my way, and freezes—mouth hanging open—when he sees I am not laughing. Or smiling.

I say, "Not quite three thousand. The price fluctuates daily. It was only twenty-six hundred dollars a week and a half ago."

This does not appear to make Alan happy. He grimaces.

Helena says softly, "So it's true."

Alistair's eyes pop wide. "Are you fookin' kidding me?"

Who is this guy? A surprise of this magnitude and Alistair doesn't drop his English accent *for a second*? Wow. He's unshakable. Weirdly, now that I know his name is John, I can't stop thinking of him as John.

"No," I say and turn to Alistair. "I'm not kidding. I brought a sack of these to give away."

I jingle my hip for emphasis.

Helena starts to cry.

"Oh god," Alan wipes his hand across his face. "It's true. You're a thief."

"Thief? No. I bought these."

Nobody speaks. Helena wipes her face, and my heart sinks. They think I stole these coins. It's the explanation that makes sense to them. *That's* why Alan's so serious. I don't know why I'm surprised. I took precautions for a misunderstanding like this. I thought legitimizing paperwork would be necessary if the police somehow got involved. Police often get involved on my King Weekends. Karma for me, I guess. I'm never quite done with the cops. But I hadn't thought these guys, my Burning Man friends, would assume I was a thief.

Ow. This hurts.

Alan says, "These can't be yours. The coin guy said the only way to amass a collection of Roman coins was to steal them."

I owe them an explanation. "Guys, I bought these coins a month ago."

"Bought how?"

"Online. From a reputable gold exchange. I have proof of authenticity and my purchase invoice. I bought the coins as giveaways for Burning Man."

Alan presents Nero in the palm of his hand. "You expect us to believe you're randomly handing away gold coins worth three grand to—to just anybody you run into this week? These have to be stolen, man."

"Two days ago, I gave one to a lawnmower salesman who gifted Alistair and me water and a place to sit. He tried to sell us a lawnmower with no wheels. I saw a woman crying at the Temple of Joy a few days earlier. Gave her one, too, and told her a story. I've given away a handful already."

Alistair says, "Holy shite. We handed them out yesterday to total strangers. For volunteering stupid answers."

"Not stupid answers. They played along. They got a prize."

Alistair says, "You gave them each three thousand dollars?"

"Technically, Alistair, *you* did."

This makes him jerk and say, almost pleading to Helena and Alan, "I didn't know."

"Bullshit," Alan says. "You—this is bullshit. Nobody takes a bunch of gold coins to Burning Man. What are you, rich?"

I nod. "Yes. I am. I'm rich."

Nobody speaks.

"I'm rich."

With hesitation, Alan says, "Bullshit."

Alistair says, "Like, outside-Burning-Man wealthy? Or did you mean *rich* as a metaphor?"

"I'm wealthy. Technically, the money is mine. However, I can't spend it on myself."

Alan's vigor returns. "Dude, by all means, assume we're stupid—"

"Why?" Alistair asks. "Why can't you spend it?"

I look at him. "The money is only for Found Kings. Or finding kings."

Alistair backs up a foot and winces. Softly, he says, "No."

Alan opens his mouth, but Helena puts her hand on his chest and indicates he should look at Alistair, whose face has transformed.

Alistair says, "You're a bloody millionaire who can't spend any money on yourself because it's only *for Found Kings*."

"Yes."

Alistair says, "Oh my god." He turns to Alan and Helena. Tears fall out his eyes. "I don't think he's lying. I think this is all true. This is a king thing. He lives his life based on this...some imaginary code."

He turns to me. "Do you swear on last night's erection this is true. *You're rich*."

"I swear on last night's erection."

He turns to Alan. "It's true. He's not lying. Don't get me wrong, he's a liar and manipulator. I'm being manipulated like crazy. He's also a good person, and he believes this king stuff is real."

"What king stuff?"

"It doesn't matter. All you need to know is he lives by his king code. Vin is telling the truth. I know all this sounds crazy, but he's different from other people. He's not normal."

Tears well up. I know I'm not normal. I know. But Alan and Helena were my friends last night, and their *first* thought—*first* reaction—was to believe I'm a thief. I had so much fun with these guys. We hustled together at the disco! They think I'm a thief, and the only way Alistair can describe me is "not normal."

Alistair sees my face and touches my cheek with the back of his fingers. "In a good way, Vin. I meant it in a good way."

I wipe my eyes. "I know. It's hard to hear sometimes, even though it's true."

Helena takes command. "Okay. We all hold hands. Right now. Vin's going to explain this. C'mon. Everyone take a hand. Vin, talk."

This is also Burning Man, moments like this, in which four almost-strangers hold hands for a truth circle, some commitment to being real. Which means I have to tell the truth, the shitty, awful truth. It's the only way we'll get through this without them hating me. Okay. I can do this. Telling the truth is my deepest bow to their king- and queenship.

They remain silent.

I say, "Years ago, I kinged a beautiful man who later died of cancer. His generous father bequeathed me his son's inheritance to help me find other kings. I'm a millionaire, many times over, who can't spend the money on himself. You want to hear something crazy? I got it in my head I would retire from kinging men once the money ran out. To that end, I opened the account to the Found Ones, so they could access the money as well. Figured we might all drain the account faster and I might retire. But guess what? They keep replenishing it. The balance is always eleven million dollars. I'll always be rich for the rest of my life. No matter what.

"My day job is as a mechanic. I hate cars. I hate my job. But I can't quit because I'm not rich and I'm not good at anything else. I do well at making friends for short periods of time, but they always end up regarding me like you guys do right now. Skeptical. Afraid. I give off a creepy, don't-trust-me vibe. On the other hand, men trust me with their sacred hearts all the time. I guess I also give off a very trustworthy vibe, too. It's confusing. The more someone gets to know me, the creepier I seem. At Burning Man, I belong. Friendships here are intense and only last a week. I can keep my weirdness at bay for a week."

I look to their eyes. Helena's have softened and are filled with tears. Alan's face is softer too.

Alan says, "You brought these coins to deliberately give away. To strangers."

"Yes."

"Why?"

"Because Burning Man is the closest I have ever known to feeling at home."

Nobody speaks. I guess I'll continue.

"Every year, when I get here, I can breathe. The art, the random acts of kindness, the radical acceptance and gift economy...this is how I want to live every day. So, I express my gratitude. Not always with money. I like to knit. One year, I gifted homemade scarves. They were pretty. I didn't knit much this last year."

"I'm sorry," Alan says with no trace of animosity. "I'm sorry I got mad. Accused you. I just—I've never heard anything like this. That guy said the coins had to be stolen, it was the only explanation. We thought you'd involved us in something illegal."

"I'm sorry, Alan. I'm sorry, Helena, to have caused you guys worry. Maybe I shouldn't pass these out. I brought paperwork showing proof of ownership. It's sewn into my tunic, the one in your tent. I worried I might have to prove myself to the police."

Helena says, "Did you want us to have that coin?"

"I did," Alistair says with surprise. "I wanted to give away a coin to Alan, gratitude for dinner."

Helena starts to cry but cannot wipe her eyes. We bear silent witness to these confused tears from a queen. Finally, she says, "You do this because you have such a hard time making friends?"

I squirm uncomfortably. "Yes."

I feel Alan's grip squeeze me tighter. Alan leans over and bumps his forehead into mine. His voice cracks when he says, "We'll be your friends, you idiot. You don't have to buy our friendship."

His words hurt my heart.

I say, "In the past, people tried to become my friend. I'm not good at it. I don't return phone calls for weeks at a time, and then months. I make plans to get together but get scared, and I cancel. I can read people incredibly well, but I'm not good at being me. If we try to be friends outside Burning Man, I'll fuck it up. I'd rather not put you through that, and I don't want to feel worse about my inability to make friends than I already do."

Our handholding comes to its natural conclusion, and all four of us drop hands at roughly the same time. The intensity, whatever happened, has passed.

Alistair says, "This is the truth?"

"Yes, well, with one little exception. I do have a handful of friends outside Burning Man, I guess. I'm sorta friends with the prison guards on Alcatraz Island. They don't know my name, but I consider us friends. We were pen pals for a few years. But now when I sleep over on the island, we hang out and talk."

Alan wipes his face. "Alcatraz? Who the fuck are you?"

Tell him the truth. "I'm nobody."

"Sit with us," Helena says. "Just...sit. Let's all sit and be quiet for a moment."

I nod. I don't want to damage our new friends any more than I have. We sit on the coolers. They spent their night worrying I had involved them in some sort of coin-stealing scam. I owe them this.

The heat intensifies a little. The sun grows stronger by degrees. Those degrees will make an even bigger difference an hour or two from now.

Alan says, "Alistair, how exactly are you involved?"

Before he can answer, I try to explain King Weekends, but it's like trying to explain an eclipse to someone unfamiliar with the sun. It's like explaining Chinese New Year to someone who never celebrated a holiday. My explanations are a sloppy compilation of details and ideas, crisscrossing stories, intersecting—and then disappearing. Alistair interrupts to verify what he knows, what he's heard, and I can tell that despite my explanations, neither Helena nor Alan have a clue what a *kinging* is.

Do I?

Even after all these years, I can't explain what happens, how what is necessary is brought into reality. I don't *make* it happen. I am the witness. The Found Ones made me an emissary, not a trusted partner. But I don't want to talk about the nature of Reality with these people. I don't trust Reality, with that shifty capital *R*.

After a silence, Alan says, "I'm getting us water."

He returns from the bigger tent with two full cups, offering them first to Helena and Alistair. I know it's stupid, but it hurts he didn't offer one to me. It's stupid, I know. Especially since he's already gone, returning to the tent for ours. When he comes back, he nods briefly, making eye contact. For the first time since I've known him, I see him as a father. Three daughters. He and Helena will have three daughters.

What's wrong with me? Why would I think that?

He and Helena, *he and Helena*, the word *he* completes part of Helena. She pulls him in, *he and Helena*. Turn the words inside and out until I can ban the details, not remember, not remember.

"Vin," she says in a soft voice.

I hang my head in shame. A Found Queen sees me.

"Alan," she says, "give him back the coin. We haven't been good friends to him."

"No. Please, keep it. Dinner and dancing...it was amazing. Alistair and I both had fun—great fun. Please keep it and stay our Burning Man friends."

"So, we can't be friends beyond Burning Man?" Alan asks.

I try not to look pathetic. "I'm not going to be a good friend, Alan. I'm sorry."

He nods, takes this in. He glances at Helena and something passes between them.

She raises her glass. "To Burning Man friendships."

We toast.

We drink.

Alistair and I collect our robes, deciding, for now, to wear them. With the promise to visit again before the weekend is over, we leave in silence and walk into the desert sun.

TEN

"I underestimated you," Alistair says. "Again."

"I swear, I never met Alan and Helena before this weekend. They are not—"

"I know," he says. "I could tell. But obviously, you manipulated them, too. You knew we'd come back here this morning. I wouldn't be surprised if you planted the coin expert among their 'new friends.' In fact, of course you did. He probably followed them all night waiting for the right opportunity."

"I didn't."

"Oh, please. Everything you do, everything you say. It's both honest and a lie. You're the absolute definition of a bloody forked tongue."

Look who's talking.

Alistair reaches for my hand. "You're also just lovely. It's quite confusing."

My heart softens again. He really does see me.

"Vin, I must admit, you've surprised me. As a lawyer, I think of myself as a man ready for surprises, yet you keep pulling it off. If a clown jumps out and puts a pie in my face, I will nod and say, 'Of course.'"

"I'm not a fan of clowns."

Alistair says, "Did you see those clowns yesterday, yeah? The ones with the spider undersides?"

"Thankfully, no. Did you notice those tambourine ladies who passed us a while ago?"

"Vaguely."

"Very sweet sounds, like a brook babbling."

We fall back into making observations, wondering about camps now open, as we stroll down Mainmast Avenue. A nearby Camp Inferno seems sluggish, reluctant to face the day. At the next camp, a giant wooden sign entices passersby to DISCOVER YOUR MUTANT POWER.

My mutant power must be alienating people. I can't shut it off.

John stops. "Where are we going?"

Damn it, he's not *John*. Not yet. Don't blow this.

"I don't know. We're wandering. Where should we go? Any thoughts on how to spend today?"

"No, no," he says. "No games. We know wherever we go, your people will meet us with mysteries and secret notes. Bit of a farce to make me choose, yeah?"

"It's not a farce. I'm still contemplating how much to explain. Seriously, any thoughts on today?"

"What do *you* want, Vin Vanbly?"

This conversation is headed nowhere, a stalemate until we have a bigger conversation about control. Well, shit. Maybe I could explain things to him without fucking the dynamic. It's a risk. In the meantime, it doesn't matter what we do. I lied last night when I told him he will lose his King Weekend in the day or two before the final event. For some men, yes. For a man like John, it all comes down to the final minutes. This is how it is with a shower man. Tears, fears, power, *shower*.

I say, "Let's get ice from Center Camp. We now have two water pouches. Let's fill them with ice. Maybe pick up a copy of the Black Rock Gazette. We could eat breakfast, too. I brought food from my truck. I have peaches."

"Lead the way."

I don't love his smug expression right now. He assumes he's got it all figured out. I dunno, where's the harm in letting him believe that? Wasn't this always part of my master plan to make him believe he is not in control? Isn't this what I wanted?

We wander through Black Rock City, admiring the inventive bikes people have constructed, inventive costumes, and inventive ways of carrying around water. We see parents dragging two kids in a Star Wars wagon, and in a separate wagon attached to that, their family-sized cooler. R2-D2. Don't see a ton of families out here. I think there's a Kid's Camp somewhere in the city. More nuns, another snake guy with a rubber tire around his neck, two naked men. A see enough parasols dotting the morning landscape to make me think of Victorian England.

"Do you think the snake guys put sunscreen on their butts?"

Alistair says, "Absolutely. They all seem to have shaved heads, yeah? You think it's a requirement?"

"Must be. I hope they sunscreen their heads."

"You mention sunscreen a lot."

"I worry."

After another block or two, it feels as though everyone is headed toward Center Camp. The trickle of people becomes a stream. The stream becomes a river. While we slow our pace to accommodate the growing crowds, I hand him his peach. I savor my peach because it is juicy and hot, and the liquid is refreshing in a way no peach in the real world can ever hope to be. John eats his groaning the way I do.

A peach in the desert is magic enough.

As Center Camp comes into view, I can't help but see it as an alien gathering place on a faraway planet, like the planet where Luke Skywalker grew up. The dull silver tent—if you can call something this humongous a tent—creates roughly an acre of shade and has no real sides, just long tarp flaps flowing from the roof to the sand, creating an entrance every twenty feet around the entire perimeter. A dozen flags made from old windsurfing sails—yellow, red, green, and blue—wave proudly overhead, declaring their allegiance to some intergalactic alliance not yet formed. A hundred or more bikes, floats, and hard-to-interpret constructions on wheels park around the exterior, many guarded by their owners, who chat with nearby friends or simply make new friends.

"Look over there. Is it a bike? What is that contraption?"

Alistair says, "Funny, I noticed it, too. No idea. Perhaps it gets dragged behind a bike, yeah?"

"Possibly. I see coils coming out the side. Does it spit fire? Smoke?"

"I'm guessing fire. It's some firebug's wet dream."

We stop to examine it, but after a moment with no further insights, we decide to go inside.

I put the underside of my open palm in front of him. "Hand over your moop."

"Thanks, mate."

He hands me the peach pit. "I'm surprised it took you this long to mention the word *moop*. I would have thought it was one of your favorites."

"I've loved it off and on over the years. You know, even I get tired with my word obsessions. I had to retire moop."

Apropos of nothing, Alistair says, "If you can only spend your money on Found Kings, how do you know the people who received your coins are Found Ones?"

"I don't. But they might be."

If this answer satisfies him, he does not say so.

Inside, hippies chat with skinheads, nakeds discuss shade strategies with people dressed for a fashion show. I know they do amateur drag, poetry slams, and environmental lectures all day on either of the two massive stages in here. With *literally* a thousand people or more lounging on battered couches and folding chairs, or lying in the sand itself, you'd assume the interior would be nothing but chaotic noise. It's quieter than you'd expect. This is where first year burgins come to hide from the sun, having not figured out their own best shade. Experienced burners come to nap on couches when they need a break from their camp. Everyone else comes because, well, because. They come to socialize. They come for relief. They come for coffee. The Center Camp Café is the only place at Burning Man where currency is accepted. Four things are sold: coffee, ice, tea, and hot chocolate, essential items not stored easily in our temporary civilization.

Alistair says, "Last year, I hung out with a camp that made shrimp pad thai one night for dinner. Quite an elaborate preparation."

As we make our way to the long café line, we reminisce about some of our best and strangest Burning Man meals. Mac and cheese with trout, vegetable lasagna cooked by the sun, tuna jerky casserole, and the many, *many* ramen noodle meals we've subjected ourselves to over the years. People get creative. A few years ago, one camp brought nothing but vegan burgers—good ones for every meal. They cooked and traded for all kinds of goodies. It became quite a foodie scene in their camp, everyone showing up to trade their quality items. I should Alistair if he remembers them.

Alistair nods to the people in line in front of us. It's them. We sorta followed them in, I guess. The bald men with rubber tires painted like snakes around their necks. There sure are a lot of these guys. I've never seen them in previous years, I don't think. Of course, that doesn't mean anything. They could have been here for four years and I wouldn't know. This thing is so huge now.

"No visible sunscreen," he whispers.

I shake my head.

"Sixteen," says the one with a reddish-colored snake around his neck.

It's got white stripes. Maybe it's a coral snake. The detail is amazing.

"It's legal," says his friend. His snake is green. "Look, weren't we just complaining this place is lame? No risk-taking. None of the orgies that everyone talks about. Let's do this. Let's at least sit and talk about it with him."

"How did he know to talk to you?"

"Because he's as bored as we are. He's tired at looking at shitty art and saying 'no thanks' to assholes who want to hug. This was a mistake, for us to do a national chapter meeting here. It's that asshole Marco's fault we're here. It's boring as fucking hell until night when everyone gets drunk. Let's do something crazy. Let's do this."

"The age doesn't bother me," says his friend. "It's legal. But it's a *guy*."

"Don't think of it that way."

Alistair and I cast sideways glances at each other. Are we hearing this correctly?

Green Snake unfolds a piece of paper. I try to peer over his shoulder to see it, but I can't.

Coral Snake says, "Are you serious? Because this is serious."

"Wasn't my idea originally," Green Snake says. "But it could be fun."

Alistair steps back and whispers, "Are they talking about a sixteen-year-old?"

I nod cautiously.

"We wouldn't do anything technically illegal. Just party with him. See what happens. Put a wig on him. It'll be dark."

I feel sick.

With a glance, Alistair and I communicate our mutual desire for silence, waiting for the conversation to resume in front of us, but either the serpent men have finished that topic, or they discuss their plans in quieter undertones.

Sooner than we expect, we reach the front. The two snake men order coffees and stand aside. I've nearly forgotten why we're standing in line. A young woman stands before us expectantly, half a shaved skull and black eye makeup deliberately applied to appear as if she finished bawling her eyes out only seconds ago.

"Two cups of ice, please."

She walks away.

Alistair points to a flyer on the counter before us. My stomach flips.

A sixteen-year-old Los Angeles boy, Mickey Flynn, ran away from home. The flyer says it is suspected he has come to Burning Man. The picture shows a cute kid, barely in his teens, big grinning smile and brown hair covering his ears.

This kid! The serpent men were discussing *him*.

"Huh," Alistair says and shoots me a guarded look. "Isn't this a bit off."

They were babbling. Just shooting the shit. Of course they were. They're not... they couldn't find him if they tried. In fact, he's probably already found and on his way home, this kid. Right?

I feel sick.

The serpent men trudge away with their coffee, and I watch where they sit, with two other snake men. They had to have been kidding. Obviously.

Our mascara friend returns with two cups of ice. "Six bucks."

I absently pull out my jingling purse, and Alistair draws in his breath sharply.

"Vin, are you sure?"

I unzip it and pull out a twenty-dollar bill.

Alistair exhales sharply.

While she counts out our change, I say, "Are you a volunteer? Working the café?"

"Yes," she says. "We all volunteer."

I hold a gold coin out for her to take. She accepts it and reaches toward the tip jar.

"Wait. Put the change from the twenty in the tip jar. The coin is for you. For volunteering."

She smiles brightly and says, "It's heavy."

Alistair says, "It's heavy because it's real gold."

She smiles sweetly. "Well, aren't you thoughtful. Real gold. Fuck your burn."

"Yes," I say absently. "Fuck your burn."

We collect our ice.

"Hey, I'm bothered by the conversation we overheard."

He nods. "I thought you might be."

I don't know what that means.

"There's an empty couch near those serpent men. Can we sit by them and listen in? Make sure those guys in line were just talking trash?"

Alistair says, "Of course."

It's funny how challenging it is to walk casually when you're consciously trying to be at ease, but I manage it, wandering to a couch adjacent to theirs. I nod at Alistair, a casual sort of "sit here," and he plays along. I feel sick to my stomach. I know I will feel better when I hear them *not* discussing it with their friends.

Alistair and I sit. Given the spacing between us, we aren't exactly right next to them, yet close enough to eavesdrop if we remain silent. I see a few of them in my peripheral vision. I fill my canvas water bag with ice, pretending to concentrate on the task, while Alistair sucks a piece of his own ice and leans back, closing his eyes.

"How do you think four peopl are going to find this kid," says the fourth man.

His snake is earth tones. Something flesh colored. I don't know what it is. Fleshy.

Another man speaks up, and although is voice is low, quiet, it is also quite clear. There is power in it. "Not just the four of us. We get the camp. We get everybody. Say we're doing a service project or something and tell the men if they find this kid, they hand him over to us. We're going to *talk* to him. Straighten him out. One of us says we ran away when we were a kid, and this is our chance to make things right, some bullshit so whoever finds him alerts one of us four. And then we take him to the rangers." He pauses. "After a while."

"What makes you think we can even find him, even with everybody looking?"

I shift slightly. From the corner of my vision, I see his snake tire is different. He's mutilated the rubber into a raised, flared head, poised to strike. It's a Cobra poised to strike.

He says, "Because I know something that's not on the flyer. We can get this kid. We party with him. See if he's game."

"I'm not gay," says Coral Snake.

"Neither am I. But how many chances in life do you think you'll get to nail someone this young?"

"And where do you think this *nailing* is gonna happen? In front of our whole camp? I know some of the other men hate it here, too. This was a bad idea. But they'd never go along with that."

"Of course not. I have an idea for the location. I've given this some thought. I'm just so goddamn bored. I wanna party like I was promised."

Oh god.

Green Snake says, "We were talking about this earlier. Nothing has to happen if he doesn't want it to happen. But we're in a gift economy, right? He's probably totally unprepared. We share some weed, some booze. He gifts back to us. Sixteen is *legal* in Nevada. It'll be dark. He won't even be able to identify us. It would be totally legal."

Alistair spits a laugh. I glance his way and he remains still, eyes closed.

My heart stops.

Cobra says, "Of course, we are kidding. If we found him, we would return him to rangers right away. For his own safety."

The other men remain quiet.

"Also, we should not discuss our rescue plans here at the Center Camp where other fuck-nosy burners might listen to our private conversation."

The sentence strikes me, jabbing like fangs into my neck, causing my hair to stand up. He means us. He knows we're eavesdropping.

I glance at Alistair. He's...he's smiling. Why is he smiling?

Cobra says, "'Sup, bro?"

The greeting is obviously meant for me, but I ignore it, fiddling with the ice.

He says, "Not cool to listen in on private conversations, *bro*."

Play cool. Ignore this.

Alistair speaks up. "Actually, *bro*, it's not cool to take advantage of a sixteen-year-old runaway."

Oh god.

Cobra says, "You heard me say if we find this kid, we're going to turn him over to the rangers. Immediately. That's what you heard. We're just concerned citizens on the playa."

Green Snake and the Fleshy Snake snicker. Coral Snake does not look amused.

Alistair lifts his head and turns to face them. "You fucking gits couldn't find the exit to a paper bag if the top was open. You won't find this kid."

They regard him with surprise.

Alistair! What are you doing?

"If you do find him," Alistair says, propping himself up on his elbows, "do it. Fuck his brains out. I suggest you all wear the same snake tire while you're having sex with him so he can't identify you. But hey, just a suggestion."

My god, he's offering rape tips!

I grab his arm. "What the fuck are you doing?"

Alistair ignores me. "You Lost Kings will never get the chance. You won't find him. We'll get to him first."

Green Snake frowns. "What the fuck are you talking about?"

Alistair says, "This. This whole setup. I'm sure Vin arranged this run-in, you guys with your symbolically evil snakes, your shaved heads. Obviously, our next assignment is for us to rescue a prince in distress. All that's missing is one of Vin's friends delivering us a note. Don't worry, I'm playing along."

I jerk him to face me. "Hey, don't taunt these guys. This isn't a joke. This isn't part of your—"

He wrests his arm free and shakes a fist at them. "We'll defeat you, you dastardly Lost Kings!"

"We should go," I say, rising. "Now. C'mon, Alistair."

Cobra rises from his couch. "Don't appreciate your tone, *bro*. Or being called Lost Kings, whatever the fuck that is."

Alistair laughs. "Don't bro your bro, *bro*. You sound like an idiot, you know that?"

"Alistair!"

Coral Snake speaks with a snarl. "Fuck you, you fucking Arab."

Alistair turns to me. "Don't worry, Vin. I trust you. I know you have this all under control."

"I don't! This isn't part of your King Weekend!"

"Right," Alistair says. "We *happen* to see some snake guys outside this tent—again—and then *happen* to stand in line behind them—"

"They're the ones we followed in. It's not manipulation, it's logistics!"

Green Snake says, "Dressed like fucking girls wearing dresses."

Coral Snake says, "You guys are pansies."

Cobra chuckles.

Alistair shakes his head. "They *happen* to discuss this runaway kid who needs saving...so we *happen* to sit next to them and hear the plotting. Please, Vin. I'm not an idiot."

There's nothing I can say at this moment to convince him—no explanation.

"How much did Vin and his people pay you to do this? To pretend to be interested in finding this kid? Is this kid even real? What am I saying? Of course, he's not. Is Vin paying you in gold coins?"

"You're making this much worse," I say, my voice getting desperate. "Let's go. Now. I'm ordering you."

"We have to go. *Now.*"

Alistair stands.

I stand.

Alistair says, "I'm offering you nine thousand dollars in gold coins if you find him first. Genuine gold. I swear on my reputation as a seven-year burner."

Cobra says, "You're on, you asswipe."

I'm about to cry. How did this get so out of hand? "*Please!* We're sorry, snake men. We're leaving right now. Ignore him. He's not even English."

Alistair jerks his head at me.

"You guys stay," Cobra says. "We're on our way out. We have work to do."

Cobra smiles at me. "Good luck finding the little cherry."

No. *No!* This is all wrong! How do I convince him to drop this? Any words I say are poison!

I don't know how to stop this! Everything is spinning out of control!

The other snakes murmur to each other as they shuffle away.

One of the men mutters, "Assholes."

Cobra stares at me, his eyes hard and glittering. In a low voice, he says, "Fuck your burn."

ELEVEN

Alistair, *Alistair*.

Precarious word, a heavy *A* on the front end, leaning on a slender *l* and shorter *i*, slipping on a stair to tip over, and over, the Alistair stairs, *i* and the *a* in the front, in the back, slipping and sliding all around the damn word. Do not scream at Alistair, for he's topsy-turvy and wonky-bonky, and behind the fake *Alistair* is a name that is strong.

John.

How the fuck do we find this kid?

"Vin? Something you want to say?"

He grins.

"Yes. I'm trying not to scream. I'm doing word tricks in my head to not scream your name and then start crying. I'm trying to keep my shit together. I spend a lot of time trying to keep my shit together."

"Ah," he says. "The master of all plans is trying to keep his shit together. Well, we're sure in a pickle, aren't we?"

"If you knew as much about people as you think you do, *Alistair*, you'd realize adults with serious control issues come from kids whose lives are incredibly out of control. Control is an illusion we use to comfort ourselves. Look at my face. Do you think I feel in control? Hear the tension in my voice? So, yeah, your name's swirling through my brain's salad spinner to see if there are more ways I could love you. This, so I don't scream your name."

He frowns. "About my name, yeah? You don't believe I'm English? Where did this come from?"

"No. We can't get into that. We have to figure out how to find this kid. That's the top priority."

He might argue, but I see his face change. He's picking his battles. He knows I will not answer him right now. Good, Alistair. Because you're right. I won't.

"Okay," he says. "I'm following orders, Captain. Where would the evil rubber tire snake clan search first? If we beat them—"

"Alistair, this isn't part of your King Weekend."

"Don't patronize me," he says gruffly. "I'm playing along. I'm in it. I just don't like all the smoke and mirrors. You could have said, 'Next we have to pretend to find a runaway' and shown me the flyer. I would have played along."

"I swear to you this is real."

"Okay, okay. I'll react more authentically. I won't fourth-wall you."

"That's not what I—"

I stop.

I don't know how to convince him this is real and how much *worse* he made everything. I don't have time. I need…I need help. I've got to signal an emergency. We need more of those flyers. Call for help, then get a ranger to get some flyers. Shit. Talking to rangers is not a good idea. But they have the flyers. I have to.

Shit.

Don't freak out.

One thing at a time. Send up the flare.

I search the couches around us for any burners with a—water bottle. Right there, only two couches away. I stride in that direction and with Alistair following me, we arrive almost as soon as we leave. Two guys and a girl, all in their late thirties or early forties, chat among themselves.

"Hi, I'm sorry to intrude. May I borrow your water bottle? I'm not going to drink from it or harm it. I'd like to hold it for about thirty to forty seconds."

The man says, "It's my only bottle to carry around all day. What exactly do you need?"

"I need to toss it into the air. Someone here will see it. A friend waiting for a signal from me."

He looks at his companions and then says, "Okay. But do it right here."

"Yes. I'll step a few feet away from you so I don't drop it on your head."

"Ah," Alistair says. "Flying water bottle. I wondered about an emergency flare. I haven't figured out how you communicate with the note messengers, though."

"Be cool about this," the man says and hands me the bottle.

"I will. Promise. Thank you."

I step a few feet away. Nobody's near me. I toss it five feet above my head. After catching it, I toss it higher, two more times, roughly ten feet above me. High enough for a relay to see.

I return the bottle.

While he accepts it, the man says to his friends, "Weird."

Alistair says, "You don't know the half of it."

Absently, I say, "Fuck your burn."

The bottle man turns to his friends and says, "I've always hated that phrase."

The woman laughs. "What does it even mean?"

The second man says, "I never even heard that phrase until last year."

I ignore their chatter.

Ranger.

Gotta find a ranger.

I scan the area, the dozens of couches and folding chairs, cots, and miscellaneous seating devices. People have brought some very strange homemade seats. A small ranger cluster over there, chatting, but I would avoid a group if possible. Unless one of them is briefing the rest on the runaway situation. I see others scattered around the area, a few lounging. I could ask any of them.

There's a Jabba the Hutt whose costume is made out of a bean bag chair. He's sitting on his own flesh. I don't have time to notice this.

"What now, Vin?"

"We wait. Someone will come. No one I recognize."

"Hello. I'm here."

The low voice behind me makes me jump, and I realize I've got far too much adrenaline. Black guy. Young. Great afro. Blue shorts and a faded button-down shirt.

Those men are gonna rape that kid.

We have to stop it. I have to stop it. Keep cool. Keep it together. Remember to breathe.

"Hi, what's your name?"

"Reggie."

"Hi, Reggie. I'm Vin. Thank you for your help. How many are near?"

"One by a south exit. One on the northeast exits."

"Go get them both. Meet me at the northeast side. Hurry. This is important."

"Okay. Northeast corner. Ten minutes?"

"As soon as possible. Every minute counts."

Alistair laughs. "I underestimated you again. I thought only one person followed us."

I nod. "Hurry."

Reggie says, "I will."

He takes off.

I turn to Alistair. "We have to get more posters from a ranger with the kid's picture."

Alistair says, "Right. Good idea."

Why am I explaining this to him?

I resume staring down rangers, looking for Ranger Ron. I don't see him. Good. He probably doesn't remember me anyway. I'm paranoid.

Alistair says, "If we're looking for flyers, why don't we ask the chick who served us? She can tell us who gave her the poster."

"Yes. Good! That's *good!*"

Okay, maybe Alistair can help, though he's in the dark. I can't think about Alistair right now, tripping down stairs after stairs is *Alistairs*. What the fuck is happening? Is this happening? *He fucking taunted those guys.* We have to fix this.

I trace our steps back to the café, stepping around those in line. We get a couple dirty looks and a snarky, "Be cool, guys," but I explain we're not ordering, just have a question for our cashier.

She's busy helping someone else.

I say, "Excuse me, miss, who gave you this missing kid flyer? Which ranger?"

She looks at me, puzzled, and says, "I don't know. It was hours ago."

Our interview is over. She begins helping someone new.

Okay. Pick a ranger. Go.

The group. Fine. I'll ask the small ranger group. They stand near one of the exits, in the direction we're headed anyway. Customized ranger shirts and name badges distinguish them. Okay. It's going to be okay. Easy exchange with a small group. Nothing will go wrong. Wait. Yes, it could.

"Alistair, please do not say anything. Okay? Please. Don't say a single word. Let me speak to the rangers."

"Hang on. Is this one of those tests where you *want* me to talk, though you're telling me not to, because a *true* king speaks out when others are afraid?"

"Oh my god, no. It's not a test. Okay, wait, *yes*, it's a test. The goal—*swear-to-god*—is to keep your mouth shut. It's not reverse psychology. I promise."

"Unless you're using reverse psychology right now."

I spin around and try to keep panic from my voice. "Please, please believe me this once."

"Okay, okay," he says backing up with slight alarm. "Message received."

Crossing this wide-open room feels like walking a rocky coastline, sand beneath our feet, maneuvering to avoid ocean boulders. Here, the boulders are couches. The ambient noise all around us, constant but not loud, feels like seagulls you train your ears to ignore. I have to swirl his name around like water in my mouth, thinking of new ways to love him. Alistair, *Alistair*!

Wait.

How can I be mad at *him*?

This isn't his fault.

This is *my* fault.

I refused to explain how much I controlled this weekend. He's assuming I control *everything*. I didn't think about the potential consequences of not explaining, of not finishing our conversation from this morning. I didn't realize there could be consequences! Of course, this is all my fault!

Oh my god. Oh my god.

This is all my fault.

Can't deal with that right now. I'm here, in front of them. Start talking.

"Excuse me, I hate to bother you rangers, but at the café, I heard about this runaway kid. The sixteen-year-old?"

One of the men, the bandana guy says, "Yeah?"

"So it's true? He's a runaway and he's here?"

"Suspected. Told his best friend he was coming here, so, that's the fear. You seen him?"

"No. Actually, I wanted to help search. My whole camp wants to help. We're worried."

The other ranger, probably a more senior rank, speaks up. She says, "That's cool. But we don't want to make a big deal of this. So, no thanks."

Another ranger says, "She *means*, yes, it's a big deal. It's a big deal. But let us handle it."

The woman ranger says, "That's what I said."

"No, you didn't."

I say, "How about a flyer? Can I have a flyer to show around my camp?"

I don't want to come across too desperate.

The first woman says, "No."

I want to scream in their faces. I want to tell them what Alistair said, and now *rapists* are hunting this kid. I can't reveal that. I can't betray Alistair. But, I'm betraying this kid, aren't I? Oh my god, am I? No. I'll get someone else to approach the rangers, anonymously, and tip them off regarding the serpent men. That's what I'll do.

Alistair nudges me.

I'm not moving. I'm not talking. They're staring at me.

The fourth ranger, the only one who hasn't spoken, says, "We're not spreading paper all over camp. If you want his picture, use your cell to take a photo."

Great idea!

"Hey, thanks. Great idea. We'll do that."

The first woman ranger, lanky with red curly hair says, "Hey. Seriously, we've been briefed on this situation and you haven't, so stay out of it."

I look too intense. Too worried. Dial it down.

I nod. "Okay. Good luck finding him."

Alistair steps up from behind. "We'll give you each a gold coin worth three thousand dollars if you give us a flyer of the missing kid."

Oh my god. I grab his arm and lead him away.

He calls back to them, "Three thousand dollars!"

"Alistair, stop, please. I begged you."

Alistair says, "What did I do?"

"Alistair, *please*. Please don't talk until you and I get a moment alone."

"Why not now?"

My fury rises. I can't talk to him. We navigate furniture again, and while in years past I have been impressed with how huge Center Camp is, I'm angry about its size today. We can't get to the doors fast enough. We can't run. I bet those rangers are watching us. My rage dances around me—blinding me like a desert whiteout—tiny grains of anger fighting each other, making me feel crazy inside my head. Don't get mad at Alistair, get mad at the true source. You're the fuckup here, Vin Vanbly. You are a fucked up fuckup.

Alistair says, "Hey, slow down. Don't get the next clue without me."

Alistair.

Is this the same man who sobbed in my arms last night? The man who is afraid of sex because it will remind him of happier and sadder times? He's a cheerful fucking robot right now, playing and laughing like he's having the time of his life.

Oh.

Which means he's *not* having the time of his life.

I have to be kinder to him. I have to love him. He truly thought he was playing my game, making it more intense. He tried to show me love, not fuck this up. But he did make it worse. He must take responsibility for his actions. I have to take responsibility for mine. That's how we survive this.

After.

First we find this kid.

We make our way outside, making room for a trio of cat women, Sparkle Ponies in last night's costumes, presumably. Behind them, two topless women in leopard vests smirk at the felines. Behind those women, a group wearing butchered business suits, satirizing corporate America. Outside, I scan the crowds and find Reggie with two other men, roughly the same age, at his side. They look like typical burners, teased hair, long shorts, tatted and pierced. I wonder who they are. Get names later. Reggie sees me and touches his companions.

I say, "We have a situation. It's serious. There's a sixteen-year-old runaway who snuck into Burning Man. We have to find him. Some very bad people are pursuing him, so this is top priority. Everything else gets suspended. Understood?"

Two of them nod.

The man to Reggie's right says, "What about the Twinkies? The shirt?"

"Suspended. Alistair's King Weekend is on hold. We have to find that kid. Do you each have a cell phone? Yeah? Good. Go to the café and take a picture of the flyer on the counter. Get a close up of the kid's face so we can show it around. Show the picture to everyone. Get all the kings together and have them form search parties."

I pause and consider, then offer my suggestions for how the search ought to be run, but I emphasize if someone among them formulates a better plan, do it. I explain they need a meeting place, somewhere not Center Camp but near it, not too public, and we need to have relays in place to move with greater frequency.

"Please, someone bring me my cell. Julian has it."

Reggie says, "Okay."

Julian. Saying his name makes me miss him.

"Wait. Take a photo of the kid's picture with my phone and then bring it to me."

"Where are you going to be?"

"Good point. I don't know. One of you hang back. Leave Alistair and me alone again, tailing us, keeping your eyes open for this kid. Which of you has everybody's phone number and the mobile hot spot?"

One of the men thumbs himself.

"You? Great. Okay, you're on me, same as before. Instead of throwing a water bottle, I'm gonna turn and signal you. You don't have to hide, just stay back."

"Decloaked. Got it."

Reggie says, "Do you want us to bring one of the kings to you?"

Oh. I hadn't considered that. "Hang on."

I had decided Alistair shouldn't meet any other kings until he was ready to cross over tomorrow morning. I can't have Alistair meet any of them early. He's already chasing his kingship too hard. I shouldn't have attempted this. Alistair wanted it too much. A man threads his kingship through an impossible needle, not caring and caring, wanting and not wanting, allowing failure to be an option while striving harder than ever. Men have to surrender. A man who wants it with his ego can never surrender. I knew this and still heard the *yes* anyway. Why? *Why?*

"Okay, let's...keep using relays. No direct communication."

"This is unbelievable," Alistair says with excitement. "I love watching this. I *love* seeing behind the scenes!"

"Ignore him. He doesn't believe this is real. It's real. No joke. Guys, we have to find this kid. I fucked up something bad, and I have to make this right. Please. Tell everyone to take this seriously. Okay? Thank you. Wait, what are your names? Please. Reggie, I met inside."

Reggie nods.

The one with an elaborate tat down his arm says, "I'm Ko Ko, with two *K*'s."

"Andy," says the third, "but this year, everyone is calling me Mars."

"Ko Ko. Mars. Reggie. Thank you. *Thank you.* We have to make this right. I fucked it bad. We need to find this kid."

They nod, accepting the urgent warning I wanted them to hear, the one Alistair refuses. They take off, except for Ko Ko, the man who pointed at himself and his phone.

He turns away. Over his shoulder he says, "Twenty-five feet away?"

"Yes. Thank you."

"No problem, Ghost."

My heart sinks.

He freezes. With his back to me, he says, "I'm sorry. I didn't mean to call you that."

"It's okay. I know that's what the kings call me."

Ghost. They all think of me as a lost cause.

He turns, and I see a bashful, apologetic expression cross him. "They don't. None of the kings would ever say that. Honestly. Only a few of us—guys who know kings from our outside lives—we keep in touch, too. We call you Ghost. It's short for The Ghost Who Walks Among Us. We don't know what it means exactly. We saw it online. There's a website..." His voice trails off. "I'm sorry. I didn't mean to be rude."

I'm dying inside. "Don't worry. It's not rude."

Everyone, *everyone*, knows I am a Lost King. Apparently, the Internet knows, too. How could I ever become a Found One with so many who know me this way? Every single person who gossips about me binds me to my current identity with an invisible silver strand, like Gulliver tied down on the sandy beach in Lilliput. The Human Ghost. The Lost King destined never to be found. The Ghost Who Walks Among Us. I know who I am. I don't need the whole world reminding me I am a loser.

He jogs away.

Alistair says, "Bravo. *The Ghost Who Walks Among Us*. Very oogie boogie, yeah? I love it."

"Really? I don't."

How do I convince—?

Stop.

Doesn't matter. Despite being surrounded by thousands, Alistair and I are isolated in a very confusing dust storm. Explaining makes things worse.

"And the marshalling of the troops," he says. "Color me impressed. You're very sexy being all commanding. I think perhaps this kidnapping drama could lead to serious kissing. Give me time."

His face changes. "I'm also sorry you're a Lost King. I believe that part, too. I know you weren't kidding about how much it upsets you. I saw it last night during our show. That was real."

Alistair's big compassion for me, another reason to love him.

I say, "You absolutely believe finding this kid is part of your King Weekend?"

"Yes. Let's find him."

Okay, then. Fuck it. He can believe what he wants, as long as he helps me find the runaway.

"Where should we go first, Vin?"

"I don't know. Where would a sixteen-year-old kid hang out?"

"Here," Alistair says, indicating the tent behind us. "Especially if he had no real camping supplies."

"Yeah, good insight. However, this place is teeming with rangers."

He chuckles. "It's not much of a king challenge to find him if he's right here. Not for all that drama."

Ignore his grin. Ignore the attitude.

"Let's start here. We'll do a full tour and hope we get lucky."

Alistair smiles. "Lucky. I love it. Let's hope we get *lucky*. So what do we do?"

I'm already scanning all young male faces in my visual range.

I'm distracted when I say, "Now, we search."

For the last hour, Alistair has interrupted me regularly with questions about the hunt, the players, how long before the kid is found. For the first hour and a half, he remained a cheerful, helpful partner. He participated as I hoped he would, scanning and pointing out anyone who might fit the description. But we can't find Mickey. Nobody can find him.

This is not like television, where a manhunt lasts the length of a video montage. Those searches end with some late-realized clue, some ironic little twist someone should have noticed all along. As in, "he likes ice cream" or something equally basic, and then they find him in an ice cream parlor. We could use one of those lucky breaks.

"How long until the next clue?"

"Alistair," I say in a warning.

This is how I now answer his questions.

"I feel like we're not learning anything new," he says. "Maybe it's my fault, like, maybe I'm supposed to take greater charge of this part of the weekend, yeah? Should I drive this? Is that why we found no additional clues?"

"There are no additional clues," I say and realize there's nothing more to say. "I can't get into this again."

"I'm sorry, Vin. I tried to act surprised with those snake men. I'm sorry if I embarrassed you by not believing in your show."

"It's not a *show*. This isn't performance art, Alistair," I say, while thinking, *John.* "Even though it's one hundred percent *my* fault, this entire situation, it's also *your* fault because you made it worse. I'm trying to get you to see that."

"Nice maths."

"It's not about the math, it's ownership. You made it worse, Alistair. You did so by accident, believing it was part of my plan, but I tried to stop you, and you ignored me. Why wouldn't you listen?"

"I *have* been listening to you. Doing everything you wanted. I'm totally in, Vin. I am. We've been hunting this kid for almost three hours and I haven't complained once, yeah?"

"Except now. And your needling questions for the last hour."

"I'm not complaining," he says coldly.

He's accidentally reminded me it's almost three hours, which means it's nearly time for another check-in. Find out if any other search team has experienced success. Maybe this kid is already found. Maybe they found him. No, don't get your hopes up. Black Rock is a huge city. Thirty thousand people, and roughly half of them are mobile. The likelihood of any hundred searchers physically seeing Mickey Flynn is close to zero. Through a relay, Perry's note observed the kid's picture looks dated, if he's currently sixteen. The photo shows a boy thirteen or fourteen. So he could look mighty different. Facial hair. Anything. At the time, Alistair asked, "Is this a clue?"

My heart thudded when I saw Perry's handwriting.

"I'm not complaining," Alistair says with more insistence.

"You are. We have to find this kid. Yell at me later."

"I just want a clue or something. A nudge. Should I take over? Are we getting nowhere because I'm letting you lead, and a real king would step up and take the power from—"

"No. A real king would not do that or not *not* do that."

"Lost me."

"It's about sharing power. Sharing the burdens together. Nobody wrestles power free when you share it. Instead of getting stuck in one person, it bounces from person to person. Lots of people get to touch it, and the way you touch it is to willingly knock it to someone else, like a beach ball at a rave. I know this is true, because I see the Found Ones do it. Clearly I don't get it on a personal level, because I'm as manipulative and clumsy as I was ten years ago. If you have ideas and want to lead, great. Lead. I will follow. But all your ideas must relate to finding this kid. No throwing a 'bubble bath parade' or inventing a song only he can hear. No bullshit."

"I know, yeah? Find the kid. Find the kid. I'm on it. I do have an idea."

He explains.

I don't see how his idea improves much on what we're already doing. Still, I am desperate to work smarter. He's a lawyer and I'm a high school dropout. Let him lead.

I say, "Let's do it."

Be smarter than me, Alistair. Or John. Whoever you are.

Find this kid.

Three hours later, Alistair seems as unhappy as I am.

He stops, right in the middle of Forecastle Avenue. "This is ridiculous. This is our second time down this street. On this same block."

He's right, but so what? Could be five hundred new faces on this block since our last time here four hours ago.

"Stop," he says. "We have to talk about this."

Streams of cheerful people move around us.

"Do you need a water break? Food?"

"No. Vin, what the fuck are we doing?"

"We must—"

"Stop. Stop. We're not doing anything different than we were three hours ago. Or five hours ago."

"I know. I *know*."

He pauses.

I say, "Let's find some place to step out of traffic."

We pass two New Agey camps, one promising five minute sessions of "deep listening," and its neighbor is a place where you may marry yourself, reciting vows of love and self-reliance. The idea of being married to myself horrifies me, especially in this moment. This is all my fault.

Once we find a niche as private as is possible on this busy street, Alistair is ready to argue. "If our check-ins with the other search teams are to be believed, your people found the Snake Camp. It's now under surveillance in case this kid shows up."

"You heard the same updates I did. There are *three* Snake Camps. The serpent men have teams of two and three leaving the camp and returning regularly. They could take this kid to any of those other ones or maybe a fourth we haven't discovered."

"So, let's go to the big Snake Camp and force a showdown. Fight them. Get the next clue. *Something*."

"You and I can't go there. They know our faces. Besides, we sent two kings to explain to the rest of their camp. You heard the update. Cobra and his pals warned their friends we were obsessed and to not talk to us. He said we were Christian missionaries making up tales."

Alistair looks around. "Right, right. But there's so much else we could do. It's like we're at the circus and you're obsessed with finding a single ticket on the ground."

"He's not a single ticket. He's a human being. His name is Mickey Flynn."

"It's pointless."

"Not if they *rape* him, it's not pointless. As long as we keep them from getting Mickey, we can prevent that. We will call rangers the minute Mickey shows up in Snake Camp."

"Yes," Alistair sounds weary. "I know. We've been over this so many times. Find the kid. Get the kid handed over to the rangers. Go back to my King Weekend."

We stand facing each other, unsure. I've felt this showdown brewing for hours. Unless I come up with a compelling reason, he's not going to keep searching.

Four bikers pass us, one after another. Couples walk by. Two guys in silver garb wearing wispy capes. Long-haired, short-haired, bald, and green-haired pass us. Fauxhawks. The river of people flows around us, none of them carrying this kid on the current. Where are you, Mickey?

"I can't do this anymore," Alistair says. "I thought there was some lesson to learn, but I'm not learning it."

Stay cool, Vin. Keep it together.

"How about this lesson? Clean up your fucking mess."

Wow, way to keep your cool, you moron.

"Alistair, *we* made this worse. *We* have to fix this. You and I. We aren't responsible for those four serpent men's actions. They were going to hunt this kid anyway. But we turned it into a sporting competition. You offered a nine thousand dollar prize. Don't you feel any sort of responsibility?"

"No. By the way, this is the most conversation we've had in the past hour. You're not asking me anything, you're not answering any of my questions. You still won't explain why you think—"

I frown. He knows I refuse to discuss his English heritage. He wants the reasons. The lawyer wants arguments he can counter.

"We have to keep looking."

"Wait, wait," Alistair says. "Hang up, mate."

He takes in everything around us, the camps, the people drinking shots, the sand swirling in small eddies. Two people play volleyball nearby, keeping the ball alive, back and forth, back and forth, back and forth.

"How does this help my King Weekend? Finding this tosser?"

"Maybe your King Weekend is less about you and more about helping others. Maybe that's how it relates."

"You think I'm selfish."

"I do right at this moment, yes. Nothing matters until he's in safe hands."

"We spent all day looking."

"We will spend all night, too."

Alistair says, "I know this is part of your plan. In last night's story, the two kings wandered lost in the desert for hours. That's us today, right? Wandering from camp to camp, street to street, lost like they were, yeah?"

Well, fuck. Yet another part of this weekend returns to bite me on the ass. Fuck. How can I ever persuade him this isn't part of the plan?

"How long do we wander? I mean, isn't six hours enough?"

I do not answer. All the arguments have been made.

"Do we have to sing Christmas music for the next clue?"

I say nothing. I stare into his eyes. Let's get it out there.

The showdown.

Alistair says, "I can't do this any longer."

"Would it help if I told you the king story again? Would that remotivate you to help find a teenager who is emotionally wrecked, homeless, and at the mercy of whoever has food and—"

"How did you get the rangers in on it? None of them acted surprised when we asked for a flyer this morning. I wouldn't think those guys would be bribable."

"What do you want me to say, Alistair?"

"What was the point of the stories with the sleeping king and the girl locked in a prison with her father holding the key? The thirsty kingdom with the water well?"

"No. Not explaining."

"Yes. *Yes*, explaining. You gotta give me something, Vin. I'm not having fun."

"Good."

"I am very happy to *wax on* and *wax off*, like a good grasshopper, but give me something to focus on, the rule we're learning or whatever. Something."

I don't know what to say. Doesn't happen very often, but here we are.

A dusty breeze rises and we cough it away. After a few seconds, it's gone.

He stares at me.

"The kings—"

"There is no magic kingdom," he says. "Look around us, Vin. Half the people here are drunk, and it's not even six o'clock in the evening. This isn't your world of blessed kings, this is a big, drunken drug fest in the desert, full of losers pretending to be someone they're not."

My eyebrows arc up in surprise, wondering if he caught what he just said.

He did.

Losers pretending to be someone they're not.

His face wrinkles into something angry. "I'm sick of your snarky little tones, yeah? Your askew glances, like that one now, and the funny pronunciation of my name. I'm not stupid. Why do you think I'm not English?"

Get ahold of yourself, Vin. Don't make this worse. Love this man. *Love him.*

"Alistair, I'm sorry. I'm *sorry.* I promise you we will get back to your King Weekend as soon as we find this kid. I promise we'll figure a way to make it right."

"But," Alistair steps closer to me, his face twisted into a furious question mark, "this *is* my King Weekend. The kid, the hunt for the kid, yeah? I have to use *all my love* to find him? He's—this is a setup."

"It's not."

"Yes, it is," he said. "I heard the tales, the elaborate schemes, the lies, the way you twist information out of men to trick them into revelations."

This is it. Right now. I'm being punished for my lifetime of lying and manipulation. A kid is going to get raped because I am so untrustworthy.

"Yes, yes, I've done all that. Sometimes it works. With some men. It doesn't work with everyone. Alistair, that kind of King Weekend would never work with you. Honestly, I didn't have anything planned for us after our pirate escape this morning. I thought maybe we'd sleep for a while. I'm really fucking tired."

Alistair shades his eyes with his right hand, blocking me out. "I don't believe you."

One last chance to reach him. "Alistair. Can you not feel it? Feel how this is our shared responsibility, how we are both necessary? Be quiet in yourself. Listen."

"No. I don't feel it."

"Just take a deep breath with me. Let's breathe together."

"No. A million things led to this kid running away—you know what? I can't argue this because this runaway kid isn't *real*."

"He is."

"Quit it," he says. "I'm serious. I'm not falling for this. Give me the *reason*. Teach me the *lesson*."

"Here's the best lesson I can offer. What would you risk to find a lost king? And what if he doesn't remember you? This young king needs our help."

"No," he says. "*Fuck your cryptic, bloody kings*! Fuck 'em, mate! Tell me the goddamn truth. Were you *ever* going to king me?"

How do I answer this honestly without revealing the truth—it was never within my power to king him? If I reveal the truth, he may never cross over. Yet, I have to find a way to answer him. Choose the words carefully.

"If you're asking me if the King Weekend was real, yes. It was real. My intention was you would be recognized by the Found Ones after our time together."

"*Bollocks*. You're lying. You took a long time to answer."

"King's honor."

"Well then, what was your big plan?"

"I can't reveal that."

He pauses, stares at me. "What did the notes say?"

Perhaps sharing the truth is the way I show him all my love.

"Honestly? The notes were about cheeses."

He waits for my elaboration.

"I wanted you to believe secret plans were happening all around you, so we passed notes. Notes were never necessary. Instead, we argued about various cheeses and their usage. The notes were a distraction."

His face grows red, redder. Tighter.

"I'm telling you the truth, Alistair. I'm trying to make things right with you, to keep you by my side, because I don't think I can do this without you. The secret to finding Mickey is both of us working together. I don't know how I know that, but I *know*."

"Bullshit. You still have a note in your pocket. Show me."

I retrieve it from my pocket and hand it to him.

He reads it aloud. "Camembert is a fussy cousin to Brie. No way is it suitable for omelets, a blue-collar egg dish." He looks up. "You've got to be bloody kidding me." Alistair puts both hands to his head. "I can't believe this. I cannot believe I trusted you. I thought you were somebody...you're not anybody...you're *nobody*. There is no magic. None."

"Yes, I tried to tell you. The only magic is what happens between two people— us searching for Mickey. Miracles, I've witn—"

"Fuck that! Fuck you and your stupid kings! Why would I ever take the advice of a *Lost King*? Why did I—"

"I *told* you I was a Lost King."

"Fuck the king business," he says. "You're not anybody—you're *nobody*. A big nobody, and I followed you around like a baby duck, like a fooking duckling, because I thought you were special."

"I'm not."

"You're *not*," he says vehemently.

"I tried to tell you, time and time again. You wouldn't listen. You kept seeing what you wanted to see."

"Yeah, a *king maker*."

"The first time we met, I told you not to call me that. I can't *make* kings."

"Yeah, yeah. You told me. You preyed on my bloody hero worship and downplayed yourself so I would grow it even bigger. You truly are the most manipulative person I have ever met, and I, like a first-class twat, fell for it, believing in you fully, believing you could make a difference. You're a fake."

The hurt raging inside him...I hate seeing it. But he's not wrong. I am nobody. I am a terrible, manipulative person. He's not telling me anything I don't already know.

"After we find—"

"Oh, for bloody Christ's sake, stop *already*. You're nothing but bollocks and bullshit, mate. I did everything you wanted, everything. I submitted over and over. You failed me."

Okay. Enough. The time for gentleness is over. My lover tried to win him back, now it is time for my warrior. Time for the sword. Clean cuts, Vin.

"You're right. I failed you, Alistair. In my defense, you never submitted as you agreed to do. Every time you said, 'Yes,' you winked at me with your English accent, your personal rebellion to prove I couldn't force your submission."

"About bloody time," he says. "Finally, you're going to say it instead of hinting at it over and over."

"Yes. I'll say it. You're not English. You're good at the charade. You didn't say anything to give yourself away. Honestly, you could spend your whole life waiting for someone to catch you in your lies, someone clever enough to unmake you, but guess what? Nobody can force you to confess to anything you don't want to reveal, whether it's the English bit, your HIV status—"

His eyes harden.

"Or any other secret. So stand there with your arms crossed. Be furious with me. You win. But guess what? You lose. The real you will always be trapped inside Alistair. Trust me on this one. Hanging on to your secrets isn't much fun. I know how my story turns out. There's no castle. No prince charming. You should look upon me as a cautionary tale, one potential future, unless you do what needs to be done. I can't do it. I'm weak. But you still could. It's not too late for you. Last night, you walked right into that fear and chose the most graceful way out, sharing your heart with me under a million watchful stars. You were amazing."

He glowers at me, face twisting into fury, replies storming inside him, justifiable, gritty potshots he could take.

His voice is tight. "I did *not* say 'go get him' to a bunch of asshole rapists. I know this is part of your plan. I *know* it."

He is his own private sandstorm. He doesn't know what to believe.

"Tell me what I'm supposed to learn from all this," he demands. "Tell me right now."

I choose not to speak. I'm out of words.

When his mouth finally opens, he spits out only two words.

"I quit."

Do I argue? Do I try to—no. Years ago, a different version of me would have tried everything in his power to stop him from this irreversible action. I've learned a few things along the way.

I nod. "Okay. Have a good life, John."

I turn from him before seeing his reaction. I don't need to see it.

I start walking down Forecastle Avenue again, stepping aside for three women on recumbent bikes and two men dressed in fish costumes.

In a few short hours, sunset, then darkness.

The neon tarantula will stretch awake. This kid is out there.

I've got to find him before something terrible happens.

TWELVE

Alan says, "They will recognize you."

"Maybe. Probably. But I can't send anyone else over to the main Snake Camp. We've got to get some undercover intel. I'm already on their shit list. I don't want anyone—"

"No, I meant they *will* recognize you. Even bald, you don't look different enough."

I rub my hands against my shaved head. I'm bald. This feels so alien.

I say, "What's missing? What do I do? Keep in mind I'll have a rubber snake tire around my neck."

"For one thing, your bald head is too shiny. Too white. You gotta rub some sand into it, see if you can make it darker somehow. These guys run around in the sun all day. You gotta be burned or brown or something."

"Right. I can do that."

Alan looks down the road. "Where are they?"

"All reports said any minute."

"Good," he says grimly.

Not good. Helena is seducing one of the serpent men, bringing him back to Robot Zamp for what he hopes will be a sweeter reward than coconut water. I need one of those rubber tires if I'm going to get into their camp. Helena and Alan are going to help me get one.

"Alan, what's missing? What can I do to look more different?"

Alan says, "Take off your shirt."

I yank it over my head.

"Same thing. You're too clean. Too pale. How are you not sunburned?"

"Sunscreen. Moisturizer."

Alan says, "It's dark. Your pasty skin won't be as obvious. Maybe some of Helena or Lisa's makeup to rub under your eyes, make you look party haggard. I'll also see if Lisa has some bronzer or something to put on your head and chest. Shoulders, too. Too fucking pale."

Alan dashes away.

I move to a less densely populated part of Robot Zamp and drop to the ground, rolling myself in dirt and sand. It doesn't stick, so I do rapid jumping jacks until a small sheen of sweat emerges. Doesn't take long. When I get up from the ground the second time, Alan is watching me.

"Better," he says. "But rub more on your skull."

Thank god Alan and Helena's camp agreed to help with my latest plan, the infiltration. I explained how desperate the situation had become. Alan and Helena were horrified—everyone in their camp was—by the idea of a sixteen-year-old being taken advantage of so ruthlessly. I hinted at our accidental involvement. When they agreed to help, I suggested the plan. Helena would seduce a snake man with her beauty. Invite him to a Robot Zamp party. Get him so drunk he removed the snake tire around his neck. I told them ideally, only nine people would be necessary for the party—important to the dynamics interplay—but thirteen people are currently present, including Alan. Fourteen if I include Helena. It's too many people. The wrong number.

But I can't control everything.

A relay appears, one of yesterday's deliverers of cheese notes. He says, "They're coming. One block away."

With that warning, Nitro, Tuck, and their guests bring a party to life, someone stroking a guitar, and beers are rapidly distributed. Manufactured laughter begins immediately. Nitro's friends stand and chat with strangers in the street, making the Robot Zamp seem quite social in their approach to humanity.

Alan leads me around a tent corner, shoving the makeup case into my hands. "Use this on your head. Rub it in. On your way to the snake guys, stop at another camp—anywhere really—and ask someone to smooth it out. Once this dick is here, I won't be able to help you."

"Alan, are you truly okay with this?"

He says, "Yeah, I guess. It's not gonna be great seeing her flirting with this tool, but I know who she loves. I know she's doing this for that kid. We all are." He pauses. "I'll be glad when it's over. I'm not secret agent guy."

"Alan," I say, feeling overwhelming gratitude. My heart is full of him. Of *them*. The love I offered them reflected back on me tenfold. "I love that you're not secret agent guy. *Love* that. Thank you for helping anyway."

He says, "No sweat. I would only do this for a good acquaintance. I would have said 'a friend,' but you'll break out in a rash, apparently, if someone calls you that."

"I didn't—"

"Relax. I'm teasing."

I can never relax, Alan. If I relax, you'll see weird and awful aspects of me.

We wait for Helena and her new snake beau to come into view.

"You're sure these snake guys are still looking?"

"We think so. This afternoon, my...friends...discovered two other Snake Camps. Well, satellite camps. They keep their food and supplies there. Sleeping tents. The main Snake Camp is the party playground. Cobra said he had a plan for taking this kid somewhere else but we don't know where. The rest of his camp refuses to listen to our warning."

"You've told the rangers?"

"It's complicated. This morning, they insisted I stay out of it, but by now, it's obvious I haven't. Our guys warned them of Cobra's intentions. They don't even know who 'our guys' are exactly, but the last time we sent an envoy, rangers asked a million questions. They asked if the envoy was related to the "gold coin Arabs." Our relay had to run away and ditch them. We can't go to rangers anymore."

"Alistair?" Alan's voice sounds hopeful.

I already explained this part to him earlier. "He's definitely out of the picture."

Alan says, "I liked him."

"Me too."

Where are you, Alistair? I can't believe we never kissed. I only got to hold you once, from behind. But you cried in my arms last night and I saw the stars in your tears. Can you love someone you've never kissed? Yes. I know the answer. Yes. *John.* I never quite got to meet John.

Helena comes into view, shirtless, wearing many layers of beads around her neck, like the day we met. She wears a men's khaki-colored kilt, a very industrial contrast to her long, smooth legs. She's got her arm looped through a snake guy's arm, and he doesn't seem to mind. He's thinner than me, which makes me worry they won't accept me wearing his rubber tire.

I duck behind the tent. He mustn't see me. Although he's not one of the original four snake men from Center Camp this morning, he can't know our plan until it's too late to make a difference.

I hear a chorus of party cheers welcome Helena back into the fold, and one voice rises above the others to call for more beers.

Alan whispers, "Time to join the party."

I must wait patiently. Our scouts targeted this guy because he wandered on his own and stopped for free drinks at other camps. He seemed the easiest to get drunk.

My plan shocked Helena and Alan at first. They don't think like I do. They're not used to exploiting someone and turning a situation to a tactical advantage. They caught a glimpse of the real me, and I think they understood—more than this morning's explanation—why I end up alone. I'm not a good person.

But this kid, this *sixteen-year-old*, is innocent.

Alistair, where are you?

Why is it taking so long to get this already semi-drunk guy drunk enough to remove his snake?

Because it takes this long.

Be patient.

The party surges every now and again, some big laugh or whooping, and I hear lots of toasting. They're knocking off beers quickly. Be patient. Let them do what they're doing.

The snakes haven't found the kid—we know. We *think* we know. The kings continue to search, trying to imagine what exotic flame will attract a sixteen-year-old moth.

No theory has worked out.

I never should have tried to king Alistair. He was always far beyond my abilities.

So why the fuck did I get a *yes* in my gut?

Don't peek out from behind the tent. Don't do it.

I wait.

Impatiently.

Why is this taking so long?

Seems like an hour, though surely it is less, before I hear Alan laughing louder, closer, and he slurs out a comeback to someone. Then, I hear a whizzing in the air. With a barely audible *plop*, the rubber snake tire lands twenty feet from me, almost into the camp behind Robot Zamp.

It's here! I can go!

Have to move quickly. Have to get to Snake Camp and see if I can uncover something before this guy sobers up and realizes he's missing his tire. I assume they got it from some sort of truth or dare drinking game, because I heard them all chant, "*Take it off! Take it off!*" more than once. I'm assuming Helena lost some beads, too. Poor Alan. Could I try to befriend them outside Burning Man?

No. I will fuck things up.

There's no time to think about this.

I merge onto Mainmast Avenue, and take the first cross street to get further away. Wheelhouse Avenue is where I will find the main Snake Camp. It's a fifteen minute walk, which means I have fifteen minutes to practice my swaggering confidence, swinging my arms differently, carrying myself differently. I can do this.

When I put my mind to it, I can become anybody.

As I stride toward its entrance, Snake Camp is not what I expect. I'm not sure what I expected, a shambling gothic mansion surrounded by giant iron railings? Metalwork snakes coiling around the front gates? This is Burning Man, not vampiric New Orleans. Their camp—easily four camping spaces merged together—is surprisingly crowded with people but not structures.

There's a main tent, a party tent, in the center of their property. Drab olive green, an Army surplus store find, I'm guessing. Big enough to hold ten. On the right side, two fire barrels blaze alive, the flames punching a hole in the night. A dozen men gather around each one. That's where I'll go for information after I establish my credibility. On the left, a dozen pup tents, crammed close together. If Cobra and his pals have the kid squirreled away in one of those private tents, I couldn't search them all before they caught me and kicked me off their property. But they said they couldn't seduce him here—others would object. No, the kid won't be here. But we need more information. Cobra said he knew something not on the flyer that will help him find this kid. What is it?

I got updated moments ago by a relay who said the snakes still don't have Mickey. We think. Nobody has seen a young boy leaving or entering this camp. That was good news. However, nobody has seen Cobra for hours. That's the bad news. Maybe the serpent men have given up for the night. I hope so.

I stride into their camp with a confidence I do not feel. All it takes is one of them recognizing I do not belong. I will shrug it off as a big joke and leave camp. They may chase me. Beat me. I can handle beatings. On the other hand, I look like them. Mostly. I'm counting heavily on this rubber tire granting my admission and concealing my identity. I'm glad to see I'm not quite as pale as expected, the makeup, sand, and darkness conspiring to conceal me. We overheard they are part of some national gathering, which means they may not know each other well by sight. Maybe. This could work. Or fail miserably.

I wish Alistair were with me. He could do this. He could pull this off. *Alistair.*

I stroll over to a snake man standing alone near the pup tent area, sucking down a liquid in a plastic tankard. Yup, it's beer. I need to make sure the fire barrel men witness this. I need to establish I *know* people here. I casually glance over at the fire barrels, nodding to an imaginary friend. A few curious looks find their way to me.

"Got change for a twenty?" I ask the man gruffly, and then clap him on the shoulder, laughing at my own joke as if it were hilarious.

He turns to me with an irritated, "Huh?"

I clap my hands together and make some inscrutable hand gesture. "I'm fucking with you. Beer cold?"

He looks at his mug and then me. "Yeah."

I laugh and nod, walk away, shaking my head and smiling to myself. I hope our brief exchange convinced anyone watching that I know this guy. In another twenty seconds, I'll be at one of the fire barrels. I've got four conversations ready to launch. Two not-too-subtle and two much more subtle. Let me see which one I need to whip out first.

"What's he doing?"

The snake man asking me nods in the direction where I came.

I look over my shoulder, stalling for a split second. I turn back and say, "He's drunk."

"Yeah, no shit he's drunk. He said he had to go piss."

I say, "He told me he forgot where he was going."

Two of the snakes laugh. The man who spoke first says, "Typical."

The guy who spoke to me has a big snake tire, a long one. I'm not sure what kind of snake it is, possibly a python. Maybe not. It's hard to see clearly across the flickering flames.

One of the women, long-haired and wearing a short shift exposing her midriff says, "I'll get him."

Python says, "Leave him. Stay."

Python puts his arm around her, claiming her, and she does not fight it.

As conversation resumes around our barrel, I am free for a moment to observe. There are women, I see now, three at our fire barrel and a few more at the one beyond. Two are making out with snake men and some just enjoy the party. A fairly steady stream of people travel from the main tent to the second fire barrel. No man here is without a snake, which means no guests are welcome. Every man is bald. No man wears a shirt, regardless of body type. I'm glad to see I'm not the only chunky guy, or else I'd stand out too much. I'm sucking in my gut as it is.

The conversation is nothing spectacular, the quiet chatter you'd expect around a fire, conversation about the day, people seen, and plans for later in the night. Some of them talk about going dancing. Some talk about ditching their snake tires and trying to get laid.

"I just got back," I say. "Hadn't heard the latest."

They look at me expectantly. One bears a curious expression on my face, as if he can't place me.

Shit.

"Where's Cobra," I say in a low voice, grinning while I speak.

Holy shit—so much for subtle. What happened? Why am I *not* subtle right now?

Because I'm obsessed. The recognition that this is an obsession flits over me—I've been obsessed all day. No time for this. Obsessed people aren't in control. Get in control.

"Dunno," Python says. "I assume out in the desert."

The desert? Why?

Don't act too interested.

Python says, "He said he was going out there after they delivered the runaway back to the rangers.

"Oh shit," I say and I'm sure the surprise on my face is genuine.

They found him? How did we not know?

Python skewers up his face. "Why do you care?"

My heart is pounding. "I don't. He said he had something for me is all."

Python says, "Well, he's gone. Headed to Center Camp an hour ago to return the kid and then he said he was gonna go chill out in the desert. Unwind."

Oh my god. *Oh my god.*

They're in the desert. *Right now.* I have to go. I have to stop this.

I turn away from the fire and start stumbling away, into the dark.

It's all I can do not to run.

He's in the desert.

The rapist took him into the desert.

The city disappears behind me but I'm not far away. I'm beyond the temple, beyond the last art installation—the chapel with stained glass windows made entirely from Chinese takeout condiment packets, hot mustard, duck, and soy.

I stop.

I listen.

I thought I saw people out this direction.

I'm still in what I call the "explorer zone." Many burners want to explore the desert at night, want the dizzying sensation of feeling lost out here without actually being lost. So they wander with flashlights, headlights, glow sticks or homemade fluorescents—bring a six-pack of beer and dance naked. No music required. When they grow bored or cold, or finish their booze, they return to the real party with a vaguely affected story to take home: one night, we left it all behind and communed with the desert.

Don't be that way. Don't be so goddamn cynical.

Let them have fun in the desert, to love it the way I do, the way we all do, the vastness, the loneliness, the unflinching hardness. People dance into the explorer zone to share their love for the hard earth, a landscape empathizing with dark nights and parched longings. Let them come and love. The playa makes you feel small, isolated, and connected to something greater.

Right now, I see tiny lights swirling, and they zigzag like fireflies, darting in and out of my peripheral vision. Glow sticks. I'll go to them. Ask if they saw two men pass this way. Well, one man and a boy. I run toward them and when I get close, I ask.

They've seen nothing.

Well, one of them might have seen people in the direction I originally pursued. Out that way.

I thank them.

I keep running.

Run faster.

I race ahead, though I barely know what that means. I could be running in place. I can't see. If Cobra brought Mickey this way, wouldn't he bring a flashlight? I'll catch it flicker on and off. I'll see some sign; I'm far enough out here that it's the only light to catch my eye. Plus, Cobra won't be alone. His three rapist pals will be with him. Groups make noise. I will find them.

I see nothing.

I hear nothing.

I have to find this kid. *I've got to find him.*

I'm obsessed with him. I know that now. I know why.

I can't keep running.

I stop, panting as quietly as I can, staring in every direction. I can see The Man, a grape-glowing toothpick, standing tall. How far away am I now? A mile? Not possible. When was the last time I ran this far?

I need x-ray vision, x-rays, something to pierce the darkness, to rip through the nothingness, to see something. *X, x, x, X, x, X* lining up in the crosshairs, a plus symbol on its side, +, +, +, scanning the horizon, scanning, *x, x, X,* +, *x,* +, *X, X, x,* +.

Stop it.

Okay, kings. If ever there were magic—if any of what you men believe is real—send it to me now. Please. I've served you for so long. Send me a message. I can't see my own feet out here. Point me in a direction. Am I near the orange netting? I have to be. This is a kid. Nobody deserves to be raped, especially not kids.

Nothing.

No sign.

Keep running.

After a few minutes, I see blackish-orange, the orange plastic netting. Where is the perimeter patrol? Where are those guys? I'd tell them. I'd definitely tell them and they could get other rangers out here. Why didn't I tell anyone? I thought someone would stop me, a relay, someone, and I'd tell them. But now I'm here and nobody knows it.

Here I am, right at the fence. Right here. Do I go over? Are they on this side? Would Cobra risk being spotted by the perimeter patrol? How far would he go?

Stop. Be still.

Deep breath.

God, is it cold out here.

C'mon, kings! No mystical insights on which direction to run?

Figures.

I cock my head to listen. If I could hear him cry out, if I could hear a weak, little cry.

Anything?

Nothing.

There are five of them out here! Why don't I hear noise?

The answer comes immediately: because the desert swallows everything. Even noise.

Okay. I'm going over. It's hard to climb because I'm big and it's not meant to support my weight, so I pull the fence down more than climb over it. I try to return it to the same condition I found it, while keeping an eye open for the perimeter rangers. Why isn't someone catching me? I always attract police and guards whenever I try something. Why not tonight? I don't see any fucking headlights!

Calm down. Scan the black horizon for anything, any trace of light or sound...

I'm running toward the Calico Mountains, still far on the horizon. I cannot see the mountains exactly, but I discern the jagged peaks perfectly. The mountains are the only thing out here that's not stars.

Oh god.

The stars.

The brilliant, immeasurable sky. It's ridiculous to say "the stars are out." That's like observing the ocean is wet. Looking up as I run, my eyes feel almost assaulted by the stars' true power, as if they had held back, twinkling like little Christmas lights for our amusement, but now—out here in the desert—they throw off our pedestrian expectations and blast the fucking light they are. My god! Some animal instinct demands they be counted, recognized and honored, fireballs dangling in space, but the instinct is instantly thwarted, the sheer immensity, the numbers, as if my brain both wants the total count and yet can't comprehend numbers that immense. The vastness fries my brain circuits.

Star light, star bright, first star I see tonight.

No! I can't play the Star Game.

I stop.

Anything? Any noise? Seriously, kings, *help me the fuck out.* I'm trying to do a good thing here, help out this kid. So lend me a fucking hand, will you?

Be patient, Vin. Be patient.

Maybe magic is real. Be patient.

Oh, please. Magic? Capital *M*, Magic?

What are you, ten? Don't be a child.

Don't freak out. Keep it together. Look up.

It's hard to fathom a concept like eternity, but staring above, I have a clue. An insight. I gape. The sheer rawness of it makes me want to assume nobody else in the history of everyone ever saw the stars. I must be the first to bear witness and understand how truly insignificant we are, how we are nothing in this insane, black eternity where almost nothing ever lives. If I could comprehend the sky above, I would spend the rest of my animal life screaming in terror at the sheer emptiness.

Oh, man. I feel dizzy.

The stars. The stars are out.

Fuck it.

At the top of my lungs, I scream. "Mickey! Miiiiiiiiiickeeeeeeeeeeeeey!"

He could be twelve feet away or a mile. I wouldn't know.

I cup my hands to my mouth and yell, "You're in daaaaaaangeeer!"

The stars jerk my eyes up again, and the impact is almost blinding. So bright. So many. I stare at pinpricks, light blazing from distances impossible to comprehend, and the same message bounces from each pinprick light in the sky as all around me: nothing.

Silence. *Silence.*

They never tell you in the word *silence*, the *l* is sharp, blood drawn at its peak. *L*—is a knife. Slicing off all those letters, who were probably taller at one point. Silence cut them off.

Kings. Seriously? *Nothing*?

Why am I out here like this, alone? This darkness.

It's like…it's like Alcatraz. The isolation chamber. I used to sit in there for hours, silent. Unmoving. As if I could trick my brain into ceasing its unending chatter. After I had sex with Perry in that cell, I was never alone. Whenever I visit, his ghost always accompanies me.

Damn it, think of this kid.

I stop running. I think. I think I was running. Am I running?

I cup my hands. "*Miiiiiiiickeeeeeeey.*"

The darkest dark I have ever known.

Perry is with me now, standing a few feet away. His face creases in hurt and resistance, his face on Pier 33, but he's wearing his golden king shirt, crackling gold light as if he is made from the constellations above. He moves, and a galaxy twitches. He was so brave, all night on Alcatraz. I need to be brave. I need faith like he had.

Silence.

Quit cutting me in half, silence.

Wait, is that noise? Do I hear sounds? Are those footsteps coming toward me?

I see Perry standing there, and oh…it's Liam, laughing in his sparkling crimson shirt, running at me from the darkness, the bulk of his big frame an unstoppable force, a powerhouse with a big thick head and goofy brown eyes, as he plows through pitch black—no wait. Nobody's there. It's…it's so dark. My eyes play tricks on me. The sound I heard was nothing but the wind.

The wind.

Oh shit. *It's the wind.*

It gathers force, growing around me, pelting me with tiny little ice crystals, cold sand, sssssssssssssssand, a never ending supply of *sssssssssssssssssssssssssssssssss* in sssssssssssssaaaaaaaand, because the letters are without count, without end, like the stars above. If we counted the sand we'd understand the stars.

Be quiet, brain!

Other kings approach me in the darkness, their shirts ablaze, and I am too ashamed to meet their eyes, to gaze into their loving faces, because they possessed the courage to cross over, and I do not. I clench my eyes because the wind berates me, yelling, like a thousand screaming *v*'s, jagged and pointing, sticking into my skin, calling me a liar, a *fucking liar.*

I cough. Put my hand over my mouth.

How can I blame Alistair for hiding his real name when I don't like mine either?

Everything's spinning, the letters, the sparkling colors, the *v*'s, the men standing around me, a thousand million stars swirling in sand.

It's getting worse.

I put my hands over my face.

I can't breathe.

I can't tell if I'm real anymore. Am I real? I wave my hands in front of my damned face. Wait, are my eyes even open?

No, don't open your eyes!

The desert wind screams, pelting me with *v*'s and *x*'s and other letters too, razor sharp *o*'s and steely *l*'s, cutting me like knives. I can't see anything. This really hurts my skin. Oh, shit. *A dust storm.* I'm trapped in a dust storm and nobody knows I'm here, alone in the desert. The last light I saw traveled millions of miles to silently witness me.

I've failed.

I've failed Mickey.

I bury my face in the crook over my arm, covering my eyes and mouth. Sand at this speed could do serious damage to my eyes. My eyes!

Here comes Perry, sparking gold. Rance in orange, adjusting his cuff links. Jamie wears translucent yellow, and Peter laughs in his peacock blue—the most beautiful colored shirt I had ever seen. Peter laughs with all his big teeth. I miss him. A man so strong he never cried in his whole life. Mai strolls out of the darkness in sparkling hunter green, a cross look on his face, and he says, "Well, shit."

Seeing them gathered so near makes me dizzy.

I'm still in love with them. All of them.

The wind screeches around me, screaming my true name.

Something feels funny.

I feel faloopy.

I might be falling over, maybe not.

A hard thud convinces me I was right, that sensation of not being vertical was real. I'm coughing out sand, absolutely delighted. I thought maybe I was a ghost, the world is a ghost, the sky, ghostly. As I lie on my stomach, hands covering my face while the wind rips me to shreds, it's a comfort to know *something* out here is real. I hear the stars bellowing their powerful names. Capital Reality, small reality, what does it matter? Sssssssssand. Endlesssssssss sssssssssssssssssand. The *v*'s attacking me are real.

Yes, I know. I know I'm not Vin Vanbly. Vvvvvvvvvvvvvin!

Protecting my face with my hands is pointless. I'm coated in sand. I'm being pelted by tiny chips of mountain. A mountain is crushing me.

I roll over onto my back. After a few moments, I remove my hands.

It's safe again.

The wind is gone.

I wipe the thick layer of sand from my face, trying to clear my eyes. My fingers remain gloved in pure alkaline powder, so it's hard to tell if I'm successful.

My eyes keep blinking, trying to cast off sand, *sssssssand*, but in between the fluttering, I stare into the billion blinking stars. What are your names? Please tell me again.

The stars.

I feel so heavy.

So sleepy.

The universe is squeezing into me, and I'm already so cold.

THIRTEEN

The universe. It's so big.

A million gold-flecked stars amidst the green-cinnamon light waves orbiting the impenetrable black circle of—why does my jaw hurt? Black circle? Green light waves? This...this isn't the universe. It's...eyes. I'm opening my eyes into his wide-eyed, terrified gaze. His gorgeous hazel eyes.

It's John.

The kiss ends.

We were kissing?

John's lips withdraw from mine and the whole world spins around me, light, elbows jostling. Noise, too. His eyes stare into mine.

"He's awake," a woman yells. "He's okay."

They have him. I don't know what these words mean, or where they come from, but they echo inside my throbbing skull. They have him.

I hear general expressions of relief.

John jumps back, wipes his lips.

We continue to make surprised eye contact.

Alistair—*he's John now*—rises from crouched to standing, playa dust coating his jeans, his whole body. Shirtless. Has he been rolling around in the desert? How did he get here?

Where is here?

Holy crap. John *kissed* me.

A woman rises with him, short brown hair, shaved into a mohawk. She balks with open surprise.

"You kissed him," she says. "And he woke up."

John says softly, "No."

"Yes," she says, her surprise stronger and more forceful. "That's exactly what happened. We all saw it."

All?

Who is—oh. There's a small crowd. Eight or ten people. A man, late fifties, leans down and stares into my face. His gray and white hair dangles over my forehead, grazing me. He says, "Stay with me, buddy. Stay with me."

I don't want this guy staring into my eyes. I don't know him.

Where am I?

I want to sit up, but hands, lots of hands, press me back down.

Where's the sun? Over that way—just about to leap over the horizon.

The dangling hair man says, "Stay with me." He clutches my cheeks. "Do you know your name?"

What happened with John? How did John get here?

I was in the desert last night.

The mohawk woman says louder, "We *all* saw it. He woke him up with a kiss."

"Do you know your name?" The gray-haired man repeats this forcefully, as if I were in trouble.

"Fa-tu-wah," I say.

The man says, "Fatuwah?"

I cough. I had attempted to say "far too well." My throat feels like sand.

I have to sit up. Cough. Get this shit out of my lungs. I don't remember what happened.

"Stay with me."

He tries to push me back down. I push him away with my hand.

"Sit." I croak out the word.

Mohawk Woman says, "Everyone saw it. You *kissed* him and he woke up."

John glances at her, as if he wants to argue the point.

Instead, he takes off running.

What the fuck is happening?

My caretaker keeps saying, "Easy, easy." I wish he would back away, because his hair smells disgusting, and it's making me nauseated. How long have I been asleep? Where the hell am I?

The Man.

Find *The Man*.

There he is.

The mayor of Black Rock City is surprisingly close. Well, far enough away, but I'm in the explorer zone, near the art installations. I was much farther out last night. Did I cross the orange fence, or did I imagine that?

Mohawk Woman turns her attention to me with the same blinking surprise, her upper body covered in a purple afghan. She turns to the others. "We all saw it. He *kissed* him."

A black man in a top hat, watching John's retreat, says, "Dude can book."

"He woke up, yes," says a man in a kimono. He's next to a woman wearing a matching robe. White girl with long dreadlocks. "Maybe it wasn't the kiss."

"It was *the kiss*," Mohawk Woman says, growing almost defiant. "For ten minutes, we've been trying to revive this guy. We talked to him, slapped his cheeks, poured water into his mouth. You two arrived right after my boyfriend slapped him hard. The sleeping guy rolled onto his side and yakked, right there."

She points to the spot.

Ew. Gross.

"For *ten minutes*," she says. "We weren't the first on the scene. The guy who ran was already here. We saw him dragging this guy through the desert by his legs, toward the city. Look at that trail. He dragged this guy for a long ways. He said he couldn't wake him either."

Now that she mentions it, I notice my back is incredibly scratchy and sore.

"Okay," I hear someone say.

I don't like this. I don't like people talking about me. I turn over onto my knees and cough more, emptying my lungs. I wish she would let this *kiss* thing drop.

Mohawk Woman says, "Those two arrived next."

I glance to the side to see her pointing at the couple wearing colorful, flimsy kimonos.

The kimono girl with dreads says, "It's true. We couldn't wake him. We sent a friend for the rangers."

Shit. *Rangers?*

"He just blacked out," Kimono Man says. "Probably partied too hard and passed out drunk."

"We got here next," Mohawk woman says, pointing to her boyfriend.

I attempt to stand. The long-haired man tries to force me back down. I won't let him. He keeps telling me to take it easy, and I want to punch him. I'm furious with him, making him the target of my rage because I don't understand what has happened.

Ow. Why does one of my nipples hurt? Why am I wearing a shirt two sizes too small for me? This isn't my shirt. This is Alistair's shirt. No, *John's.*

Top Hat says, "Okay, so he awoke while being kissed. Correlation does not mean causality."

A man in banana-yellow longboard shorts turns to him and says, "Scientist?"

Top Hat says, "Physicist."

Banana Shorts offers his fist to bump and says, "Sweet."

Mohawk Woman throws her purple afghan to the ground. She says, "Unbelievable! We were all standing here. He kissed him! The dude woke up. We saw it! It's like a fairy tale!"

I don't want to hear any more of this.

Rangers are coming.

I stand and take off running—galloping more likely—in the same direction Alistair ran, though he's long since disappeared from view. Oh, god, *my back!* Agony! Distract from pain. So many people are out now, sunrise worshippers ready to catch the early show, and late night revelers waiting for the official sunrise to end their night. People will provide cover. I run straight to the biggest crowd, standing near Lotus Land.

I hear surprised yelps behind me.

My back feels raw, so I try to outrun this ripped-to-shreds feeling. If it's bloody back there, if I *think* it's bloody, oh god. I feel vomit rising. I feel bad about leaving my spew behind, and I should have thanked them for their efforts to revive me, but *what the fucking hell happened to me and why did John's kiss awaken me?*

I remember asking for king magic last night but—that was for Mickey, not me. If the Found Ones consider this a gift, they are painfully inept. You fuckers. *Mickey.* You were supposed to protect Mickey! Oh, god. I failed him, too. Another person I've let down in the world because I'm me.

I hate being me.

My brain is a mess.

My back feels like gravel in blood.

Is anyone chasing me?

I thought I'd heard footsteps behind me, and maybe I did, but they're not growing stronger, and I don't feel the presence of bodies near. I don't think I'm being chased, but I cannot stop until I'm near other people.

I don't feel like barfing anymore. Okay. Stop.

I stop under a lotus flower, stop and wheeze, attempting to breathe life back into these lungs. How could I run with all this gunk in my lungs? I feel like I swallowed a handful of sand and—delighted by its grainy deliciousness—went back for seconds.

My back is agony. I'm sure it's bloody and raw. Sand embedded in blood, all sticky—

Oh god.

I move a few feet away from the sculpture. *Here it comes.*

I barf.

While panting out the last of it, I look behind me.

Yup I was chased, at least part of the way.

At some point, Banana Shorts, my pursuer, gave up. I see him returning to the small crowd assembled around my first vomit. I'm sure he could have caught me. He's younger and in better shape. I see Top Hat pointing my way, and Yellow Shorts glances over his shoulder.

That's my cue.

I'm too far away for him to catch me, but I run hard anyway, straight to the mayor of Black Rock City, like a child dashing to his beloved parent to complain of sibling injury. A sister. I would have liked a sister.

I push hard, knowing once I reach the front of the lighthouse base, I can enter the city on any degree street, and they will never be able to guess where I am. I'll be safe.

Rats do not like being exposed in broad daylight.

I arrive at my tent. I need to think. Do I try to find John? What the fuck happened? How soon can I get a Mickey update? Where are the relays?

I've got to check in—shit. *Someone's inside my tent.*

The serpent men? Or is this a thief? People get robbed here. I haven't been, but I know it happens.

I try to sound in command as I say, "Feel like coming out?"

My throat is scratchy, my back feels like bloody sandpaper, and my legs are wobbly. I'm not much ready for a fight. What could I do, anyway? Vomit on the thief? I'm out of juice. Right now, my strongest defense mechanism is dry heaves.

John's head pops through the flap. My tent is tall enough to stand in, comfortably, so he leaps out standing up, thrashing through the nylon, unnecessarily rough on the fabric. I feel a protective pang regarding my stuff as I glance inside, but I instruct myself not to care. I wouldn't leave anything in the tent I wasn't okay with having stolen. Although, I guess I left fifty thousand dollars in gold coins behind. Perhaps not so smart.

"Yes," John says in a clenched voice. "I just finished rifling through everything. I'm trying to understand what kind of game this is, what you're doing."

"You've been crying."

"Yes, I've been crying. Last night was the scariest fucking night of my life. You put me through hell."

"I don't understand."

His voice cracks as he says, "Please, man. *Please* stop fucking with me."

I put my finger tips to my forehead. I don't know if I can have this conversation. I'm tired. Sore. I should be trying to find Mickey.

"This note," he says, thrusting the folded paper at me.

I take it and review the words. Everything in me sags. "I can't do this fight today. I can't."

He glowers. "*Pizza, soup,* and *Caprese salad*. What do they represent? Are there other camps involved? Are these locations?"

"These are my three best uses for mozzarella."

"Nothing more?"

"Nothing more."

I don't know why I didn't see this until now, but he looks as exhausted and fragile as I feel. Dark bruises, like hammocks, are tucked under his eyes. Sand clings to his hair and naked chest. He looks terrible.

He says, "I don't know how to believe you. I don't know if this is a note about cheese, or a secret message. I'm so fucked up."

When I speak, my voice is quieter than normal. It's all I have left inside me. "I know. When you dance like you and I've been dancing, it's hard to know when the music stops."

The fury leaves his face. "I'm so confused. So fucking tired. Last night terrified me. I pissed myself. Look at my shorts. See all the sand stuck to me? That's because of the piss. I pissed myself three separate times."

"I see. *Wait*." My face crinkles in surprise. *He has no English accent.*

"Yes," he says, defeated. "I'm not English. I'm from Kansas. But please, *please* tell me the truth about last night. I'm so scared and freaked out. *Please* tell the truth."

Wait, wait, *wait*. My whole body tingles awake. Something happened to him. Wake up, Vin. He abandoned his English persona. This is big.

"John, I will tell the truth. I promise. I will tell you anything within my power to answer."

Liar.

I will not reveal his path to his kingship. As exhausted as I feel right now, a spark reignites inside me. *Our dance isn't finished.*

"What happened last night, Vin?"

No more games with questions. This one, I answer.

While the city awakens around us—the daddy longlegs spider stretches each wispy appendage forward—I explain. Helena's seduction at the Robot Zamp party. Getting a rubber tire snake. As I tell the tale, I watch him closely, waking up to my responsibilities as his guide. I'm responsible for this man. He's mine to love with all my love. When I explain how Cobra took the boy into the desert—meeting the other rapists out there, I'm sure—he interrupts me.

In a tired voice, he announces, "They played you."

"I don't—I don't think so."

Oh god. What if he's right?

"Definitely. Classic misdirect. Got you to race into the desert while the kid was somewhere else."

His whole face collapses into something a defeated resignation. "*If* you're telling the truth. I can't tell anymore. Maybe your running into the desert was a trick to lure me out there."

The brutal morning sun is unkind to us both, all our dust-creased wrinkles and physical defects are magnified in this revealing light. He's sweating already, and I suppose I am too. I touch my head and remember I'm bald now, which I'd forgotten. I need to get some sunscreen on my head.

Oh shit. Fuck.

I know the way through this. I know exactly what must be done.

Fuck. Knowing what to do and wanting to do it are not the same thing.

"John, the only way I know—"

This makes him cry. "How did you know my name?"

"John," I say again, quieter. "The only way to navigate something like this is to rebuild honesty. I'm going to tell you something from my childhood. Something horrible for me to remember. I spend so much effort trying to forget this memory, yet I never can. Okay?"

John wipes his face. "Okay."

Oh god. Oh god. I'm going to tell this.

Breathe.

I feel so raw I might burst into tears at any second.

"Fewer than five people in the world know this story. If you listen and then say 'bullshit,' it will hurt me a lot. You have to be gentle with me right now."

I can't quite read his expression. Something powerful unraveled him last night. This is a different man. He is changed. I see it.

He says, "Go on."

"When I was a kid, ten years old, I lived in a foster home, a nasty one. The place was owned by this man named Billy. Billy pretended to be married to the lady next door, and they would hang out at her house as if they were a family. It's how they got foster kids."

Take a deep breath. Say it.

"He and his friends raped. They'd have a poker night and get a kid. They tried to get me, but I hid in the basement with the rats. Billy feared the rats as much as anyone, but he used them to scare the kids into obedience. The first time he showed me the rats, he promised to throw me down the stairs unless I played nicer. I wrenched my arm free and raced down into the darkness. I spent the next three days and nights down there until Billy opened the door to find me sitting on the stairs, covered in rat bites."

Alistair's expression does not change, the wariness, but I see two tears come out. I don't know if he's aware of their presence. He's been crying a lot. What's two more?

"Billy and his rapist pals never got me."

Careful with the truth, Vin. Careful with the words. Don't reveal too much. Keep the story about Billy's basement. Nothing else.

"How long did you live there?"

"I ran away when I was eleven. I lived on the streets and in the Chicago sewers. I got caught a few times and put back into foster care or juvie. No place could hold me long. I always escaped. During the summer, when the sewers stank, I used to sleep under cars. To make sure they didn't start suddenly and drive over me, I got very skilled at breaking into cars, opening hoods, and disconnecting necessary plugs. But that's not.... I'm stalling because I don't like talking about Billy."

I look around. I don't want to be overheard. I hate this. I would never tell this story except we've reached such a dangerous place, he and I.

"During my year at Billy's house, the other foster kids were terrified of me. I got a reputation and even a nickname. In fact, Billy would show me to the new kids. There I was, sitting in the dark on those basement stairs. Billy would say, 'This is what happens to kids who refuse.' I was good advertising for them. It's my fault other kids got raped. One time, I tried to persuade an older boy to stay in the basement with me. Keep him safe from Billy and the rapists, but the other kid couldn't handle the rats. He freaked out and ran up the stairs. I failed that time, too."

"Jesus," he says, covering his face with his hands. "Why are you telling me this?"

Don't throw up. Don't throw up.

"John, yesterday I got obsessed trying to prevent Mickey from being raped. I'm sure it's too late. I failed him the way I failed the kids at Billy's house. But I had to try. I swear on Billy's basement, this runaway situation is *not* part of your King Weekend."

"How old were you?" he says, choking out the words. "With the rats?"

"Ten."

This makes him cry harder.

I hate when people cry for me. I hate that pathetic, scared kid covered in rat bites. I hate his weakness. I feel myself clenching, followed by an intense desperation to get away. Run! *Run away.* No. Calm down. Something is unfolding here, supposed to happen. Don't run.

"You were ten," he says. "You were a *child.*"

I hate this.

The softness in me shrivels, and I feel anger rising. That's it. This Billy conversation is over.

He cries harder and drops to his knees. I know he needs to be held, but I don't want to do it, not if he's crying for me. He cries harder. He's bawling.

Wait. Something shifted in him—this isn't about me, not anymore. Okay. I can do this. I kneel and wrap my arms *almost* around him, not touching, just letting him sense me until I gradually close in, allowing my flesh to contact his. He falls against me with all his weight. He sobs in unrelenting howls, enough to attract the attention of wandering burners.

Two people stop.

"He's okay," I say. "Having a good cry."

I'm not sure I'm all that convincing.

I cradle him on the desert floor. His broken posture, his rough appearance. Everything suggests a dying man.

"I dared them to rape him," he says in a hoarse, broken whisper.

I say nothing. I squeeze him.

We stay like this for a while, until he wipes his eyes and pulls himself into a sitting position. I adjust myself so I'm behind him, arms around his waist. I put my head on his shoulder. A dozen people wander by, ignoring us, creating small dust clouds as they pass. Through touch, I feel him tremble.

He says, "We have to find Mickey."

I inhale deeply, breathing the sweaty, tangy scent of him.

It's John.

I breathe the scent of King John.

FOURTEEN

"**M**ickey may have been found already. I've been gone all night and had no updates."

"He's still missing," John says. "There was a relay waiting at your tent when I arrived. The one named Ko Ko. I sent him away, told him you were safe. I told him to update the others and asked him to come back in thirty minutes, preferably with a first-aid kit. Bandages. Aspirin."

"I've got Advil in the tent."

The dull throbbing pain up and down my back pulses, like a.... I don't know what it's like. I've never felt anything like this. My back feels wet and sticky and hot. I want to take off this confining shirt, but I'm afraid it's stuck to raw skin. If it's stuck, I'll vomit again. I feel like someone threw a pizza against my back, fresh from the oven, and the cheese has melted against me. Oh god. Don't think that.

Face it, I'm thinking about my back pain as a diversion to ignore the hard truth of what I just heard.

They haven't found Mickey.

I'm not sure if it's my heart that sinks, or my stomach, but something inside me trips over and over, down the basement stairs. Over and over, I keep failing. My eyes fill with tears. He's sixteen. He's a kid. I really do belong down in the sewers.

John says, "I know how to find him. I got an idea. When we kissed."

I drag myself back to listening. "Say that again?"

"When we kissed. I got an idea."

We haven't even discussed the kiss. His night in the desert. What happened to him out there, to make him drop the Alistair act?

"John, what happened—"

"Wait. No. Do you swear on Billy's basement you had nothing to do with what happened in the desert? The dogs? The music?"

"I—I swear."

My voice is thick. I can't imagine a more vile swear than to swear by Billy's name. Billy's rape house. I know I just swore by it, but to hear the words in someone else's mouth makes me sick. I want to vomit again.

John says, "I will tell you everything about the desert. Later. First, we have to get Mickey back from Cobra."

"I thought you said he was still missing."

"I think Cobra and his friends already have him. Based on what you told me, I'm sure they already had him last night when they sent you into the desert. Classic misdirect by the defense. You can't send your opponent just anywhere—you have to lead him far from any real discovery. Why send you into the desert? Because they knew he wasn't out there. Kept you out of the way."

"But the whole camp wasn't in on it. Why would they lie?"

"why not? Early in the day, Cobra told his camp mates that your kings were Christian missionaries trying to stir up trouble. He discredited whatever message you—or you kings—brought. He obviously told his camp mates last night to send you into the desert if you came around. His Snake Camp friends didn't have to know Cobra's real intention to lie to you."

Was I really manipulated that way? Seems plausible when John says it. I was obsessed with finding him. I did some stupid stuff.

"So, where is he?"

"I don't know. But I have a guess why we couldn't find him yesterday. We were looking for the wrong person. We were looking for a missing boy."

From his sitting position, John pivots his body around to face me.

We are distracted by barking and hissing.

Across the street, the space cats theme camp welcomes visitors from other planets, offering cream in bowls and shots of rum. A dog, well, a man costumed as a dog, black leather jockstrap, tail included, growls at the space cats. They hiss at him, baring sharp claws, yelling things as the dog's master tugs at the pup's leash. Where's Animal Control when you need them?

"That picture of him was old, right? Maybe two or three years old?"

"Maybe."

"So when the police want a picture of your runaway kid to use for flyers, they ask for a recent photo."

"Okay."

"Why didn't his parents use a more recent photo? Why? Because they don't have any. Why not? Well, maybe they got lazy with the camera and stopped taking pictures. His friends must have taken more recent photos with their cell phones. So, why no recent photo? Maybe they stopped taking photos because they didn't like who he was becoming."

"Becoming?"

"What if Mickey is transgender? We've been seeking a sixteen-year-old boy. What if—"

"He appears more like a *girl*."

"Yes."

A girl! I never—it never dawned on me. Goes to show my own biases and limitations.

John says, "If he started wearing makeup, or acting more feminine, ashamed parents wouldn't photograph him, nor would they want an accurate photo of their transgender kid on a flyer."

"But an old photo won't help—"

John says, "I know. Maybe they don't care about finding him."

We both let those words sink in.

Mickey's parents don't want him? Don't care if he's found? This story keeps getting worse. John's theory might be correct, yet it's only a theory.

John says, "Yesterday morning, Cobra said he had an advantage to finding this kid—something not on the flyer. I bet this was it. He knew to look for a girl. Your kings watching Snake Camp never saw Mickey because they were looking for a boy."

"It's possible."

John says, "I know how we find this runaway and free him from the serpents."

"You don't know for sure that Cobra's men have him."

"I know." He is quiet. "I *know*. I feel it. Don't you?"

I look inside myself to see if I know something, if this is a thing I know without knowing how. I'm so tired. My back is sticky and sore. I can't remember what I know or don't know. But I remember the first thought when I came to consciousness after this morning's kiss. *They have him.*

I failed. He got raped.

"Vin, don't cry. I could be wrong. We're going to Snake Camp to confirm it."

"Okay," I say, wiping my eyes. "Let's go."

"No," John says. "We're going to wait here for your relay to return with the first-aid kit. Get your back addressed. Clean ourselves. We can't let them see us this battered. We go into court strong."

"Court?"

"Yes," John says. "I'm a lot of things, Vin. A liar. A coward. A quitter, it turns out. But I'm a damn good lawyer. We're not going in unprepared."

John and I limp into my tent. In the tossed mess, he searches for clean clothes to wear, and I search for a pencil and paper. I have a note to pass along to the relay when he returns. While John's back is turned, I scribble the words in all caps.

THE KINGING IS BACK ON.

Snake Camp is decidedly less impressive in full daylight. The fire barrels are big, ugly cylinders, stained black with smoke and tar. Fire made them special. Without the dancing, jagged light, they are empty, cavernous mouths, begging for purpose, for some meaning to their gaping existence. The earth is littered with plastic cups. I see one serpent man stumbling around, picking them up. One of the camp's neighbors chews him out while he ignores her.

"Clean up your damn moop!" she yells. "Do you not understand the concept of leave no trace?"

We stand at their camp entrance, not daring to go farther.

Two of the serpent men see us, consult with each other, and move briskly into the big tent. A moment later, two different men emerge. Definitely not the man, Python, who said Cobra was in the desert. I wanted to see him. I wanted to look in his eyes and determine if he intentionally misled me.

As they clomp toward us, I see one of the men is Green Snake. "You're a fucking *idiot*, you dumb Arab."

I know he's addressing me because Alistair does not wear his jubba and keffiyeh.

Green Snake laughs. "Heard you raced off last night into the desert."

I guess I got my answer.

The other snake man says, "So fucking gullible."

John says, "Don't say anything, Vin. Not a word. Guys, we want to talk to the guy wearing the Cobra snake tire. Is he here?"

"Fuck off."

"We want to make a deal."

"Fuck *off*."

John pulls out a sack—a familiar sack.

Wait! No!

He says, "I promised him nine thousand dollars in gold coins."

I'm so beside myself with horror, I can barely think. "You can't!"

John ignores me, pulling open the drawstring and fishing inside, extracting three coins and displaying them. "Check it out. It's real gold from the Roman empire. Each one is worth roughly three thousand dollars."

"John, I'm begging you!" My voice is shrill.

Green Snake says, "Give them to me. I'll see that he gets them."

John says, "That's not going to happen."

I never saw John pocket the sack of gold coins from my tent. When? How? I reach for it and he moves it out of my grasp, puts up a hand to stop me.

One of the men reaches out, saying, "Lemme see."

John says, "Not a chance. Look at them in my palm. Photograph it with your cell phone. Each coin is worth three thousand dollars."

He jiggles the sack and the coins make a believable, satisfying clang.

The rapists can't walk away from this making a profit!

When I speak, my voice is low. "John, please. I *beg* you. Don't reward them with money. Don't give this to them."

John says, "Tell Cobra to meet us at The Man in an hour and to bring Mickey. I'll bring the gold coins."

Green Snake looks uneasily at his camp mate. "Cobra turned that kid over to the rangers yesterday."

The other snake man says, "Why do you want him? Who are you people?"

John says, "Too bad. Seeing Mickey Flynn was the only acceptable proof for collecting your reward. Plus, I had a new deal. Fifty thousand dollars in gold coins to hand the runaway over to us."

"John!" I cry out his name as if I were stabbed. I think I was. "*Please!*"

Green Snake stares at John hard.

They still have him. John was right!

The other snake man laughs. I have no idea what his snake is. It's albino white with blue stripes. "You're crazy. Go the fuck away."

He turns away.

Green Snake says in a quiet voice, "How do we know these coins are legit?"

"My companion has paperwork proving their authenticity."

Green Snake says, "We don't have the kid."

John says, "I think you do. Meet us at The Man in an hour. Bring Mickey or there's no deal. No reward."

John turns away and, with a nudge, expects me to do the same.

"No," I say, one final protest. I turn toward Green Snake. "We'll get the rangers!"

John spins around to face him. "No we won't. Ignore him. I promise you we will not involve rangers. If we did, we'd look as monstrous as you, buying a kid for fifty thousand dollars. No rangers. Bring the kid in one hour to make the trade."

Green Snake crosses his arms.

John leads me away by the elbow. "Vin, I need a bunch of your crew to help me with this. We need a Hacky Sack. I need a small group of five men, young guys—like your relays—for what I'm planning."

I can't believe this. We aren't out of earshot when I jerk my arm free. "What the fuck! What are you doing?"

John says evenly, "The smart thing. Settling out of court."

Though noon remains two hours away, the sun burns as if it does not fucking care, reserving nothing to escalate during the midday hour. It's so fucking hot. We swelter with every step as we approach The Man. He is our judge and jury, presiding over today's exchange. I can't tell if I'm sweating in terror or from the heat. Salty beads trickle down the bandages on my back. John rewrapped them in his tent, after our exchange at Snake Camp, using materials from his own first-aid kit. He'd wanted his own clothes, and we had an hour to kill.

When I asked him how my back got all scratched up, he said, "When I couldn't wake you up, I dragged you across the desert."

"How far?"

"A mile, I'm guessing."

I did not ask further questions. He will tell me when he's ready. I'd probably ask more, but I'm so obsessed with getting Mickey away from these men, I can't focus on anything else.

Five relays play Hacky Sack near the lighthouse base supporting The Man. I recognize three of them. I met Reggie and Ko Ko in Center Camp yesterday. I know one of the other three as a cheese note relay, but I don't know his name. The remaining two are unfamiliar to me. They have assumed the position John requested. As we draw near, none of them acknowledge they know us. John said to assume we are being watched.

"Are you okay?"

"No," I say. "I'm nervous. I want to throw up. Please don't give them the gold coins."

"I'm not used to seeing you nervous, Vin. You were incredibly calm yesterday for all those hours we searched."

"Yesterday was different. I hadn't failed yet. I still had hope. Today, I have to look my failure in the face. I have to apologize for letting him get raped."

"You didn't fail him, Vin." John stops walking and takes my hand. "I failed him. You told me we had to find him *together* and you were right. I quit because I was terrified to believe you. I couldn't take responsibility. But I'm taking responsibility now. I failed *him*. I failed *you*."

The grief between us is palpable, like the heat, it's a presence engulfing us, searing this pain onto our hearts. We could each argue our personal responsibility for the next hour, using all the hot air around us to create more hot air, but I see our nemeses approaching.

I squeeze his hand and say, "Here they come."

The serpent men appear as badass as you could imagine, kicking up dust with their black boots, walking bare-chested across the desert. They wear their snake tubes around their necks. One snake sticks up. It's Cobra. Only two of his companions are with him. Green Snake and Fleshy Snake. Where is the fourth one, Coral Snake?

John and I remain silent. He lets go of my hand.

I'm not sure I can watch this. When we were alone, I protested bartering the gold coins. He said, "Vin, I ask you to trust me the way you asked me to trust you."

I will.

I will trust him.

I must do whatever I can to repair the damage between us. That doesn't mean I can't also feel sick to my stomach. Please, *please* don't give fifty thousand dollars to rapists.

They arrive in a cloud of dust, like a chariot that dissipates around them.

Cobra nods at me. "Shaved your head. I'm flattered you want to join us. But I decline your membership application."

The other two serpent men snicker.

Cobra says, "Was the desert cold last night?"

I say nothing while his two companions laugh outright.

He snickers. "I almost wish I had been there to see it. Chubby little sheep goes squealing into the night."

John says, "Vin, don't say anything. We're here to make a deal."

The Hacky Sack rolls to a stop between John and I.

John picks it up and tosses it back to Reggie. He says, "Hey, do you guys mind taking your game farther away?"

Reggie says, "Yeah, we do. We were here first. You guys move."

Cobra says, "Just fucking move, you little bitch."

Reggie says, "Nice attitude for the playa."

John holds up his hand. "Never mind, never mind. We're fine."

Cobra says, "Let's go over there. Away."

John says, "No. This won't take long. Do you have Mickey? Or are you wasting our time?"

I resist the urge to look behind me at the Hacky Sack players. I know their role in all this, and I must not give away a single clue.

Cobra says, "Let me see these gold coins."

John takes the bag from his cargo shorts pocket and hands it to Cobra.

Cobra opens it and peers inside. Shakes it. He offers the bag to Fleshy Snake on his left, who sticks in his fingers and pulls out a coin. Odd. Why didn't Cobra fish one out himself? Cobra offers Green Snake the same opportunity, but Cobra immediately takes the coin from Green Snake. Inspects it. Tries to scrape off the gold paint he believes he will find. Green Snake pulls out another coin.

I'm going to be sick. How can John negotiate with these guys?

"Any proof these are real?"

John turns to me and says, "Show them."

John warned me this moment would come. I pull up my jubba's underside and find the secret pocket. I rip it open from the inside and draw out the paperwork. With reluctance, I hand one of the pages to John, the page describing the coins and their authenticity.

Cobra says, "What's the other page?"

"Proof I paid for the coins legally. I'm not handing it over."

Cobra says, "Fair enough."

John hands over the sheet of paper. "This should prove the coins are authentic."

Cobra reads the paper while Fleshy Snake bites the coin.

"Tooth mark," he reports to Cobra. "That means it's real."

Green Snake says, "That's not a thing. That's just from the Underdog cartoon."

I want Mickey free from them, yes—anything—but I hate the idea of them profiting. I hate it. I'm sure they can all see it on my face.

After a moment, Cobra says, "What's to stop us from turning and taking off with your gold?"

"This," I say holding my piece of paper. "I'm still holding the proof of ownership. I'll report you to the rangers."

"Fair enough." Cobra laughs as he speaks. "And why exactly did you bring fifty thousand dollars in gold coins to Burning Man?"

John says, "Not your business. The exchange is for Mickey Flynn. Not information. We've seen no proof you have him."

The Hacky Sack crowd behind us explodes in a cheer.

Cobra says, "We'll tell you where to find him."

John says, "Nope. You bring him right here, right now. I know he's near. You know it. So quit fucking around."

Cobra says, "Relax, guy. We're still negotiating."

John says, "No, we're not. Bring Mickey to us."

Cobra crosses his arms. "What if we bring you Mickey, and he doesn't want to go with you? You gonna force this kid to go because you bought him?"

"Let's let Mickey decide," John says. "He might be eager to have another option besides your camp."

"He might," Cobra says. "My question was whether you'll force him against his will. You didn't answer."

John says, "If he doesn't want to go with us, we will all escort him to the rangers. Get Mickey now, or give back the gold coins. All of them, including the one Green Snake slid into his front shorts pocket with terrible, terrible subtlety."

Cobra laughs. "Okay, fine. You need to chill. Maybe get laid. Trust me. Best thing you can do at Burning Man is dump your load into a hot little hole. Maybe two or three times."

I wince. I'm going to be sick.

Cobra waves his arm over his head in a big *c'mere* gesture.

Fleshy Snake laughs, and says, "If you didn't pick up on that, he's talking about fucking your sixteen-year-old friend. We all took turns."

In a sharp voice, Cobra says, "*Hey.* Don't say anything specific."

A small bit of wind kicks dust up to our faces, and we cover our eyes for a moment. When the breeze fades, I stare across the open playa. I see men wearing tie-dyed sarongs and big floppy hats. More bikers cruise by us, leaving small dust wakes. I hear the megaphone of the whale watching tour—another school bus converted into mutant car. This one is an elaborate "Whale Watching" tour bus, and their host narrates facts about whales as they whiz across the playa. The sound is distorted, so I can't hear any words. I keep scanning the horizon. Don't see—there.

Two people walk directly toward us. A woman in a black leather skirt and a snake man. Probably Coral Snake. Oh, right, the skirt. Mickey. My heart pounds in my chest. *We failed you.* How could I possibly apologize for failing in this unforgiveable way? We let you get raped!

John says, "Is this Mickey?"

Cobra says, "She prefers Michelle."

As they approach, I wonder if I could ever have pictured her as a sixteen-year-old boy. She's got long legs, and wears torn, black hose, a popular style with some women here, a "fuck you" to conventional beauty standards. She wears a white blouse, more tube top than blouse, and a heavy black jacket totally impractical for this weather. Her long, brunette hair falls behind her, untamed. It's obvious this poor kid has been used hard.

I want to die. I failed to stop another rape.

John says, "You have to let us present our case to Mickey without interfering."

"Naw," Cobra says. "We don't."

"For fifty thousand dollars, you owe us *at least* giving Mickey—"

"Don't owe you crap," Cobra says. "Your money doesn't buy our silence. Nice try, though."

As Mickey draws closer to our group, I see that his angular face and accentuated features make him appear more sophisticated than his age betrays, more like a woman of twenty or twenty-one. As he—she—surveys us with haughty disdain, it's hard to remember she's a vulnerable teenager. His—her—eyes are unnaturally blue, some kind of enhancement with contacts, I'm guessing. She scowls at John and me, as though this entire transaction is an inconvenience to his plans.

Or rather, *her* plans. I have to respect her gender.

Cobra reaches out an arm and says, "Hi, babe."

Mickey curls into him and puts her hand on Cobra's naked chest, scratching gently with her nails.

"Doesn't she look fantastic?" Cobra asks us eagerly. "We found a camp to do his makeup."

Mickey, I failed you. I failed you!

John says, "Mickey, my name—"

"It's Michelle," she says. "Not Mickey. I'm not him."

John says, "Michelle, we worried—"

Cobra says, "Babe, they want you to go with them. Do you want to go with these guys?"

Michelle says, coldly, "No."

John says, "You don't have to be afraid of them."

"I'm not afraid," she says sharply. "They're hot, and you're lame. End of story."

Now, what? I assumed Mickey would be eager to get away. John asked to do the majority of the talking, but we both anticipated a smoother transition than this. Do I jump in?

John says, "Michelle, these guys are using you."

Michelle says, "Yeah, for sex. I know."

Coral Snake snickers. Apparently they succeeded at persuading him to join in.

Cobra turns to Michelle and she turns her head to face his.

"Babe," he says. "I don't love you."

"Good," Michelle says with relish. "Because I don't love you, either."

John says, "You're sixteen. You shouldn't have sex with these guys you don't know."

"I know what I'm doing," she says, looking squarely at John. "They aren't the first. I'm no virgin, you pinhead."

For the first time, I thought I heard her slur two words together. Drugs.

"Are you doing any drugs?"

Michelle offers me the hint of a smile when she says, "Some."

Green Snake says, "Ecstasy."

Cobra says, "What the holy fuck did I just tell Jim about shutting *the fuck up*? Jesus, man. Don't volunteer anything."

John turns to me. "Give Michelle some water."

Cobra says, "Don't. Michelle, I command you not to drink water."

She pushes away from him and says, "You don't get to boss me around. You're not the boss of me."

She walks my way. I hand her the canvas water bag.

"Well, you heard her," Cobra says. "She didn't obey my wishes. She makes up her own mind, and she doesn't want to come with you."

"She's sixteen," John says. "She says a lot of things."

How do we persuade her?

Michelle pauses with the canvas bag halfway to her dark maroon lips. "Fuck you, dickweed."

Cobra says, "You're right. Sixteen-year-olds can be unpredictable. That's why we recorded this."

He produces his cell phone, and with a few button taps, plays back a recording at full volume.

"*I, Mickey Flynn, promise I am indeed sixteen years old, and I want to have sex. With a bunch of these guys. I am into it. I am not coerced in any way. Here's proof. Mom, you can go fuck yourself, you self-righteous bitch. All I needed was one good reason to leave your shithole home. Dad, you're a complete loser. There. Anyone who knows me, knows I hate them both.*"

Cobra says, "Convenient, huh? You know, in case she changes her mind in a few weeks and decides to cry rape."

Michelle hands the water canvas back to me without making eye contact. "I won't cry rape. I wanted it."

"You were drugged," I say.

"I wanted it," she says. "Fuck you, Arab."

John asks, "Did you practice safe sex?"

Michelle crosses her arms. "None of your beeswax." She laughs. "I don't even know what beeswax is. Is that a real world? Wait, did I just way *word* or *world*?"

Cobra says, "I have another recording to play for you assholes."

He holds up the phone.

"*I, Mickey Flynn, god, do I really have to make another recording? This is so stupid. Okay, fine. Fine. I'll do it. I, Mickey Flynn, don't care if the guys don't use condoms. We decided on a don't ask, don't tell policy when it comes to sexual history and diseases. Ew, gross. I'm not saying that next part."*

Cobra turns it off and says, "Bases covered."

I'm going to vomit. They thought of everything.

I say, "You coerced her."

"Nobody co-nursed me, you dumb bear," she says. "I knew what I was doing. I wanted to forget."

Oh, Michelle, what happened to you? What do you want to forget?

Fleshy Snake—whose name Cobra revealed as Jim—says, "Hey, slut, you wanna go fuck some more?"

Michelle says, "Sure. I'm tired of you, though. Get some other dudes."

Cobra says, "Does it matter who fucks you?"

"No. Not much."

It hurts to hear her casual tone. This sounds like someone who knows sexual abuse. What can we do? We can't *force* her to come with us. Cobra and his crew have taken pains to cover themselves. How do we get her to the rangers?

"We done here?" she asks.

I look at John's face, and even he looks confused as to our next steps.

"But," John says, "you...what about sexually transmitted diseases? Aren't you worried about syphilis or HIV?"

"No," she says, tired of our conversation. "Can't worry about what you already got."

Cobra says, "Let's go, ba—wait. Wait. Already got what?"

Michelle looks bored. "The HIV. That's why I got kicked out from my folks' house. My parents found out I've got AIDS."

Nobody speaks, but all four serpent men pivot in the sand toward her, as if that would clarify their understanding.

John says, "Wait...are you HIV positive, or do you have AIDS?"

"The first one," she says. "I just found out. They said my viral load is high. Like me!"

She laughs.

None of us speak.

"Why isn't anyone laughing?" Michelle asks. "That was funny."

Finally, Cobra says, "No. No, you little cunt, *tell me* you didn't just say that. Tell me—"

Michelle pouts. "Oh, c'mon, baby. Don't ask, don't tell. You said we weren't going to talk about that stuff, just fuck."

Cobra bristles, his whole body somehow tightening or compacting with the same cold menace I saw in his eyes yesterday.

"Hang on," John says, stepping forward. "Hang on, Cobra. Let's get some more information first. Michelle, do you remember your T-cell count?"

"No," she says. "I don't care. Why should I care? I'm going to be dead in a year or two anyway."

"No, you're not," I say firmly. "That's not going to happen."

She shrugs. "I don't want to talk about this. I thought this place was a party."

Jim turns his head away. "Oh god."

Then, he vomits.

Coral Snake puts his hands over his face. He says, "This can't be happening."

Cobra says, "You fucking whore cunt. You *whore*! I'm gonna rip your—"

John says firmly, and loudly, "Stop! *Enough.*"

John's voice is so different from Alistair, who always wore a hint of doubt, a solicitousness I found difficult to swallow. John's voice is strong. I would imagine when he argues in open court, his timbre dominates.

John says, "You're going to do two things, Cobra. First of all, hand back the gold. All of it. Right now."

Cobra hasn't removed his murderous glare from Michelle, who—sensing a shift in affections—now stands behind me.

"*Cobra!*" John yells.

The man's head snaps to John. I would not want to be John right now, feeling the attentive rage.

Green Snake has been breathing in shallow breaths and not spoken since Michelle's revelation. Until now. "I will kill you, bitch. I will fucking kill you."

"Michelle, are you coming with us?" John doesn't look away as he speaks right at Cobra.

"Yes," she says, hesitant. "I guess so."

John says, "Great. Cobra, give us back the gold. One of the Hacky Sack men has been filming this entire exchange. Outside of Burning Man, I'm a lawyer. A good one. By selling us Michelle, you engaged in human trafficking which, depending on whether you're charged on a federal or state level, carries penalties similar to murder. You could end up in prison for the next twenty-five years, though any reasonable DA would recognize you as a small fish and make a deal for ten years."

Cobra doesn't appear to be listening.

"I'm going to kill you," he says, returning his gaze to Michelle.

She coos a soft response over my shoulder, but the words are unintelligible.

John says, "Excellent! Add death threats to the human trafficking, and we're back to twenty-five years for you and Green Snake. Fleshy Snake and Coral Snake will get only ten. Five, if they testify against you."

I say, "Fleshy Snake's name is Jim."

Jim speaks in a trembling voice. "We didn't do anything."

John turns his attention to him. "First off, you're in Nevada, which is not to your advantage. Prostitution is legal in this state, so they beefed up human trafficking laws to make sure fewer violations slipped through the cracks. Second, you each held a gold coin, which was payment. Do you honestly think you can deny you didn't understand money was exchanged for a human life? Men, your only chance to avoid human trafficking charges is for our Hacky Sack friend to keep filming, and for you to hand back the gold coins. Do it *now*."

He was never going to let the rapists walk away with that gold. John! King John!

Cobra chokes the neck on the bag of gold coins.

John yells, "Right now!"

Cobra's head turns slowly to John, pronouncing a death sentence with his eyes.

In his strong, calm tone, John says, "A good lawyer might get you off, arguing we entrapped you. Here's the thing. Your names, your *real* names, will be famous nationwide, synonymous with seducing a vulnerable teen at Burning Man. Those clever recordings on your phone? Court evidence. The world will be aware you knowingly, willingly, engaged in drugged sexual relations with this child."

Michelle exclaims, "I'm not a child!"

John turns to her and says, "As your lawyer, I need to tell you this. Shut up."

Michelle says, "You're not the boss of me. You're not my father."

"No," John says. "I'm your lawyer. I'm ten times worse than your father. He can only threaten you. I can ensure you spend the next few years in juvie, and sweetie, you need help. Big help. Much better help than county juvenile hall. So, *shut up*."

She crosses her arms.

John turns to Cobra. "I don't have your real world names. But once I show our video to the event organizers, Burning Man will happily and eagerly release your four names—and all your camp mates' names—distancing themselves as much as possible. They will issue very loud, public statements condemning you as violating the spirit of Burning Man. These statements are what draws national media attention. Oh, and your camp mates who you tricked into searching for the runaway? The ones who thought they were doing a good thing? They will crucify you. They will eagerly assist the police investigation in every way possible. So, hand over the gold."

This latest speech seems to attract Cobra's attention.

Each man holding a coin deposits it back in the bag and hands it to Cobra. Cobra tosses it to land at John's feet.

John says, "Pick it up."

Cobra says nothing.

John says, "By returning the gold, you avoid a lawsuit. That was smart. We can still go to Burning Man organizers with this video. Whether your actions were legal or not, they will denounce you. Instant celebrities for the rest of your lives as date rapists of the barely legal. If any of you have professional careers, they are over. Pick up the bag of gold coins and hand it to my friend."

John's powerful command leaves little room for doubt as to what happens next. It's assured. Why would John want to be Alistair when this kick-ass lawyer was here all along? I'm in love all over again.

Cobra picks up the bag of gold coins, and my stomach twists. With his every slow movement, I worry he's debating a violent response. He turns to me in slow motion, and the rage, the hatred, is undeniable on his face. He wants to kill me. Instead, he drops the bag of coins in my hand.

My fingers tremble.

Now, I understand. John didn't reveal his plan because he wanted my face to show authentic agony watching the money exchange.

John says, "Thank you. That was the first thing. Second thing. All four of you apologize to Michelle for using her. For seeing her vulnerability and using her to your advantage. Tell her that you're monsters."

Cobra looks at the Hacky Sack man filming our exchange, and if I were him, I'd debate the odds of grabbing the phone and destroying it before we stop him. I see it in his eyes.

"Feel free to use the exact words I spoke," John says.

Cobra must have decided his odds are poor, because he turns toward Michelle—still hiding behind me—and says in a distinctly unapologetic voice, "Sorry."

John says, "Feel free to use the exact words I spoke."

Cobra glares—this latest verbal shove almost too much—but John doesn't back down.

"Tell her, 'I'm a monster.'"

Cobra says, "I'm sorry we took advantage of your vulnerability. I'm a monster."

More than an apology, this feels like sinister intentions.

Timidly, Michelle says, "I didn't mind. You didn't force me."

Cobra's other three pals mimic the same words, but without the malice. They seem ready to tip over. Jim puts his hands on his knees, ready to spew again. Coral Snake looks terrified. I almost feel sorry for him. Almost.

John says, "Thank you. Michelle, apologize to these men for not revealing your HIV status."

Michelle says, "Hey, they didn't tell me, *none of them* told me—"

"*Michelle,*" John says the name and ends her words. "As your lawyer, I'm *advising* you to apologize to these men, right now."

She relents and spits out the word. "Sorry."

"Michelle," John says. "Apologize the right way. Now."

I suspect John doesn't lose many cases in court.

"Fine," she says. "I'm sorry I didn't tell you about the HIV. I didn't think you cared."

Cobra takes a step closer to her, his fists curling again.

John shouts, "*Huddle!*"

The five Hacky Sack players leap together into a tight, closed circle with their backs to us.

Cobra turns to his men and says, "Get that one with—"

Before he finishes, the huddle breaks apart and all five men start running toward Black Rock City in different trajectories.

John speaks calmly. "There's no point to chasing. Any one of them could have the phone with the video. They decided amongst them who would carry it. Even we don't know. There's four of you, five of them. Vin and I would delay two of you, so the odds of your successfully catching the right man are slim. But let's forget about the video for a moment and talk about the HIV situation."

Green Snake jogs impotent steps in their direction, already aware of how correct John is in his assessment. They'll never catch the video. Cobra stares at the running men and then turns to face John. I think he might explode.

John says. "Researchers agree tops are significantly less likely to contract HIV than bottoms. This does not mean *no* risk, but it does mean *less* risk. You could take hope in that. Of course, if you guys were rough with Michelle and she bled, different story. Plus, high viral load. You might want to consider getting to the nearest hospital—Reno—and ask for post-exposure prophylaxis. It's a regimen of HIV drugs that will dramatically reduce your risk of seroconversion. Side effects are brutal, but it might be worth the risk. You only have a short window after exposure for taking these drugs. You've got to get to a hospital right away. I don't remember if it's within forty-eight hours or seventy-two hours."

I know. It's seventy-two hours, but I suspect John is narrowing their timeframe so they feel a certain urgency to leave Burning Man. The way John rattles off these facts tells me that since his own diagnosis, he has not been idle. I'm betting he researched everything about HIV. Of course he did. Duh. In his sorrow, he probably read everything he could.

"What's it called again?" Jim asks.

"Shut up," Cobra says with a snarl. "Don't talk."

"No, you shut *the fuck up*, David," Coral Snake. "You talked us into fucking a sixteen-year-old with AIDS. If we get AIDS—oh god! *We could get AIDS!*"

Cobra is David.

"Shut the fuck up," David says. "I didn't make you do a goddamn thing you didn't—"

"What's it called?" Jim yells, cutting him off. "The drug?"

Quietly, John says, "Post-exposure prophylaxis. Just ask for the HIV post-exposure drug. Now, I have no idea if the Reno hospitals will have enough in stock for you four. They might, but they might not. I read an article last year about how the local hospitals near Burning Man get hit hard this week every year, treating a ton of dehydration cases and a million STDs. So, maybe you shouldn't rely on Reno having enough. You may have to drive farther. If I were you, I'd hurry. Pack your gear and go."

Coral Snake and Jim take off running back the direction they came. Once they gone, Green Snake says quietly, "I hate you guys."

He turns and begins walking slowly.

Cobra's whole body is rigid and trembling, as if he's repressing a seizure. His clenched fists can't seem to find direction. Is he more furious with Michelle or with John? Or me? He's not sure whom to attack.

He decides to attack John. I see the slight shifts, putting his weight on his back foot, preparing to throw himself.

Words will end this. Unbidden, the right words come to me.

"You're a dentist," I say.

His furious snarl freezes, and his head jerks my way. The alarm on his face shows me I'm right. How do I know he's a dentist?

"After this weekend, you might be a dentist with HIV. Your career will be over."

Horror comes into his eyes.

"You should go. Your crew will converge on Reno's hospitals. You seem selfish enough to try to beat them there. Also—and don't ask me how I know this, I just do—within the next fifteen minutes, your three snake friends will destroy your tent and everything you brought. Then, they'll come after you. It would be safest if you went straight to your car."

David breathes heavily, sweat pouring over his bald skull.

He stares at me, disbelieving.

I say softly, "It's time for you to go."

He backs up a few feet, unsure if he's going to spit a final curse at us or not.

I can't resist saying it. I can't. People change.

As he retreats, I yell, "It's not too late, David. *Remember who you were always supposed to be.*"

He flashes his loathing at me, but turns and jogs in the same direction as the other men.

John turns to me and says, "Really? *Really?*"

"All men are kings. That means *all.* This might be what changes him."

As we watch him retreat, Michelle says, "Well, whoever you people are, you sure know how to ruin a party."

FIFTEEN

As soon as Cobra disappears, John starts asking questions. What kind of drugs? How high do you feel on a scale of one to ten? Have you done drugs before? She answers with the snark and hesitation of a teen, yet fights back with her adult desire to appear in control. She remains breezy throughout. None of this is a problem for her. Not her lack of food and water, prospects beyond this week, her health, her future.

"Hey, I'm thirsty again," she says.

I hand her the canvas pouch, and she takes several long pulls.

"Let's go somewhere fun," she says. "Really fun."

"We can't hand her over to the rangers," John says. "Not like this."

She ignores us, scanning the horizon.

"Was the human trafficking law stuff true?"

"In theory, yes. The case would get thrown out before trial, undoubtedly. The video most likely didn't record everything, including every spoken word. Intent is everything, and I'd have a hard time proving intent. Eighty percent bluff."

"Where are we going?" Michelle asks.

John and I look at each other with surprise. Planners that we are, we never anticipated this scenario where we couldn't take her to the rangers. What happens next?

John says, "We need to sleep. Both of us."

The energetic, whimsical Purple Sarong Man I met a few days ago is not here. In his place stands an exhausted parent, a depleted lawyer, a man carrying burdens not his own. We still haven't discussed his night in the desert. It changed him.

I say, "Let's head to my tent. We will find a relay who can take her to the kings. They will watch her while she sobers up. Feed her. Get her medical attention. Two of them are doctors."

"I don't need medical attention, girls." She pauses. "Although, a house call from Doctor Vodka would be welcome."

John says, "Michelle, do you realize the trouble you're in?"

She leans closer to confide in us. "I didn't make that up about Doctor Vodka, my friend Natalie did."

John says, "Currently, there's a nationwide hunt for you. Your parents—"

"Fuck those douche bags."

"Yes," John says. "Fuck those douche bags, but they have all the power over your life. They make decisions for you. If they don't want you at home, they could stick you in a state mental institution, or an intensive drug rehab. Hell, maybe you need exactly that. Maybe not. We'll talk once you're sober. Right now, let's keep all your options open, including the best ones."

"Damn," she says. "Don't hold back."

"I'm your lawyer now. I'll never hold back. It's my job to make sure you get better than you deserve."

"I didn't hire you," she says loftily.

"Self-appointed, which means you can't fire me. Well, technically, yes you can, but you need a good lawyer. You need me to drive you back to Los Angeles. You need me to file your emancipation paperwork. Which, by the way, if you're high, you will never get. The court will find you unstable."

"I can't pay no lawyer."

She crosses her arms and turns away.

I say, "I can."

I hold out the bag of gold coins. I raise John's hand and place the bag in his palm. "Your legal fee."

"I can't," he says slowly. "That money is for Found Kings."

"I have a good feeling about you."

"No," he says, and his eyes fill with tears. "I failed you. I failed myself. I failed Michelle. I will learn to live with knowing I quit exactly when my trust was needed most. That hurts, but I'm in a much better place than I ever was. She's my future, this crazy sixteen-year-old. This is the kind of lawyering I always wanted to do. But I can't accept this money. I'm not a Found King."

He speaks the last few words with raw hurt, as if the words scratch his throat. The desert offers hard truths to wanderers. Not always what you want to hear, but the wind whisks it into your ears and it sticks. Like sand.

I take his free hand and raise it.

"No." His voice cracks. "Please don't."

Despite his gentle protest, he cannot stop me.

I kiss the underside of his palm. "My king."

Hell, he cannot stop what's already in motion. He *will* become King John, exactly as planned. He will boldly claim his destiny through the Eastern Gates. I see the truth of him. His kingship is coming.

We make eye contact. Tears stream down his face.

He says, "I can't."

"Well, take the coins for Michelle. I assume she'll need housing, or a place—"

He looks over my shoulder and, amid tears, he says, "Holy shit!"

He darts around me, chasing—I turn—*she's gone.*

Michelle is arm in arm with another woman, fifty feet away, pointing at something on the horizon. Where the fuck is she going? John chases after them and extracts our charge. Michelle sways while John talks to the woman. A moment later, they return to us.

Michelle calls over her shoulder, "Love those clogs, girl!"

She smiles as she stops in front of me. "She had perky boobs. I'd like mine to be perky. Hey Arab, you have a sad face. You look sad."

I say, "I'm worried about you."

She smiles. "Don't be, baby. I'm doing great."

John's eyes dart across the horizon. "We'll get her sober and then sneak her out."

We lead Michelle in the direction of my tent, well, if leading is possible. I feel like we're walking a cat. A social cat who likes to admire peoples' shoes. John explains the need for keeping a low profile, but she says in response, "You have bags under your eyes."

John watches her chat up someone new. "Oh yeah. She's my responsibility. We're going to have a long talk on the drive to California about sexual ethics and HIV status."

"The serpent men must be panicked."

"Yeah, I don't envy them, but I laid it on a little thick. The exposure risk is fairly low. Definitely possible, but low. Still, Michelle owed them the explanation."

I squeeze his hand.

He says quietly, "I'm finding it hard to not scream at her for not telling. If my ex had only told me..."

We are quiet. Michelle starts chatting up another someone new.

"She's sixteen."

"I know," he says. His words are quiet. "She's sixteen, and she has some hard times ahead."

Michelle turns to us with a dreamy smile. "You sad sacks are so boring! Let's go shopping!"

We have to visit almost every theme camp to satisfy Michelle's huggy curiosity. Cobra was right. This girl has a mind of her own and she doesn't take instruction well. After a few times of John proclaiming, "As your lawyer, I don't think we should visit this camp site," she wises up to his cheap manipulation. During those slim moments when he gets her to focus, he outlines the plan, how they will leave Burning Man tonight after she's sober.

After leaving behind a theme camp devoted to the worship of yams, John's plan finally sinks in.

She says, "Wait, so, we'd miss tonight's burn?"

John says, "Yes."

"Oh, I can't miss that," she says matter-of-factly. "This is my first Burning Man. I have to stay to watch them burn The Man. David said it's magical."

John says, "No, absolutely not."

She stops walking in the middle of the street. "Oh, sweetness, I'm definitely staying."

A small party dressed as Native Americans walk by, and as they pass, I suspect that they aren't in costume. They're Native Americans wearing traditional garb. Interesting. I always see a few teepees in Black Rock City. I wonder if those are theirs.

"I love your tits!" Michelle calls loudly after a shirtless woman headed in the opposite direction. Before either one of us can apologize to the object of her praise, she says to John, "I wasn't paying attention to the gold stuff back there, but I know you don't own me."

"Nobody owns you. I'm trying to keep it that way, Michelle."

"Well, you're a doll. And I'm not leaving before tomorrow. If you try to make me leave, I will scream you kidnapped me."

John flashes me a panicked request for assistance, but I have no words of wisdom. An emotionally unbalanced, high-as-a-kite teenager has us over a barrel. Well, only if John wants to preserve some quality options for her.

She's walking ahead of us again, greeting people and complimenting whatever she notices.

I say, "Once she's not high, she'll more reasonable."

John grumbles. "Are you absolutely sure *every* woman is the one true queen? I find this philosophy very challenging right now."

Michelle's now making friends with a shirtless, sunburned stoner. I smell the pot from over here. He's got shaggy blond hair, falling in thick, dirty strands over his face. She squeezes his bicep, impressed by the modest bulge. He doesn't realize she's a sixteen-year-old boy.

John cries, "*Michelle.* No! No. Do not kiss that man!"

Something tells me they're not going to leave until tomorrow.

Which is great for me.

Tonight, John gets kinged.

Arriving at my tent, Michelle takes one look at my bland, ordinary quarters and says, "I'm not sleeping in a turd hole." She turns to John. "As my lawyer, you got to get me better hotel than this."

I notice Reggie thirty feet away. When I make eye contact, he tilts his head, an almost-visible question mark rising above him. I nod and wave him in. He turns and signals to someone else.

Soon, Reggie and another man join us.

We explain our situation. Michelle interrupts to offer her perspective, which mostly consists of complaining about the lack of soda machines and how the porta potties are disgusting and full. No place for a lady. She takes an interest in Reggie and requests to run her fingers through his afro.

He laughs, amused and vaguely uncomfortable.

Michelle says, "Baby, ignore me. I'm high as a kite. I've always wanted to try ecstasy."

John takes Michelle aside to explain how she must go with these men, and how she will not be harmed or sexually used.

She pouts and says, "Why not?"

Her good cheer about being used hurts my heart. I recognize sexual abuse. Although I was not physically raped in Billy's home, I definitely share qualities with sexually abused kids. I've read all the books. The violations in sexual abuse are violations of spirit. Yes, body. But the spirit sustains the most damage. In that regard, I was raped. Some days, I fear I'll never get out of Billy's house. Did my experience at Billy's make me more vulnerable to what happened years later? *Don't. Can't think about that.*

As John re-explains, I pull Reggie aside, away from the tent. I have specific instructions for him, and John mustn't overhear.

"Mobilize everyone. This happens tonight at sunset. Get the Twinkie tent ready by six o'clock and confirm with everyone to show up fifteen minutes after we go inside. Be absolutely silent. Ask Captain Graybeard to arrive with minimal noise. Ask if he can push the bus into position with the engine off. Tell him I owe him a walk under the stars discussing kings. This all happens at sunset."

Reggie turns his full attention to me. "Sunset? Doesn't the king have to greet the dawn?"

I'm surprised by his surprise. How do people know so much about this story? Who's retelling?

"Yes, normally. But this man. Well, he's unique. He crosses over at sunset."

Reggie nods slowly, as if wanting to contradict me. "If I may, how do you know? I mean, how can you know it's the right call?"

While I don't like to talk much about the kingings, this one I can answer easily. "You know, I don't even know anymore. Ideas or conclusions pop into my brain and I don't know why. I just know they're true. The other day, I looked at a guy and knew he would father three daughters. One day."

Reggie jerks his head toward me, eyes wide. "Seriously?"

Oh. I freaked him out.

Of course, *you idiot.* He asked you a simple question, and you made it creepy. You can't help but freak people out, can you? *You goddamn fucking moron.*

"I'm not giving you a good answer. What I meant was, I read a ton of stuff. I don't remember it all, not consciously. Maybe I read some statistics about fertility in biracial marriages and added that to my assumption the two of them fuck like bunnies, so it wouldn't surprise me if they brought a lot of kids into the world. Statistically, girls are more common than boys—" *I'm babbling. Someone stop me.* "It's ordinary, really. It's not...it's not weird."

"No, no," he says apologetically. "I didn't say it was. Just curious."

"Oh, okay. Great."

"It wasn't weird," he says.

"Great."

Okay, *now* it's weird.

I'm so tired. So tucking fired. Fucking tired. Whatever. Swear to god, I'm making everything worse because I need sleep.

"Any other messages?"

I pause to consider this. I try to contemplate final details, but my brain mostly wants to stop feeling like an idiot in front of Reggie. We've got the Twinkies, La Contessa, the people, and the kings. Oh. Shirt.

"How's his king shirt coming along?"

"Stunning. Probably done by now."

"Done? Fantastic!"

"Yeah, people were up all night and didn't have anything to do. So, they worked on the shirt."

"They looked for Mickey all night?"

"Yeah, that and worried about you."

"Oh."

I'd forgotten about last night. My back instinctively responds, itching and sore. Less right now, standing still, but I haven't forgotten how scratchy I am.

Reggie says, "What happened? Where were you?"

Try to answer this one normally. Be normal.

"Oh, I took off on a half-assed idea and started searching the desert alone. Without a flashlight. No real plan except running around." I sound like an idiot. "Turned out I was tricked by the serpent men."

"You were out there all night?"

"Yes. Not searching all night. I guess I...somewhat passed out."

After a vision of all my ex-boyfriends gathering around me, and then I was attacked by the letter v. So, you know, normal stuff.

"How did you get back to Black Rock City?"

"I woke up in the desert."

Be normal. Try to sound normal.

Reggie says, "You slept all night in the desert? Alone?"

"No, not quite alone. John woke me up. Not terribly far from the city, just behind The Man."

"Who's John?"

Oh shit. John hasn't given me permission to use his real name. They know him as Alistair. Is it my place to tell his story? Here I am, once again, protecting his identity.

"John is a guy I know."

"Some *other* guy ran out there, some guy named *John*?"

"Yes, he was...he was searching for me."

Reggie frowns. "We didn't know about this guy, John. Last night, Alistair caught the relay assigned to you—after you left Snake Camp but before he could make contact with you—and sent the relay to tell us he himself would bring you back. Said to keep everyone else looking for the kid. So, now you're saying *two* guys, Alistair and John, were both running around in the desert looking for you, and John found you asleep?"

"Sort of."

Okay, yes, that sounds a little crazy. I can't spin this into normal. What I wouldn't give to sound normal. To be normal. To have a normal life.

We watch John and Michelle argue. Finally, John found someone willing to debate him, point for point. Unfortunately, it's a stoned sixteen-year-old who doesn't listen.

Reggie says, "If you were out running around in the desert, how did you wake up near The Man?"

Oh god.

"Well, I was, um, dragged. By my legs. For roughly a mile."

What the fuck is wrong with me? Keep your damn mouth shut!

"Who dragged you? John or Alistair?"

How do I—okay. I'll say this. "There's a tricky answer to this question. I'd rather not share it. Not right now."

Reggie says, "If one of those guys dragged you, your back would be scratched to hell."

"Yeah."

Vin, do *not* offer more details. Quit being a freak.

"Is your back all scratched to hell?"

"Yeah. It is."

I sigh. I guess there's no fighting it. I'm a freak on every level. I don't know why I try to hide it. I just want to fit in somewhere. Out in the real world, I feel like I'm lost in the desert.

"Did he drag you because you were still asleep, and he couldn't wake you up?"

Reggie is a bright guy.

"Yeah."

He ponders this only briefly. "What finally woke you up?"

Why fight it? Why fight it at all? I'm a freak.

"He kissed me on the lips. I woke up. Don't ask me to explain why that worked."

Reggie is startled by this answer. He takes a step backward, and we both turn to watch John hug Michelle. Or rather, Michelle throws herself around him.

"Any other orders?" Reggie asks with forced cheer.

"That's it."

"Great. I'll convey the messages."

"Thank you, Reggie. For everything. Also, please have someone wake us around forty-five minutes before sunset, okay? Give us time to clean up, amble over to the tent. Maybe some wet towels?"

"Will do."

He strolls back over to the tent in a manner meant to convey casual indifference. Yup. I freaked him out.

John extracts himself while Michelle wipes her eyes and fixes her makeup with her fingertip.

She says, "This place is horrible. Who knew there'd be so much sand in the desert?"

Michelle introduces herself to Reggie, clearly not remembering her earlier offer regarding his afro. With Michelle in safe hands, the pure adrenaline coursing through me evaporates under the hot desert sun. I am so fucking tired. I'm baking in my Arab uniform. I'm baking like a cake under here, and I don't care. I want to sleep.

As the two men depart with their new charge, Michelle turns back to say, "Hey, Arab. How did you know he was a dentist?"

Thankfully, I can explain this.

"Yesterday, he checked out my teeth in Center Camp. I didn't realize he was staring at my teeth until I saw him checking—"

Which name should I use? Alistair or John?

He says, "Go ahead and say John."

"Okay," I say, relieved.

"—checking John's teeth today. Then I saw how he handled the bag of gold coins. He let his two buddies dig out the coins themselves. He's a selfish man. What kind of selfish man would let others touch his gold first? He thought there might be some sort of trap inside that bag, maybe a spider or something. Who knows. But he protected his fingers. His fingers are his livelihood."

I don't think Michelle is listening anymore.

Reggie says, "*You're* John? I thought you were Alistair?"

The other relay says, "There were *gold coins* involved?"

John says, "Rest now, explanations later."

Reggie says, "Wait, you were British yesterday."

"I was. Explanations later."

I'm getting dizzy. I need to lie down.

We watch them walk away, Michelle between them. Reggie glances back twice.

I made him fear me. I screw up everyone I talk to.

John says, "Tired?"

"Yes. Dead on my feet."

"Good. I was going to propose sex. But not now. Sleep."

I nod at him. "Sex is nice. Sleep is better."

We unzip the flap and step inside my warm tent. It's like a rat's nest, piles of clothes in the corners, broken granola bars, and papers ripped apart. Wow, I am a slob.

"Real sorry about the mess," John says. "I was pretty freaked out while I was searching in here this morning. I don't know what I expected to find. I'm sorry."

I strip my keffiyeh and toss it to a corner. When removing my robe, I move slower as I drag the fabric across my back. John helps me so I don't disrupt the bandages.

As John strips, I rebuild the "mattress" I've used all week, folded towels, sheets, and unworn costumes under my thick sleeping bag. Bending over hurts. My back wrinkles with quiet pain, but not as much as a few hours ago. I should take more Advil.

"John could you dig out some Advil from that bag in the corner, the brown one? Thanks."

As I work to reposition the sleeping bag over this makeshift bed, I say, "You were great with the serpent men. I never even told you how impressive you were. Your voice. Wow."

"Thank you. Lawyering is easy for me. Trust is harder."

Trust is hard for everyone.

We lie down, not touching, because it's already way too hot in here. But our faces are close together.

Quietly, he says, "Thank you for trying to king me. I'm sorry I pushed you so hard."

"You're welcome. And I love you."

He laughs. "I know."

"I love you, too, Vin. I feel about you the way I feel about a lover. Someone I want to have sex with. Someone I want to wake up next to and go for brunch with. I understand that won't happen. While part of me mourns this, I also celebrate it happened at all, this impossible feeling. After my ex, I never wanted to be in love again."

"Alistair was fantastic. I miss him. But you, wow, you're so easy to love."

His voice is sad. "I can't talk about Alistair. I am so ashamed of myself. I've never been loved like this, when I feel so small and ugly. It's like nothing I've ever experienced."

His words make me smile. I feel hot and dreamy.

I twist the wrong way and my face winces.

"How's your back?"

"It's sore. I'll sleep on my stomach. But until I fall asleep, I want to be close to you for as long as I can."

"Okay," he says, and his tone is soft, loving, warm.

Almost as if he meant to softly utter the words "I love you," but what slipped out instead was the word "okay." How often does that happen to me? I intend to be my own version of John but what slips out is my own version of Alistair? Authenticity is a choice and a hard one at that.

Our noses touch.

The touch feels like fire, as if we're falling asleep on the lip of a volcano. Every touch, every movement, results in heat and steam, orange and yellow touching bodies, oh man, am I tired.

"You love me," he says.

My lips ease forward an inch to touch his.

We kiss, but barely. Our lips are scorching, so we lie close to each other and breathe the fire.

The world is growing dim.

He asks, "Do you want to know how I knew you loved me?"

"Yesssssss." The word appears an orange-tinged yellow as it slides out of my mouth.

"I'll tell you," he says, his hot breath the smallest whisper, smaller than when he said "I love you."

He loves me!

"You said, 'Have a good life, *John*.' It was your victory moment, Vin, the moment you proved me a liar, because I was so shocked you knew my real name, I couldn't hide the truth."

Mmmmmmm. I love you, John. I should say it out loud.

"You triumphed over me. But you turned away without seeing my humiliated and shocked face, denying yourself any sort of victory. Why? Because you loved me. You actually *loved* me, as shitty as I had been to you. At that moment, I began to realize how I was wrong, though I had convinced myself I was right. It's why I trust you weren't fucking with me last night in the desert, because you *love me* and you would not devastate me that way. You had your chance to humiliate me, and you didn't take it."

I love you, John. I loved you right away.

"We weren't alone out there," he says in a soft, soft voice. "In the desert last night."

Those are the last words I hear.

SIXTEEN

"It's time."

A man's voice says this, and I feel something shaking.

"It's time," the voice says again, and I realize my foot really is being wobbled, a gentle way to wake me. Why do so many of my mornings start this way?

"John," I wrap my arm around him.

He groans. "It's too hot to snuggle."

Nevertheless, he pushes himself back into me and tugs on my arm to curl it around his chest.

I like this.

I squeeze him tight for a moment. We can be late by a few minutes. Unfortunately, now that I'm awake enough to be aware of the time, I can't relax and enjoy this. I kiss his head in several places, softly at first, then more persistent, gentle reminders.

"Okay, okay," he says. "Aren't you still tired?"

"Yeah. Exhausted. But we have to go."

"Why?" he says, half-groaning. "Why can't we sleep?"

I don't mind lying in this moment. "We're going to a party to show gratitude for all those who helped in the search for Michelle."

"I'm awake," he says quietly. "I'm awake now."

When we emerge from the tent wearing only underwear, we are greeted by two relays who offer us each a small bucket of cold water and a washcloth. John thanks them both heartily, as if he had requested this water himself as a personal favor. One of the relays is the tattooed note deliverer from yesterday. He's got another lollipop in his mouth. Don't recognize the other guy. I probably won't see Reggie again. I scared the shit out of him.

They leave.

We're passed by a half-dozen people every thirty seconds. The exact same Burning Man crowd but different. Bikers, Maxers, people in homemade costumes of glittery blue and green. Women with parasols. They can't help but intrude on our private master bath. A few ice cubes float in each of our small buckets, which is cause for great joy. *Ice!* We make pleasure faces as the cold washcloths touch our steaming flesh.

He picks up his bowl and stands in front of me. He looks at me with great seriousness and says, "I do this because I love you."

What?

He dumps his cold water over my head, making me gasp and shriek in icy delight. The cold water runs down my sore back, and while my jerking causes pain, the water cools me, expertly, and I realize my back is slightly less sore than when we fell asleep.

He laughs and dances back a foot, which kicks up enough dust to undo the recent washing, at least of his legs. I laugh too, because it feels surprisingly great, this cold water dripping down my ass crack and over the tops of my thighs.

"Your turn," I say, picking up my bucket.

He spreads his arms apart and closes his eyes. "Hit me."

While he waits for my revenge, I do nothing. After ten seconds, I say, "Once there was a tribe where every man was the one true king…"

He opens his eyes. "Why—"

I splash him across the face and chest with my icy water.

He squeals, dancing in place as the cold water finds every crack and crevice.

"You got me," he says laughing. "Wasn't expecting that."

His whole face changes, everything in him sags with instant grief.

"I'm so sorry," he says, choking out the words. "For everything I said. I was horrible. I said you were nobody."

"It's okay. I am nobody."

"No." His tears fall freely. "I was talking about myself. I hated you for not making me special. But *nobody* could make me special. Nobody could touch that. I'm so sorry for what I said."

Shit.

I don't want him to feel everything right now. I need him to retain a little sorrow. He will need it soon, that deep compassion for others—and certainly for himself. So, instead of hugging him, I put my hand on his chest, the smooth, clean plane of muscle right above his heart. It's already dry.

"Look at me, John. Look into my eyes and listen."

He resists. It takes a moment before he can allow his gaze to settle into mine.

When he submits, I say, "Forgiven."

He nods, breaking eye contact. "I'm not sure I could, Vin, if I were you. I hate my—"

"Hey. Look at me."

He does.

"*Forgiven.*"

He wipes his eyes. "Thank you."

The relays return. I'm not sure if they stood nearby, watching, or just happen to have perfect timing. They bring us clothes. White T-shirts and joyfully colored sarongs. John picks a green and yellow tie-dye. I choose red with fat blue flowers.

We wrap them around our waists, adjust them, and admire them on each other. So much cooler than pants. Why don't men wear these more often? John and I both opt to tuck our T-shirts into the back of the sarong rather than wear them.

The relays leave.

After grabbing our footwear, we abandon my tent. We wander my street and observe camps we'd previously raced past without seeing. I have an agenda, of course, so we don't visit any of them for long. He is amenable to following my lead. At the nearest intersection of streets, he tugs me in the direction I want us to go anyway, so I follow and we come one street closer to the city's outer perimeter. I chuckle to myself, wondering who leads whom right now. When two magicians dance, it's hard to say.

Holding hands, I lead him with more purpose through the last block. I'm not sure we're late, but the sun determines our timetable, so we can't dawdle.

Minutes later, we reach the end of the city. The last city street, the last block. I chuckle. Assplanade.

Just beyond the assplanade is a strange no-man's-land with few art installations—just two this year. Because this space borders the area where mutant cars roam freely, the organizers deliberately underutilize the area in case of a speeding-out-of-control accident. With La Contessa chasing the white whale bus around the desert all week, an accident seems not only possible but probable. Black Rock residents live on the edge.

As casually as I can muster, I say, "Have you seen any of the art over here?"

"No. I've never wandered this far. My camp is on the opposite side."

I might feel sorry for the artists whose work is displayed out here. The city's enchantments lure folks far away. Yet all creative gestures are a gift. Whether appreciated by twenty people or two thousand, the beauty remains the same. Perhaps these artists are thrilled to display in such a private, remote area. Perhaps they chose this. Not everyone chooses the Esplanade.

Beyond the two art installations is a tent, colorful with its fat blue and yellow panels. It's not huge, like a circus tent. It's not exactly a camping tent either. This must be an event tent someone rented for the occasion. Or created? Who knows? I love it. It's perfect. I can't wait to see inside. As we draw closer, I notice the subtle ropes ready to yank down the front panels.

John says, "Right before you fell asleep, did you hear me tell you anything about what happened last night in the desert?"

"Honestly? No. The last thing I remember is—let's go check out that tent, okay?—is you saying we weren't alone. In my brain, I started gazing around in the darkness, trying to remember what I saw, and that was it. I was out."

"Okay. Well, I'd like to get your perspective. I need to understand what happened, if that's even possible. I want to tell you everything."

We reach the tent.

"As long as we're being honest with each other, I have to confess something, John. I have one more surprise. Go inside."

He smiles bashfully, as if receiving a birthday present. "Have you been to this tent? What's inside?"

I growl at him. "You and your damn questions. Go inside!"

John pulls aside the blue flap. He gasps.

I love hearing him actually *gasp*.

As I join him, I see a beautiful, four-tiered cake covered completely in thick, white frosting, each tier supported by plastic columns. It's not even bumpy. Amazing. Flawless. A thing so white and pure cannot possibly exist in this gritty desert environment. Not for long. Yet, here it is. Icing bags filled with colored frosting are scattered around the table base. The cake commands most of the tent's space; there's only enough room to circle around it. John is wide-eyed.

"Why is there a cake?" His voice shakes while he asks the question.

"This is your cake. That's not the surprise."

John shakes his head. "I'm drained and weary on every single level, Vin. I'm not sure can cope with more surprises."

"Oh. Well, that's too bad. Because the surprise is it's time for you to get kinged."

"No," he says, almost in anguish, as if I'd punched him. He puts his hands to his eyes. "No. I failed."

"But you returned."

He keeps his hands over his eyes. Does he want not to be seen by me, like a child playing peekaboo? Or is he trying to hide from himself?

Behind his hands, he says, "When it was my opportunity to rise up, I shit all over you. I chose what I always choose. Cynicism and doubt. I'm no king."

"Men fall down. Kings get back up. You got back up."

He wipes the sweat from his head and looks at me at last, his eyes red and almost angry. "No. This isn't me. Not all men are the one true king, Vin. I'm a fuckup."

"Are you sure? Was it the fuckup who found a place for John to play piano? Did you fuck up when we did our crazy improv? When you used your great compassion to beg King Perry to come back across the rope bridge for me, who was that fuckup?"

"That was Alistair," he says with sadness.

I say, "Alistair is real. His feelings, his love. Alistair is one aspect of who you're becoming."

John cries. "What's happening to me? Why am I constantly inside out around you? I cry. Then we laugh. Then we cry. Everything is exposed and raw. I'm no king. Please don't tease me."

"You are a special king. Pick a tube of frosting and watch me. I'm going to draw something on the cake."

He picks the lipstick-red frosting tube. His hand quivers.

I choose ocean blue. On the side of the third tier, I squirt out a fat question mark.

"I have questions about you, John. I know you on some levels, but parts of you I do not understand. I will only know those parts if you choose to share them. If you love me enough, love yourself enough, you will share those parts you find unlovable. I shared with you my horrible story about Billy's basement. Did it make you hate me?"

"No," he says.

"You can share what's unlovable and not be hated for it. Or, spend your whole life hiding your shit, like me, fighting it. Gotta tell you. This approach hasn't worked great for me, but I'm too stubborn to try something different. You can do it. I know you can. You can let your unlovable story be heard. But will you? Will you risk telling your story? Who knows?"

I draw another question mark.

"Go ahead. Put a few question marks on this cake. We both have a few questions to answer. I'll start. At last, I can explain how your King Weekend differs from other men. I will tell you why I hesitated when you asked me if I ever intended to king you. I'll tell you how I knew your name was *John*. If these questions aren't important anymore, ask me something else. Then, choose another color and add a few more question marks. Fat ones. Long thin ones. Make them look pretty."

He smiles at this, a sloppy smile, his lips wet with tears.

"Answer whatever you'd like, Vin. Your choice. I'll just listen."

"You asked me if I ever intended to king you. The real answer was *no*. John, I could never king you. A man like you walks through the Eastern Gates of his own volition. Holding your hand, I can lead you there. But no trickery, no manipulations would ever force you inside. A man like you chooses to cross over when the moment presents itself. It's so much harder this way. But for you, it's the only way."

He adds a few questions marks and pauses when he picks up the purple. "I don't think I'm the man you describe. I don't have enough faith in myself."

"No man ever believes he is. Just wait. When you stand on the threshold, you will decide. Your decision in those seconds will feel less encumbered than right now. It's less an issue of faith in yourself and more an issue of simply saying 'yes.' I can't cross over myself, but I know how this works."

He shakes his head a little, as if he does not believe me.

"Did I intend for you to be a Found King after our weekend together? Yes. Could I ever cross you over? No. Thus, my hesitation. It was never within my power, John. Still isn't."

The tube of frosting quivers in his hand, and the question mark he's currently forming will truly be in question.

"Your whole weekend had no design other than for me to soften you for these final moments. Pour love into you no matter what. How would we spend our forty hours together? Didn't much matter."

"But the Temple of Joy?"

"You arranged that. I played along."

"But his name was *John*."

"Yes. Interesting coincidence. You shot me a crooked glance when you heard his name, and the look registered with me. The truth of what it meant did not signify until we fought. You let it slip that it couldn't have been an accident we ran into a man named *John*. Which meant the name was significant to you. Because, most likely, your name was John."

"Oh," he breathes heavily. "That tortured me for hours, how you knew my name."

"Cues and clues from yous," I say, a phrase I thought was so cute I adopted it.

King Ryan the Protector taught me that. I miss him. I *miss* him.

He nods. "When you called me John, I thought to myself, *this is magic*. But I get it. There's no magic." John peeks around from the other side of the cake. "Keep frosting question marks?"

"Until you run out of questions inside you. In this non-magic tent, questions get answered."

"Okay. But there is magic, Vin. I can't explain last night."

"Please, tell me. I promise not to fall asleep this time."

While he speaks, I will listen carefully for noise outside the tent.

He says, "I don't know where to begin."

"Earlier today, Reggie told me how you caught the relay chasing me into the desert. How did you find him? Or me?"

"After we...parted." He looks at me with a remorseful expression. "I started to realize I might be wrong. My arrogant confidence unraveled. My brain was on fire, debating every option. I knew I couldn't do anything else all night, so I decided to go watch Snake Camp myself. From a distance, with my binoculars. See if I could learn anything. I never saw Mickey—Michelle. Of course, I wasn't looking for a *Michelle*. Hours later, you showed up, strutting like one of those assholes, and I thought to myself, 'Here comes Vin.' I wasn't surprised to see you bald and wearing a snake tire around your neck."

"Was it that obvious?"

"I don't know. I guess so. But I knew before I could see your face. I looked down the street and recognized you before it was possible to distinguish you. My heart knew. *Knew*."

This makes me smile. "The only real magic is between two people."

"Maybe," he says.

We keep circling the cake, picking up frosting tubes and creating new flavors of questions—sunflower yellow, shamrock green, soothing violet, hot pink—and thick black question marks. I come upon his handiwork, three black ones. They look like heavy brothers, chunky men who walk their kids to school.

"You left Snake Camp. I followed. I caught the relay following you and told him I'd bring you back from wherever. He raced off to tell everyone, and I followed you into the desert. I tried to stay far enough back you wouldn't notice me, which is hard when there's no trees or landscape—and after a while—no people. Of course, I lost you."

Wait, do I hear them? I requested absolute silence. But do I hear them gathering?

John says, "You're quite fast, Vin. I think you underestimate your physical stamina. You're not exactly a marshmallow bear. You're more muscle bear. I was surprised when you stripped down two nights ago."

Muscle bear? Maybe I am. I guess I do eat better these days. Exercise. Too much junk food in my past. Strange how food is so much less important on the playa. It's one of my biggest distractions and obsessions, but out here, I barely think of it for a week.

He says, "I heard you yell. Couldn't make out any words, but I ran in the direction of the sound. I was terrified running out there."

"Yes, I remember. You feel like you're running in place. Or going insane."

"Yes, it was like being insane, but you *know* you're not insane, which makes the insanity worse. Then, silence. After a long time, I called out to you. Nothing. I ran in every direction at some point, I think. I spent an hour searching, I bet. I would have quit, but I knew you were still out there. Out of nowhere, I felt something brush my leg, like the tips of a pine tree branch."

I add an orange and then a pink question mark to balance out the crooked green ones he added.

He finishes frosting a question mark and says, "I screamed. Pissed myself— the first time. To be physically touched in that primal darkness...it's...I don't know how to describe it. It's...unforgiveable. If it were you—or your kings, as I first suspected—I would have hated you forever."

I understand what he means. Plenty of burners try to explain our experiences out here. The cognitive dislocation, the extreme minute-to-minute fluctuations in feeling powerful and insignificant...a person's very sanity is brutalized by merely witnessing this landscape. My Burning Man kingings always required less psychological manipulation, because the landscape does the work for me. But to be *fucked with*—especially at night—in this vulnerable place of temporary insanity... well, he's right. It's unforgiveable.

We stare at each other.

Even now, he seems haunted.

"I wanted to die, Vin. I was so scared, I wanted to die so I wouldn't feel more fear."

I nod. "I don't know what to say."

John pauses and puts his fist in his eye. "Gimme a minute."

During his quiet moment, I worry about him hearing the noise outside the tent, but if he has, he does not let on.

"I'm freaked out thinking about it," he says. "But I want to tell you. I began to understand I wasn't alone out there. That was the true terror. My company in the desert wasn't a tree, either. I shined my flashlight in front of me and saw a thick shadow scurry off in the periphery. A short, squat shadow, like a dog. I swear I saw paws cross in front of the beam two or three times."

"A dog?"

"Dogs. Multiple. I assumed I was about to be eaten alive. A pack of wolves was hunting me. I know I pissed myself again. Once, I heard growling. I froze. I turned and walked a few paces opposite the sound, and I felt more at ease. Less...this is hard to describe. Less *wrong*."

I'm glad we're frosting every inch of the cake with question marks, because I have no fucking clue what to make of this. Desert dogs? Wolves? There are no animals out here. Hell, dogs aren't even allowed at Burning Man.

"I could feel them near me, not too near, never far. I would feel a *whisk* on my left, so I'd jog right. When I'd feel a slight presence on my right, I'd change course to the left. I was completely petrified yet at some point, I realized they weren't attacking me. You'd think this knowledge would have calmed me, but it didn't. When I wasn't close to vomiting, I bawled my eyes out and swore."

"I have no idea what to say to this."

John stops frosting. "I know. I don't know what to say, either."

He picks up another frosting tube, the kelly green. "At one point, I flashed the beam ahead, just off to my right, and saw three of these dogs, or wolf things, scatter. I screamed. Seeing them scatter was official confirmation that living creatures were near me. I had been trying to convince myself it was a trick of peripheral vision, or that you and your kings were fucking with me. But after they ran off, I found you. They had been hovering around you. I assumed you were dead. Arms folded across your chest, hands on your shoulders, like a corpse ready for burial. I screamed my lungs out for about two minutes."

"My god."

"Vin, I'm still scared, just talking about it. What happened?"

We are silent. This is a moment. Something inexplicable happened to us. Of course, I was unconscious. But I believe him. I have no idea what to say to this.

John says, "I have a confession. I don't want to reveal this, but at the same time, I want complete, transparent honesty. I had eaten two pot brownies earlier. I was high. Not crazy high, but enough to know I was high. Does that make sense?"

"Not to me. I've only done pot once, and it was horrible. But go on. You were high."

"Yeah. Less so after running around out there for hours. I don't think I was hallucinating. But I want honesty with you, even if you judge me. Because..." He hesitates. "I am tortured. I will never know if what I saw was real or the result of my being stoned."

"I thought you said pot doesn't make you hallucinate."

"It doesn't! I swear it doesn't. I will show you science reports proving hallucinations are not possible. But then, in a tiny corner of my brain, I wonder if I'm being honest with myself. How else could I have seen what I saw? How could I have felt a whisker brush the back of my leg and then flipped around to find nothing? It's possible the brownies had something in them, LSD or shrooms. I ate a few brownies earlier this week and didn't hallucinate. All night I felt terrified and alert. What do you make of all this?"

"I'm not sure. Ironically, your honesty about being stoned lends your story more credibility with me. But I was unconscious, so how could I argue your experience?"

"Right," John says, holding up the tube of turquoise frosting. "It's a good thing we're putting question marks all over this cake. I have a terrible feeling I'll never know what happened."

He stops. "My whole life, I wanted something remarkable to happen to me. An experience no one else had. Turns out, a life-changing, mind-blowing experience isn't as much fun as I thought. I will always remember last night with terror. I will always doubt what happened because of the pot."

We say nothing for a while. I'm listening for noise outside the tent. I'm sure I heard something a moment ago.

John says, "It's a rainbow cake."

I hear the noise now. They're gathering. Stall for time. "What happened after you found me?"

"I was relieved when I realized you were breathing, but I couldn't wake you. I cried. Pissed myself a third time. I dragged you by your shoulders for a while, but you were too heavy. Any time I tried to stop and rest, I'd hear them, the dogs, always just out of range. They were behind us, following us. I put my shirt on you to help protect your back and dragged you by your legs. That wasn't much better."

"Thank you for trying."

"How's your back?"

"A dull throbbing. Not bad."

"Sorry about that."

"Not at all. You were doing your best to rescue me from a dangerous situation."

"Thank you for understanding. I thought those animals were going to eat you. I know better now. They were protecting you."

"We don't know that."

"I do. I know. I heard the singing."

"Singing?"

"Yeah. There was *singing*. I remembered a few lines of it this morning, but now, nothing. It was the song."

"What song?"

"I don't know. *That* song. *The* song. They sang in a circle around us, all the voices. The three dogs were singing, too. I fell to my knees and wept."

"I don't understand. What song?"

"I don't know. I can't explain. The one song. It calmed me. The song was...it was pure love. It was a song about love, but it was math and science and poetry all wrapped together in the lyrics, the voices. When it was over, I wasn't afraid. I dragged you for a long time until the sky got lighter. You know the rest. I tried a ton of ways to wake you up. I yelled. I whispered. I tickled you. I twisted one of your nipples really hard. Like, really fucking hard. The two people in kimonos found you. Then, that woman in purple and her boyfriend."

I say, "But only the kiss."

He nods. "The kiss. I think I might have known all along what would wake you, but I didn't want to believe it. I kept hounding you for answers about magic. When it was my turn to experience something miraculous, I denied it. When a crowd started forming, I realized I would have only a minute or two left to see if kissing you would break the spell. It worked. I panicked. I don't know why. It was too..."

John's face is grave. "Vin, we will always have unanswered questions between us."

We stop. Put down our icing bags.

"Why did kissing you work?"

"I don't know."

The cake is decorated, covered in question marks.

"John, I know your king name. Wanna guess it?"

"No. I want to tell you about me. About Alistair. I want you to know why I pretended."

I hope they're ready with the ropes.

"If that's true, we've reached the moment of the weekend which determines your kingship."

"Oh," he says. His face grows anxious. "No, Vin. I'm not a king. I'm not ready."

I turn to face the tent entrance.

I yell loudly, "*Pull the ropes!*"

The tent frame shakes, and John raises his arms to protect his head, but the earthquake is over immediately, as four of the tent panels are yanked free, exposing our cake to the desert and two hundred people. In the middle of our crowd, a giant pirate ship sitting atop a school bus. Boy, they *nailed* the silence. They obviously turned off the engine and pushed it here.

John's astonishment refuses to fade. He looks to me, to them, to me, to the ship. To the sky. To them.

"John, to cross over, you have to tell the truth about yourself to *them*."

With his mouth open, he surveys the crowd, the large assembly suddenly amassed. My heart finds the kings easily. Liam sends me a searing look across eighty people. Lucian smiles at me and bows his head. I see Ryan the Protector, and over there, Perry. He wears a pink, button-down shirt and watches me.

I'm dying.

I turn back to John, whose expression has changed little.

"This is your kingship moment. Your moment to decide. To tell everything about yourself, the very worst you believe to be true, and see if you drive people away."

He stares at me in horror.

"You don't have to do it, John. However, this is the moment I alluded to. You walk through the kingdom gates on your own, or you don't. Who are you? That's the question. Who are you, John?"

"I don't know," he says, his voice the tiniest whisper.

"John, you hold the key to your own prison. You're dying of thirst, but you have a bucket and rope. Quit waiting for me or someone else to ride into your kingdom and save you. It's *time*. Because of the kind of man you are, you have to king yourself."

A small cloud of dust rolls in, possibly residual from freeing the tent panels, blowing around our feet and swirling around the cake. At least a few pieces are going to taste gritty. Nothing stays pristine in the desert. We are nothing but sand.

John moves to the center of the open panels.

"Who are all these people?"

He whispers as if they cannot hear or see him.

"People who wanted to meet you. People who want to see the real you. Random burners we collected and a few faces you might recognize."

I spot Alan and Helena standing together, her arm draped casually over his shoulder, watching. Waiting.

John, our piano player friend, is out there somewhere. I don't see him. From what I understand, it was challenging to chase him down.

John—my John—turns to me.

His eyes fill with tears. "I'm terrified. But I don't want to stay a Lost King."

I nod and two pirates make their way to us, and with a big show of fanfare, plenty of *Arrrrghs* and pirate-speak, they announce John must walk the plank. They reach for him, and he steps back, instinctively.

I say, "If you want your kingship, you have to surrender. Nobody forces you. Nobody chooses this for you. If you're not sure in this moment, keep your options open and go with them. Decide in two minutes while you're staring at the plank."

John casts his bleary eyes my way, as if he resents my suggestion. Perhaps he always knew he would never be forced into submission. Maybe he knew it was always up to him. He just never wanted to choose it, for to choose felt weak. Like so many others, he thought his kingship meant unconquerable strength.

He offers his arms to the pirates, and they march him away.

They're the only ones playacting. Everyone else watches in curious, controlled silence. I asked for this. Restraint. No cheering, no encouragement. Let this be hard. Let this be John's moment to do something extremely hard.

After all, he is a shower king.

Some men need tears to cross over. Others face their worst fears. I've worked with men who need power. The fourth type of king has his kingship showered upon him, but only if he first believes it himself. He has to say *yes*.

He emerges on the deck of La Contessa. His pirate guardians continue their *Arrrrrrgh*-fest, guiding him to the edge. As he stares at the silent crowd, a long wooden plank is pushed out over the edge and secured in ways I cannot see from the ground.

They prod him with their fake swords and bark orders at him.

"Walk the plank, you scurvy dog. Yarrrrrrgh!"

"The ocean deep calls for you," the other says.

I grimace. I wish they wouldn't make it campy.

"Take off your shoes," yells one of the pirates.

John does so, glancing at me. Tears stream down his face.

I know, buddy. I know this is hard. I couldn't do it.

He climbs the stairs leading to the plank and takes one tentative step. Then, another.

As he edges toward the plank's end, it bends. It's not going to break, but his weight creates a slight arc.

I clear my throat. "This man is going to speak to us. Please remain silent. Let him speak until he's done. If you identify with anything he says, if anything rings true for you on a deep level, raise your hand for just a moment. Don't wait for him to make eye contact, just raise your hand. Let him know he's not alone. And if it's not true for you, don't pity party him. Keep your damn hand down."

I turn to John and nod.

He knows what he has to say. This is it. Let it begin.

"Hello," he says in his English accent. "My name is Alistair. Or rather, some of you have met me as Alistair. This is the fourth Burning Man where I pretended to be English."

He stops.

"I'm sorry about that. I really am. I never meant to lie to you."

His accent falls away.

"I started doing Alistair at parties for fun. I would entertain friends. I read English history books and studied maps so I could answer questions when pushed. I mastered English colloquialisms. I know all of London's tube stops, the big ones. At the first Burning Man I pretended to be Alistair, I felt...I felt special. I felt like I was somebody. Because the real truth is—"

He pauses.

"The real truth is, I don't believe I'm special at all. I don't think I've ever met anyone as ordinary and boring as me."

Several hands shoot up in the crowd and then go down again.

John stops and covers his eyes. He says, "Thank you."

Everyone remains quiet while he pulls himself together and wipes his face.

"*Alistair* was special. To me and my shitty self-esteem, the most common English person was more fascinating than boring, flat-voiced me. Alistair was more outgoing than I often feel. I get anxious in groups."

More hands shoot up.

"Ha, thanks. Yeah, this is freaking me out right now. This group. All of you. My biggest fear is I am exposed as a liar in front of a group of people. Then they all laugh at me and shame me. This fear is happening right now. But none of you are laughing."

He cries again and holds his palms against his eyes. "Nobody's laughing."

I see Helena cry against Alan's shoulder. Alan's eyes meet mine, and he mouths the word, "Friend."

I clench my eyes shut.

What's wrong with me?

Why can't I cross over?

After a moment, John can speak again. "My life is ordinary. I grew up in Kansas. My parents were great. I still love them. They love me and my two sisters. I had a dog. A few friends. I went to college, then law school. I'm smart, but not Harvard Law smart. I'm fun at parties, but easily overshadowed by more dynamic people—"

Another few hands rise and fall.

"Even my name is ordinary and common. *John*. There's not a more ordinary, bland name than *John*. I feel as though I was destined to not be special."

Hands go up. Hands go down.

"I come here, and I see all the amazing, beautiful people, and it makes me sad. I'm not one of you. I'm not...I don't belong. I'm not creative enough to make art. I'm not brave enough to wear elaborate costumes. Or go naked. When you're boring and small, it hurts to know you'll never be remembered."

A large number of hands rise for this comment, more than half. More than three-quarters.

This makes John cry.

After a moment, he says, "No...no, it's not true. You guys are...you guys are amazing. You're so beautiful. I watch you. I'm envious. So big. So joyful and strong and..."

He puts his hands on the top of his head. Oh good. Classic sign of giving up.

"I'm HIV positive."

Almost a dozen hands shoot up. Interesting.

John shakes his head. "A second ago, I was afraid nobody would put up their hand, and I'd feel so alone. I hated this diagnosis. It wasn't fair. I played *safe* except for my lover, whom I trusted. This wasn't supposed to happen to me."

Numerous hands go up, more than volunteered their HIV status. Maybe many of us feel life wasn't supposed to happen to us this way—not to me—but it did.

"I spent my life angry about being ordinary, and when this diagnosis made me more unique, well, I fought it. Not unique like *that*. That's not the uniqueness I wanted. I thought if I kept it secret, like everything else, it wouldn't be a big deal. But secrets pile up."

Hands go up and down.

I give the signal, and the kings start working through the crowd, moving in, moving closer to him.

He unwraps his sarong, letting it fall to the wooden plank. He's stripping. Interesting. He pulls off underwear and cautiously kicks them on top of the sarong.

"This is my body," he says, spreading his arms. "It's average. I'm not athletic. Hell, yesterday I had to climb the side of this ship, and I couldn't manage it without being dragged up."

A few people chuckle but it's not laughter. Not laughter at him, just acknowledgment of his dark humor.

"Even my dick is average. I always wanted it to be bigger. Huge."

A bunch of men raise their hands in response, more than several. Two dozen. John's honesty is contagious. None of us want to feel alone in our fear and dissatisfaction.

John laughs. "I can't believe this. If someone promised me they could get me naked—in front of a crowd—discussing, well, *anything*, I would have laughed. Let alone these confessions. I could never, *never* do that. I'm not that kind of man. I'm not special."

Someone in the crowd, one lone man's voice cries out, "You are!"

John chuckles, and it turns into a laugh.

That's how it works for men like him, men whose horrible secrets—once exposed—almost instantly transform into something more loving, more sustainable for life. The horror for these men is not that such secrets exist. They can be brutally honest with themselves. The horror is that someone else should know them. Once relieved of that specific burden, these men float.

Look at him! No one at Burning Man will ever top this story. At last, John achieves a moment in time as unique as he.

I give Liam the signal.

A few seconds later, a quiet chant begins with a few people in the crowd. The words are hard to recognize at first, only the dull thud of dum-DUM...dum-DUM...dum-DUM...until the syllables gradually become recognizable words.

"King...*John*. King...*John*. King...*John*."

The chanting surprises a very naked John as he stands spread-eagle, gaping in disbelief, the words like heat, rising to greet him.

"King...*John*. King...*John*."

The chanting grows louder. While they chant, the kings below him switch shirts.

He turns toward me, completely broken. It's too much for John to bear, their adoration.

I cross my arms in front of me, Egyptian-style, tucking in my elbows. I make it obvious how rigid I am making my body. I turn around and pretend to fall backward, stiff as a board.

John nods. He understands.

He sees the kings gathering beneath him, all wearing their sparkling shirts. Ryan in blue. Crimson Liam. Perry wears his shimmering gold. I loved shopping for his shirt. Dewey and Paul emerge from the crowd, and my heart twangs because I didn't expect to see either of them. My stomach twists. *Dewey!* I was the first man you ever kissed! I love you. I miss you talking about bluegrass music. I miss all of you. Do any of you still love me? Oh god, I'm dying inside.

He faces away from the men who will catch him.

He makes himself stiff as a board, arms crossed in front of him.

My heart is bleating with confusion and hurt. To love so many powerful, beautiful men and not be in their lives. To not be their one and only, or be able to call them and say "I'm thinking of you." There they are, thirty feet away, the men I *love*, all friends with each other.

What's wrong with me?

They arrange themselves below him, readying themselves while the chanting grows louder.

"King *John*! King *John*! King *John*!"

John takes a deep breath.

Do it, John. Wake yourself up.

Trust.

He falls.

He falls for an eternity—the longest seconds—until their interlaced network of arms catch him easily, the weight of him, and he bounces in their embrace until they circle around him, cooing.

Everyone else screams, howling at the sunset, joining the burners' sounds from far away.

We scream, harnessing the intense power and desolation of the desert. We howl for the sheer decadence of naked touch, and we howl for life-changing experiences with strangers. A mighty phoenix, born of two hundred roaring souls, screams straight into the blue cosmos far above us, and in this cacophony of sound, John is raised above all our heads, lifted high, his arms spread wide, as the world screams his name.

"King *John*! King *John*! King *John*!"

This is it. The shower.

I see his body react, see it on their strong hands, his chest lifting higher as if someone forced the air out and he must open his lungs. His whole body vibrates and shakes. He falls back and a high-pitched howl leaps from him, a wolf scream transcending the other yelling. It's not howling so much as gasping and screeching, dying and birthing, all at once. His fingertips flex rigid and release, a gesture that seems to send his consciousness into the new phoenix, the creature skidding into the cosmos—that's it.

There!

He's crossed over.

During the time we spent together, I witnessed no sparks on him the way I have other men. But right now, I see creamy light go coursing through him, the peanut butter light I sensed so long ago, or has it only been two days? Three? There's peanut butter, golden brown, thick and gorgeous, swimming in and out of him in long, creamy ropes of light. It's beautiful. I've never seen anything like this.

He is passed around, mosh-pit style, riding the crowd, all of whom are eager to touch him, to touch this king as he is honored and applauded, his name screamed and chanted. On his second circuit back to the kings, instead of passing him forward, they carry him to La Contessa where he is restored to the deck.

He stands and faces everyone, beaming with light, with joy. His athletic frame seems more powerful than it did a moment ago, his cock more plump. How can a dick be average when it's attached to such a powerful man?

He shakes his fists over his head, laughing and crying, unashamed, beaming his great love for us all, until the two pirates approach him. With their fake accents, they direct his attention to the mainmast, covered in ropes and rope ladders.

A smallish purple flag ripples in the breeze above the crow's nest. I'm eager to see it up close. Reggie said it was stunning. As the crowd chants his name, lower again, stronger, like the electronic beat to a song, he climbs, butt naked. And really, it's a glorious butt. It's not muscular, it's not flabby. It's perfect and ripe. I feel my lust grow and wonder if we're going to have sex after all. Right before we got to my tent, he said he wanted to. Or I hallucinated him saying so. Higher up the pirate ship mast he climbs, higher and higher, until he reaches the crow's nest, and everyone cheers again.

He climbs inside and reaches above his head to unknot his king shirt. The chanting dies down while he frees it. While we watch, he buttons it up. The ship is safe enough when it's standing still. Their crazy careening around the desert terrifies me, though the deck ride back to Black Rock City was thrilling.

Okay, I admit it. It was fun.

At this moment, the sun does something spectacular, which is also quite ordinary. It sinks. In fact, it's been slowly sinking all this time, now reaching that glorious point where hot yellow melts into scalding orange, a misleading egg yolk color convincing you the sun is nothing but friendly and wants to be your pal.

Wearing his purple shirt, arms wrapped around the mast of the pirate ship, John takes a moment to stare at the setting sun, the six shades of yellow, four hues of oranges, a hint of pink, and other colors you never realize are essential to a sunset until you stare, unflinching.

For a moment, we all watch him in silence, but the chanting begins again, low at first, until it becomes recognizable again, the King *John*, King *John*.

He climbs back down with easy agility.

When he reaches the deck, applause takes over, and with an endearing, bashful pride, he returns to the plank. His ears stick out as they always do, and I'm reminded how much I like them, also his eyes, the way he cried in my arms. My heart swells. Oh man...that butt. I want to bite it.

He edges to his sarong, still balanced on the end, and his casual gestures carry more assurance—like a cat who understands it can go anywhere, climb anywhere, get higher than anyone ever expected. Once his sarong is adjusted, he surveys the burners. His people.

Our crowd has grown. Those who saw La Contessa on their horizon have wandered over to discover her story.

"Thank you," John says. "This was the very *best* experience of my life. If you've never watched a desert sunset from a pirate ship's crow's nest while hundreds chant your name, I highly recommend it."

People laugh.

He says, "I heard a song last night in the desert. Today, I could only recall snatches of the melody. I couldn't remember any of the details, the lyrics, what it meant."

He turns to face me. "I remember now."

Oh, wow. I *knew* it.

He faces his admirers. In a calm and commanding tone, he says, "Though our roots be earthed in misery, and nurtured with our humbled tears, tomorrow's hope is today's firm, green sprig, pushing upward, barely seen. Eager to unfold, to manifest the unknowing directions, we grow." He pauses. "We are all destined for Spring."

He drops his head.

Prickles race up my neck and skitter over my bald head.

After a moment of stunned silence, everyone screams. This noise feels more frantic, more *unscrewed*, if I dare use that word. What's happening? The primal howling explodes everywhere around me, raw and writhing, inside out, in ecstasy or sunburned surprise, I cannot tell. In my head, I picture every single letter of the alphabet shooting above this crowd like fireworks, unspooling, unforming, meaningless chaos, every letter banging together. Small *f*'s are swirling and uncurling, becoming *t*'s, and the letter *i* keeps dotting the barren landscape, overwriting consonants and vowels alike. A dozen capital *S*'s break into *c*'s and *u*'s, spinning in circles, circling the spinning. I'm drunk. *I'm drunk with this.* I glance at the Found Ones. They whisper to each other excitedly. I am not privy to their secrets.

He said he heard the song. *The* song.

The screaming dies, and all the letters circling above the crowd turn to dust, spraying me with their leftover powder. I cough and wave my hand in front of my mouth a few times, reluctant to let the chaos of untamed letters inside me. I can't tolerate any more chaos inside me. I'm barely keeping it together.

Wait...keep it together. Keep them here.

I raise both hands and yell, "Don't leave! There's cake!"

Over his shoulder, John offers an unfocused smile.

I yell, "In gratitude for your witnessing him, John will serve you each a piece of cake. Well, it's not cake. It's about four hundred Twinkies frosted together to appear as cake."

Cheering loudly, the crowd collectively approves of this latest direction. While John steps back to the ship, our crowd shuffles into a line. My heart sinks. I'll have to face them all, the kings. One by one. I don't know if I can.

As soon as John disappears into the belly of the ship, Captain Graybeard strolls forth and grasps the railing. I mouth the words "thank you," and he nods.

He points at the sky above and grins.

One starry night, I owe him an explanation regarding the secret kings of Burning Man.

I give him a solemn nod and mouth the words "I promise."

John emerges, wearing his sexy sarong, and he strolls to me, unescorted. I finally see his king shirt. *Stunning* is the absolutely the right word, *stu* the stuttered surprise, *stu*! *stu*! followed by all those *nn*'s tumbling over each other, *n-n-n-n-n-n-n-n-n-n-n* each of them trying to see it twice, three times, and ending with that satisfying ring of *ing*. *Stunning*! Unlike any other king shirt and gifted in sacrifice. I can't wait to describe it to him.

When John arrives, he throws himself around me and sobs.

I squeeze back equally hard, the same emotions filling me. We went through awful times together. We each witnessed the other at his worst. Then, we loved each other back to our best. I inhale the smell of him, the peanut butter brown still gliding in and around him, sliding over his shoulders, creamy, soothing, and fresh. As our bodies untwine, I become aware of the soreness in my back. I didn't feel it while he held me. We pull apart enough to stand cheek to cheek. I feel the wet of his hot tears.

"I love you," he says, the words breaking apart.

I squeeze him and for a moment cannot reply. I love him, too.

He is already deep in my heart, intertwined with the exquisite loves I have known. My heart will always yearn for him, for us to play together on stage, for us to joyfully yell *sahiiiiiib, sheehiiiiiiiib*. In the future, I will jack off thinking of our intimacy in the hot springs, how we made love without physical sex. His eyes. I will always miss his eyes. Over time, my love for him will grow, not diminish. I've kinged men for so long, I know how this works. My heart grows bigger, my love for them grows stronger, and I grow more despondent.

Who could ever fall in love with me? They'd have to accept I'm already in love with more than two dozen other men. *Three* dozen including the dead. Jamie. Evan.

"I love you, John." I squeak out the words, and already it pains me that I won't have enough opportunities, enough time together, for me to explain how much.

We draw apart and touch foreheads.

I sputter a laugh. "I promised cake. Any second now, we'll have a riot."

He laughs. "You promised *I* would serve cake."

"I did."

"Well, I'd better get serving."

"Yes. First, we must explain your king name."

I wipe his tears and he wipes mine. Our wet hands find each other, and we turn to face the populace. Inexplicably, I feel shy. Maybe because of all the kings out there. But I must shout so all can hear.

"Thank you for your patience. Soon after John and I began our time together, he requested a king name unlike any other. Something almost hard to pronounce, or so uncommon, whoever heard it would have to say, 'How's that again?'"

A few people laugh, which is nice.

I wipe my eyes.

"What John did not realize is a king name often presents a burden as well as a blessing. A call to remember the best of yourself, and the stumbling blocks to choosing your best self. John happens to be one of the most inquisitive men I know, and he pounded me with questions. Why are we doing what we're doing? What happens next? Is this part of my King Weekend?"

This last question reminds me of our terrible struggle, the division between us. We will not forget it, either one of us. We must acknowledge it and love ourselves for what we could not give each other.

John squeezes my hand, a sad acknowledgment. Yes, questions sometimes create strife.

"His questions are his gift. He works hard to understand the world around him. He wants to deeply know and understand the people he meets. Questions also become his curse, his way of hiding. His way of not trusting. When you meet John and he showers you with questions, you must ask yourself—and then him—'Are you trying to know me? Or are you trying to hide from me?'"

John cries at this.

I squeeze his hand.

"Whoever encounters his king name must also wonder, 'Am I myself authentic in this moment? Or am I using my own methods to hide?' This is a conversation you can easily initiate with him. His king name invites this conversation. His king name says to the world, 'Let us question and wonder together, and in doing so, show our deepest, truest selves.' His king name will be a hard mantle to bear some days. Yet his king name is a gift to all he encounters."

I go silent.

As I had hoped, someone finally yells, "What is it?"

"You just said it," I say. "Of course, I can't pronounce it. Nobody can. It's unspeakable. However, we frosted the entire cake with it."

I step aside to show off our masterpiece, the colorful question marks rippling over the white frosting. Those in front step closer, eager to see.

John asks, "My king name is 'question mark'?"

I want to involve everyone in this conversation, so instead of answering the man at my side, I speak to all. "His king name is the symbol, not the words. If you call him, 'King John the Question Mark,' you will not have addressed him with the respect he is due. Everyone must find their own way to pronounce it. Go ahead. Please. Draw it in the air. Dance it. Make a question mark out of your body. Find a way to express his king name, right now. He is King John, the..."

I let my voice trail off, and a few people appear confused. Others laugh and clap their hands. A few draw question marks in the air. A man I do not recognize hops straight up and down, curving his arm over his head to represent the hook.

"Let's try this again. I introduce to you, King John, the—"

I jerk my arms—spread them wide—indicating I want their big responses.

More people participate, someone making a "boing" sound, one guy drawing a fat question mark with both hands in the air. Perry spins around in a 360-degree circle and presents John with jazz hands. Three people imitate the first guy who jumped up and down, with the curved arm over his head.

John laughs at all the creative expressions and claps his hands. He wipes away more tears.

I yell, "One more time! I present you, King John, the—"

This time, our crowd squeals in wild appreciation, bouncing, drawing, making noises and someone makes a *caw-caw* sound. I'm not sure how that's a question mark exactly, but who fucking cares? Everything is acceptable, offered in the spirit of love.

John laughs and cries, cries and laughs, and turns to me. "You son of a bitch."

"Well, you wanted unique. No other man I kinged has a symbol. But I chose it because of its truth."

He laughs and hugs me, squeezes me again, and this time, I have to pull away and remind him of my back. He apologizes and throws his arms around my neck, watching people finish their boingings, their curved arms, their jumping up and down.

I must give them their final instructions. "As you come for Twinkie cake, friends, take note of John's special shirt. It was sewn together over the last two and a half days. More than a dozen burners cut up their own purple shirts, scarves, skirts, pants, anything to contribute. This shirt represents the sacrifice some of you went through all weekend to see him kinged."

Another mighty roar rises from the crowd, and John falls to his knees, fists in his eyes. He didn't know how much he was loved by all these people. Ordinary John is loved. So loved. When you are loved, you cannot possibly be boring.

I kneel with him on the playa and hold him until he can stand again.

Under the cake table, I spy our serving tongs. No plates. No napkins. Paper plates are a wasteful luxury out here. Everyone will eat off their dust-covered hands and lick their fingers clean.

John mangles the first few, jabbing the serving tongs into them, trying to find where one Twinkie ends and the next one begins. Once he feels the structure beneath the frosting, he serves with more grace.

The line moves slowly at first as people want to bless him. He cries and is unable to wipe the tears away, because he's busy serving with both hands. I think people prefer this anyway, to see his broken, humbled face as he whispers to each person, "Thank you."

I cannot assist. They want *him*. Everyone wants a blessing from this Twinkie-serving king.

One by one, our relays come through the line. John serves them each two Twinkies. Reggie shoots me a sly grin. He says to John, "That was amazing. Stay beautiful."

John whispers, "Thank you."

When Liam approaches, I almost can't look at him, so bright, and so beautiful. His big head and his lopsided grin.

To John, he says, "Two years ago, brother. I saw you."

John yelps, as if struck, and hugs Liam, crying in his big arms.

As they hug, Liam shoots me a fierce and knowing look. I nod and return his gaze for as long as I'm able without breaking down.

Helena and Alan step up and throw themselves around John. They embrace for as long as they can without tipping over. Before they leave, Alan caresses the side of John's face and says, "John."

I worry John might physically drown in all this juicy attention.

But he deserves it.

Michelle approaches, skipping the line and justifying herself by turning to those waiting and saying, "It's okay. He's my lawyer."

She hugs him with great dramatics.

"Oh, baby," she coos into his ear. "I wasn't paying attention to most of your speech, but I'm glad you gave it."

John laughs at this, a great belly laugh, because, after all, Michelle is sixteen.

She pulls back and stares into his eyes. "Also, I just smeared frosting on the back of your new shirt. Sorry."

John smiles. "Of course you did."

She says, "We're staying for tonight, right?"

John says, "Yes. We're staying. No drinking. No drugs. You're in bed by two o'clock."

"How about four o'clock?"

John says, "How about midnight?"

She says, "You're no fun."

John says, "We have people assigned to you. Please show them respect. Don't give them the slip."

She saunters away, complaining to anyone who will listen.

Soon after, Perry approaches and it's hard to be near him. I knew it would be. His face is so kind and open. One of those beautiful people who thinks you're beautiful, too. He's living in Australia these days, happy and in love with a rancher. I'm happy for him. I wish it could have been me.

He hugs John and says words to him I do not hear. Whatever he says makes John cry.

Perry accepts his soggy, frosted Twinkie in his right hand. With his free hand, he touches my face and says, "Always."

I wince.

Me too, Perry. Me too.

He steps away and disappears into the crowd.

I want to die.

I can't keep doing this. Loving men and sending them to better lives while I stay behind. I love witnessing the birth of their power, their sudden awareness of kingship. I know John will never describe himself as ordinary ever again. It's breathtaking. But then I go home. Dinners eaten out of cans, and television while lying for hours on the couch. It's worse being in a house, a whole empty house. I thought I would love owning my own home. All that space for myself. It's so much worse than I had imagined. I never got lonely in the sewers. I was too busy trying to survive.

Quit complaining. Quit feeling sorry for yourself. It's pathetic.

The only reason you don't cross over is because you are too weak to face your demons. Too cowardly to let the world know you're a fuckup and to accept the consequences. You're not like these men, bold and brave. John confessed his darkest secrets standing naked on a pirate ship. I could never be that brave.

Twinkie by Twinkie, the cake gradually disappears. Sugary snacks are a luxury on the playa. Most people don't bring them, because you can't store them. Calorie-wise, they offer no survival value. Frosting? Melts to liquid in half a day without refrigeration. The kings went through a lot of effort to create this magic cake in the desert. As an experienced burner, John will realize the magnitude of their extravagant gift, if he doesn't already.

Right now, he's busy serving cake.

The sun sinks lower, close to disappearing. Those with Twinkies stroll away. Probably going to prepare for tonight.

I tense as the remaining kings come through the line, and I thank them with my eyes. Try not to let them see how much I miss each of them.

Piano John steps up.

"*Sahiiib, sahiiiiiiiiiiiiiiiiib!*" he cries, throwing his arms around King John.

King John winces and cries harder. They make plans to keep in touch.

It twists my stomach. I'm glad they're going to be friends. I am. Still hurts, though.

King John serves with attentiveness, making sure the last ones in line feel as blessed and honored as the first. Every single person matters to him, even those who missed his experience and only want free Twinkies. Everyone here, they are all his people, these burners.

Captain Graybeard and his crew come for cake. John tries to convey his delight at experiencing the pirate ship so thoroughly this year.

Graybeard says, "We'll be back next year."

He gives me a meaningful look.

I nod. I will be back next year as well.

Soon, only a handful of Twinkies remain on the bottom tier. A few bashful people return for seconds, and John happily obliges them.

As the last of our party guests wander into the desert, John says, "I am speechless. My heart can't find any words."

"Sometimes life is better without words."

We look to the sky. All that remains of the sun is its echo, the afterglow.

Burners howl.

Far away, across the city, drums pound a steady heartbeat. They ready themselves, soon to be called into service, the only music necessary for fire. The lamplighters begin their evening task. After tonight's festivities, all the street signs get pulled down. You stumble home in the dark, not knowing where you are. It's tradition.

The neon tarantula stretches itself awake.

Tonight, The Man burns.

SEVENTEEN

In Burning Man's early days, we all gathered close, and someone started The Man ablaze. As the flames shot into the night sky, we danced. We howled our sins at it. We defied him, honored him, begged the damn thing to witness our destruction at the hands of time, and bless our rebirth.

That was then.

You can't allow thirty thousand people to dance around the inferno of a forty-foot-tall burning sculpture. I admit, it's less intimate these days, maintaining a safe distance and watching the fire spinners and dancers put on their show while The Man burns. I liked being up close and feeling the heat on my face. Oh well. Everything evolves. Everything changes.

"They're coming," John says and pushes back against me.

I squeeze him tighter, as if the arrival of torch bearers from Center Camp means he will disappear from my arms. Well, nothing quite so immediate. But soon. This is our last night together.

Five heartless drums pound out the executioner's slow march, waiting for the echo of each solemn stroke to die before pouncing again, implying a cruel desire to see the mayor of Black Rock City dethroned. In fire. We cannot blame the drums for executing their grim responsibilities. They only reflect the burners' mood tonight, everyone howling in anticipation—screaming with their last reserves—for The Man to burn, burn, burn.

As the giant torch is borne into the center arena to feed our ancient hunger for this grisly entertainment, John and I howl as well, howl for ourselves, for Michelle, the serpent men, for all of us living and dying on this isolated little planet.

The firebugs rush into the center, a furious mob, occupying the giant semicircle before The Man. Fifty of them I'd guess, maybe sixty, all swinging poles with fire dancing on both ends. These spinners move in synchronicity, shoving their poles out, then spinning them over their heads, and for the few seconds their hands are out of contact with the circles of fire, I remember how dangerous all of this is, the fire, the desert, the thousands gathered here, singing, howling, dancing, and grinding.

Maybe we came here for the danger.

Maybe we need the danger.

Or maybe we witness danger to better appreciate tranquility.

John says, "I love this part. Fire dancers."

He turns to face me, cranes his neck around, and our lips find each other. *This* kiss I am awake enough to appreciate. He turns further so our kiss can extend itself, and the warmth of his lips is the only heat I will welcome. The firmness of his mouth against mine alternately yields to my power then demands my submission, and we dance together as we have danced in all our time together, pressure and release, pressure and release.

I stare into his hazel eyes. The reflection of fire allows me to see the earnestness in his gold-flecked irises.

"I love you," he says. "I love you."

Our lips touch gently.

He says, "I never thought I would love again, not after my ex-boyfriend."

"I love you like fire," I say.

He throws himself at me, and our next kiss is wet, hungry, fueled by the raging fires inside us, around us.

There's nothing better than being in love at Burning Man.

Eventually, John faces front to watch the fire spinners worship their beloved, tossing sticks into the air and retrieving them with grace.

Looking around, I am surrounded by thousands in glitter, feathers, and transparent silks, people in various stages of nudity and neon, costumes and noncostumes, and what they all share—what we all share—is the dust. We've slept, eaten, and played here for a week, and we are all acutely layered in dust, in grit, in grunginess. We sweat together. We wear the planet's dust together. This is what binds us, not our uniqueness, or our giftedness. No one can escape our commonality— dust. It's who we are. Where we're going. If we're lucky, we get enough dust on us to feel as though we've truly lived.

The Center Camp torch bearers eventually reach The Man.

John and I wail with everyone else. We can't help it.

I am always grateful no one gives speeches or offers explanation for what Burning Man means, or what it should mean, or what it means to the organizers, and so forth. So much better to apply our own meaning, our own experience. To stop filtering through someone else's reality and find our own.

Years ago when he was helping me buy the Kearns' farm, Rance told me no matter how many stories I tell about the kingdom, the men I king find a way to believe and yet *release* the stories as merely stories—allowing them to experience their kingship directly. I wonder how it would feel to touch that primal reality, our primordial origin where all stories are born. Maybe I already do, more than I know.

The Man's arms—limp at his side all week—are gradually raised by unseen crank turners. Crank, crank, crank! Whether his arms above his head suggest abject surrender or if he's signaling his desire to party with us, it's not clear. Doesn't matter. His arms rise.

The screaming grows louder.

This is Burning Man's gift, really. This geographic space outside reality, this moment in time, where raw ideas get birthed into existence. With radical self-reliance and radical acceptance, anything we imagine can be true. Some fashion the world through metal sculpture. Some create a pirate ship on the back of a school bus. Working with fire, or with thoughtful gifts. Some reality-makers invite you to marry yourself or they love strangers by trying to sell them a lawnmower in the desert. A beautiful woman changed my reality this week by offering me a cherry Popsicle.

Cobra and his friends imagined a hell where people are used, use each other, and the only victor is the least manipulated. Michelle's omission was wrong, no doubt. She should have told them. But she is a young adult who is not an adult, though worn and discouraged beyond her years. The serpent men created hell and invited her participation. They didn't expect her to accidentally participate so fully in the reality they created.

John was wrong—or rather, Alistair was wrong—when he said this place is nothing but a loser-populated drug fest. Yes, the reality some people create is darker. There is crime here. There are real problems. But this reality-shaping event creates a life-affirming allure so powerful, so *essential*, people travel the globe to this desolate environment—this imitation of Death Valley, but without the charm—just to taste it. Be a part of it. To look around and say, "I belong. I have always belonged."

The Man shouts his belonging, his neon purple arms fully raised over his head, and his people—all of us who consider ourselves his people—wail before fire consumes him. John and I break apart so we can pump our arms into the air, screaming our wishes, our last prayers of love and acceptance, and gratitude—*deep* gratitude—for the gift of this desert, this tiny carnival existence.

Is Burning Man an oasis, the future of a civilization rooted in abundance, gratitude, and principles of love-centric survival? Or is this the opposite, a prehistoric escape from civilization, an essential part in calibrating our sanity? Lawlessness and screaming at three o'clock in the morning with the fire of life coursing through you?

"Yes," Burning Man says. "Yes!"

Fire explodes out of his chest and head.

Fireworks burst behind him, big and blue, purple and orange. The sky is alive.

The dancing begins.

The fire dancers warmed us up, throwing their juicy wares over their heads and twirling about. The rest of us now join in as The Man burns, burns, burns.

Thousands of people dance together.

Tens of thousands.

The number is hard to appreciate without seeing everyone at once, turning, swaying, jumping.

We are legion.

Fireworks overhead detonate in soft *pffft-kow* sounds, their quiet beginnings producing unexpected brilliance, light and light-patterns, afterimages of long hairy, ashen legs, suggesting the neon tarantula tickling across the night sky, just out of the light's glow. The center arena of Black Rock City becomes one unified nightclub, all of us whirling and spinning, celebrating the destruction and the new life promised us.

John and I dance near each other, in each other's arms, front-to-back and back-to-back, anything allowing us to be near, feeling the intensity of our days together. We dance with men in kilts. We dance with two fiftyish women, topless, proudly bouncing their boobs and waving sparklers. We hug. I hug people I know are drunk and some who are high, which is sometimes hard for me. I dance with a young woman in a wedding dress, a *real* wedding dress, and when we finish our duet, I see she's been crying.

Somewhere out there, Michelle is dancing under Liam's watchful care. During our last communication with a relay, we discovered she has a crush on him. Which is good, because Michelle might flit away without someone drawing her in. Helena and Alan dance somewhere in this crowd, kissing, celebrating. Perry is out here somewhere, one of the thousands, and the sting of this thought is lessened knowing I am loved by and loving a powerful man, John, right here in my arms.

We twirl and watch the stars above us.

We dance with a man dressed as a snowman. Hell, snow woman for all we know.

Together, John and I hug a snow person in the desert.

I am home.

We dance for how long? Who knows? Chronological time ceases to exist. The only time that matters is now o'clock.

John leads me from the party, the thousands of dancers, and it takes us a solid half hour to get to the perimeter of the crowd. The desert chill had been staved off by body heat and the fire we all circled. Now, the cold feels delicious, a first head-to-toe shiver after eating ice cream.

The unbearable daytime heat and the surprising nighttime cold.

Just another day at Burning Man.

John leads me. When I ask where we're going, he looks back and says playfully, "Try not to ask questions. They get in the way of the experience."

He laughs.

I delight in seeing him this way, happy and relaxed. I saw a lot of this in Alistair when we performed and wandered through the city, but *this* man is so much more. More assured, more relaxed, more of everything.

Ah, Lotus Land.

A sizable crowd parties under the purple lotus leaves, drinking and dancing. They yell, "Fuck your burn," so we yell it back and they growl. Then, they invite us to join them.

John thanks them but promises we have an engagement to keep.

He leads me deeper into the desert.

We walk beyond the art sculptures, the cool shark fins circling a life raft art, and while we occasionally pass another couple or small group, the gatherings are quieter this far into the explorer zone. They came here to observe The Man burn from a distance, so when we briefly meet in darkness, we nod and pass them, leaving them to their own reality and their own reflections.

We go far enough I wonder if we will spot the orange fence. Did he have time to arrange something? After the Twinkie cake, we strolled the city, watching others prepare for tonight's big burn. We visited my tent, confirmed with a relay our revised timeline for tomorrow's departure.

John had wanted to leave early—extremely early—but our relay explained when men drove into town for Twinkies and frosting, each car was searched thoroughly. Rangers still seek Mickey Flynn. John doesn't want Mickey/Michelle discovered here, feeling it will adversely impact her emancipation. Better Mickey has been "hiding out" at a friend's place all this time. We decided the best strategy would be to leave after ten in the morning. Maybe eleven. Most everyone stays until Sunday but tomorrow a good number will depart by late morning. Hopefully the inspectors will work quickly, wanting to minimize a lengthy delay and backup.

"We're here," he announces and releases my hand.

Here seems relative, since the spot he chose is indistinguishable from any other spot. It's inky-black in every direction, well, all directions save Black Rock City, where flames are visible, though smaller and turning into their next state, ash. I feel the ash all around us, tiny grains of it brushing my ankles. Ash or playa dust.

We look around.

In the desert at night, outer space isn't a concept. The cold emptiness of space is something you touch and taste. I always have a lot more empathy for astronauts when I'm out here.

John slips out of his sarong, and I'm surprised when his cock springs free at full attention.

"I love you," he says. "I want you to know what it means to me, the love you have shown me. I want us to make love."

"We don't have to do this," I say, already regretting the words. I want this. I really, really want this. "If you're not ready."

"Vin, I'm so ready. And it has to be with you."

I can't see his eyes, but I hear his voice crack.

I jump toward him, pushing my lips onto his.

He grabs for my cock under my sarong, and he finds it already half-hard. His earnestness, his hunger for me, serves as an aphrodisiac. Yup. I've wanted this man since he joined me in his Arab costume. I accepted we might not fool around beyond some light touching. I accepted that, though I hoped for this. Apparently, we're going to fuck under a billion stars.

Works for me.

With hesitation, he says, "I haven't negotiated safer sex as an HIV positive man, so, are you okay with me sucking your dick? Without a condom?"

"Hell, yes." I yank off the sarong. "In fact, I insist."

We kiss again, surprisingly wet despite our dry hours around fire, and as we grope each other, my hands exert extra pressure on top of his shoulders, lest he forget his promised destination below the belt. He likes this, I feel it in the way he responds, raises his shoulder to feel my strength pushing down. I grip his neck hard and he likes that too. He hasn't had sex in eight months, his self-imposed isolation. I bet he's hungry.

He drops, and without hesitation, launches his throat onto my cock.

Whoa!

So much for foreplay. Like a man dying of thirst in the desert, he attacks my cock with a thirsty ferocity I absolutely love. I respond instantly, hard, because as great as gentle lovemaking is, I am a man. Men are sometimes rough. Sometimes gentle, but right now, we celebrate the power of men having rough sex.

I grab his head and pull him deeper, the only inch he hadn't already devoured. He makes a sound in his throat, a wet sucking grunt, and I'm suddenly thinking of his dogs out in this desert last night. What the hell was that? What happened to him out here?

I can't get too distracted. He won't let me. His throat works my cock, making it fatter and harder and incredibly slobbery. He indulges his hunger and makes no pretense of holding back. Dude loves to suck dick. I love when freaks show their love for their own freakiness. I have much to learn from this King Weekend, including loving myself for being a freak.

In a low voice, I say, "Suck it, John. Suck that big dick."

He throws himself on it with abandon, this man who loves cock.

Oh god, that's good. I grip the sides of his head and stare up, the stars, the stars, the mighty bright stars. *Star light, star bright, first star I see tonight.*

I feel John's saliva drip over my balls. Oh god...he's good at this. I want to hold off, not come so quickly, so I pick one single star and begin to play my Star Game, pretending we are friends. Before I can ask it questions about its life and feel it express fascination with mine, I feel a familiar tug, a rippling through my nuts which communicates "I'm not at the final destination. But I'm in the neighborhood."

I pull his head off my cock and suggest we slow it down, just a tad, so I can last longer.

"Yes," he says wiping his mouth. "I was hoping you were in the mood to top."

"I am."

He grins. "Okay, well, I stole condoms from your tent."

I laugh. "Thinking ahead."

"I'm a lawyer. We examine all the possibilities."

We lay our sarongs down on the ground, lying atop them. They offer little relief, none almost, from the parched, cracked earth. We feel each clod beneath us as we shift positions. I suck him, his luscious, perfect cock. He sucks me again. He tells me of his attempts to "clean up" for sex tonight, and we laugh about our barbaric conditions and our longing for cleanliness. Sometimes, Wet Wipes are your best goddamn friend out here.

He maneuvers on top of me, enjoy a rowdy tongue-sucking, face-fucking slobberfest. We gradually transition to something gentler, gasping for air between delicate kisses. With playful skill, he puts the condom on me, and while praising my cock for its many virtues, reminds me he last got fucked nine months ago. He asks to ride me, so he can control the entry and depth.

"No problem," I croak, as best I can.

Sand in my mouth and our intense kissing have left me gritty, dirt-covered, and feeling raw, physically and emotionally. I love him. God, I *love* who he is. I just want to be inside him, however it happens. I hunger for this, for him.

After applying lube, he lowers himself inch by half inch, pausing repeatedly to stare at the sky, or at me, or in one instance, some burners who wander by, giggle, and say, "You fucking fucks," before jogging away. I wouldn't be surprised if other burners wandered by. Maybe. The city parties in full force. Every now and then a roar rises, far away.

When he lowers himself to the last inch, he moans, and I can't help but buck up, to show him there's more to me. There's more of me to experience.

His eyes pop open, and he looks into mine. We move together, riding together, measuring our slow responses to each other, knowing when to push, when to sag, when to gasp and let it all out, slowly.

It's good. It's really, really good.

His ass grips me sometimes, other times he surrenders, inviting me to have my way, which is what I want. When I am balls deep, I see his satisfied grin. Everyone knows the bottom holds the real power. The top only loans it out. During sex, we toss power back and forth like a beach ball, offering each the right to push away, to push deeper, to welcome my cock or to resist. Each thrust renews the invitation.

I love the resistance, so vital to the core of John.

Just over his left shoulder, the infinite universe hovers in black, watching us fuck. The universe is right there. Watching us fuck. Fuck. Fuuuuuuuuuuuck! F-f-f-f-f-f-*f-f-f*like feathers floating to heaven, the start of the word, such a friendly fervor in *f,* and then *uuuuuuuu*-my god, John feels amazing! Enough to snap off the word with a *ck*, a cock, a cock *you, fuck you,* oh feathers to heaven, I love fucking inside him! No wonder the word is so dramatic. It's feathers and groaning and a hammer slamming down on a plank, cracking it in half, all in one word.

In the middle of our exquisite desert dance, I realize he won't give up on Michelle. She's got some rough times ahead, some hard growing up she must do, but he will be there for her, loving her through it. He will be her lawyer, yes, but so much more. This makes me want to fuck him deeper, to indulge the paradox of loving someone and wanting to cause that slight discomfort in them, making myself a literal pain in the ass.

He winces and it melts into a grin, loving this as well.

He says, "Come with me."

He lowers himself, and the feeling of being pulled in overtakes me. I find my eyes fluttering closed. Oh god. I love this deep plunge—oh *god*.

I stare up into the universe behind his hazel eyes.

Softer, he says, "Come with me."

The stars seem brighter than they did a moment ago, no longer soft and jolly balls of light, but a revelation that they are each powerful suns.

He pulls himself up and slides himself further down, and I buck up involuntarily because my cock wants that half inch more. My eyes squeeze shut—everything black—and then I open them to see the stars are falling, like a meteor shower inside him.

"My foot's getting scraped," John says.

Sex has its awkward moments. It's not always comfortable on parched earth, so without pulling out of his ass, we manage to wrap his foot in my T-shirt, giggling, me occasionally thrusting into him, to continue our manly fuck. Now, we can't stop giggling, laughing at our own "tee-hees" in the desert, the funny ways we laugh. Distractions like these only highlight our pleasure, the intense, unfunny beauty when our bodies reconnect. The oneness we feel. I'm sweating and I don't mind one bit. I welcome our heat.

"Come with me," John says.

He stares into my eyes, his hands cupping my pecs as he rides me.

Nothing matters except me inside him, the connection between us, the black road under our naked feet, the two of us holding hands, walking through meadow after meadow of stars. We stroll together, our bodies mere outlines, the presence of outlines, and I look at my hand—the ghost version of my hand—and it comforts me to know I have found my true form at last. I am a ghost. I am the Human Ghost.

"Whoa," I say, suddenly very much ass-on-the-ground. "What the hell was that?"

A black road? A meadows of stars?

He leans over to kiss me, squeezing his ass as he bends. While my cock does not actively fuck him, every time he clenches his ass, I squeeze my balls in response and it results in vibrations, a cock massage, a delicious twisting, and I understand something else about John. He knows what he's doing. Power bottom.

Our lips find each other, gasping for air and stealing each other's breath, this union on yet another level. Our mouths taste pure desert heat and lingering sweat. We've already released all the toxins, sweated them out days ago, so what remains is what's truly ours. I could get drunk on these kisses.

"What was that?" I say, still gasping. "With the stars?"

He closes his eyes, and juts his chin skyward. "No questions."

He kisses me again, eyes open, and the stars come out. I thrust into him until we merge into one, a union of soul and body that feels like witchcraft. Why does making love feel so amazing, so connected, so...everything?

He's waiting for me, reaching out to me, and we resume our ethereal stroll. The landscape is light, a thousand million stars projecting enough light to guide us, illuminating in softer light and then stronger light, the fields around us. The black road with miniscule pebbles composed of stars. Different intensities convey texture. The light creates all.

We f-f-f-f-fuck the feathers to heaven!

And buried in this fuck—this love made physical—the light of a thousand stars, is the shimmering version of him and the sparkling version of me. The light beneath our feet creates the illusion of stone paths with no sharp rocks. We're walking on light. All around us, stars grow on trees, and I see us traversing a million orchards, the endless black is the tangle of a billion intertwined tree trunks, bearing hundreds of billions of stars, tiny universes next to grown-up stars, stars so ripe they will go supernova and blow love onto growing galaxies—

What the hell?

I pant, gasping, looking around me. We're still on the playa, right? The dirt rises in small clouds near us, making me cough, the distant cry of fire worshippers—

"Come with me," he whispers.

Okay. This is weird. I will follow.

The orchard is less overwhelming when I see it in my mind's eye, and maybe this mirage is fueled by sleep deprivation and adrenaline, fear for how things could have turned out, and love for how they did. Maybe my brain is processing every grain of sand tickling my every exhausted nerve and fiber, convincing me I see intricate trees bearing suns as fruit. That's probably it.

Or maybe it's not an illusion.

Maybe I know exactly what I'm seeing.

These are the ancestral fields from the story.

This is it.

The true home.

John kisses my neck and pushes me down, leaves his lips locked on me, as if I am wrapped around him, him around me, both of us swirling in smoke and light while wandering the stone path, the mountains of stars, the orchard, the—*it's everything at once*. Millions of miles away, I see kingdoms and lovers, people beaming light, histories and cultures I will never know, or wait, are those earlier times on this planet? Who knows? We are all made of stars. The same light comes from them as me, different, always different, but the same goddamn light.

He sucks my neck.

"*Remember*," John whispers into my mouth.

I scream and I come, my hips jacking upward as he clenches me and lets me pound him open. I scream and he cries out, a sharp sound, over immediately, and

I'm afraid of opening my eyes and discovering where I am, where I'm not. I just exploded over the entire universe, and I'm too spent to open my weary eyes.

My god, what happened? What was that?

When he said the word *remember*, when he said that, the world rushed into me—I don't, oh my god. I am still coming inside him, still shooting.

I squeeze my nuts and jerk my legs together in exquisite and almost painful release.

What *was* that? It's fading. Already, it's fading.

He kisses my neck and I don't remember when his lips left my neck but when he said the word *remember*, he said it right into my mouth. But I don't think his lips left my neck.

I smell peach trees and green life.

And then, nothing.

EIGHTEEN

I wake up. Sit up. Look around.

I'm in my tent.

How did I get to my tent?

Oh, right. We walked back. Well, dragged ourselves would be more accurate.

The sex was great, but the post-coitus wake-up in the desert was less than sublime. Covered in grit, mouths dry, sore in some places. His foot is chafed. I now realize I did not once think of my scratched-up back. It hurts right now, but not half as bad as the first day. Much better. Last night, I never even considered it as I fucked him, lying on my back. We fucked for a long time in that one position, and I never noticed? How is that possible?

We woke up, laughed at ourselves, fastened our sarongs, and he dusted off his new purple shirt. We half limped our way back to Black Rock City—which was still partying—and back to my tent, which took an inordinately long time. We were spent.

Through the screened tent top, I see the sunlight overhead, which makes my heart leap. *We have to part by noon.* I get weird after noon, thinking it might work out, maybe *this* time I could be better, maybe we could date. I can force out those thoughts until noon. But after noon, I start to wonder and feel hope, a dangerous quality when you have no basis. I have no hope for us, though I would dearly love to see him on a date where we wore real clothes and walked near a river, holding hands. We need to part by noon!

John wakes up beside me, rubbing his face, rising on an elbow.

"Bloody fooking hell," he says, and then he chuckles. "Whoops. Sorry about that. What I meant to say was fucking hell. I feel like I got hit by a truck. What time is it?"

"No clue."

John lies back down and puts his arms over his head. "I would like to float down a river right now. Doesn't that sound refreshing?"

"Maybe eat some ice cream for breakfast?"

"Start a snowball fight."

"Ice cube on your back."

"Cold thunderstorm in late March."

After a while, tormenting ourselves with things we most certainly cannot have at this moment, the real world leaks in. We both start worrying about Michelle, getting her to safety. We decide to be responsible and yell out the tent flap, *what time is it?*

A stranger answers us.

It's okay. Only nine o'clock. We have a few hours.

John pops out into the hot sun, naked.

He calls to me, "Hey, where's our relays with the cold water baths?"

I join him outside. "Yesterday you were a king. Today, you're a common chauffeur to a surly teen."

He leans against me. "Never. I'll never be common again. Ordinary, yes. Common, no."

We kiss and make our plans. The wind picks up and assaults us, driving sand into our naked skin.

"Hey, watch it, sandy," John says at no one in particular.

A garden gnome in a tall, pointed red hat strolls by and says, "Windier than yesterday."

We dress ourselves. Beige shorts and a tee for me. John wears clothes I've supplied. From my truck, we grab granola for our breakfast, bananas too, and we eat while applying sunscreen. This breakfast doesn't satisfy. None of my food looks appealing. Sometimes there's just nothing good in the fridge.

John's got decent food back at his camp. He hasn't much about where he's staying, which surprises me. Then again, how often do I volunteer information not directly asked? We're a lot alike. We visited his tent for his clean clothes yesterday but did not stay long. Nobody was around.

He explains his camp as a loose connection of experienced burners who knew each other, sort of, and they didn't have a theme or plans to hang out. They felt friendly toward each other and counted on each other for supplies, transportation, and interdependence in living together. That was it. No cooking or cleaning schedules. You were there, you cooked and ate. You weren't, go have fun.

He explains their camp philosophy, saying, "I didn't abandon them to spend time with you."

His camp seems far, and we are feeling lazy. We decide to visit Alan and Helena. They're only fifteen minutes away. I'm nervous to see them. Also, eager. Of course, I won't call them outside of Burning Man. I already warned them I wouldn't. But maybe we could be Burning Man friends next year. Maybe I could be in their camp. *Maybe* is the best, lightest word flitting around me right now with translucent wings.

Maybe.

I don't even mind the capital *M*.

Burners today seem different. Satisfied. The energy, the appetite for fire has been satiated. The burn happened. Tonight, the Temple of Joy and all other wooden structures get roasted, the dramatic Burn Two to last night's Burn One. Most everyone sticks around for the second night of fires, though a few sneak out early, eager to avoid tomorrow's traffic clusterfuck.

To our dismay, Alan and Helena are not in Robot Zamp. Nitro needed their help with something urgent. We didn't have specific plans to see them, so there's no reason they would stick around.

"Wait," Tuck says, and he starts backing away. "Stay here. They left notes for you both on the off chance."

John says, "*Ooo*. Notes!"

I smile weakly, and he sees me.

My note will tell me to *keep in touch*, I'm sure, and it will be the first big way I disappoint them.

Tuck returns with two halves of a ripped paper and hands us each one— handing us what I would expect. Love notes with contact information. Next to the words "call us," I see in Helena's handwriting the word "please." Alan wrote "Don't be an idiot, you idiot."

Burning Man friends.

Maybe. *Maybe*. Maybe!

If Michelle is happy to see us, she's skilled in hiding it.

She wears different clothes, a skirt she loves to twirl in, someone's donation to her shortage of outfits. A shirt that doesn't quite fit her—too big—but she clutches it like a wrap and complains, "Someone's sweat is inside this!" She wears big sunglasses, like a celebrity worried about reporters. Which is the reality, isn't it? John is taking a huge risk for her, sneaking her back to Los Angeles. This is serious stuff.

She is escorted by one of the relays who brought me a cheese note, the man who brought us bikes the other night. The two of them laugh back and forth, and he is genuinely entertained by her. Not in a "she's a freak and a novelty," way, but rather, "I like her crazy-ass company."

Burning Man friendships. This place is the best.

When I ask about last night, what she thought, she admits it was cool, but would have been so much better had she been allowed to smoke weed and drink vodka, "like every other single person on the playa." She is more subdued today than yesterday. Her snarks are spaced further apart, less dramatic. Maybe the weight of her predicament is sinking in.

The relay asks if I need anything else.

Before I can answer, the wind kicks up, blowing dust all over our faces. We all do what's normal, cover our eyes and wait for it to pass. This one takes longer than usual. We wait.

Michelle says, "Was that a tornado?"

John says, "Not even close. But it was a pretty good wind."

"It's disgusting," she says. "Nobody tells you how dusty it is out here. They talk about the cool music and parties and sex. Nobody says, 'it's like French-kissing dirt.' And it's also scorching hot. Like, really hot."

I finally answer the relay. "I don't think I need anything. But just in case, could you send someone in an hour or so? Also, tell the kings to use the bank account for reimbursing Twinkies, frosting, bikes, supplies, anything. Great. Ummm...I don't know. I can't think of any other wrap-up stuff right now."

I don't want to think about wrap-up stuff.

I'm about to lose John, and I hate it.

The relay teases Michelle a little longer. She takes his arm and makes him stay.

With possibly our final moment alone, John says, "Brace yourself. I'm going to ask you a question."

Don't ask. Please don't ask.

"Is there—is there any way we could date?"

"I'm a Lost King."

"So? Let's break the rules."

I look down. "There is no official rule. Only my rule. You would grow to hate me. I couldn't bear it, not after the way you loved me this weekend."

I glance up to see that the lawyer in him wants to argue, but if he's learned anything during our time together, it's the futility of that approach.

We chatter a little longer, delaying the inevitable.

The relay kisses Michelle's hand, her palm, just under the thumb.

My stomach twists.

After a slight lull in the conversation, John says, "I don't want to go."

I say, "I don't want you to go."

I can't believe I said that aloud! It's getting close to noon, I bet. I'm weakening.

"I wanna go," Michelle says. "Let's get the fuck out of here. It sucks here. I have to get some cold caffeine in me or I will have a fucking stroke right now."

John and I smile weak, unconvincing smiles at each other.

"Do you have the gold coins?"

John jingles the bag tied to his belt.

We stand in silence until Michelle says, "I'm going to go check out that camp, right over there. They look cool. I promise I won't leave."

The tent in question is close, close enough John doesn't have to worry about her bolting.

She's gone before waiting for a reply.

I nod after her. "Good luck with Michelle."

He stares into my eyes. "You, too. I mean, with your...things."

We are silent.

His eyes fill with tears. "I have so much to say to you."

I wince. My heart is exploding, and I'm trying hard not to cry.

"You kinged me." His face bears surprise.

I look down at the ground. *Don't leave me! Please don't leave!*

I clear my throat. "No. Don't misremember this weekend. You kinged yourself. I was your witness."

"Vin," he says. "You were my *guide*. Do you know what that means?"

I have to interrupt him before he says anything else. Before I cave on my resolve.

Instead, we're interrupted by another strong wind, a big one, kicking playa dust to our faces. I cover my face and wait, but the wind doesn't die down. Not much. This is growing.

Oh shit. It's growing.

Through squinting eyes, I see the white wall coming toward us.

Whiteout!

"Michelle!" I yell at him and point in her direction.

Though we stand less than a foot apart, the wind steals all the senses, including all sound. Only two streets away, the white wall. We're about to be erased.

He's yelling? What is he yelling?

Through a slight downshift in the wind, only seconds—

"Don't give up, Vin!" He shouts the words at me through cupped hands. "Don't give up!"

I want to scream, "On what?" I'm not sure he could hear me if I did. Also, I know what he means. I know.

He turns and races toward Michelle, who of course, I can't even see.

The white wall hits us with physical force, and it pushes me four feet before I drop to the ground. I put my arms over my head, protecting myself in case something big blows on top of me. This exposure is dangerous. I shouldn't be out here!

There's not much to do but wait it out.

Could be over in three minutes or an hour, depending on, well, everything.

How much time passes? Can't tell. Maybe thirty seconds or maybe fifteen minutes. A landscape this alien, this foreign, bends the brain, tricking it into believing what is not present. My exposed arms and legs are scraped hard with sandpaper, so hard I wonder if my knuckles will be bloody when this is over. I wish I'd worn my jubba today! The intensity is so great, I crawl in a direction—any direction, hoping to accidentally crawl into shelter, a tent, a stand, something to hide behind. I'm now worried.

When the wind disappears suddenly, and the air is not blinding white, I discover I'm in the middle of the street, a half block from where I started. Burners emerge from the cubbyholes where they had been crouching. People shake themselves off, laughing and throwing around blessings, proclaiming, "It wasn't that bad."

John and Michelle are gone, of course.

Maybe hiding nearby, recovering from the storm. I could go back and look for them but why? I will drift away, leave them before they see me.

My greatest magician trick.

I always disappear.

I return to my tent and pause outside it.

My back is sore, my arms are sand-scratched and weary, my left nipple still tingles with every brush against my shirt. I miss him. I want him. I want to play word games and fence verbally and be delighted by him. John. *John.* I take off my shirt and shorts, teasing out as much sand as I can. Not that it will make much difference. Inside the tent, I start making piles, trying for something more livable. I'm leaving tomorrow, so there's really no point, but I fold my clothes into neat, little stacks and then sit in the middle and weep.

I miss John. When I think of this weekend, I will always feel like I met Alistair at a party and had fun with him, but then met his *hot* friend—his hot, open, honest friend—John. He was dazzling, berating those serpent men yesterday, and he was in love with me. He loved *me.*

Crying makes me laugh at myself.

Idiot!

I open a warm bottle of water.

I'm not going exploring today. I want to lie here and feel miserable.

Prickly sensations rising up my spine indicate that someone's talking about me. A moment later, I hear my name called at the front of the tent.

"Vin Vanbly? Are you in there?"

Kings? Relays? I did ask a relay to come by.

I unzip and step out.

I find five people standing in front of me. Three rangers. Two bald guys in T-shirts. I don't recognize them, but my heart beats faster. They're from Snake Camp.

"That's him," one of the serpent men says.

"Definitely him," says the other serpent man.

Is that guy Green Snake? I think so. But honestly, I would only recognize him with the green snake inner tube around his neck. If it's not him, who are these two?

"Are you Vin Vanbly?"

I look at the lead ranger's face and oh—oh fucking god. It's *him.*

The one I've been avoiding for *years.* Ranger Ron.

Oh shit.

He saw me—all those years ago—walking back to Burning Man from my night in the desert. He's got a square face, a fat square nose. He's a guy who gets into bar fights. His nose has been broken at least twice. He's dressed in traditional ranger gear, the khaki explorer shorts with a million pockets and a T-shirt that says "Don't fuck with a ranger."

He is famous among the rangers. He *is* the rangers.

He stares at me. "You fucked a sixteen-year-old runaway kid?"

"What? *No!*"

One of the serpent men says, "He said he was going to. First he offered to buy this kid, like a piece of meat. He tried to pay us in gold coins. When we said 'No, we're looking for a ranger,' he got mad and talked the kid into going with him. Threatened him."

What? *What?* Stay calm. "Sir, that's not what happened. Not at all. These snake guys—"

"We have proof." One of the serpent men produces a phone, photo already displayed. Is that me?

Ranger Ron does not remove his gaze from me. "I saw the photos."

Another ranger takes the phone from the serpent man. She's tallish, maybe— wait it's *her*, from Center Camp yesterday! She was one of the four Alistair and I talked to. The one with curly red hair.

She holds up the phone for me to see. A photo of Michelle talking to me and John. Who took this?

"That girl is the kid," the first serpent man says. "He's a tranny. Or whatever. He dresses like a girl."

Ranger Ron will not stop staring me down!

The woman ranger says, "You sure were eager for a photo of this runaway. Kept hassling us for one. Your friend—the other Arab—he offered us gold coins for a flyer."

I am horrified by how this sounds. "No, not like that. I didn't want—"

"Shut up," says Ranger Ron. His angry, square face leans closer to me. "Where is he now, this kid? Where's Mickey Flynn?"

Oh shit. I can't tell him. I've got to give John and Michelle as much of a head start as possible, especially now that these rangers know to look for a girl. They have a picture, too. Fuck. If I don't stall for time, John will be pulled over on their way out of camp. *Fuck.* They're probably not even in John's car yet!

I have to stall.

I scan Black Rock City before me, as if looking for Michelle myself. "I don't know. I swear to god, I don't know where they are right now. I mean, where *she* is."

Draw suspicion to me. It's the only thing I can do to help.

"Who's they?" says the other ranger, the younger man who hasn't spoken. Buzz cut. Maybe Hispanic.

"He's lying," says one of the serpent men.

"You guys leave. Now," Ranger Ron says over his shoulder. "Go to Center Camp and get some Wi-Fi. Text me those photos you took of this perv. Grech, give them my number."

His eyes never leave me. "Is this your stuff? Are you part of a camp?"

Ranger Ron's tone demands the truth.

"No, I'm here alone."

He snarks a laugh. "Shocker."

He turns to the other male ranger. "Call this in. Get two rangers to pack up his tent. Bring it to the front gate."

"Wait—"

"Your job is to shut the fuck up," he snarls, stabbing a finger at me. "We're gonna drive you over to Front Camp. You're gonna get arrested by the cops if you don't tell us where to find this kid."

The one who might be Green Snake speaks up. "What's going to happen to him?"

Ranger Ron gets angry. "I told you two to fuck off. This is ranger business now."

While I try calm my heartbeat, I admire Ranger Ron's fury. He's outraged that I would take sexual advantage of a sixteen-year-old. This means he's a good person. The truth will come out in a day or two, when John steps forward at a press conference and reveals Michelle is petitioning for emancipation. How should I stall? How much heat do I want until the truth comes out? I can't mislead them. That would be hindering a police investigation. I will tell the truth. Sort of. I will say I honestly don't know where they are at this second. John's name? Well, when we met, he told me his name was Alistair.

That works for now. Though this is going to get very ugly.

Wow. The serpent men screwed me. As they shuffle away, one of them flips me off. Nobody can see it but me.

Ron tells Grech to search my truck and the attached trailer, while the young ranger disappears inside my tent. I'd protest, but every minute stalls for time.

Now that we are alone, Ranger Ron steps forward. I can smell his hot breath.

He says, "You think I don't recognize you? You think I don't know who you are?"

Uh-oh.

"Nineteen-ninety. Monday after Sunday's burn. Our first year out here on the playa. You were just a punk. Came strolling out of the desert, pleased as punch, as everyone was packing up to leave. Your clothes were pressed. Creased! You think I'd forget something like that?"

My heart pounds.

He's wrong. My clothes weren't *pressed*. I don't know what he's talking about. Hell, I don't remember what I was wearing. I barely remember that day.

Play dumb.

I ask, "You remember me?"

His face clenches. "I'll never forget your face. Your freshly ironed shirt. You terrified all of us. You know we almost didn't come back the next year because you fucking freaked everyone out. You walked out of the desert followed by three wolves. Three…dogs or whatever. They walked behind you at a distance. As soon as you reached people, they turned and ran off."

Dogs? *What the fuck are these dogs?*

Ranger Ron steps back, and behind his rage, I see something else gleaming. Fear.

"You're not human. I don't know what you are, but you're *not* human."

I look down as tears form. How many times have I leveled that very charge at myself?

"You know there's no fucking wildlife out here, right? That was your mistake. You're a fucking devil in human skin! They just trotted away, happy as can be. Tongues wagging, like suburban, backyard pets."

Weakly, I say, "I never saw them."

"Bullshit. You're evil. Thank god, you didn't come back the next year. I thought I saw you a few years later, but I wasn't sure. Those of us who witnessed that morning convinced ourselves we were hallucinating. Now that I know you like to fuck sixteen-year-olds, I know I wasn't hallucinating. You're evil."

The young ranger steps out of my tent with a piece of paper. "This!" He holds my paper in his hands. "It certifies he owns almost seventy-five thousand dollars in gold coins."

Ranger Ron turns to me. "Where's the kid?"

"I don't know."

"What's the money for?"

"Nothing. Giveaways."

He sputters. "Bullshit!"

The younger man eyes me with disgust and returns inside. All I can think about are my nice folded piles. It's all I can focus on. I'm about to lose it.

Ranger Ron says, "I don't need either the kid or these gold coins. I'm not a real cop, so I don't need real proof. I'm on the senior executive committee, and you're banned from Burning Man. For life. You can never return."

My head shoots up. "*No!* This—is my home!"

"Consider yourself homeless." He makes this pronouncement with satisfaction. "Trust me, I'm the kind of crazy bastard who will personally patrol the front gate next year, and the year after that. I will distribute your photo to every ranger, to every volunteer. I will tell them you're a predator. You might be tempted to sneak back three years from now. Four. I will be here, protecting these people. I will make you my personal cause, you evil piece of shit."

I'm going to be sick.

It's the only place where I feel at home.

"Sit. Sit your ass down until we pack your tent. Once we find Flynn, he's going to tell us you forced yourself on him, you ugly fuck. Then you go to jail."

No. No!

Do I run? Do I—I can't run. They know my name. Plus, every minute they investigate me is a minute John gets further away.

I've been banned for life?

Oh fuck.

Reggie?

Across the street, Reggie watches the scene with apprehension.

"Sit your ass down, you freak."

I lower myself to the ground. *Reggie, don't come over here. Don't do it.* I try to communicate this with my eyes—without giving him away. Ranger Ron steps back and speaks with someone on his walkie-talkie. He keeps his eyes fixed on me, ready to pounce if I attempt to flee. In fact, I think he wants me to try.

My camping neighbors watch me, and the unfolding drama, with undisguised interest. Rangers tossing a tent and kicking someone out? In a culture dedicated to radical acceptance, this is about as bad as it gets.

My god. I can never return to Burning Man?

Shit. Reggie's crossing the street. Coming over.

I look the other way. Don't come over here. Don't get involved in this!

I can never return to Burning Man.

Reggie says, "Vin?"

Ranger Ron silences the person on the walkie-talkie.

I calculate the odds. The two other rangers are busy.

"Run," I yell. "Run hard!"

Reggie takes off, instantly obeying, and shit—*shit*!

Ranger Ron takes off after him.

I scramble to my feet. "If you chase him, I'll run away!"

Ranger Ron jerks to a halt and spins back toward me. He yells to the ranger searching my tent, but it's too late, Reggie is gone. Ranger Ron calls it in. "We're looking for an early twenties male, didn't catch white or black. Afro. Blue jeans. Knows our suspect."

Run, Reggie!

Why is it that every life I touch—if I'm not kinging a man—is made worse? What's wrong with me?

Oh god, I'm going to jail. I can't go to jail. I won't do well in jail. I need my secret entrances and exits. I need to escape! I can't live in a cage! Don't think that way. This will all get straightened out soon. John said he will stage a press conference within a day or so, and this will all be over. Stay calm.

Calm down?

I just got banned from Burning Man!

Ranger Ron snarls, "When I'm done here, I'm going to kick your teeth into your throat."

Don't vomit, Vin. Don't do it.

I clench my eyes shut. The world is spinning.

There's nowhere I belong anymore. I get sad visiting New York and Atlanta. It's not fun driving through the Midwest because I think of Mai and Ryan and Preston. Oh god, *Preston*. Not just places. Orange reminds me of Rance. Blue reminds me of Ryan. I can't eat tiramisu without thinking of Pietro, and when I see scrambled eggs, I hear Jamie's laugh. Oh, how I miss his beautiful laugh! I can't even visit Alcatraz without being in love with Perry and wishing he were at my side, calling himself Nevada. He haunts me.

No, no, no, *no, no, no*...keep it together. Keep it together. Don't freak out.

V-v-*v-v*-vin Vanbly.

Maybe it really is time to go back to the sewers. Back where I belong.

I crouch down in the dust and put my arms over my head.

I rock back and forth.

Reggie's on the run now. I'm *poison*.

I can't keep my shit together much longer. Colors, places, foods, everything. It's all becoming too much. I didn't know I'd remain a Lost King for this many years. I always thought one of the men I kinged would realize I'm not among them and come back for me. I thought one of them might miss me.

Like a complete loser, I'm still in love with all my kings. Every person's worst nightmare is their ex-boyfriends getting together compare notes. Mine actually do. Do they laugh at me? Maybe they think I'm pathetic? No. No, don't think that way, Vin. They're not like that.

No, no, no, no, *No*. Capital *N*, strong and safe, like a friendly Neighbor who intervenes and says, "No. Leave those kids alone." His sidekick is *o*, a letter constantly surprised by its own strength its own—

No, Vin. Keep it together. *Keep it together.*

I can *never* return to Burning Man.

Oh god, oh god, oh god.

I'm begging you, kings. *Please.*

I can't keep it together much longer.

Please.

Somebody.

Come back to me.

Epilogue

St. Paul Pioneer Star, Saturday, March 19, 2011

Neighbors Upset Over Cemetery Desecration

Local residents of the West Saint Paul neighborhood are upset by what might have started as a St. Patrick's Day prank but is being treated by police as a property crime. Sometime between Thursday dusk and 6:00 a.m. on Friday, March 18, a plot was excavated at the Oak Hill Cemetery. The cemetery, off Marie Avenue, is occasionally the target of summer nighttime pranks or homeless activity, due to trees throughout the grounds capable of hiding trespassers.

Police describe the damage as limited to one gravesite, but have been unable to locate records on the interred. Only a smashed tombstone revealed the last name. St. Paul police request anyone with a loved one buried in Oak Hill Cemetery bearing the surname Vanbly to contact the authorities.

Coming in 2016

Book 6, *King Daniel*, Chapter 12. One chapter. Everything changes.
Book 5: *Come Back to Me*. This is the one. It happens here.
Book 6, *King Daniel*. Daniel's fate. D.C. revealed. What happens to Lost Kings?

Thank you, beloved strangers who became readers, readers who became friends, and friends who became companions, for your patience on this journey. Are you ready to come home?

Futher Reading

If you enjoyed *King Perry*, *King Mai*, and *The Butterfly King*, you may enjoy reading chapters from *King Daniel*, the sixth book in this series. *King Daniel* takes place in 2013 and continues the modern-day adventures with the men who were kinged. Some mysteries are solved...new mysteries are introduced. Visit www.edmondmanning.com/blog/wp-content/uploads/2015/04/King-Daniel-Chapters-1-10.pdf for the first ten chapters of Book 6 in The Lost and Founds series, *King Daniel*. Another chapter will be added before the next full novel is released. Visit me on Facebook for details.

REVIEWS

I wanted to find some way to thank the readers who take time to write reviews. So here's the deal.

- Write a review for Goodreads and I will email you a document titled, "Secrets in The Lost and Founds." I reveal a number of behind-the-word clues and foreshadowing plots.

- Write a review for Amazon.com and I will email you a not-yet-released short story about the Bubbas from *King Mai*.

- Write a review for some other website (Barnes & Noble, ARE, etc.) and I will email you a haiku about any topic you request.

Doesn't matter if your review is one star or five stars. As long as you write at least one sentence about your reaction, I'll count it! And you can copy the exact same review for each site. After you write your review, email me to let me know. remembertheking@comcast.net.

ACKNOWLEDGMENTS

King John takes place in a straaaaaaange and loving community. This is good. I am also part of a straaaaaaange and loving community. With gratitude as big as a desert I would like to say, "Fuck your burn" to the following people: Ann Batenburg (who inspired me when I wandered lost in a whiteout), Tony Ward (I miss you), Rhyss DeCassilene (who sent a McGuffin), Joe Keiffer (who hand-crafted me an awesome Butterfly Tree), Craig Ball (who feeds me), Keith Jarvis (who challenges plots that needed to be challenged), Kaje Harper (who conspires with me), L.C. Chase (who creates amazing illustrations), AJ Rose (who loves Vin more than I do), and Kate Aaron (who helped me fake being English). Oh, and for those English folks who caught a few of Alistair's mistakes imitating your language (like how he uses the word 'toff'), those are not Kate's fault. Despite her advice, I left Alistair a few missteps, clues he's not authentically English. A big fat thanks to Scotty Millay King who answered my questions about Burning Man. I would give you a cherry Popsicle.

I had a fantastic editing team: Jonathan Penn (Romantic Penn Publication Services) led the charge, fretting over italics in one-word sentences and whether phrasal adjectives are hyphenated (They are when preceding the noun, and they are not when following the noun.) Excellent proofreaders followed: Samantha and Ashley E. Thank you for the many corrections. If there are still errors in this book, it's because I changed shit after they saw it. Sorry, team.

I thank my goofy and wonderful Facebook friends and readers who delight and entertain me with love, cat videos, and proof of their own king- or queenship. Where would a story be without someone to believe in it?

I end with a private note to the Bear Walker king, Theo Bishop. Come home, Theo.

ALSO BY EDMOND MANNING

The Lost and Founds series:
King Perry
King Mai
The Butterfly King

AWOL (in the *Men of Honor* anthology)
Filthy Aquisitions
Hunting Bear: A Fariy Tale with a Very Hairy Ending (in the
A Taste of Honey anthology)

Non-Fiction:
I Probably Shouldn't Have Done That

ABOUT THE AUTHOR

EDMOND MANNING has always been fascinated by fiction: how ordinary words could be sculpted into heartfelt emotions, how heartfelt emotions could leave an imprint inside you stronger than the real world. Mr. Manning never felt worthy to seek publication until recently, when he accidentally stumbled into his own writer's voice that fit perfectly, like his favorite skull-print, fuzzy jammies. He finally realized that he didn't have to write like Charles Dickens or Armistead Maupin, two author heroes, and that perhaps his own fiction was juuuuuuust right, because it was his true voice, so he looked around the scrappy word kingdom that he created for himself and shouted, "I'M HOME!" He is now a writer.

In addition to fiction, Edmond enjoys writing nonfiction on his blog, www.edmondmanning.com. Feel free to contact him